Conquering the Darkness
The Darkness Trilogy - 3

Cassie Sanchez

Conquering the Darkness

© 2023 by Cassie Sanchez

All rights reserved. No portion of this book may be reproduced, stored in a retrieval system or transmitted in any form or by any means—electronic, mechanical, photocopy, recording, scanning, or other—except for brief quotations in critical reviews or articles, without the prior written permission of the publisher.

Publisher's Note: This novel is a work of fiction. Names, characters, places, and incidents are either the product of the author's imagination or used factiously. All characters are fictional, and any similarity to people living or dead is purely coincidental.

Cover and Interior Design by:

Karen Dimmick

ArcaneCovers.com

Published in the United States of America, by Silver Labs Press.

ISBN 979-8-9868224-4-0

Author's note: This story is intended for mature readers as there is sensitive subject matter throughout, including alcoholism, sexual situations, and violence.

To Louie, my amazing husband. I love that you are the Yin to my Yang, that your half-full glass fills my half-empty one, and how your cheerfulness in the morning makes me smile—after I've had a cup of coffee.

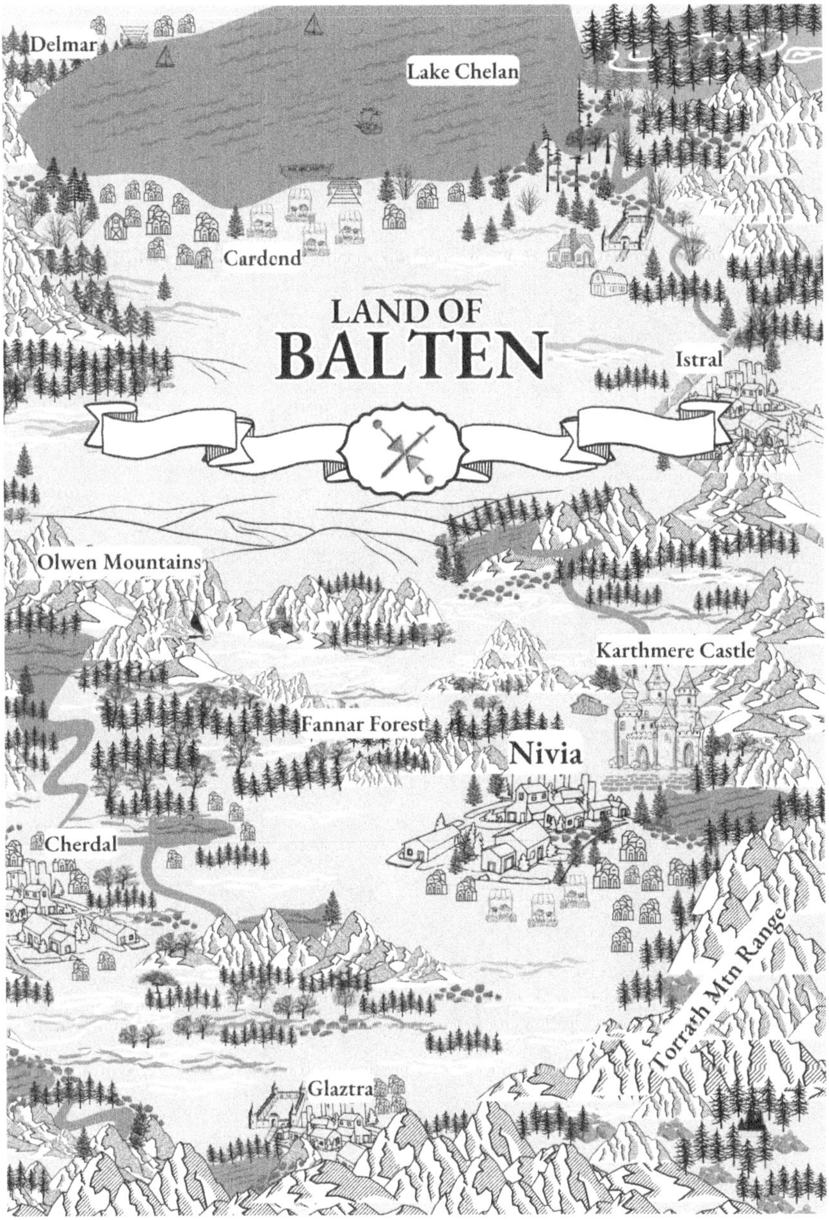
Delmar
Lake Chelan
Cardend
LAND OF
BALTEN
Istral
Olwen Mountains
Karthmere Castle
Fannar Forest
Nivia
Cherdal
Torrath Mtn Range
Glaztra

Prologue

Somewhere off the coast of Opax
Three-and-a-half years after the first war with the Vastanes

The spindly fingers of death wrapped around Amycus's throat. Drexus Zoldac, the commander of the Watch Guard and the most lethal man in Pandaren, was coming.

The wind and rain battered Amycus's face, but the storm couldn't compete with the chaos pulsing through his veins. Horror at what he had done attempted to drop him to his knees. His motives and intentions were noble, but somewhere he lost himself to the notion of "what if."

What if he had more power? What if he could defeat Drexus? *What if?*

The Empower Stone, an almost clear gem with a tinge of blue, thrummed in his hand. His magic responded as if to a lover's caress.

He closed his eyes to the churning surf, knowing what he had to do. He had to let the Stone go. No one should ever have this much power. And what if someone, like Drexus, acquired the Heart of Pandaren?

Two magical beings had created the Heart, which consisted of four Stones, to sustain magic and maintain balance across the land. The pieces of the Heart had remained hidden for centuries, but a sliver of the Empower Stone had gone missing, until recently. Drexus discovered the king of Pandaren had worn the sliver as a ring, and in his hunger for power he had killed the king and taken the ring.

A shiver racked down Amycus's spine and his hand trembled. In his quest to stop Drexus's tyranny, he'd stolen the sliver and used it to locate the Empower Stone. Magic from the Stone pulsed, and what felt like thousands of spiders crawled along his skin. The smell of smoke and burnt flesh—the body that had been his friend Cerus—stung his nose as he overlooked the churning surf of the Merrigan Sea.

Through the sound of crashing waves came the pounding of hooves. Amycus turned to see dust billowing from the road, heading straight for him.

How had Drexus found him so quickly?

"Forgive me, Cerus," Amycus whispered to the air in memory of his friend. "I'm sorry I didn't listen to your warning. But I will do everything I can to make things right. And I will make sure no one else follows in my footsteps." With a grunt, he threw the Empower Stone off the cliff and into the dark waters of the sea.

He didn't wait to see where the Stone fell, satisfied with hearing the splash as he ran toward the cave. Time ticked down while the sound of racing hooves grew nearer. Hiding his journal from Drexus was imperative. He feared his capture was imminent—there was nothing he could do now to prevent it, not with the masked riders approaching. And deep down, he deserved whatever misfortune was in his foreseeable future. Maybe someone would discover his journal, use the information inside, and stop this war against Spectrals. But for now, all Amycus could do was hide the book and pray. Pray he would survive to right his wrongs.

Voices drifted in the breeze from the ocean.

His time was up.

Drexus was here.

Chapter One

Nivia, capital city, Balten
Five months after the Gathering

Darkness clung to the frozen land like a greedy lover. The strike of a hammer sent sparks into the air as Jasce Farone, assassin, blacksmith, and man without a home, pounded on a piece of molten steel in an attempt to break the metal into submission. The wind howled and snow swirled through the crack under the door. A Khioshka, the large snow cats occupying the glacial landscape, roared, silencing the cry of its prey.

Jasce couldn't remember the last time he'd seen a blue sky or felt the warmth of the sun on his face. He had heard stories of the harsh winters in Balten, but not in his wildest imagination could he have prepared himself for the drudgery of months in a constant state of twilight.

Despite the dreadful weather, he had comfortably stepped into his new role among the Balten warriors since he grew up at the Bastion, the military compound in the kingdom city of Orilyon. His life, on the outside, looked respectable. He instructed younger recruits in the mornings and worked in the forge in the afternoons. It was the nights when he would drink himself into oblivion, either to block the chronic pain in his back and leg or silence the nightmares tormenting him in his sleep.

Sparks fluttered as the clang of metal resounded through the forge. This was his third attempt at making the double-headed ax the Baltens were known for, and so far he'd been unsuccessful. With every strike, an image flashed in his mind, but would vanish before fully forming. The last thing he remembered was his life as a Hunter in the Watch Guard, second in command to Drexus Zoldac, and volunteering to receive the Amplifier serum. He vividly pictured a cold metal table, leather straps crossing his chest, and pain like he'd never known as magic pulsed through him. The next thing he knew, he'd woken in the medical facility at the Bastion, missing an entire year of his life.

Ever since Kord Haring, a Spectral Healer, had removed his magic, and consequently his memories, vague impressions of the previous year flitted through his mind like mist, giving him nothing solid to hold on to. As the months progressed, the hole in his heart grew into a cavernous pit that no amount of training or whiskey could fill. Even working in the forge, which usually brought him comfort, now left him empty.

When Jasce was a child, Braxium, the blacksmith from his hometown of Delmar, would sneak him into his forge and secretly teach him how to craft steel into weapons. The first dagger he had ever owned he'd created with the blacksmith's guidance. The man's forge became a refuge from his father's paranoia and drunken tirades, and even now Braxium's words drifted to the front of his mind.

"Life can be like this metal here—no purpose, no function. But the forge, the hammer, and the anvil will shape and temper you. And if you endure, then your character, resilient and purposeful, will emerge from the flames."

Jasce thought it ironic that he could recall a conversation from when he was ten, and yet he couldn't remember pivotal events from a year ago.

As a Hunter, Jasce had a purpose. But now with this missing chunk of time, a time that seemed to have transformed him into a man he didn't recognize, irrelevance and aimlessness clung to him like a noxious odor.

With a final strike of the hammer, he thrust the glowing metal into a pot of oil to temper the steel. Holding it up to the light, he frowned at

Conquering the Darkness

the hairline crack running through the center of the blade. He ground his teeth and, with a yell, threw the ax across the room, where it landed with a resounding clunk and joined the ever-growing pile of worthless and broken blades.

The motion caused him to swear as his leg gave out. His knee cracked against the ground and pain like a molten blade pierced his back and side.

He rested his palms on the cold stone, his long hair forming a dark brown curtain around his face that puffed out with each breath. He crawled to a side table and, with shaking hands, reached for his flask. The whiskey warmed his throat and belly and eased the pain. Sighing, he leaned against the wall and frowned at the pile of worthless weapons. He huffed out a bitter laugh, able to relate to the mound of junk. He'd been the most feared assassin in Pandaren, and now pain and weakness had him quavering against the wall.

Pain is inescapable. Suffering is a choice.

He shook his head at his mantra and lifted the flask to his lips. Suffering wasn't really a choice. The choice was in *how* someone suffered, and right now he wasn't making good choices, but he couldn't find a reason to care.

Under a pile of discarded tools and papers, he spied a dusty leather journal, one he hadn't opened since leaving Orilyon. Curiosity got the best of him. He blew the layer of dust off the cover and opened the book to the inscription on the first page.

This is the journal of Amycus Reins—Blacksmith, Air Spectral, Murderer, and Traitor. The first three are correct. But I am no traitor.

Jasce frowned. Of all the stories he had heard about Amycus, not one of them mentioned him being a murderer. And as for a traitor, the blacksmith had been accused of killing King Dietrich Valeri after the Vastane War, but the queen cleared him of all charges. He found it interesting that he shared a few qualities with Amycus, who had sacrificed himself and saved Jasce's life. Based on what Caston, a fellow Hunter, had told him when he'd awoken from having his magic removed, Jasce had also been labeled a traitor after he'd escaped Bradwick Prison and joined the Spectrals to stop Drexus.

But there was one trait on that list that bothered him, one that woke him in the middle of the night covered in sweat with his hand gripped around his dagger and the blank eyes of his father staring back at him.

Murderer.

Drexus had ordered him to kill Barnet Farone, but he could have said no and forfeited his aspirations to become a Hunter—and most likely his life. A part of him had craved retribution for his father's betrayal, though, and the hunger for vengeance made him greedy for more, where no amount of blood would satiate him.

Icy wind stung his face as the door to the forge opened and his younger sister, Jaida, marched in. For years, Jasce believed his sister had died the same night as his mother, but he later learned Drexus had taken her, keeping her existence hidden from him.

A lavender gown peeked out from the opening of her fur-lined cloak, and she'd twisted her golden hair into an intricate braid. Her face was flushed from the cold, and her gray eyes reminded him so much of his mother that it hurt to look at her at times.

Jaida kicked the snow from the bottom of her boots and closed the door. "Jasce, we're supposed to be attending the celebration . . ." She frowned at him, still sitting on the floor, clutching his flask with the open journal on his lap.

She tilted her head. "What are you reading?"

"None of your business." He pushed off the ground, wiping the dirt off his leather pants, and limped toward his worktable.

She reached for him, but he waved her off. "Why won't you come to the Santoria? We could help you. They've created a tonic to relieve my headaches. They might have something for your back."

His sister, it seemed, had an aptitude for healing and medicine. She had found work in the Santoria, the medical facility near the palace, and even made friends with Princess Irina and the other Balten menders. Jaida had adjusted well to her new life among the warriors, since she too grew up in a military compound. Her experience with Drexus, however, differed greatly from his. It seemed Drexus, in his sick and twisted way, loved Jaida and was proud of how strong her Psyche magic was. After all, there weren't many Spectrals with the ability to move objects with their minds. Drexus became the father she was robbed of, the one Jasce took from her.

"I've told you, I can't let them see me as weak or injured. There are enough soldiers striving for a piece of the Angel of Death," he said, balling his fists, unable to mask the sharpness of his tone. Many of the warriors craved the honor of defeating the mighty Azrael. Unfortunately, more Baltens than he would have liked had already claimed those bragging rights. "Besides, I have it handled."

"Fighting and drinking every night is not what I call handling it."

He turned toward her and scowled. "Back off, Jai. I don't need a mother."

"I'm not trying to mother you, but escaping to the tavern won't solve your problems."

"You know nothing of my problems." He raked his fingers through his hair and searched for a leather strap to tie it back.

"I thought you wanted to start a new life, but this isn't living, Jasce. This is barely surviving. What would Kord or Kenz think?"

"I don't know who they are, so why would I care what they think?"

Jaida sighed. "Please, talk to me."

"What exactly do you want to talk about? The fact that I killed our father or, based on what you told me in Orilyon, that you chose Drexus —the very man who murdered our mother—over your own brother."

"I thought you'd forgiven me for that," she whispered.

He turned from the tears lining her eyes. "Just go, Jaida. I have work to do."

Hurried footsteps strode for the door, and the cold washed over him once more before the only sounds were the shifting logs in the hearth.

He rested his palms on the scarred table while the smell of snow, smoke from the fire, and molten steel filled his nose. He supposed the "old Jasce" would have handled that confrontation differently. But he didn't know that man, the one with genuine friends and a woman he supposedly loved.

In Orilyon, after he'd awakened in the Sanctuary, he'd played the part expected of him with Caston, Kord, and Kenz. But now that he was away from them and the person they wanted him to be, his old self, the one from before he'd received the Amplifier serum, became more comfortable, like a worn pair of boots.

He was broken, and the sharp edges of revenge that defined his life fueled him once more. Now he had a face for the Spectral who killed his mother—Drexus Zoldac, his former commander and the man who had molded Jasce into his image. He deserved to die, and Jasce would be the one to kill him. He just needed an opportunity, a reason to leave this frozen wasteland.

He tried to continue his work, but too many thoughts assailed him as he glanced once again at the pile of damaged and useless weapons. He wasn't in the mood for the dinner celebration he was supposed to attend, and he didn't want to go home where loneliness threatened to suffocate him. Exhaustion weighed heavily on him, but sleep never came unless he deadened the chaos of his mind. The restlessness and resentment flowing through him made his skin crawl. Only two activities settled the frenzy—sex and fighting. He couldn't remember the last time he'd been with a woman. Besides, fighting was less complicated and some nights he won more than he lost.

His sister's words grated on his nerves. *Escaping to the tavern won't solve your problems.*

"The hell with it," he said, extinguishing the fire in the hearth. He threw on his heavy cloak and tugged on his gloves while shoving Jaida's disappointment into the dark recesses of his mind.

Hopefully, after someone was beaten into submission, even if it was him, he would make it through the night without an assault of nightmares, the alcohol and exhaustion catapulting him into a dreamless sleep.

He slipped Amycus's journal into the pocket of his cloak and buried the promise he'd made when he left Orilyon—to do better, to make the blacksmith proud. He filled his flask and strode into the bitter frigid night.

Chapter Two

A yell lodged in Jasce's throat, forcing him to wake from another night of restless sleep. He lurched from the bed, barely making it to the wash chamber before throwing up. His stomach convulsed and expelled the whiskey and what little food he had eaten the night before. The hammering in his chest kept time with his throbbing head. Fear, anger, and shame racked his body as he heaved. If only it was as easy to purge the emotions infiltrating his dreams as it was the contents of his stomach.

The nightmare always started the same. A blur of random memories, as if he were witnessing the events through a veil. As the dream progressed, the visions became clearer, more substantial, and no matter how hard he tried to wake up, the images devoured him like quicksand.

He saw himself in a forge, holding a small gem while power coursed through him.

The vision shifted.

His hand stabbing a sword through a leathery black creature with white eyes and bloodstained teeth.

Shift.

Panic and unfathomable rage coursing through him, followed by suffocating failure as a woman lay in the sand, her side ripped open and blood pooling around her.

Shift.

His body controlled by a queen as he murdered a defenseless man.

Shift.

Wrinkled blue eyes gazing lifelessly at the sunrise with the sounds of war surrounding him.

Shift.

A sword exploding through his chest, then waking up to an enormous man wearing an eyepatch, the visible green eye peering at him as if he could see all the way to his soul.

Jasce slowly rose to his feet, gritting his teeth against the pain in his back, and wiped the sweat off his forehead. It was the same nightmare over and over. Based on what he'd learned at the Bastion, the woman bleeding out in the sand was Kenz Haring, his supposed fiancée, and the man lying dead in the street was Amycus, accidentally killed by Jaida. He also had discovered it was Drexus who had stabbed him in the back, literally and figuratively. The man with the eyepatch was Kord, his alleged best friend and the one who had stolen his magic and his memories.

He sat on his bed, holding his head and staring at his bare feet. He was so tired, mentally, emotionally, and physically, but knew from experience that sleep would evade him. Glancing up, he noticed the journal on his bedside table next to a bottle of whiskey. He reached for both with shaking hands, took a long pull from the bottle, and thumbed the book open.

> *Orilyon is in a state of chaos, and my heart is breaking. How is it that you think you know someone, only to find out you have seriously misjudged them? One of my friends has betrayed me and the other one is dead. And I feel partly responsible. I should have seen Drexus's ambition, especially after King Valeri defeated the Vastanes. Drexus killed Dietrich and is now hunting me, and he will not stop until I'm dead. I fear there is nowhere safe in Opax for me to hide.*

Conquering the Darkness

Caston had told Jasce about Drexus's betrayal and his obsession with creating a Spectral army to rule Pandaren. Based on what Jasce knew of his former commander, this didn't surprise him in the least. The man had always craved power and would do anything to obtain it, including betraying his second in command. The notion set his teeth on edge.

Shaking his head, he flipped through the worn pages and stopped at a word he'd never seen before: Saldrakes.

I've never sailed on a boat before and the journey across the Merrigan Sea was anything but pleasant. I will miss my home, but visiting the island of Alturia has a certain appeal. I've read about the Shade Walkers and hope to see the Saldrakes, the infamous sea dragons that live off the coast. The captain of the ship is working me to the bone, but having an Air Spectral aboard speeds up the voyage. Thankfully, we've not experienced any of the deadly storms that plague the channel between Pandaren and Alturia.

Jasce couldn't remember any stories about Amycus spending time in Alturia. Maybe Kord or Kenz hadn't known. He scanned the next few entries of Amycus settling in a town called Havencrest and creating a new life as a blacksmith.

Eighteen months have passed since Dietrich was killed. I thought distance from Pandaren would make the pain go away, but grief over Dietrich's death and the queen's loss makes it hard to breathe. To make matters worse, Queen Valeri has been stripped of her power because of Drexus and his sniveling advisor. But what can one Air Spectral do against the Watch Guard and Drexus's Hunters? Rumors of these ruthless assassins have made it across the sea, and I feel like a coward hiding while Spectrals are suffering.

~~~~~

I think I've found a way to stop Drexus! I was returning to my cottage, had made a wrong turn, and ended up near the art district. Colorful murals lined the wall depicting scenes of a great battle, and amid the carnage was a warrior, taller than the rest, eyes filled with purple fire and holding a sword with lightning dancing along the blade. The warrior had unbelievable strength and speed, similar to an Amp, and could wield all four elements. A tall woman with hair like the midnight sky, also a warrior based on her ivory armor, stood in the distance, her arms raised and her eyes shining like molten silver.

Underneath the mural were the words: Theran, Sovereign of the Corporis, and Cerulea, Sovereign of the Sensus. *Excitement beat through my chest. I thought the legend of Theran and Cerulea was a myth, a bedtime story. I stared at the image for what seemed like hours while an idea took root in my mind.*

Tomorrow, I plan to travel to the kingdom city of Cartennae to visit their libraries in the hopes of obtaining more information about these magical beings. If I have any chance against Drexus and his army, then I need more magic. My Air magic is relatively strong, but what if I could be more powerful?

It seemed magic was a common thread between Drexus, Amycus, and himself. Drexus sought to create a magical army, and Amycus needed more magic to defeat Drexus. Jasce receiving the Amplifier serum and unlocking his Vaulter magic had turned his life around. He'd had a family and friends, had become the hero instead of the villain. And because Kord had stolen his power, he'd lost all of that, even a part of his humanity as evidenced by his bloody knuckles and bruised face.

Jasce rubbed the soreness from the muscles in his neck while resentment and anger writhed through his chest at his supposed best friend. How dare Kord remove his magic? Even though he couldn't remember having magic, he could imagine the lethal fighting skills of the Angel of Death combined with Amplifier and Vaulter powers. He would have been the most powerful Spectral in Pandaren, and some stranger stole that from him. Surely Kord could have found another way.

He resisted the urge to throw his flask across the room and

Conquering the Darkness

continued reading. The writing in the next entry differed slightly from the previous ones, with the ink blotted in a few places.

The seas are rough as I return home, and I'm not sure how long I have until I'm heaving over the railing. My time in Cartennae proved fruitful. I found scrolls of information about Theran and Cerulea, the two powerful beings who had created magic in Pandaren, as well as the four Stones that formed the Heart of Pandaren. According to legend, a sliver is missing from the Heart, namely the Empower Stone, and because it's incomplete, magic has been at an imbalance for centuries. Based on my readings here and back home, the royal family has passed down that sliver, usually as a piece of jewelry.
I've seen this crystal on the late king's finger, and the last time we were together, I had felt a tremor in my magic. I brushed it off at the time, but I believe this is the missing sliver of the Heart. Now all I need to do is break into the palace and find that ring.

Jasce raised his brows at the blacksmith's bravado. He wanted to read on but the pounding in his head made the words blur together. Before he closed the journal, he noticed a sentence written off to the side, as if scrawled as an afterthought.

If I do not deal with my past, I am condemned to repeat it.

It seemed Amycus had also been haunted by a past.

Jasce lay back on his bed with a sigh and covered his eyes with his arm. Thoughts of the Heart of Pandaren echoed off the caverns of his foggy mind. He'd heard a lot of talk about the balance of magic. The Heart consisted of four Stones: The Empower, Creator, Inhibitor, and Abolish Stones. Drexus already had the Empower Stone, and who knew what he was doing with it. But if Jasce found the Creator Stone, then maybe he would get his magic back, and therefore his memories. With his magic restored, he'd be able to fight Drexus, and this time he would not fail.

"Condemned to repeat it," he mumbled. He was tired of being tormented by his past and the image of blood splashing across his face as he drove a dagger into his father's chest, and he didn't want to analyze why hate and revenge compelled him. He just wanted to forget.

He let out a harsh laugh at the irony. He wanted his memories back, and yet he wanted so badly to forget his past.

"No wonder I drink," he said, before rolling over and falling asleep.

∼

Jasce tucked his head and pulled his cloak tighter to block the frigid wind as he plodded through the snow on his way to the Terrovka, the Baltens' primary training center. The beard he'd grown helped protect his face from the harsh conditions, but the temperature this morning was especially cold with the blustering wind and the sun still low on the horizon. He thought by now he would have adjusted to the watery light, but found he missed the blue skies and the salty, warm air of Orilyon.

He passed a herd of Ornix in a meadow, chewing on straw brought in from the many barns dotted through the countryside. The Ornix's large antlers might impale someone if they weren't careful, and their long, thick fur kept them warm in the frigid climate. He'd seen the animals pulling sleds loaded with supplies headed for the dangerous mountain passes separating the many towns in Balten.

Even though he was late for his teaching session, he trudged along a carved trail through the snow to the nearest stable, needing to check on his horse, Bruiser. The stubborn beast was the closest thing to a friend he had. Granted, he recognized that was mostly his fault. He had learned early at the Bastion not to trust anyone. Balten was no different, and habit kept him keeping people at arm's length.

He pulled open the stable door and breathed in the sweet smell of clean hay. Walking past the occupied stalls, petting noses sticking out over the doors, he thought about what Jaida had said the previous night. What would Kord think? Or Kenz? How had he come to trust them? Even though Kord had told him how they'd met, Jasce still found it hard to believe he'd put his life in their hands. It seemed he'd also trusted Amycus and the rest of their team: Caston, Aura, Delmira, and Flynt. What had happened to him to allow these people past the iron fortress of his self-preservation? It couldn't only be about the magic. However, discovering his mother was a Spectral and he was a Vaulter seemed to have been the catalyst for many of the changes in his life.

Bruiser poked his majestic head over the stall door and blinked his chocolate-brown eyes.

"Hey, boy," he said, scratching the horse's midnight-colored ears. Bruiser nuzzled his hand, searching for a treat. He chuckled and revealed a sugar cube he'd hidden in his pocket. Bruiser nibbled the cube while Jasce looked out over the stables. Blackness crept into his peripheral and the ground shifted underneath him. A blurry image of him pressed up against a woman in a barn flashed through his mind and then disappeared. He shook his head and his balance returned.

He knew who that woman was. But why Kenz continued to haunt him, in his dreams or at random times like now, he didn't know. Sure, he had found her attractive back in Orilyon, but so were a lot of women. He did know he was getting more and more frustrated by her incorporeal presence. Supposedly, she was somewhere in Pandaren searching for Drexus. Something he should have been doing, but was instead stuck in Balten because of his sister's banishment from Pandaren.

He sighed. It wasn't Jaida's fault. She had simply become an easy target for his arrows of accusation.

Bruiser chewed on his pocket in search of another treat. He pulled out a sugar cube and gave it to the horse. "I'll see you later." The horse snorted as Jasce returned to the frigid air and headed toward the Terrovka.

He entered the enormous complex and found his class running through one of the four different obstacle courses on the ground floor. Clanking metal echoed from the weight room and laughter sounded from the adjacent dining hall. The hairs on his neck stood to attention and his gaze drifted to the second story, where soldiers sprinted around the indoor track. King Morzov's consort, Natasha Lekov, along with the king's son and daughter, Prince Andrei and Princess Irina, observed him from the balcony.

He swore under his breath at being caught arriving late and strode to where the kids had gathered next to the sparring rings.

Every morning, he worked with recruits from the ages of twelve to eighteen on their fitness and swordplay. He had adapted his Hunter training for the young soldiers and was proud of how they responded to the new methods.

"Whose idea was it to run the obstacle course while you waited for me?" Jasce asked, as the recruits circled around him. A few of the kids glanced at a fourteen-year-old boy named Stepan.

Stepan jutted out his chin. "I did."

"Well done. Who won?"

Stepan rolled his eyes and pointed to Eva. She was sixteen, one of the best recruits in the class, and also the niece of a soldier named Matvey, who Jascc had injured during the Gathering. Eva laughed whenever she recounted the story of Jasce and Matvey's first encounter. Her uncle had cheated during their arm-wrestling contest, and Jasce had used his dagger to pin Matvey's hand to the table. Jasce never liked cheaters and wasn't surprised by his actions, but he was positive Queen Valeri had not appreciated his behavior, especially as commander of her Paladin Guard.

Jasce smiled at Eva, whose cheeks turned pink. "Everyone, grab a practice sword. Eva and Stepan, lead the group in our warm-up and then we'll continue the slash-and-parry maneuver we worked on last time."

After an hour of instructing, Jasce stepped into the sparring ring with one of the older kids to demonstrate a complex series of movements while combining the moves they had learned. The young man attacked quickly, and when Jasce twisted to block his strike, his back spasmed and he fell to his knee.

The recruit rushed to his side. "Commander, are you all right?" He reached out to help him up, but stopped when Jasce swore, lifted his head, and glared at the young man. Fear replaced the concern in the recruit's eyes.

A tremor racked through Jasce's body as sweat dripped from his temples. He took a deep breath, forced a smile, and rose to his feet.

"Thanks, Lev, I'm fine. Just an old injury." Out of the corner of his eye, he noticed Consort Lekov and the two royal siblings watching him. The prince smirked and whispered something to his sister, who glared at her brother.

He raked his fingers through his hair and dismissed the kids for their lunch break. His hand trembled as he reached for his flask and took a quick sip to ease the pain throbbing down his spine. When he glanced over his shoulder, the upper balcony was empty.

He chose an unoccupied table in the dining hall and kept his back to the wall while he ate his lunch. He dipped a sizable chunk of bread into a steaming bowl of stew loaded with meat, vegetables, and spices unique to Balten—the perfect comfort food. The hall had long, wooden tables and the benches were filled with trainees and seasoned fighters, many of whom snuck glances at him. He recognized a few of the men and women from his training sessions and the nightly visits to the taverns.

The scarred wooden table rattled as Princess Irina dropped her sword and sat across from him.

"Your Highness," he said with a quick nod.

"How many times have I asked you to call me Irina?" she asked, ripping off a chunk of his bread.

He examined her face as she scanned the crowded room. A cunning intelligence shone from behind her warm brown eyes and the corner of her lip turned up from a small scar, suggesting she always found something to be humorous. She had braided her hair, and the strands of red and brown hung over one shoulder. She wore the customary fighting leathers, lined with fur, and a cream sweater that looked as soft as silk. Inked vines decorated her collarbone, and he briefly wondered how much of her skin was marked with tattoos.

She turned back to him and smiled. "You really are an excellent teacher."

"Thanks." He dipped a hunk of bread into his stew.

"We noticed you're still having trouble with your back."

"We did, did we?" He was afraid of that. It was no secret that Prince Andrei didn't approve of Jasce living in Balten, let alone training his soldiers. He had yet to spar with the future king, but knew it was inevitable. The man was talented with the spear, another customary weapon of the Baltens, and one he hadn't mastered.

Prince Andrei stood a few inches shorter than him, but was solid muscle and lightning-fast, even without using his magic. Pre-injury, Jasce would have had his hands full with the warrior. But now? He wasn't too sure if he'd be victorious. And now the prince knew of his weakness. He bit back a curse and took a long swig from his tankard.

"Why haven't you come by the Santoria? We have some unique remedies that might ease the pain. We have Healers from Pandaren, too. Perhaps their magic could help."

Jasce huffed out a breath. "Pandaren Healers aren't fans of Hunters. Or me."

Irina arched a brow. "You might be surprised."

"Speaking of the Santoria, don't you usually work the same shift as Jaida?"

"Normally yes, and against my father's wishes since he doesn't like me working there, but duty calls. My father wants to meet with you."

Jasce wiped his beard with the back of his hand. "When?"

She smiled. "Now."

"I have a class in twenty minutes."

"Consort Lekov is covering it."

Jasce tapped his finger on the table. He hated being summoned—always had. He couldn't imagine he'd enjoyed his position as commander of the Paladin Guard, constantly subjected to Queen Valeri's orders. No wonder he'd gone insane.

Sighing, he slowly stood, hiding the grimace from the shot of electricity down his back. "Lead the way," he said, and followed the princess out of the dining hall.

Chapter Three

Princess Irina led Jasce from the training center to Karthmere Castle through a maze of underground passageways. The unassuming structure differed from the palace in Orilyon, with its conglomeration of mismatched buildings made of wood and stone.

"What matters is on the inside, yes?" Irina said, and he couldn't agree more as they wound their way through the musty corridors and up a spiral staircase to the central foyer.

The castle was nestled at the base of the Torrath Mountain Range, surrounded by imposing cliffs and a dense forest of pine trees resembling watchful sentries. And if the surroundings weren't deadly enough, the magic-wielding warriors inside would make any attacking clan think twice. Having increased speed and strength, along with the ability to unleash an ancestral power to fight alongside them, the Baltens were a force to be reckoned with.

Jasce turned, heading for the throne room, but the princess continued up another set of stairs toward the king's personal receiving room. She glanced over her shoulder and caught him wincing as he trudged up the steps.

"You are very stubborn." She took a small bag from her pocket and handed him what looked like a dried mushroom.

Jasce frowned. "What's this?"

"Makovus. Something to help with the pain until you come to the Santoria. Be careful, though. Too much of a good thing."

He arched a brow and sniffed the herb. It smelled like dirt. Shrugging, he popped it in his mouth and continued up the stairs. It tasted like dirt, too.

Two warriors guarded the entrance of the king's room, one Jasce recognized from the night before in the fighting ring. The man scowled, making his black eye pucker.

"Viktor," Jasce said, dipping his head.

"Ahren."

Jasce's spine stiffened at the nickname, meaning Angel, that some of the soldiers had given him. The guard smirked and opened the door.

Windows lined the west wall of the king's receiving room, displaying a magnificent view of the city and Fannar Forest clinging to the horizon. Clouds hung low and snow drifted lazily to the ground. In the distance, the Olwen Mountains towered over the landscape like an impassable giant.

An enormous fire crackled in the corner of the room, and a colorful rug lined the stone floor. King Leonid Morzov sat behind his mahogany desk with his crown resting on a pedestal behind him. His thick red hair, laced with gray, hung just past his collarbone. The man looked intimidating with his goatee, tattoos, and impressive size. His eyes, though, were like his daughter's, warm and kind—most of the time.

Two wing-backed chairs, embroidered with crimson and gold thread, sat in front of the desk. Prince Andrei turned, his face free of any emotion. The two siblings were opposite in appearance: Where Princess Irina resembled fire with her amber hair and warm eyes, Prince Andrei was like ice. His blond hair, almost white, and blue eyes matched the frozen landscape.

Irina and Jasce approached, and the man in the other chair grinned as he stood. His black and crimson tunic seemed out of place among the fur and leather of the Baltens. Silver hair matched his eyes, which sparkled in recognition.

"Ah, Commander. It's good to see you again. Although, I'm not sure the beard suits you," the man said, smiling. He grabbed Jasce and hugged him.

Jasce's spine turned rigid and his eyes widened. "Umm," he stammered, stepping away.

"Jasce's memories haven't returned," said the king, with a bored expression on his face.

The man's smile fell. "Oh, I'm sorry to hear that."

King Morzov stood and walked to the other side of the room, where couches and chairs surrounded the fireplace. "Jasce, this is Prince Nicolaus Jazari from Alturia. How you could forget such a character, I simply do not know."

So this was the Alturian prince who had vouched for him to Queen Valeri. He hadn't met the prince after he'd awoken, since the man had returned to his island to bury his commander.

Jasce dipped his chin. "Prince Jazari."

Nicolaus lifted his palms. "There are so many princes around here. Let's just call me Nicolaus. It's much easier, don't you think?"

Jasce shrugged in agreement. "Very well, Nicolaus."

The group followed the king to the sitting area. Jasce tried not to look too eager as Prince Andrei grabbed a decanter and five glasses and poured a shot of whiskey into each. Princess Irina tried to stop Jasce before he swallowed the contents in one gulp.

Everyone stared at him. "What?" he asked, glancing down, wondering if he'd spilled stew on his fighting leathers.

Princess Irina rolled her eyes and took the glass from him. "This is a sipping whiskey, plus you shouldn't mix it with the Makovus."

"Irina, seriously, you gave him Mak?" Prince Andrei asked, shaking his head.

"Just a little. I wanted to see how quickly it affected him."

"He isn't a test subject. That needs to be done in the Santoria, not on the way to a meeting. Nor with someone who drinks as much as he does."

"You two stop squabbling. I'm fine," Jasce said, even though he had to blink a few times to bring the room into focus. A numbness spread through his body, and his mind settled as if he lay floating in a warm sea.

Nicolaus chuckled. "Fine, indeed."

The king rested his ankle on his opposite knee. "Prince Jazari, please fill the commander in on what you've told me."

Nicolaus sipped his whiskey and placed the glass on the table. "A few weeks ago, Drexus attacked Vastane. Practically decimated the island."

Jasce leaned forward. "Vastane? Why?"

"Well, despite the fact that he's a vengeful wretch of a man and didn't take kindly to the Vastanes removing his magic, I believe he was looking for information."

"What kind of information?" Princess Irina asked.

"Now that he has the Empower Stone, I would assume it'd be obvious. Drexus wants the other three pieces of the Heart. He needed to wait to rebuild his strength, and Pandaren was too dangerous for him to be snooping around. He'd never make it over the mountains to Terrenus, and coming here would be disastrous until the opportune time. Which left Vastane and Alturia. We also have scrolls of information regarding the Stones, as did Vastane. But since Jasce left Vastane without a ruler—thanks for that, by the way—their island was the safest choice."

"You said Vastane did have scrolls of information. Do they not anymore?" Jasce asked.

Nicolaus smiled. "As you're aware, or maybe you aren't, I come from a long line of powerful Shade Walkers. We are excellent spies. My father put me in charge of infiltrating Vastane and removing the information on the Stones. I was in the middle of this exploit when Drexus and that abomination, Vale, attacked. My team retrieved most of the documents and helped evacuate the survivors to Alturia." Nicolaus filled his glass and took another sip of the amber liquid.

Jasce tapped his finger in an attempt to harness some amount of patience. Thankfully, Prince Andrei had less than him.

"Get to the point, will you?" the Balten prince said.

Jasce snorted, which earned him a glare.

Nicolaus arched a silver brow. "Yes, well, it seems Drexus is intent on making a magical army and therefore needs the Creator Stone. That is his next target, which means he's heading this way."

Jasce's heart thumped as excitement thrummed through him. Finally, a lead on Drexus. At least he now knew what his former

Conquering the Darkness

commander was planning and that the Creator Stone was nearby. If he secured the Stone, he'd get his magic back—and possibly his memories. Then he would have his revenge on Drexus once and for all. Finally, after months of aimlessness, he had a sense of purpose.

"You're about to break my chair." The king nodded to the armrest creaking under Jasce's grip.

His head jerked up. "What?"

Princess Irina smiled at him, pointing at his shaking leg.

"I need the Creator Stone," Jasce said. "Where is it?"

"What makes you think we know?" the king asked.

Jasce crossed his arms and held the king's stare.

Nicolaus grinned over his glass. "Of course the king knows where it is. Queen Valeri would like you to believe none of the other kingdoms knew about the Heart, but alas, that wasn't the case."

"You really do have a big mouth, Nicolaus," King Morzov said. He leveled his gaze at Jasce. "Why would I let you near the Stone?"

"Because Drexus is mine to kill." Jasce absently rubbed the scar on his chest, reminding him daily of Drexus's attempt to murder him. He didn't remember being stabbed in the back, but the nightmare of a sword exploding through his chest was as vivid as any memory. "And I need my magic back."

"Not good enough reasons." Jasce bristled as the king tapped his lip. King Morzov's eyes darted to his son and then to his daughter. "I might let you use the Stone, on one condition."

"Father, no," Princess Irina started, but snapped her mouth shut when the king raised his hand.

Jasce had a sinking suspicion. "What condition?"

"You agree to marry Irina," the king said.

Princess Irina covered her face and mumbled an apology to Jasce, who had fallen back into his chair. Was this the reason the king had wanted him to come to Balten after Jaida's banishment? King Morzov's words came back to him. *You're an excellent warrior and we could use a man like you. Plus, I think we could learn from each other.* Surely, marrying his daughter wasn't what he'd had in mind. He glanced at Irina, whose cheeks flushed as she glared at her father.

Prince Andrei swore. "Father, why are you intent on marrying my sister to this man?"

Nicolaus lifted a finger, but the king interrupted him. "I've told you, Andrei, I have my reasons. Besides, Jasce was the commander of Queen Valeri's army. I'm sure I can convince Lorella to reinstate him. An advantageous match, yes?"

Jasce shook his head, unsure if it was still attached to his body. "Don't you think the princess and myself have a say in this? And what the hell did you give me?" he asked Irina, swaying in his chair.

"Yes, well, I told you to not mix them," she said, a flash of annoyance crossing her face.

"There might be one minor problem with your plan, Leonid," Nicolaus said.

"One?" Prince Andrei asked, slouching in his chair, his brow furrowed.

"And what's that?" the king asked.

Nicolaus's eyes darted to Jasce, and his white teeth sparkled as he grinned. "Kenz Haring might have a problem with your marriage proposal."

"Who?" Prince Andrei asked.

"Kenz Haring, Jasce's betrothed," Nicolaus said, tracing the edge of his glass with his jeweled finger.

Jasce rubbed his temples. "We're no longer engaged, since I don't remember her."

"Really? Well, I assume she still remembers you." Nicolaus turned his smile on the king. "She'll have something to say about any arrangement you make."

"She's not here, and I don't answer to a Spectral. I make my plans, which are good plans," the king said, tossing back his drink.

So much for a sipping whiskey, Jasce thought, desperate for another glass.

"Father, if the commander is not available, then we will need to explore other options," Princess Irina said, her eyes darting between the king and Jasce.

Jasce stared at her. She was kind and not at all what he'd assumed of a princess, spoiled and arrogant. She was also a warrior and beautiful, and she'd make an excellent partner—he could see that. A smart man would jump at the king's offer.

He shook his head. He needed to focus on getting the Creator Stone before Drexus did. "Do you know where Drexus is? Has he returned to Pandaren?"

"My spies reported he left Vastane a week ago, so I'd assume he has returned, but I'm not sure where. My people unfortunately lost him during a storm," Nicolaus said.

Prince Andrei spun his glass on the table, making the liquid swirl. "He couldn't sail to Balten, not with the ice. Havelock is the closest port."

"Agreed," the king said. "Send Matvey and his cadre to gather intel."

The prince finished his drink and marched from the room. Princess Irina mumbled something about returning to the Santoria and followed her brother.

The crackle of the fire filled the silence. Finally, Jasce looked up. "I do not appreciate being a pawn in this game of yours. My life is not up for negotiation, nor your daughter's."

The king's eyes hardened. "My daughter is aware of her responsibilities to her kingdom."

"Then a prince would be a better match." Jasce pointed to Nicolaus. "Like him."

Nicolaus had been sipping his drink and sputtered the contents onto the front of his tunic. King Morzov swore in his native tongue while the Shade Walker dabbed at a stain on the silky fabric.

"I already said I have my reasons. You want your magic back, therefore you need the Creator Stone. My daughter needs a husband. It's simple."

Jasce's knuckles ached from clenching his fists. Getting into an argument with the Balten king wasn't a smart move. "I need time to consider your offer." *And to come up with an alternative plan*, he thought.

The king's eyes narrowed. "I'll not allow Drexus near that Stone. If you want to go on the mission to retrieve it . . ." He waved his hand and let his sentence trail off. His meaning was clear. If Jasce wanted the Creator Stone, he'd have to cooperate.

Jasce nodded and rose to his feet. "I understand."

Nicolaus crossed his ankle over his knee, the glass of whiskey dangling from his fingers. "I look forward to catching up at the festival tonight, Commander."

Jasce scowled and trudged across the room. Even though the Mak had dulled his senses and his pain, an invisible weight pressed against his chest. But at least now he had a direction and a purpose.

Chapter Four

Sweat dripped down Jasce's chest and his hair had fallen loose, hanging damply around his shoulders. Instead of working in the forge, he'd spent the afternoon training with some soldiers and then soaking in the hot springs adjacent to the Terrovka.

When Jasce and Jaida first arrived in Balten, they had marveled at the kingdom's ability to produce hot water and taking his first shower had been an amazing experience. Hot springs underneath the Torrath Mountains created enough energy to heat and pump the water through pipes, along with providing unique lighting that illuminated the halls of the castle, the Terrovka, and the Santoria. The wealthier citizens in the city could afford the hot water and lighting, but most could not. Jasce heard plans were in place to change that, but lately the king's focus had been on the threat from neighboring clans.

Jasce kicked off the snow from his boots as he opened the door to his and Jaida's lodgings. All he wanted to do was collapse into his chair in front of the fire with a bottle of whiskey in his hand. He wasn't expecting, however, to find Jaida sitting on his bed with Amycus's journal on her lap.

"What are you doing?" he asked, his nails biting into his palms.

Jaida didn't look up as she scanned the pages. "Reading."

"That's mine."

Jaida's eyes narrowed. "Did you know Amycus loved our mother?"

He clenched his jaw. He hadn't read past the entries detailing Amycus's return journey to Pandaren or his mission to steal the sliver of the Empower Stone.

Jaida flipped a page and read. "*. . . helping my people escape the reach of the Watch Guard and its Hunters is my new mission—and keeping Lisia and her children safe if I can. Barnet Farone is an angry, jealous man. Granted, his behavior is justifiable if he knew my feelings for his wife. But I will not add to my list of wrongs. She is off-limits even though my heart doesn't know the difference.*"

Jasce ripped the journal from her and placed it on the dresser. "Why are you doing this?"

"He's the reason she's dead."

Jasce spun so quickly he almost lost his balance. "What did you say?"

She pointed to the book. "Just a few pages over, he says it. Amycus led Drexus to our village. Because of him, our mother is dead."

He towered over his sister and pointed at her. "No, because of our cowardly father, she's dead. Because of Drexus, who *you* chose. Because of him, my mother is dead!"

Jaida stood and jammed her finger into his chest. "Don't yell at me. You have no idea what my life was like with Drexus. Grieving the loss of my mother, my brother, and my father." Her chest heaved, and her hair floated off her shoulders. "But what do you care, since you murdered him!"

Jasce fell back into the dresser as if her words had been a physical blow. "I had no choice. I was ordered—"

"Don't give me that. You had a choice. You wanted to be a Hunter, and your need for revenge blinded you. I'm sure you took pleasure in killing him."

Rage pulsed through him as he shoved her against the wall. How dare she judge him? She hadn't known what his life had been like, either, and he had the scars to prove it. Frustration, loss, and shame threatened to drown him where he stood, and the need to lash out overwhelmed him. Her eyes widened, and she lifted her hands. With a yell, his fist collided into the wall next to her head.

Her hair swirled around her face. The journal and his dagger rose off his dresser. The lamp next to his bed rattled. He tried to step away but his body was no longer his own.

Jaida released a quavering breath. The journal and dagger clattered onto the floor, and Jasce's body relaxed. She slumped into the chair and ran a shaking hand through her hair.

Guilt at losing his temper and frightening her made him wince. "I'm sorry I scared you. I . . . I'd never hit you."

She looked up, her eyes flitting across his face. "I know. But you're more like him than you want to admit."

"I'm not like Drexus," he said through clenched teeth.

"I meant our father." She swiped at a tear escaping down her cheek.

His legs almost gave out as her words extinguished the fight in him. He slowly lowered himself onto the bed, his gaze catching on the blade of his dagger resting on the floor. "Was that your magic?"

She nodded. "It's been slowly coming back. I guess Kord and Maera's procedure didn't work completely."

Did that mean his magic might return all on its own? "Why didn't you tell me?"

"There are a lot of things we don't tell each other, Jasce." She lifted her hand and Amycus's journal floated across the room and landed in her lap. She ran her fingers over the worn leather but didn't open it. "For so many years, I hated you for what you did, and reading this brought up feelings I tried to bury. I'd hoped Amycus had some shred of wisdom in here, because until we learn how to forgive each other, I feel you and I will never be whole."

He rested his forearms on his legs, as if the weight of her admission was too much to bear. "I despise Barnet for what he did to us. A father is supposed to protect his children, not offer them up like a lamb to the slaughter." He lifted his head. "He deserved to die."

She rose from the chair. "That's not your choice. Can you hear yourself?" She thrust the journal at him. "Maybe you should spend more time reading this than fighting in the taverns."

"Be careful." Jasce's knuckles whitened as he held the leather book.

Cassie Sanchez

"Or what?" She lifted her hand, and the journal struck the wall, falling to the floor with a thump. "What can you do to me?" She spun on her heel and stormed out of his room, slamming the door in her wake.

His jaw ached from clenching his teeth. He stood and picked up the book to where it had fallen open.

My heart is shredded beyond repair. Grief and rage are swallowing me whole. And it's all my fault. Once again, death has tainted something beautiful in my life. It's been four years since I was blamed for Dietrich's murder. Four years of living as a fugitive and losing those I care about.
The burnt husk of the cottage is all that remains of my beautiful Lisia. If I look close enough, I can see the blood staining the ground, calling out for retribution.

He closed his eyes, easily recalling the black flames circling his mother, hearing Jaida's screams. Of all the memories he wanted to lose, this would be the one. Shaking his head, he mindlessly thumbed through the pages until he saw his name.

He's alive. How could I have let this happen? Jasce Farone has been in the Watch Guard all this time and now I've discovered he's a Hunter, but not any Hunter. He's the Angel of Death.

He scanned the pages where he and Amycus had first met, learning about Drexus killing the king, and how his magic was released, the story familiar since Kord had told him all of this after he'd woken without his memories.

I know I should tell him, but I fear he will kill me when he learns I was the reason for Barnet's betrayal, that his mother's and sister's deaths are my fault. There is so much rage and bitterness in him. It's drowning him and his full potential, not just as a Vaulter, but as a man. One day he'll have to learn, as I have, that

Conquering the Darkness

these emotions will destroy his soul. One day, he'll have to learn to forgive.

His vision blurred, and the journal slipped from his hands, tumbling to the ground with a thunk. Fury and guilt battled for dominance inside him, and his entire body trembled, his skin tingling as if thousands of bugs crawled over him. He took the bottle from his nightstand and drank, but the whiskey didn't relieve the pressure in his chest. The room crowded in on him, and he suddenly found it difficult to breathe. Falling to his knees, he groaned. He wasn't strong enough to do what Amycus wanted.

"Do not ask that of me, old man. Do not take away my hate."

∼

A hand reached for him, and within seconds he flipped the assailant over and pressed his dagger to their delicate throat.

"Jasce, it's me!" Irina said, pushing against his chest.

The image of a blonde woman clung to his subconscious. She was beautiful, wore a crown on her head, and her ocean-blue eyes sparkled in victory. Was this Queen Siryn, who had manipulated and controlled him, turning him into Azrael?

Realizing he had pinned Irina to the bed, her lush body warm under his, he finally lowered the dagger.

"I'm so sorry..."

She pressed a finger to his lips. "It's okay. I should know better than to wake a tormented man while he's sleeping."

He barely remembered crawling to his bed and falling asleep. He swallowed, noticing a thin line of blood along her throat, and wiped it with his thumb. His body responded to the way her breasts molded to his chest, her strong thighs pressed into his. His gaze drifted to her slightly parted lips.

Only a breath separated them.

A knock on the door had him pushing off her.

"Jasce, are you okay?" Jaida opened the door and froze. "Oh, sorry... I—"

Irina sat up and straightened her sweater. "It's fine. I startled him in his sleep."

"Well, now I know never to wake him up, if that's what he does," Jaida said with a smirk.

Jasce got to his feet. "What did you want, Jai?"

The smirk melted from his sister's face, and he inwardly scolded himself for being so harsh.

"I heard you call out. Plus, we need to get ready for the festival."

"That was another reason I was here. My father sent me to remind you that your presence is required." The princess winced. "It will be fun, I promise."

He groaned. The last thing he wanted was to take part in the Zima Festival, the Baltens' annual week-long party celebrating the end of winter. Plus, he didn't appreciate the king ordering him to attend. He figured it was bound to happen, as he'd successfully avoided many other dinners and celebrations over the last five months.

Jaida smiled at Irina as they walked through the living room, whispering the entire way. He could only imagine what they were talking about.

He closed his eyes and took a deep breath. Her body had felt so good underneath him and a part of him desperately wanted more. If Jaida hadn't barged in, he would have kissed her, for he sensed she wanted more, too. When was the last time he'd been with a woman? He couldn't even remember. Maybe it was time to change that, and what better opportunity than during a festival celebrating new life?

But first, he needed to apologize to his sister. He'd been unfair to her. She had her own struggles and ghosts in her past to deal with. He admired her for how well she was handling their new life and was ashamed at how he'd failed these past months at being present and supportive.

He found her perched in front of her vanity, humming a familiar tune. A glass of pale purple liquid sat next to combs, gold clips, and containers of what he assumed was makeup. She twisted her golden hair into an intricate knot on the top of her head. The ivory dress she wore made her gray eyes brighter.

Her humming stopped as he entered her room and sat on the edge of her bed.

"Is that the tonic for your headaches?" he asked, pointing to the glass.

"What's it to you?" She wove pearl-lined pins into her hair, securing the strands in place.

"I thought they were getting better."

"It's amazing how irritating people can make them flare up." She dabbed a pink powder onto her cheeks.

"I'm sorry for yelling at you, and for my behavior," he said, resting his arms on his thighs.

She crossed her arms, and her reflection stared at him until she finally sighed and shook her head.

"I'm sorry, too. I shouldn't be so nosy. I'm just worried about you." Twisting around to face him, she said, "Despite my many mistakes, I want a relationship with you. We're a team—the last of the Farones." She gave him a watery smile.

He picked at the skin on his thumb. *The last of the Farones* sounded so ominous, but if he wanted a relationship with his sister, he needed to be honest and tell her his plans. "Drexus attacked Vastane and is most likely coming to Balten for the Creator Stone." He scanned her face to gauge her reaction at hearing about the man who had raised her. Her face remained expressionless, a skill Drexus must have taught her. "I'm going after the Stone, and if I find it the king wants me to marry Irina."

Jaida's brows inched up her forehead. "Well, based on what I saw, you two have some chemistry. But isn't your heart already spoken for?"

He surveyed her room. Clothes were piled up on the chair, and boots, slippers, and a dirty bowl lay scattered on the floor. He never realized his sister was so messy. He rubbed his temples to relieve his headache. "I don't even know who I am anymore, let alone what my heart wants. Besides, I've never trusted the thing, anyway."

"That's not entirely true. I've seen you with Kenz, and your heart trusted her completely."

Jasce waved his hand as if swatting a pesky bug. "All that matters right now is finding the Creator Stone before Drexus and getting my magic back. Then I can deal with the rest."

"When are we leaving?"

"We?"

"I'm coming with you."

Jasce's head snapped up. "No, you're not. It's too dangerous."

"Yes, I am, but I appreciate your concern."

"As your older brother, I forbid it."

"You can take your male dominance and shove it—" She stopped when he narrowed his eyes. "You're an excellent warrior, but my magic is returning, and I'm not too bad at fighting. Irina has been teaching me."

He wasn't sure how he felt about that, but better she be prepared. When her magic returned fully, plus the training from the Baltens, she'd be lethal. "What about Vale?"

She licked her lips. "What about him?"

"You two have a history. If he gets in my way, I will kill him, and I don't need you as a distraction."

She played with the fur along the cuff of her dress. "I honestly don't know if *my* Vale is still in there after that Vastane hag put three types of magic in him. But what if there's a chance to save him?" She lifted her head. "Everyone deserves a second chance. I have to believe that, for you and for me."

Jasce's chest tightened as he thought about his past, the decisions he'd made, the people he'd killed. Did everyone deserve another chance? Did he? He wasn't so sure. He had the resolve to kill Drexus and Vale, but he didn't think he had the strength to grant them mercy.

"Anyway," Jaida said, a look of understanding crossing her face. She patted him on the shoulder and said, "Go clean up. We're already late for the party."

Chapter Five

The festival was in full swing by the time Jasce and Jaida entered Faerseton Hall. King Morzov and Consort Lekov sat on wooden thrones laced with gold, with Prince Andrei on one side and Princess Irina on the other. The four made an imposing force with their fighting leathers, tattoos, and weapons strapped to their bodies. In the center of the hall was a wooden floor with couples performing a dance that Jasce wasn't familiar with. The hearth on the west side of the room blazed, and ale and whiskey flowed freely from the bar next to it. On the other side of the room were tables laden with meat, an assortment of cheeses, and fresh vegetables grown in the Baltens' greenhouses. Trays of decadent desserts made his mouth water. The atmosphere hummed with laughter and the stomping of boots from the dancing couples.

Jaida immediately abandoned him and joined her friends from the Santoria. He was amazed at how well she'd acclimated to Balten and their way of life, while he still felt like a stranger as he caught wary glances from soldiers as well as some Spectrals from Pandaren. A few Baltens, those he fought with nightly, nodded when he walked toward the bar. He wouldn't call them friends, but he had shared a drink or two with most of them.

Jasce filled his glass from one of the whiskey barrels and drained it.

Breathing deeply, he savored the way the smoky flavor warmed his stomach. He topped off his drink and faced the room, his eyes automatically locating the exits and threats occupying the space, which was pretty much everyone. He'd never lived in a place with so many skilled warriors. Even at the Bastion, there were those who worked in the dining hall or the medical facility who weren't trained to fight. But every person in Balten, no matter their job or station, was lethal.

Jasce rested his hand on the hilt of his dagger and felt its comfortable weight. He'd never be able to let his guard down here, and the thought left him exhausted.

"You made it," Irina said, drawing alongside him. Auburn hair cascaded down her back in a molten waterfall while her large brown eyes smiled warmly. The fighting leathers hugging her curves made him swallow.

"Princess," he said, raising his glass. "Not sure I had a choice."

She rolled her eyes. A red line marred the skin along her neck. He reached out to soothe it but lowered his hand and pointed at the mark. "I'm sorry, again, about earlier."

"No harm done." She raised onto her toes and kissed him on the cheek.

He gave her a quick smile and turned to observe the crowd. "I'm also sorry about your father and his . . ." Jasce searched for the polite word. "Proposal."

She sighed. "He is always planning. But I suppose, as king, he must. I'm sorry he put you in this position."

He leaned against the wall and faced her. "My priority is finding that Stone and killing Drexus. Can you understand that?"

She lifted her chin and studied his face. "I'm a warrior, Jasce. Of course I can."

Relief had him lowering his shoulders as he finished his drink. They both refilled their glasses and found unoccupied chairs near one of the hearths in the enormous hall.

They were soon joined by Nicolaus, who told them stories of Alturia and the exploits of his siblings and their Shade Walking. Jasce laughed and enjoyed the company—a rare occurrence—as they sat before the fire. Irina scooted closer to him as more people invaded their space, while Nicolaus's attention drifted toward the closed doors of the hall. Jasce enjoyed the heat from the princess's thigh touching his and caught himself staring at her. Nicolaus spoke to a server, who shook his head.

"Are you expecting someone, Nicolaus?" Jasce asked when the Shade Walker once again looked toward the closed doors.

"I wonder, Commander, if you've heard from anyone in Pandaren?" Nicolaus asked, picking a piece of meat from a platter and examining it. The Alturian's eyes slid to him, his tone accusatory.

"No, I haven't."

"Ah," Nicolaus said.

Another servant approached Nicolaus. "Your Royal Highness, the king would like a word."

Nicolaus curled his upper lip. "I really hate when they call me that." He stood, sliding a look to the door and back at Jasce. "Please excuse me."

Irina watched him maneuver through the banquet tables and around the dancers to the dais where her father sat. She huffed out a breath. "I thought he'd never leave."

"He is quite the character." His gaze dipped to her lips. He wanted to touch her, feel her pressed against him again, but a segment of his mind shrank away from that thought. The battle going on inside him made him grit his teeth. Why couldn't he enjoy this woman, who was kind and beautiful, and seemed to truly care about him as a person and not a conquest? He studied her auburn hair, a fire drawing a moth to its flame, and ran a silky lock through his fingers. She blushed and heat spread through his loins. The alcohol stripped the inhibitions from his mind and, shoving away any resistance, he surrendered to the cravings of his body.

"Come here," he said, pulling her onto his lap. She licked her lips and ran her hand across his chest, pausing over his pounding heart. He kept telling himself this was what he wanted. He was tired of being consumed by a woman he didn't know, by someone he couldn't remember. When had he last experienced passion? The heat from a woman or the thumping of his heart?

Irina touched her mouth to his. He closed his eyes and savored her soft lips. He brought her closer, relishing her curves as he plunged his hand into her hair. She let out a quiet moan, which caused a shiver to race down his spine. He explored every corner of her mouth, deepening the kiss, craving more as she kissed him back, matching him in desire and wanton need.

A frosty breeze brushed across his face and the hairs on his neck rose. He pulled away from Irina as two Balten soldiers entered the hall. A large man stood between them, his face hidden in the shadows. The room quieted as the stranger stepped into the light. Black, windswept hair stood up in all directions, and a patch covered one eye, but the other one, a piercing green, scanned the room and narrowed when it found Jasce.

"Oh hell," Jasce sighed.

Kord Haring entered, followed by Caston Narr, the commander of the Paladin Guard, and the Fire Spectral Flynt Culbrim, who both shook the snow from their coats. They moved to the side and Jasce's stomach dropped as the ghost from his dreams became flesh and blood. He sprung up from his chair, almost knocking Irina to the floor. But it was too late. Kenz's eyes had immediately found his and widened when she'd seen the woman on his lap.

The music stopped and everyone focused on the visitors as they made their way through the throng of people who parted to let them pass. Nicolaus, who had been speaking to the king, broke out into a catlike grin.

Caston gave a quick nod to Jasce as he made his way to the dais. The former Hunter walked confidently past the warriors, his brown hair damp from the falling snow and ice crystals clinging to his goatee. His coffee-colored eyes scanned the room, most likely searching for exits and potential threats.

Jasce's feet were immobile, as if frozen in blocks of ice. Their sudden appearance caught him off guard, and he didn't have a plan, didn't know what his next move should be. The gnawing pit in his stomach forced him to take a step forward.

Kord, Kenz, and Flynt followed Caston through the hall. Everyone rested their hands near their weapons, including the guests from

Conquering the Darkness

Pandaren. Jasce's thumb methodically tapped on the hilt of his dagger as he maneuvered to the front of the room with Princess Irina on his heels.

Caston bowed his head. "King Morzov, it's a pleasure to see you again. We received your invitation from Prince Jazari. Thank you for allowing our presence in your lands and hearing Queen Valeri's request."

Jasce arched a brow. He couldn't remember Caston ever sounding so diplomatic. His gaze drifted to Kenz. Her midnight hair, dusted with snow, was braided down her back. She wore a fur-lined coat and beige leather pants that hugged the muscles in her legs. Boots, also fur-lined, came to her knees, and a sword hung from her hip while her crossbow was slung across her back.

Her eyes slid toward him, and she swallowed. Kord cleared his throat. Jasce tore his gaze from Kenz, realizing everyone was staring at him.

Consort Lekov hid a smile behind her hand and shrugged when she sensed the king watching her, making her blonde hair skim along her shoulders.

Jaida had maneuvered through the silent crowd and stood beside Jasce.

The king narrowed his eyes and glared at Nicolaus. "My invitation?"

The Shade Walker rubbed the back of his neck. "Yes, well, I had it on good authority . . ."

The king raised his hand. "Enough with your authority." His gaze settled on Caston. "Commander Narr, to what do I owe the pleasure?"

Caston glared at Nicolaus, who smiled and feigned innocence, a mischievous glint in his silver eyes.

"Your Majesty, sorry for the misunderstanding." Caston darted a quick glance around the hall and lowered his voice. "Queen Valeri asks for aid. I'm sure you've heard about the attack on Vastane. We know what Drexus is searching for."

The king leaned back onto his throne, the gold inlay sparkling from the chandeliers overhead. "Yes, I'm aware. My men are scouting near Havelock."

Consort Lekov rested her hand on the king's thigh. "Perhaps this is a discussion for another time and place." She gestured toward the still-silent crowd fixated on the visitors.

Prince Andrei surveyed Caston and the others, his eyes matching the frozen landscape, cold and unyielding. "Agreed." He turned toward the king. "Father, allow me to escort our *guests* to their quarters."

Kord crossed his muscular arms while Caston's lip curled into a snarl. Flynt, finally tearing his gaze from Jaida, clicked his wrists and green fire coursed through his fingers. Kenz's eyes narrowed, and the bracelets on her wrists glowed.

Jasce stepped forward before the political tension turned aggressive. "Andrei, surely this isn't how you treat the Queen of Pandaren's commander and his associates."

A gasp resounded through the room, and the prince's face reddened. "You will not address me so informally," the prince said through his teeth.

Nicolaus chuckled. "Well, some things haven't changed."

Jasce held Prince Andrei's glare while Jaida reached for his hand and gave it a firm squeeze.

"Enough with the formalities. These are our friends." Nicolaus walked down the dais and shook Caston's and Kord's hands. He nodded to Flynt, who barely glanced at the Alturian as he stared at Jaida.

"Kenz, darling, you're looking well. The cold suits you," Nicolaus said, folding his arms around her and lifting her off her toes.

Kenz laughed, and Jasce's gut clenched with jealousy, his body reacting automatically while logic tried to curb the irrational feelings. She wasn't his, after all. Sensing the stares of the king and Princess Irina, he forced himself to relax his fists.

"Prince Jazari, it's good to see you, too," Kenz said, unwrapping herself from his hug. The flush in her cheeks had brightened.

"Nicolaus, please," the Shade Walker said with a wink.

The king cleared his throat and raised a hand. "I'm sure our guests are hungry from their long journey." He focused on the Spectrals. "Please, warm yourself by my fire. I will have food brought to you, and we will discuss everything in the morning, yes?"

"Thank you for your hospitality, Your Majesty," Caston said.

Conquering the Darkness

Jaida released Jasce's hand and ran toward Flynt, giving him a big hug. Jasce's brows raised as Flynt spun her around.

Nicolaus stood next to Jasce. "Your reactions are quite telling, memories or not," he whispered out of the corner of his mouth.

Jasce shoved his hands into his pockets, restraining himself from landing his fist into the smug man's face. "You knew they were coming, didn't you?"

"Of course I did." Nicolaus led Caston, Flynt, and Jaida to a nearby table.

Jasce's pulse pounded in his ears and his legs felt like stone as Kord and Kenz neared. A familiar citrusy scent, one he recognized from his time healing in the Sanctuary, greeted him and settled his racing heart.

"Hello, Kenz," he said, his mouth suddenly dry.

Kenz sighed. "Hello."

He tore his gaze from her, feeling the weight of Kord's stare. He crossed his arms and widened his stance. The need to lash out at the Healer battled with the kindness he had shown Jasce in Orilyon. "Kord."

Kord gave a sad smile. "Your memories haven't returned yet, have they?"

"No." Jasce glanced at Kenz, who kept her face blank, but he hadn't missed the straightening of her spine. He couldn't stomach the disappointment flowing off them or deal with the anger making his pulse race. It was, after all, Kord's fault he couldn't remember them. "Come on, I'm sure you're tired and hungry." He led them to the table with Nicolaus and the others.

Caston stood and hugged him when he approached. Jasce kept his hands by his side. Hunters didn't hug each other.

"You look like hell," Caston said, examining him.

He raised his brows. "It's good to see you, too."

Caston chuckled but his smile didn't reach his eyes. "What's with the fuzzy animal growing out of your face?" Jasce didn't have a chance to respond before Caston pulled him aside.

"You still don't have your memories, do you?"

Jasce shook his head.

Caston sighed. "I'm worried about you. Something's off, besides your memories."

Jasce frowned. He didn't have that close of a relationship with the ex-Hunter for him to know if something was off. Or did he? He glared at Kord, who had immediately grabbed a tankard of ale. Kenz turned rigid as she scowled at Jaida, who sat next to Flynt. Jaida looked up, and a flush crept up her neck.

"I'll catch up with you later," Jaida said, patting Flynt's hand. She rose from the bench and retreated to where her friends from the Santoria whispered around their table.

Flynt watched her go and then shot a look at Kenz. Kord shook his head while Nicolaus poured Kenz a glass of whiskey and handed it to her.

"Here, this will take the edge off," Nicolaus said.

The tension among the group was as thick as tar. Jasce had learned that Jaida had lost control of her magic during the battle with the Vastanes and had accidentally killed Amycus. Kenz obviously still blamed her. He opened his mouth to say something—the need to protect his sister a natural reflex—but snapped it shut when he saw Kenz quickly wipe a tear off her cheek. Warmth stirred in his chest with the longing to comfort her, but that was as foreign as another Hunter hugging him.

Jasce swore under his breath. This was going to be a long night. He filled his glass and downed the contents in one gulp, ignoring the concerned looks from Kord and Caston.

Caston loaded his plate with roasted meat and creamy cheeses. He speared a vegetable with his fork and raised his brows at Jasce.

He was about to tell them about the Baltens' ingenious use of the hot springs for power, running water, and the greenhouses when King Morzov raised his voice.

"Here's to the start of our Zima Festival. May this year bring prosperity in wealth, victory in battle, and honor to our ancestors." He lifted his glass and toasted the room. The Baltens banged their cups and fists on the tables. The king waited for the noise to die down and then continued. "And what better way to kick off the festivities than by

Conquering the Darkness

sharing this wonderful news?" His eyes, sparkling with victory, darted from his daughter to Jasce.

Princess Irina rushed to the dais. "Father, no—"

King Morzov lifted his hand.

Jasce's stomach dropped. *No*, he thought. Not now. He started to rise from the table.

"I'd like to announce the engagement of my lovely daughter, Princess Irina, to Commander Jasce Farone."

A glass dropped to the floor and shattered. Jasce closed his eyes and forced himself to turn.

Kenz stood, her entire body vibrating with fury.

"Kenz, I . . ."

Tears lined her eyes as she shook her head. Turning on her heel, she stomped through the hall, threw on her coat, and yanked open the doors.

A large hand fell on his shoulder. Jasce peered into one green eye, brimming with anger.

Kord towered over him. "What the hell is going on?"

Chapter Six

"You're engaged?" Kord crossed his arms and glared down at Jasce. Jasce pulled his gaze from Kenz, disappearing into the snow. The door shut with a thunk of finality as he stared at friends from another life. Caston winced and took a drink of his ale while Flynt glared daggers at him. The Fire Spectral mumbled under his breath and pushed back from the table, most likely searching for Jaida, who stood across the hall with her mouth open. She quickly snapped it shut when she noticed Flynt striding toward her.

A small hand touched his arm. "Jasce, I'm so sorry. My father had no right..."

Kord spun him around. "I asked you a question." His voice rumbled like thunder echoing off the towering cliffs of the Torrath Mountains.

"Can you give me a second?" Jasce asked, stepping away from Irina and Kord.

Princess Irina blinked away the hurt and straightened, addressing Kord. "Hello. We haven't met."

Kord bowed. "Princess Irina, forgive my rudeness. I'm just... I—"

"Kord Haring, this is Princess Irina of Balten, daughter of King Morzov," Nicolaus said.

"Yeah, I kind of figured that out," Kord said, sliding a glance at the Shade Walker.

"Princess Irina, this is Kord Haring, a Healer and Spectral Counselor to Queen Valeri," Nicolaus continued, ignoring Kord.

Caston choked on his ale, and Kord's eyes widened. "How did you know that? She just made the announcement two weeks ago," Kord said.

Nicolaus rested his hands on his hips. "Why is everyone surprised I know things?"

Caston surveyed the room. "Jasce, Kord, sit down. You're making a scene."

Kord muttered and returned to his seat. Jasce remained standing, unsure if he should go after Kenz or talk to the king.

"Best to let her cool off," Caston said, as if reading his mind.

Princess Irina sat on the bench next to Nicolaus, who scoffed as she drained his glass. "And I wouldn't talk to my father yet. He's in a mood."

Jasce sighed and sat opposite of Irina and Nicolaus. He pulled his flask from his pocket, and his knuckles whitened as he squeezed the metal, taking a long pull to relieve the tightness in his chest.

Caston's eyes narrowed as he watched Jasce take another drink. He cleared his throat. "Well, it seems you're still keeping things interesting."

"Glad you think so," Jasce said. "And quit glaring at me, Kord, before I knock that look off your face."

"Here we go." Caston rubbed his forehead.

Kord placed his large hands on the table and leaned forward. "I'd certainly like to see you try."

"Okay, boys, let's not do this here," Nicolaus said, his tone concerned but his eyes flashing with amusement.

A loud crash sounded from the other side of the room where two Balten soldiers wrestled while laughter and money exchanged hands.

"This seems like the perfect place," Kord said, getting to his feet.

Jasce's body vibrated from the anger coursing through him. Punching anyone right now sounded like a good plan.

Irina gripped his hand. "I'm not sure that's a good idea, not with your injury."

Conquering the Darkness

"I'm fine," Jasce said at the same time Kord said, "What injury?"

"It's none of your concern." Jasce stalked to the end of the table.

Kord seized his arm, his fingers digging into Jasce's bicep. "What injury?"

Without thinking, Jasce twisted and ducked, throwing the Healer over his back. With a grunt, Kord hit the ground. Once again, the hall fell silent.

"Stay down," Jasce said through gritted teeth.

Kord rose to his feet and sighed. He spun around, and before Jasce dodged out of the way, Kord's fist connected with his jaw. He stumbled and blinked back stars. His knuckles cracked as he fisted his hands, and his lips curved into a smile.

Caston swore and took hold of Jasce's arm. "Kord, I'd back away if I were you."

"Well, you're not me," he said, widening his stance.

Jasce twisted out of Caston's grasp and lunged for Kord. He swore as his back spasmed. He tried to stay upright, but his leg collapsed underneath him, and his knee struck hard against the stone floor.

"Whoa, are you okay?" Caston asked.

Princess Irina drummed her fingers on the table. "That's the injury I was talking about."

Kord lowered his fists, and the anger deflated from his shoulders like a torn sail. "What's wrong with you?"

Jasce wiped sweat from his forehead while attempting to relax the muscles in his spine. Months of pent-up frustration surged to the surface, giving him the strength to stand. "*You* are what's wrong with me. Because of you, I have no magic. Because of you, I have no memories. You are the reason for the hell I'm in!"

He shoved past a wounded-looking Kord and limped toward the double doors leading outside. Within seconds, Jaida was walking beside him. She reached out, but he shook his head. Any pretense at hiding his weakness from the Balten soldiers evaporated.

The predator has just become the prey, he thought fisting his hands.

Jasce strode through the snow, anger and whiskey lessening the pain in his back, and didn't stop until he entered the nearest tavern. He pushed past men waiting next to the fighting ring and ducked under the ropes. Yells of protest assailed his ears, but he didn't care. He needed to hit someone.

A mountain of a man named Yuri wiped sweat from his tattooed forehead as he stared at the unconscious man at his feet. Blood dripped from his cracked knuckles, leaving splatters in the dirt.

His brows disappeared behind a mop of black hair as Jasce approached. "Ah, Ahren. The angel from the north wants to fight, yes?"

Jasce twisted his head, satisfied with the crack in his neck and raised his fists. "Yes, he does." His attack was messy and uncontrolled, but with each pound of flesh, the anger settled into a simmering flame instead of a raging inferno. Blood dripped from his lip, and he was pretty sure Yuri had cracked a rib, but he couldn't stop.

They circled each other while the crowd placed wagers. Jasce charged and wrapped his arms around Yuri, lifting him and dropping him into the dirt. The move made his spine seize. Yuri used the hesitation, bucked his hips, and clocked Jasce on the jaw with his elbow.

Stars erupted as pain sliced through his skull. He tried to push himself off the ground but Yuri kicked him. If his ribs weren't broken before, they were now. He coughed up blood and tried to protect his damaged side.

Yuri grabbed him, and Jasce immediately cried out, reaching for his back. The Balten lifted him into the air and threw him to the ground, followed by a rapid fire of fists and kicks. Blood spurted from Jasce's nose, and a searing heat lanced through his back and leg.

A bell rang in the distance and cheers sounded before darkness took hold of him and dragged him under.

∼

Jasce blinked open his eyes. Lamps glowed softly, reflecting against the pale blue walls where metal pipes emitting a hissing sound snaked along the ceiling. The last thing he remembered was Yuri's sizable fist connecting with his temple. Last night was one of the worst beatings he'd received in a while. He didn't want to imagine the amount of ribbing the other soldiers would give him the next time he entered the Terrovka to train.

"Ah, you're awake."

He slid his gaze to the side. Princess Irina sat with a book lying closed on her lap. She'd replaced her leathers for the one-piece uniform worn by the menders working in the Santoria. The dark blue fabric looked durable, yet also seemed soft.

Pondering Irina's clothing made him suddenly aware he was naked, with only a thin sheet covering him.

"Where are my clothes?" His voice sounded like he'd swallowed knives. The door to his private room was shut, and he briefly wondered if Jaida was working her normal shift, hoping she wasn't. The last thing he needed was for her to see him like this, broken and defeated.

"They're being washed since you were covered in blood and dirt."

"And were you the one who removed them?"

The corner of her lip quirked. "You've seen one naked body, you've seen them all, Commander."

He closed his eyes and sighed. "I've asked you not to call me that."

"Yes, well . . ." She waved her hand as if swatting an annoying insect. "You have three broken ribs, fixed by a Spectral Healer, contusions on your chest and arms, and a dislocated shoulder, which we put back in place when you were unconscious. Plus a laceration along your cheek." She placed the book on the side table and frowned at him. "And to add insult to injury, my brother followed you to the tavern and made a lot of money off your fight."

He groaned at the thought of the prince profiting from his failure and hissed in pain, grabbing his side. His body ached everywhere as he rose to his elbows. Inhaling, he waited for the throbbing to subside in his head and his vision to settle. Irina helped him pivot, and he nodded his thanks, keeping the sheet covering him from the waist down. He didn't care how many naked bodies she'd seen.

A thousand thoughts had careened through his mind as he'd wandered through the snow and ice to the tavern—kissing Irina, the hurt on Kenz's face, the king's announcement, his anger toward Kord. Seeing Caston again had revealed how lonely he truly was. He wanted to talk to his friend and get an update on the search for Drexus. He also needed to speak to Kenz, even though he had no clue what he would say to her. He wouldn't mind going another round with Kord, but later, after he healed. He couldn't stand another beating, and he suspected Kord might do some damage.

Irina sat next to him on the bed. "Do you want to talk about it?"

Jasce rubbed his hands down his face. "Not really." What he wanted was his own bed and a drink. Too many emotions flowed through him—shame, guilt, loneliness. He was lost, floundering in the waves of misfortune, their intent to drag him to the deep where no one could rescue him.

Irina ran her fingers through his hair, loosening the tangles. He leaned into the touch, not realizing how desperately he needed the comfort she offered. She tied his hair back with a leather thong, letting her hand linger on the base of his neck.

"I'm sorry about my father's announcement. That was uncalled for."

He held her hand and rubbed his thumb along the calluses on her palm. She had a warrior's hand from years of wielding a weapon, yet her touch was gentle. The king's proposal was the least of his worries, even though he suspected the man had used Caston and his team's arrival to his advantage. The king wouldn't make a move on the Creator Stone until he received word from Matvey. Jasce hated waiting, which would now be worse with Kord and Kenz showing up out of nowhere.

Well, not nowhere. Nicolaus, the conniver that he was, seemed to have orchestrated them coming to Balten. Granted, Queen Valeri had also requested aid, but she could have sent a simple messenger for that, not the commander of her army.

All he knew was he couldn't allow Drexus to get that Stone, and he needed his magic back, especially after seeing Jaida's powers had returned. It seemed Maera and Kord's procedure wasn't completely effective. Maybe his magic would return on its own, but since his memories hadn't, he wasn't patient enough to wait. The Creator Stone solved his problems, at least most of them. Which meant he needed to speak with the king immediately. He looked down, not realizing he still held Irina's hand.

She smiled at him. "It's amazing to watch."

"What is?"

Conquering the Darkness

"Your thinking process." She pressed a finger on the lines between his brows. "These get very deep when you're lost in thought. What were you contemplating?"

"Everything."

"Was it difficult seeing your friends again? They seem nice, by the way."

"Besides Caston, I really don't remember the others. Which I know hurts them. I can see it on their faces. Except for Flynt. He acts like he doesn't like me much."

"He gave the impression of being taken with your sister, though. She's mentioned him a few times over a bottle of wine."

Jasce huffed. "Great."

"Kenz was your fiancée? Is that right?"

He rubbed the back of his neck. "Yes."

"Do you . . . Have your feelings for her returned?" A slight flush crept into the princess's cheeks.

His feelings were a jumbled mess, and he couldn't make sense of them at the moment. "How can I not remember someone I supposedly loved enough to want to marry? I just don't understand why my memories haven't returned."

"Do you want them to?"

Jasce turned slowly to face Irina. "That's a stupid question."

"Is it? The mind is a complex system, and I believe we can subconsciously do things to protect ourselves. Might be something to think about." She squeezed his hand.

He sighed, unable to muster the energy to consider what the princess had said. Of course he wanted his memories back. He shook his head and stood, bringing the sheet with him. Pain shot through him, and he hunched over to stem the nausea.

"Go slowly," Irina said, holding him by his elbow.

"Any chance you might find me something to wear?" he asked.

She crossed her arms as her eyes traveled along his chest. "I suppose. And we need to get you healed up. We have a few Spectral Healers, including your friend Kord, if you'd like to speed up the process."

"No. I don't want him seeing me like this."

"Good, because I have something I'd like to try first. We have time before the meeting."

He frowned at her, wondering if he was about to become another one of her experiments. First the Makovus and now whatever she was concocting. The scar above her lip puckered as she grinned at him.

"Trust me," was all she said.

Chapter Seven

"You've got to be kidding," Jasce said, kicking at a chunk of ice clinging to the dock. The sky had lightened with the appearance of dawn as he scowled at the lake behind the palace. He could barely make out the pine trees surrounding one edge of the water, and someone had cleared the snow from the beach. Red markers floated in the water among chunks of ice, as if outlining a specific course. Surely the Baltens weren't fanatical enough to swim in a frozen pond.

Princess Irina tugged her cloak tighter around her. "Based on my research, extreme temperatures force your body to go into survival mode, thereby speeding up the healing process."

Jasce shivered at the thought of getting into that water. He looked to where two workers from the Santoria waited near a fire they had built, both wrapped in fur cloaks. "Why are they here?"

"Just in case. Elethea is a Spectral Healer, and we might need her to revive you if you panic."

He frowned. "I don't panic." He held Elethea's stare and knew she would not be keen to help him. She'd probably push his head under the ice if she had the chance.

Irina chuckled. "Sometimes our body reacts before our mind can catch up, which is why I want you to practice a breathing technique before we get in."

"We?"

"Yes, I will be with you to keep you calm."

He huffed. Drexus's training and discipline methods had taught him to stay calm during stressful situations. "You seem to forget I'm a Hunter. Or was." He removed his cloak and started untying the laces of his boots. "I'll be fine."

"Uh huh. Whatever happens, don't go under the ice." Irina undressed and goosebumps pebbled along her toned olive skin.

Jasce had to swallow the desire coursing through him as her clothing landed on a blanket on the snow-covered dock. She only wore a camisole and linen shorts that seemed a little too short. He had wondered how much of her body was covered in tattoos and now he knew. Symbols interlaced with vines and flowers trailed from her collarbone down her chest and across her stomach. She also had intricate designs on her muscular legs and arms.

He tore his gaze from her almost naked form, burying the memory of her lying underneath him, and focused on a hole that had been cut through the ice, large enough for them to fit. The frigid air made him clench his teeth and sent a shiver down his spine.

She took hold of his hand and pressed it to the space between her breasts. "Breathe like this. Count of four in, hold for four, exhale for four, and hold again for four. Make sense?"

Her chest expanded as she filled her lungs with air. He quickly lifted his eyes from her breasts, the thin fabric leaving little to the imagination, and stared at her lips.

Silently cursing, he closed his eyes and listened to her breathe while focusing on the areas of pain in his body, effectively dousing the desire burning in his core. He copied the pattern of breathing and was soon lost to the rhythm of it.

"Good," she said, taking his hand and leading him onto the ice.

Jasce interlaced his fingers with hers, and they sat, lowering themselves into the water. A burning sensation assaulted his legs as he made his way deeper into the darkness. His heart stopped, but within seconds it thundered against his ribs. Any chance of breathing deeply evaporated in a puff of frozen air.

He swore as the water crested over his shoulders and rotated his legs in quick circles to keep himself afloat.

Irina's lips turned a light shade of blue, but her body remained calm as she breathed. "You're not breathing properly."

Jasce closed his eyes and repeated his mantra—*pain is inescapable; suffering is a choice*—and breathed as Irina had suggested. Slowly, his heart rate returned to normal.

After what seemed like hours but was only a few minutes, he stared down at his body and stopped moving. The pain in his back had disappeared. Irina seized his arm when he started to sink.

"It's gone," he said through chattering teeth.

Irina smiled. "Give me thirty more seconds."

He continued to swivel his legs and arms, the movement growing slower with each second. Lead filled his muscles, and his thoughts became muddled.

Irina waved to Elethea and the other mender, who rushed over and pulled them from the water. They wrapped warm blankets around them and gave them hot cider to drink.

"Rub your arms slowly. You don't want your blood rushing to your heart too quickly," the Healer said. The look in her eyes told Jasce what he had already suspected. She knew who he was, or had been, and wasn't happy about helping the Angel of Death. He didn't blame her.

"Thank you," he said, his entire body shaking uncontrollably.

Elethea narrowed her eyes and dipped her chin.

"You did well for your first time," Irina said.

"First time?" Jasce asked.

"Yes. We need to do this daily. You also need to be visiting the hot springs regularly. Keep your body guessing and therefore working hard to aid the healing process. Or you could just have a Spectral Healer fix you. But, alas, you are stubborn."

Jasce had to admit the underlying pain had disappeared, at least for the time being. He was curious how long the relief would last. His hands trembled as he fumbled with the ties on his tunic.

"Here, let me help you." Irina blew into her hands and tied the laces. She tucked a piece of hair behind his ear.

Jasce's vision blurred, and the ground swayed. He rested his hands on his thighs as a fuzzy image hovered, just out of reach, of him kneeling in a stream. Gentle fingers scraped along his bare chest and washed the blood off his face as he gazed into beautiful green eyes.

The image disappeared as quickly as it had come.

"Are you all right?" Irina asked.

He straightened and turned away from the concern on the princess's face. He was so tired of only having shadows of memory, fleeting like the white puff of his breath disappearing in the wind. The need to find the Creator Stone and have his memories returned lit a fire deep inside him. He thought about the princess's question, if he wanted his memories back. The answer was yes. He needed his life back, whatever that looked like. He couldn't move forward or escape the person he had become while an unknown past lurked in the dark recesses of his mind.

~

Jasce returned home and dressed quickly, relieved that Jaida was at work. He didn't have time to answer her questions or see the look of disappointment in her eyes. She would have heard about his tavern fight and spending the night in the Santoria. Hell, Irina may have even told her, as they seemed much closer friends than he had originally suspected.

He strode along the stone hallway toward the king's meeting rooms, hoping to talk with him before everyone else arrived. His mind and body were at war with each other. The ice plunge with Irina had been interesting and her tender, healing touch comforting, but the sorrow and betrayal on Kenz's face from the night before bothered him. What must she think? A few months ago they'd been engaged, and now he didn't even know who she was.

He rounded the corner where two soldiers guarded enormous wooden doors lined with iron bands.

"May I enter?" Jasce asked.

One guard glanced at the other and nodded. The door squeaked open, and Jasce marched in, the stomping of his boots on stone giving way as he stepped onto the thick burgundy carpet. A large oval table occupied the center of the room, polished to a shine and reflecting the chandelier above it. The king stood near the fireplace, his back to Jasce as he stared out the windows lining the far wall. Heavy brocade curtains were pulled aside to display the snow-covered mountains. The sun peeked over the summit and ignited the snow, making it sparkle like diamonds. It was the first time in months he'd seen a cloudless sky, the blue color resembling a tropical sea.

King Morzov turned toward him, and his eyes narrowed as he examined the bruises marring Jasce's face. The king wore a wool tunic partially covered by a leather chest piece. He'd tucked his heavy leather pants into black boots that traveled up to his knee. "I figured you'd be the first to arrive."

Consort Lekov, surrounded by papers, worked on the other side of the room. When she looked up, her eyes widened. "What happened to your face?"

"Yuri happened to my face," Jasce said, rubbing his jaw. "And Kord."

"Ah," was all she said, and she resumed paging through a ledger and scribbling notes.

"What you did last night was uncalled for," Jasce said to King Morzov, approaching the fire, attempting to remove the chill from his bones.

"Mind your tone, Commander. You are a guest in my lands and have no power here."

Jasce crossed his arms. "And yet you want me to marry your daughter."

The king arched a brow and chuckled. "Point taken. Come, sit." He led Jasce to a table with a board of colored squares and playing pieces Jasce had seen the game before but had never played it.

"May I ask why you made the announcement last night? I hadn't agreed to anything," Jasce said, sitting.

"Once Matvey returns, are you going with my son to retrieve the Stone?"

"Yes."

The king crossed his ankle over his knee. "Then you have agreed. Besides, it seems Nicolaus played us both with the timing of your former friends. I don't need them adding any more complications or reminders of your past life."

"When my memories return—"

"If they return," the king interrupted.

Jasce fisted a hand under the table. "If they return, that will not be fair to your daughter."

"Like I said before, my daughter understands her responsibilities to her kingdom."

"And what about love?" The question flew out of his mouth before he could rein it in. He'd been around politics long enough to understand that love had nothing to do with alliances.

"Based on the look on your face, I believe you've answered that question." King Morzov leaned back into his chair and fiddled with one of the playing pieces. "You must understand, this is one reason I offered you and your sister asylum here. I have plans for Balten, and now Pandaren. But first we need to deal with these Stones and your former commander."

"Queen Valeri might have something to say about all of this."

The king waved his large hand and blew out a puff of air. "Aligning with Balten will solidify her presence and protect Pandaren from other invading kingdoms." He stared out the window, his face grim. "Balten has many enemies. To the south are tribes who want my land and will die fighting for it. To the east, across the sea, is the island of Aria. We have reports the Fae are preparing their army. We do not yet know their destination, but as warriors, we must always be ready."

Consort Lekov wandered over while the king spoke and rested a comforting hand on the king's shoulder. "Alturia and Terrenus are not the only kingdoms out there," she said to Jasce.

"No, we are not." The Alturian prince sauntered into the room. He examined the paintings with images of warriors fighting alongside their magical Defenders. The Baltens' magic was the most mysterious in Jasce's opinion. Along with having increased speed and strength, a Balten could call upon an ancient descendant who would fight along-

Conquering the Darkness

side them, but only for a short while. Summoning that kind of magic drained the wielder and was only used as a last resort.

"Prince Jazari, why are you here?" the king asked, pushing back from the table. His knees cracked as he rose to his feet. The consort narrowed her eyes and whispered to her husband. He mumbled a reply but continued to scowl at the prince.

"Because I'm joining the commander on this mission." Nicolaus raised his brows as he looked at Jasce. "Do we have a plan yet?"

"We hadn't gotten that far into the discussion," Jasce said, wanting once again to smack the smug smile off Nicolaus's face.

"Yes, well after that announcement last night, I'm sure you had some details to sort out." Nicolaus straightened his emerald green tunic and found a spot at the table.

The doors swung open again, and Prince Andrei entered, dressed in a leather chest piece like his father's, with a sword hanging from his hip. He was followed by Caston, Kord, Kenz, and Flynt. Caston nodded to Jasce, but the other three found more interesting places to look.

Jasce sighed and stood, dreading the awkward couple of hours that lay before him.

"Ah, thank you, son, for escorting our guests. We have much to discuss." King Morzov sat at the head of the table. "Where's your sister?"

Prince Andrei was about to answer when Princess Irina entered, dressed in her uniform.

The king pinched the bridge of his nose while Consort Lekov took her spot next to her husband. "You know, you are a princess. I don't understand why you feel the need to work in the medical facility," the king said.

"Now is not the time, Father." She took her seat next to the consort. "Sorry I'm late. We had an incident in the Santoria."

"Is Jaida all right?" Jasce asked.

Irina smiled. "She's fine. Her assistance was invaluable."

Kord's brow furrowed. "Jaida works with your healers?"

"Yes, although we call them menders. She doesn't have Spectral Healer magic, but she has the touch. I'd love for you to visit our infirmary and get your opinion on a few matters. We also have some Pandaren Healers I'm sure you'd like to meet."

"I'd enjoy that very much. Thank you," Kord said, bowing his head. He sat next to Jasce while everyone else found their places around the table.

"I'm sorry for punching you last night," Kord whispered.

Jasce gave him a sidelong glance. "No, you're not."

Kord chuckled. "Okay, I'm not, but can we talk after this?"

Jasce's vision blurred, and he gripped the table. As if watching from afar, a fuzzy image formed. Jasce and Kord stood side by side, with Kord's hand resting on his shoulder. He couldn't see their faces but felt an unexplainable sense of calm as the Healer stayed by him, a bulwark of strength and loyalty.

Jasce sighed at the distorted memory, if that's what it was, and again found himself battling with his resentment toward Kord for taking his magic and a deep-rooted knowledge that the man was a trustworthy friend. Resolving the conflict with Kord was not at the top of his list of priorities, but he agreed nonetheless to talk with him later.

The next hour was filled with details about what type of aid Queen Valeri needed from the Baltens. Caston and the king negotiated until they were both satisfied while Jasce fidgeted, unable to get comfortable. His body ached, despite the ice therapy from this morning. Of course, it didn't help that his muscles were pulled as tight as a bowstring. His gaze darted around the room, and he sighed in relief when he noticed the table with varying sizes of decanters.

"Will you excuse me?" he asked, and all eyes jumped to him. The king arched a brow but waved as if to say *go ahead*. Jasce pushed up from his chair and made his way to the table with the drinks. "Anyone want one?" His hand shook as he poured the whiskey. After draining the contents, he refilled his glass and faced the room.

A look of sadness flickered in Kenz's eyes before she shook her head, leaned forward, and addressed the king. "If that's all settled, is it true you're using the Creator Stone as a bargaining chip for Jasce to marry your daughter?"

Jasce coughed and almost spit the whiskey out of his mouth. Awkward couldn't even describe the room as he glanced around the table. Prince Andrei smirked and the princess's eyes had gone as wide as saucers. The consort tucked her chin to hide her laugh, while the king puffed out his chest.

"Kenz," Caston said, his eyes narrowed. Kord rubbed his forehead while Flynt fidgeted with his ignitor switch.

Nicolaus cleared his throat. "Jasce, pour me one. This conversation is about to get interesting."

Chapter Eight

"Who do you think you are, questioning my decisions?" King Morzov glowered at her and his fists clenched. Jasce inched closer to Kenz, whose bracelets glowed. Sensing the consort and Princess Irina studying him, he forced himself to sit, but his eyes never left the king.

Caston pressed his hands to the table. "Your Majesty, please excuse my friend here. She sometimes speaks without thinking." He threw a glance at Kenz, who glared back.

Consort Lekov rested her hand on the king's. "We need to focus on the Creator Stone. Once we get information from Matvey, then we'll have a better idea of Drexus's location."

"I don't understand why we are waiting," Jasce said. "What does it matter where Drexus is? I need that Stone."

"There is more at stake than you getting your magic back," Prince Andrei said. "Besides, how do we know you won't lead him right to it? You were once his second in command."

Jasce tapped his finger on his glass and reined in his irritation. Everything in him wanted to slam the prince's handsome face onto the table.

"Are you questioning Jasce's loyalty?" Kenz asked, her neck flushed.

"I agree," Princess Irina said. "Andrei, that is an unfair and unfounded accusation."

The prince scowled at Jasce but remained silent.

"Besides," Nicolaus cut in, "Drexus doesn't need Jasce to lead him to the Stone. He has the Empower Stone, which will want to be united with its counterpart."

Jasce rubbed his temples. "So I'll ask again, why are we waiting?"

"Because there are two different passes we can take to the location," King Morzov said. "The goal is to get in and out without being noticed, then we can trap Drexus."

Flynt lifted a finger. "I'm sorry to interrupt, but why isn't the Stone here? This place is a fortress."

"That's an excellent question," Kord said.

The king tapped his lip as he stared around the table. "The Stone has been hidden, and safe I might add, for thousands of years, before Nivia became the kingdom city. It is well protected."

"It was until Drexus stole the Empower Stone," Consort Lekov said.

"Either way, the Stone takes priority over any vengeance you may have," the Balten king said to Jasce, his jaw set.

Jasce was about to reply when Kenz faced him, her eyes sparking with anger. "It's like we've come full circle again, with revenge on Drexus being your only priority."

"Damn straight. And from my point of view, this is my first time. But how could any of you understand? You still have your magic, your memories. Your sibling wasn't stolen from you, and I'm pretty sure none of you have been whipped or had a sword shoved through your chest." Jasce's blood boiled as his anger grew.

"Actually, I have," Kord said, lifting his hand. Jasce snapped his head around and stared at the Healer. "The sword through the chest part." Kord smiled sheepishly. "I've had that happen to me."

"Really?" Kenz said to her brother, irritation lining her voice.

Kord lifted his palms and mumbled, "Well, it's true."

Jasce shook his head. "That's why I'm going on this mission, to stop Drexus and get the Creator Stone."

"And the added benefit of getting a wife and therefore becoming a prince of Balten has no influence?" Prince Andrei asked.

Conquering the Darkness

Jasce dropped his head into his hands.

"And we're back to this again," Flynt said, pushing up from the table to pour his own drink.

"My future has yet to be decided. I do have a say in who I marry," Princess Irina said, glaring at her brother and father. She shifted her focus to Kenz. "I'm truly sorry about this."

Kenz's eyebrows shot up.

"Back to the matter at hand," the king said with an air of impatience lining his voice.

"Yes. Thankfully, the other two Stones are still hidden," Consort Lekov interrupted.

Nicolaus cleared his throat. "That's not entirely true."

"What do you mean?" Jasce asked.

Caston drummed his fingers on the table. "Our team discovered the Inhibitor Stone in the Desert of Souls. Because of Lord Rollant's connections we had a pretty good idea of where it was, and with the help of Prince Jazari we were able to locate its exact position."

"How?" Consort Lekov asked, frowning at Nicolaus.

The king crossed his muscular arms. "Yes, I'd like to hear this."

"It seems our Alturian friend acquired the sliver of the Empower Stone that was left behind during the battle with Queen Siryn. The sliver can also lead to the other pieces of the Heart," Caston said.

"And where is the Inhibitor Stone now?" the king asked with narrowed eyes.

Caston chewed the inside of his cheek. "Orilyon."

"Orilyon? Are you serious? It's not safe there," Prince Andrei said. "Father, we need to retrieve it at once."

The king held up his hand, silencing his son.

Kord bristled. "The Stone is safe. Plus, one of our top physicians is examining its magical properties to see if we can use it as a weapon to stop Drexus."

King Morzov slammed his fist onto the table. "The Stones are not to be trifled with. I will send word to Queen Valeri at once."

"That is unnecessary," Caston said. "The Inhibitor Stone is well protected."

"We need to table this discussion for the time being." Consort

Lekov made eye contact with each person in the room. "The festival games are starting soon and our presence is required. Besides, we can't do anything until Matvey returns."

The king tore his gaze from Caston and forced a smile as he gripped his consort's hand. "Yes, we will wait for Matvey. Until then, please enjoy the games. I hope you all will consider participating."

"What games?" Kord asked.

"The first is sparring." Prince Andrei pushed up from his chair and pointed to Jasce. "And I officially challenge you, if you think you can manage."

Jasce tilted his head and smiled. "Challenge accepted."

～

The Zima Festival games were comprised of sparring, a rock wall competition, a swimming race, and jousting, but riding on the Ornix instead of horses. Recalling the red markers in the lake, he realized the Baltens were insane. Who had a swimming competition in freezing water? As Jasce peered over the balcony of the Terrovka watching members of his class compete, he marveled at how strange the Balten games were. Although the jousting might be entertaining.

The entire ground floor of the training center had been set up for the sparring competition. King Morzov and Consort Lekov sat on ornate wooden thrones to witness the participants compete. Princess Irina and Prince Andrei were absent from their usual spots, but a few older nobles flanked them and acted as official judges.

The medical wing inside the training facility was already full of patients. Jasce caught Jaida helping the warriors, and a flush of pride washed over him at how well his sister was doing. He hoped she changed her mind about coming with him to find the Stone, for her sake and for his.

A group of younger soldiers surrounded one ring as two of his students sparred with short staffs. Jasce smiled when Eva swept her leg, knocking her opponent to their knees and jabbing her weapon into their stomach—a move he had specifically taught them.

"Is she one of yours?" Kord asked.

Conquering the Darkness

Jasce had been so preoccupied he hadn't even heard Kord approach and scolded himself for being such an easy target.

"Yes, most of those kids are in my class," Jasce said.

"You're a wonderful teacher. You taught Kenz and me. Flynt, too."

He wasn't in the mood for small talk or flattery. "What did you want to talk about?"

Kord leaned on the railing and peered at him with his one good eye. "About me removing your magic."

Jasce shifted his gaze to another sparring ring with two fighters he recognized from the tavern.

"You weren't angry before you left and seemed to understand why we, Maera and me, did what we did," Kord said.

"I've had a few months to mull it over. You had no right."

"Maybe not, but I couldn't let my best friend die. The two magics were killing you."

Jasce couldn't argue that point. According to everyone he'd talked to back in Orilyon, he had gone insane when his combined magic had reacted to the Empower Stone. No one knew what the lasting effects of that experience would have on him physically and mentally, and there wasn't a way to remove only one type of magic. It was all or nothing, it seemed.

"We figured you'd experience memory loss, based on Emile and your sister, but we never anticipated your memories remaining absent for this long." Kord rested a hand on Jasce's shoulder, forcing him to look at him. "I am very sorry."

"*You're* sorry." His pent-up anger boiled to the surface.

"You know, we've all lost something."

"Oh, please indulge me. What have you lost?"

Kord's grip tightened. "I lost my best friend and a brother. Kenz lost a husband. My son lost his uncle. Which hurts more? Maybe you could think of someone else for a change."

Jasce glared at Kord's hand. "Let. Go."

Hurt flashed in Kord's eye, replaced by anger. "No problem." He tromped down the indoor track, forcing a few runners to dodge around his imposing frame.

Jasce tried to inhale a calming breath but Kord's words troubled him. Best friend, brother, husband, uncle. Swearing, he squeezed the railing so hard his knuckles cracked. It seemed everyone had lost something or someone, and he realized he was the common thread. Pain and death seemed to envelop him like a well-fitting cloak.

"Self-pity isn't a good look on you."

Jasce jumped as Nicolaus emerged from the shadows.

"You really need to quit sneaking around," Jasce said, pushing off the railing and striding toward the stairs.

Nicolaus strolled next to him with his hands behind his back. "I'm a spy. It's in my nature."

"It's annoying."

"But also useful. For instance, you might want to investigate the practice area before you head downstairs."

Jasce pivoted to face the Shade Walker, but he'd already disappeared.

"Bloody Shade Walkers," he said between clenched teeth. But his curiosity got the best of him.

Familiar voices and the sound of clashing swords met him before he rounded the corner. He hid behind a pillar while Kenz sparred with Caston.

Kenz fought with two daggers called sais, used for close-contact fighting since the sharp, thin blades were perfect for stabbing. He examined her footwork as she maneuvered past Caston's guard. She was definitely formidable, and a warm feeling spread through his chest. Based on what Kord said, he had taught her some of those moves.

Caston pivoted and threw Kenz over his shoulder. She landed hard and Caston brought the blades within a centimeter of her throat. Jasce lurched forward but forced himself to remain hidden.

Caston smiled and helped her up. "You've improved a lot."

Kenz replaced the knives into an ornate scabbard she wore low on her hips and stretched out her back, wincing slightly. A familiar sensation of longing pulsed through him. He understood why he'd been attracted to her. Not only was she beautiful, but she was strong, mentally and physically, and based on how she stood up to King Morzov, she was also brave, if not a little reckless.

Kenz wiped at the sweat on her forehead. "I can't believe he still doesn't remember me. I was so excited to see him and what do I walk in on? Another woman on his lap. I almost started a 'diplomatic incident,' as you call them."

Caston chuckled. "Thank you for your self-control." He returned his blades to where they hung on the wall. "What if Jasce never gets his memories back? Would you still love him?"

Kenz wrapped her arms around herself. "I love him now. But there are things he doesn't know. Things I couldn't tell him after he woke up. He might never forgive me."

Caston wiped a tear off her cheek and another emotion rose to the surface, one that was also familiar. Jealousy pulsed through him as he fisted his hands.

"Give him time, Kenz. Let him get to know you again."

"I might not have time, not with this stupid marriage proposal." She fiddled with her bracelets. "Sorry about challenging the king like that. I put you in a tough spot."

"You did, but I bet you didn't notice Jasce's reaction. You were too busy glaring at King Morzov."

"What reaction?"

"Jasce immediately drew closer to you. Whether or not he remembers you, something deep inside him still wants to protect you. I have faith in you. And in Jasce." Caston wrapped his arm around her and led her to the door. "But for now, you need to focus on the sparring match."

The door shut, and Jasce released a deep breath. He recalled the meeting and how his instinct had been to protect Kenz. What did that mean? And what was Caston talking about with the sparring match?

"That was very touching."

He swore and seized Nicolaus by the throat. "You need to stop doing that."

Nicolaus raised his hands. "Sorry."

Jasce released him. "What do you want?"

"If you haven't figured it out yet, Kenz challenged Irina to a sparring match."

"You're kidding."

"See, being sneaky is useful. Now come on, I'm sure you don't want to miss this."

Nicolaus grabbed Jasce's arm, and together they disappeared into the shadows.

Chapter Nine

Jasce marched toward the ring assigned to Kenz and Irina's match. Kenz stood off to the side with Caston, watching two other women fight. Her eyes widened when she saw him approach.

"Can I speak to you?" Jasce asked, giving a quick nod to Caston. She raised her brows and signaled for him to continue. "What are you trying to prove? Irina is a skilled warrior."

"So am I," she said, crossing her arms.

"If you're doing this because of me . . ."

Kenz's mouth dropped, and Caston rubbed his forehead.

She poked him in the chest. "Not everything is about you. We're both accomplished fighters, and I've always wanted to spar a Balten, to see if I could hold my own. Besides, the king specifically said he'd like us to participate. So here I am, participating."

"Oh, how conciliatory of you."

Kord and Flynt joined them on the outside of the ring. "What's going on?" Kord asked.

"Your sister challenged Princess Irina," Jasce said, still glaring at Kenz.

She arched a brow. "What are you so worried about? It's just sparring."

Flynt snorted, and Jasce glared at him. "Why are you here?"

"I'm backup." Flynt smirked and fiddled with his ignitor switch.

Jasce huffed out a breath and returned his focus to Kenz. "Just sparring? Irina was bred for this, trained since she could walk."

Kenz took a step toward him. "You sound quite enamored by her." Her breath caressed his face, and his gaze immediately went to her lips.

"What?" Jasce shook his head and retreated a step. "That's not what this is about."

"Then what is it about?"

He looked at Caston and then at Kord for help. "You're on board with this?"

Kord crossed his muscular arms and peered at his sister with his good eye. "Yeah, I am."

Kenz smirked and rested her hands on her hips.

Caston led Jasce away from the group. "She's always needed to prove herself, like someone else I know. You should trust her."

Jasce ran his fingers through his hair. Out of the corner of his eye, he caught the prince and princess studying him. Prince Andrei whispered to his sister. She shook her head and then gave Jasce a small smile.

"Anyway," Caston said. "It looks like your match is starting, too. Don't worry, I'll look after Kenz, like I promised."

Prince Andrei strode to an empty ring while a student in Jasce's class signaled for him.

"Dammit, I really don't have time for this." The pain in his back and leg had returned but was thankfully only a dull ache. He needed to finish his fight with the prince quickly.

"Good luck," Caston said, and returned to Kenz's side. Kenz ducked under the ropes and held his gaze until she was called to start her fight.

Jasce stepped into his ring, and Prince Andrei handed him a wooden staff. "What an interesting turn of events. Your friend is in for a real treat."

"You talk too much, Andrei," Jasce said, grabbing the staff.

The prince chuckled and removed his tunic. He'd tattooed his entire right side with an intricate carving depicting a warrior clad in armor, wielding a spear.

Conquering the Darkness

Jasce had noticed all the male competitors were shirtless. A tradition, it seemed, to show off their tattoos and their transparency, since the rules forbade any hidden armor. He didn't want to remove his shirt, already expecting the reaction to the scars on his back, but if anyone understood, it should be a warrior race.

He leaned his staff against the ring and removed his tunic.

Prince Andrei swore. "You Hunters have a barbaric training practice." Other spectators had gasped and even the king had risen to his feet, his eyes wide.

"My commander wanted to make an example of me. It's the price I paid to become a Hunter and his Second."

"That's a steep price."

Jasce shrugged and twirled the staff to get a feel for its weight and length. *It's just a longer sword*, he told himself, wishing he'd spent more time honing his skills with this weapon.

A bell rang from the other side of the room, and metal clashed. Jasce snuck a glance to where Kenz and Irina fought, but his focus immediately shifted when the starting bell for his match sounded.

The prince attacked quickly, which Jasce had expected. But where the prince was fast, Jasce had a longer reach and used that to his advantage. Their staffs collided as they moved around the ring. Jasce maneuvered under the prince's guard and struck him in the side.

Prince Andrei glared and switched tactics.

A cheer came from Kenz and Irina's ring, but with the surrounding spectators, Jasce couldn't see what was happening.

A sharp pain to his hip made him swear.

"Best pay attention," the prince said with a smirk. His attack intensified with more powerful strikes. Jasce barely raised his staff in time to block as he retreated around the ring.

He hated being on the defensive and needed to devise a different strategy, but his focus split in two as he tried to decipher what was happening in the other ring. What if Kenz got hurt? The ground shifted and his vision blurred. Her body lay broken and bleeding in the sand, and the most unimaginable pain and anger rushed through him.

Jasce bit back a curse as Prince Andrei landed a strike in the middle of his back. Both legs crumbled, and he fell to the mat face-first. The prince was on him in seconds with his staff pressed against his throat. He lodged his knee into Jasce's spine, causing it to bow backward. The pain coursing through him made it difficult to breathe and black spots floated into his vision.

"Yield," the prince said.

Another round of cheers came from across the room. Jasce couldn't stand it. He needed to know what was happening in the other ring.

The prince pressed the staff harder against his neck, cutting off Jasce's air supply.

"Yield," he said again.

Even though it killed him to lose, it was costing him more not knowing what was going on and if Kenz was okay.

"I yield," Jasce croaked out.

Immediately, air rushed into his lungs as the prince lowered his staff, and cheers resounded from the surrounding warriors. Jasce struggled to his feet, retrieved his tunic, and limped out of the ring. Blood pulsed in his ears as he shoved through the crowd.

He found Kord, whose eye traveled down his body. Shaking his head, he rested a hand on Jasce's back. A tingly warmth running through him gave him the ability to stand straight and breathe in a full breath.

"I wasn't aware your back was this bad. With the Snatcher attack and my magic suppressed, I couldn't heal you right away. Hell, we barely kept you alive. But I had no idea the extent of the trauma caused by Drexus's blade." Regret flitted through Kord's eye.

"What does it matter?" Jasce asked, turning from the pity on Kord's face.

"It matters because if I had known, then maybe I could have tried something to help you before months of permanent damage set in. All I can do now is alleviate your pain, but I can't fix it."

Jasce waved him off. "Is she okay?" He scanned the crowd, finding Caston on the other side of the ring, yelling out instructions. Flynt and Jaida stood behind him, both transfixed by the fight.

Nicolaus appeared on Jasce's other side, again out of nowhere. "She's holding her own. Got a little scraped up, but nothing Kord can't heal."

Conquering the Darkness

Kenz twirled her knives and lunged. Irina deflected the strike and attacked with lightning speed. Jasce stiffened as Kenz barely raised her weapons in time to block.

"She's rushing. She needs to be patient," Jasce said, as Kenz leapt to the side.

"She knows what she's doing," Kord said.

Kenz and Irina continued to battle for what felt like hours. Finally, Kenz sprung forward with her blades and then dropped to the ground, sweeping her leg and knocking Irina to the mat. The crowd yelled as Kenz moved into position, but Irina bucked her hips and was immediately on her feet, catching Kenz off-balance. Irina spun on one knee and whipped her dagger around. Jasce sucked in a breath as Kenz lurched back. A line of blood ran down her arm and dripped onto the mat.

The princess said something to Kenz and the judges. One judge entered the ring, beckoned both contestants forward, and spoke to them. Irina and Kenz nodded, then Kenz glanced at Caston and smiled. She twisted her wrists, and her bracelets glowed blue.

"Excellent," Nicolaus said. "I love it when she uses her shield."

"Excuse me?" Jasce said, his shoulders tightening.

"What? She's very good at it."

"I thought they weren't allowed to use magic."

"They're not," said a deep voice.

All three turned to face Prince Andrei, who crossed his arms as he eyed his sister. "Looks like my sister is making things interesting."

Irina's eyes glowed, indicating she, too, was powering up her magic.

The gong sounded again, and the two warriors began the next round. Irina attacked, using all her might, but what Jasce hadn't realized was how quick Kenz was as she darted out of the way. Her indigo shield erupted from her left hand and she knocked Irina past her, causing her to stumble.

Irina slid on the mat, twisted, and flicked one of her knives at Kenz. The blade shot through the air, aimed at her chest. Kenz arched backward, and the dagger sailed over her.

"I didn't know she was so flexible," Nicolaus said, a catlike grin on his face.

"I think I might kill you," Jasce said through gritted teeth.

Kord glared at Nicolaus. "Knock it off."

"Just trying to ease the tension." The man chortled and focused on the two women.

Jasce shook his head. He needed this match to end now before his heart beat out of his chest. He couldn't remember ever feeling this nervous or completely useless. As second in command to the Watch Guard and a Hunter, he had never worried about his team, but standing by while Kenz fought made his skin crawl.

Kenz used her shield to force Irina off balance. In between shoves, Kenz lowered her shield and used her dagger to disarm the princess.

Prince Andrei swore as Kenz maneuvered past Irina's defense and sliced her blade through the princess's leg.

Irina cried out and fell to the ground.

"Don't do it," the prince said.

The princess tipped her head back and yelled. Within seconds, her Defender formed, a ten-foot-tall apparition wielding a sword. Kenz quickly sheathed her other blade and brought both hands up. Her shield formed a protective barrier around her while the Defender struck.

Jasce glanced at Caston, who was leaning so far over the ropes, he almost fell into the ring. He empathized with the tension stiffening the muscles along his friend's neck. It took everything he had not to run into the arena and fight alongside Kenz. His mind may not remember her, but his body and heart reacted in a way that was both familiar and unfamiliar at the same time. Approval and worry flowed through him as her shield vibrated with the constant barrage of strikes from both Irina and her Defender.

"Is she counting?" Jasce asked, leaning forward and squinting at Kenz's lips.

Kord grinned. "We had an insider tip on how long the Defender would last," he whispered.

Kenz's shield spluttered and the indigo light weakened, but the protective wall held. A trickle of blood dripped from her nose and her arms trembled, but her lips continued to move.

Jasce leaned closer to Kord. "An inside tip from who?"

Kord's eyes darted toward Nicolaus, who pointed to his chest and mouthed, *Spy*. He winked and returned his focus to the fight.

Conquering the Darkness

With a shout, Irina's Defender attacked again, causing Kenz to dive out of the way as her shield disappeared. The sword struck the ground, vibrated for a second, and vanished, along with the apparition.

Irina's chest heaved as she raised her last blade.

Kenz jumped to her feet and performed a perfect roundhouse kick, knocking Irina to the ground. Within seconds, Kenz was on top of her, both blades angled across Irina's throat.

"Yield," Kenz said, her voice echoing through the silent training center.

Irina held her stare and then tapped the mat.

Kenz sheathed her blades, got to her feet, and reached out to help Irina up.

Jasce glanced to the raised dais where both the consort and the king stood. A look of disappointment flashed across King Morzov's face.

"She fought well," Jasce said to Kord, releasing a pent-up breath.

Kord nodded, then asked, "How did your match go?"

"I lost."

"You lost?"

"It wasn't a fair fight." Prince Andrei crossed his arms.

"What?" Both Jasce and Kord asked.

"You were distracted and your injury flared up. I know you didn't let me win, but your heart wasn't in it. Tell me, who were you more concerned for, my sister or the Shield? I believe your answer is quite telling, don't you think?"

"Very telling," Nicolaus said, still focused on Irina and Kenz.

Jasce clenched his jaw. He hated losing, especially to the prince, despite the excuses. So what if he'd been distracted or injured? He was the Angel of Death and should have won that fight. He shook his head and left Kord, Nicolaus, and the Balten prince at the sparring ring. If he didn't get his reactions under control, Kenz might very well kill him.

Chapter Ten

Jasce paced the corridor outside the training center, flicking his dagger hilt to tip, back and forth in his palm. He didn't like how his subconscious had reacted to Kenz's fight or her injury, nor did he appreciate the distraction he succumbed to during his match. How had they fought side by side when they were together? He needed to figure that out before they traveled to retrieve the Creator Stone, for he had a suspicion a fight was coming their way.

He sheathed his dagger and leaned against the wall when the sound of boots and laughter emerged from around the corner. Caston, Kord, and Kenz stopped suddenly when they saw him waiting.

Kord pulled his sister close and whispered in her ear. Her eyes never left Jasce's as she nodded. Caston tipped his head and mouthed *good luck* as he walked with Kord in the opposite direction.

Jasce pushed off the wall and allowed his gaze to wander from her midnight hair to her leather boots. Her fighting leathers fit snugly to her curves and the sleeveless top revealed toned arms. He frowned at the blood staining her skin. Kord had healed her, but the results of the fight still marked her.

"Hi," Kenz said, a flush brightening her cheeks.

"You fought well. Must have had an excellent teacher."

Kenz rolled her eyes. "Still arrogant as ever, it seems."

Chuckling, he gestured down the corridor. "Can we talk?"

"Sure."

He led her through the underground tunnels to the stables. They remained silent as they walked, which suited him perfectly, since he still hadn't thought of what he wanted to say.

Kenz arched her brow as he opened the stable door.

"I don't trust our Shade Walker not to snoop. Bruiser will sense him before we do," Jasce explained.

"Ah," was all she said as she entered. The sweet smell of hay mixed with her citrusy scent. His mind emptied as he watched her walk, and the urge to lay her down in the hay and examine every inch of her made his breath quicken.

Pull it together, he thought, shaking his head. He strolled past her and leaned against his horse's stall. Bruiser peeked out, and Jasce absently scratched his ears. Kenz shivered and wrapped her arms around her waist.

He cleared his throat, tearing his gaze from her mouth, and removed his cloak. "Here. You must be freezing."

She took the covering and wrapped it around her. "Thanks."

"I heard what you said to Caston before the competition."

Her eyes widened. "How much?"

"All of it."

"Jasce, I can explain—"

He touched her lips, and fire ignited in his belly. The desire to kiss her made his heart pound. He lowered his hand and retreated a step. "You don't need to tell me anything, now or ever. I wanted to apologize for how you found me last night with Irina." He wasn't sure what else to say and waited for Kenz to either accept his apology or walk out into the cold.

"Thank you," she finally said. She stepped forward and stroked Bruiser's snout. He nudged her hand, greedy for more.

"He likes you." He couldn't believe he envied a horse, but it seemed Bruiser knew Kenz better than he did.

She smiled. "He's a good boy."

Jasce rubbed the back of his neck. He floundered like a fish out of water, unsure of what to do or say. Put him on the battlefield or strategizing an attack, and he didn't blink at the challenge. But this? Normally, if he wanted something, he would take it. His old self, the one he actually remembered, would have already pressed her to the wall and ravaged her. That's what he longed to do, but a part of him didn't want to hurt her.

That reaction was so foreign to him. He'd always known he'd been a selfish bastard, but for some reason, this woman made him want to be different, better.

"Look, let's just forget about the past for now. It was unfair to you to be suddenly engaged and expected to behave accordingly. Let's get to know each other again, as friends," she said.

He arched a brow. "Friends?"

"Yes, friends. You do know what those are, don't you?"

"Very funny." Unfortunately, he really didn't know. He hadn't had friends in the Watch Guard. Bronn, his lieutenant, was the closest thing, and based on what Caston told him, the man had betrayed him, along with Drexus and two other Hunters. In his new reality, Caston was the only friend he had. And to make things even more awkward, he'd never been friends with a woman.

"Were we friends? You know, before we became more?"

The shadow of a smile formed on her lips. "Not really. We pretty much went from hating each other to . . ." She looked up at him from under her lashes.

"To what?"

The vein on her neck throbbed and the flush that had mottled her chest spread to her cheeks. "To loving each other," she whispered.

He closed his eyes to block out the desire darkening her pupils. He was showing a lot of restraint right now, but he wasn't sure about the extent of his self-control.

"Do you think we could try?" she asked. He opened his eyes, noticing she'd taken a step back. "Try being friends?"

He swallowed and forced a smile. "I'd like that."

Her bracelet jingled as she held out her hand. "Hello. I'm Kenz Haring."

There was something familiar about the gesture, like an inside joke.

He took her hand and marveled at how her calluses matched his. "Jasce Farone."

Kenz stared at their joined hands for a moment and lifted her eyes to his. His gut tightened when she licked her lips.

"You need to quit doing that if we're going to be just friends," he said, his voice hoarse as he released her hand.

A mischievous glint sparkled in her eyes. She ran her tongue along her lower lip. "Does this bother you?"

Jasce shoved his hands in his pockets. "Were you always this feisty?"

Kenz laughed. "Pretty much." She held his arm and led him from the stables. "Take me to the dining hall. I'm starving."

Jasce huffed. "Yeah, me too." Although food was the last thing on his mind.

~

The next three days were filled with the competitions, followed by a celebration each evening. Jasce had opted out of participating in any more games, wanting to give his body a chance to heal and get stronger before they departed to retrieve the Stone. He enjoyed watching Caston and Flynt on the rock wall, pleased that Caston had come in second. Kord tried the Ornix jousting, which made Jasce laugh every time he pictured the Healer's face as he flew off the beast and landed in a heap.

His patience, however, was running thin. If he knew the location of the Stone, he would have already left, but the king insisted on waiting for Matvey's return.

Jasce pushed himself out of the icy water and wrapped a thick blanket around him. Squinting into the dark, dawn still an hour away, he could just make out the silhouette of someone coming toward him. His fingers trembled from the cold as he fumbled for the dagger he had left near his clothes.

"Are you out of your mind?"

Jasce heaved a sigh, recognizing Caston's voice.

"It's freezing out here. I can't imagine the temperature of that water." The ex-Hunter frowned as he stared at Jasce's bare feet while pulling a fur cloak tighter around his neck. He raised a brow, obviously waiting for an answer.

Jasce tried to keep his teeth from chattering. "The cold water helps with my pain. Something Irina suggested." He slid into his leather pants and pulled a wool sweater over his head. He quickly tied back his wet hair and laced up his boots.

"That looks excruciating," Caston said, picking up Jasce's gloves and handing them to him.

"It is. What are you doing out here?"

"I stopped by your lodgings, and Jaida said I could most likely find you here. Matvey has returned."

"About bloody time." He strode past Caston, who reached out to block his path.

"Are you sure you're okay to go on this mission?" Concern tightened the skin around Caston's eyes. "I can tell you're not your normal self."

He scowled at Caston's arm pressed against his chest. "Why do you think I'm torturing myself in freezing cold water three times a day? Besides, it's not up to you whether I go."

"Right." Caston lowered his arm. "About this marriage proposal. You know you can't go through with it."

"All I know right now is that I need to get that Creator Stone. That's all I'm focused on."

"I see." Caston pressed his lips into a straight line. "Jasce, you and I have been through a lot together, with or without your memories. Please trust me in saying I will do whatever I can to help you, whether that's getting your magic back, defeating Drexus, or your relationship with Kenz."

Jasce swallowed past the emotion blocking his throat, realizing what a loyal friend he had in the ex-Hunter. He gripped Caston's forearm and nodded.

They walked the rest of the way to the castle in silence. He appreciated Caston's concern, but there was no way in hell he wasn't going on this mission. And the marriage proposal? He would deal with that minor detail later.

Caston whistled as they entered the throne room. The space wasn't elegant like the one in Orilyon, but it was still impressive. Two large thrones, made of iron, if Jasce was correct, sat in the center of the raised dais. Intricate images decorated the metal, and the light flickering from the three chandeliers made the carvings look as if they were alive. As with every room in the Balten palace, an enormous fireplace occupied one wall while the other had a view of the town below. The floor consisted of slabs of marble separated by veins of gold.

King Morzov wore a crown made of black onyx with rubies and sapphires sparkling along the rim. A matching band wrapped around Consort Lekov's forehead. Both were in their custom leathers, but a cape made of fur draped the king's shoulders.

Mud covered the hem of Matvey's cloak and dark smudges nestled underneath his brown eyes. By the looks of him, he'd ridden nonstop from wherever he had been. He laced his hands behind his back and straightened to his full height.

Caston bowed his head to the king and consort. "Did you locate Drexus?" he asked Matvey.

"Yes. We found him, Vale, and a squadron of soldiers south of Havelock. If I had to guess, they're taking the northern pass."

"Guess?" Jasce said. "That's not good enough."

The consort arched a brow. "Give us some credit."

Matvey slid a glare at Jasce. "Two of my men went undercover in a tavern where Drexus had his soldiers and spread a story about the king's guard traveling northeast toward the town of Istral. Drexus's soldiers took the bait."

The king leaned forward. "It's a two-day ride to the base of the Olwen Mountains through the Vissarion Pass. My son and the consort will lead your team, Commander Narr. I'd suggest you pack—you have one hour."

Jasce's heartbeat quickened. Finally. Both he and Caston turned, but the king's voice made him stop.

"Jasce, I haven't forgotten our deal."

Jasce's spine stiffened. "I understand."

Conquering the Darkness

Anticipation coursed through Jasce as he shoved his remaining items into his bag. Finally, he had a job to do, a mission to complete. For too many months, he had felt like a ship lost at sea, at the mercy of every wave crashing upon its hull. He glanced around the room to make sure he hadn't forgotten anything and noticed Amycus's journal lying on his nightstand. He picked it up and thumbed through the pages.

> *I can't believe I escaped from the palace alive. Getting in was easier than I had thought. However, discovering Drexus already had King Valeri's ring was a bit of a shock. Which meant Drexus knew it was the missing sliver of the Empower Stone. For the sake of Spectrals, I couldn't let the commander of the Watch Guard keep it. Cerus, a friend in the Guard and a Psyche, helped me subdue Drexus and steal his ring. Should I have killed him? Probably.*
> *Drexus knows it was me and therefore, once again, I am on the run. Thankfully, this time I'm not alone. Cerus and I rode south to Delmar where some Spectrals sheltered us. From there, we made the journey west toward Paxton and then Terrenus. I need more information about this crystal, and who better to help than the Gemaris? Drexus's ring is like a millstone around my neck, but I sense the crystal's power strengthening my magic. It affects Cerus, too, giving him headaches.*
> *I have to admit, I'm not looking forward to traversing the Culmen Mountains, but it will be worth the risk, especially if I get to see the Terrenian wyverns. I've heard such wonderful tales of these majestic beasts, and I'm hoping I will get to ride one.*

Jasce scanned ahead. He already knew the passes through the Culmen Range were treacherous and was impressed the old man had crossed them. Amycus would have been a lot younger though, possibly only a few years older than Jasce.

Terrenus was home to the Gemari, a magical people who created weapons from the gems lodged into their chests. The archduke, Kraig Carnelian, ruled the lands and had visited Orilyon during the Gathering. Jasce remembered seeing him at Amycus's funeral. Short in stature, but powerful. The man had worn leather pants, woven with metal, to protect from his wyvern's scales. His gem had glowed during the funeral as tears drifted down his cheeks, disappearing in his bushy beard. It seemed Amycus and the archduke had forged a friendship.

> *Kraig was reluctant to help, but eventually he gave in and told me the same story of the missing sliver of the Empower Stone handed down through the royal family. I wonder if Dietrich was a Spectral? If so, he hid it well. Then again, so did I, and so did Drexus. The archduke is an interesting character, and he allowed us to ride the wyverns. What magnificent creatures. I hope to experience flying on them again.*
> *I can't get Kraig's warning out of my head regarding magic. Magic must have balance. We're not meant to trifle with the Stones, and I do not know what will happen to your powers if you find the Empower Stone. Now that I understand the ring will lead me to the Empower Stone, I feel the clock ticking. Cerus and I need to return to Opax and find that Stone. I'm hoping it will be a rallying point for the Spectrals to fight the tyranny that has infected our land. There is risk to my magic and to my life, but it's one I'm willing to take if it means stopping Drexus once and for all.*

Jaida burst through the door. "Jasce, do you have an extra dagger?"

He jolted and dropped the journal. Taking a breath, he calmed his rapid heartbeat. Amycus had been on a quest to find the Empower Stone and stop Drexus. And now Jasce was on a similar path.

"What?" he asked, picking up the journal and putting in his satchel.

"I asked if you had an extra dagger." Jaida looked at the journal. "Find anything interesting in there?"

He rummaged through the bottom of his bag while he told her what Amycus had learned regarding the sliver. "Did Drexus ever find the Empower Stone, or tell you about it?"

She shook her head. "Drexus kept me in the dark about most things." She frowned and stared blankly at the wall.

"What is it?"

Conquering the Darkness

"Drexus became furious with me this one time when I snuck into his study. It was so unlike him, since I'd been in that room many times. The next thing I remembered was waking up in the infirmary." She blinked and waved her hand. "It's probably nothing."

Jasce wasn't sure he agreed with her, but now wasn't the time to delve into that mystery. They needed to get going. He handed Jaida an extra dagger. "Please tell me you know how to use that."

She scowled at him. "Do you think I grew up around royalty sipping tea? The same man who trained you trained me."

"Right." His eyes drifted to Jaida's back. She didn't bear any scars from being whipped, thankfully. But she probably had scars that no one saw, and those always hid the deepest, cruelest wounds. "If you want to talk about your time with Drexus . . ."

Jaida gave him a small smile. "Thank you. One day soon, we should talk. But right now, I think we have enough to deal with, don't you?"

"Okay. But I'm here for you." He inwardly breathed a sigh of relief. The older brother in him wanted to be available if she needed him, but the part of him that was broken didn't think he could handle the hurts she carried.

"Look at you, getting all soft." She laughed and patted his beard-covered cheek.

"Get out," he said, unable to hide the humor in his words.

She waved the dagger over her head as she left his room.

He looked around again, making sure he had everything, and wondered if this was the last time he or his sister would step foot in this room.

Chapter Eleven

The Ornix puffed frozen air through their noses and stamped their hooves. Packs loaded with supplies and weapons were strapped to a few, while the others carried saddles on their backs. Jasce saddled up Bruiser despite the consort informing him that traveling on the hairy beasts was the fastest way across the snow. Leaving his horse behind wasn't an option.

Kenz and Kord were loading the last of their bags when Jasce approached. "You two ready for this?" They had donned traveling clothes similar to his—wool-lined leather pants, a sweater, and a fur-lined cloak. They also wore hats and wool mittens.

Kord stared up at the white-tipped mountains. "As ready as we can be."

Kenz shivered and drew her cloak tighter. "I honestly can't comprehend how you've lived here. It's miserably cold."

"You get used to it. And the beard helps," Jasce said, scratching the hair on his jaw.

"That furry thing is hideous, by the way."

"You don't like it?"

Kenz made a face, and Kord laughed. "It's not your best look."

Matvey and Prince Andrei approached, dressed in the same clothing, although the prince wore his leather chest piece under his cloak. "We're almost ready," the prince said. "Just waiting on our Alturian friend."

Matvey leaned against one of the Ornix and crossed his arms. "Why is he coming with us?"

"Besides the fact that he insisted," The prince spit onto the snow. "He has the sliver of the Empower Stone, which will guide us once we get to the cave."

"Cave?" Jaida asked, as she and Flynt joined them.

Kenz glared at Jaida. "Surely you're not afraid of dark places."

Jaida's cheeks flushed.

"Kenz, knock it off. We talked about this," Flynt said, taking a protective step in front of Jaida.

Kenz shook her head and walked along the snowy path to where Caston and the consort spoke to the king and Princess Irina.

Jaida stared after her. "She still blames me."

"My sister is very loyal, and it will take time. But I believe one day you two will be fierce friends," Kord said.

Flynt snorted. "Fierce is an understatement."

Jasce glanced between Kenz and Jaida. If his memories returned, would he harbor resentment against his sister like Kenz did for Amycus's death? Kord and Flynt seemed to have forgiven her. Of course, anyone could see Flynt fancied Jaida, and she him. He wasn't too sure how he felt about that.

"Finally," Prince Andrei said as Nicolaus approached. His silver hair peeked out from the edges of a fur cap and his fleece-lined traveling cloak glided over the snow.

"Why are you loitering around? We have a Stone to fetch," Nicolaus said as he passed the group and pulled himself up onto an Ornix.

Matvey shook his head and Jasce huffed out a laugh. "Quite the character, that one."

"Quite annoying is what he is." Prince Andrei strode to the front of the line and ordered his troops to mount up.

King Morzov and Princess Irina waited for them at the gates leading from the castle into the city of Nivia. The consort leaned down and rested her forehead on the king's while they whispered to one another.

Irina gripped her brother's hand and told him to be careful, then approached Jasce, patting Bruiser on the neck.

"Good luck, and I'll see you soon." She glanced down the line of travelers. "All of you, be safe."

"It is a shame, Princess," Nicolaus said, leaning forward on his Ornix, "that you aren't joining us. Your beauty and kindness will truly be missed."

Jasce arched a brow as he stared between the Alturian and the princess. Irina smiled and a blush reddened her cheeks.

"I'm sure you'll survive," she said.

"I certainly plan to."

Prince Andrei rubbed his forehead. "All right. Let's go." He gave his father and sister one last nod before exiting through the massive iron portcullis with Consort Lekov at his side.

Jasce traveled next to Jaida while Kenz, Flynt, and Caston rode ahead of them. Nicolaus, Kord, and Matvey brought up the rear, along with a small squadron of soldiers. Many of the townspeople emerged from their homes to witness the procession, bowing when they saw the prince and consort. The snow-covered road broadened as they exited the city, and frozen meadows lay on each side of them, twinkling with the rising sun.

As they rode, Jasce regarded his sister, who watched Flynt interact with Kenz. Her jaw tightened and the creak of leather sounded as she gripped the reins. Even though Kenz and Flynt acted more like brother and sister than lovers, he empathized with Jaida's jealousy.

Ever since his talk with Kenz in the stable—the way she'd licked her lips, the citrusy scent that spoke to him in a way he didn't understand—his thoughts regarding their friendship had been anything but "friendly". Especially with the way her hips moved as she rode the Ornix. Too many suggestive ideas flitted through his head.

He turned in his saddle and stared at the imposing turrets of Karthmere Castle, nestled next to the Torrath Mountains. If all went as planned, they would be returning to Nivia with the Creator Stone. Hopefully, he'd have his magic and memories, but would there also be a wedding in his future? *One problem at a time,* he thought as they rode toward the forest.

They spent the first night in a garrison between Nivia and the Olwen Mountains. Sleeping at the compound brought a welcome reprieve to his chaotic mind. The familiarity of barracks, the sounds and smells of fellow soldiers, and the camaraderie triggered a need to stay longer. If not for the Creator Stone, he might have considered it.

They rose at dawn to begin the final trek toward the cave. The wind pierced through the wool-lined leathers Jasce wore underneath his armor. The sun hid behind the mountains, giving off an ethereal glow, and did nothing to warm the morning air as snow drifted across the trail, making the visibility challenging. Conversation had all but ceased as they rode single file, each with their hoods raised and heads down to block the wind despite the trees hedging them on each side.

They rested their animals around lunchtime on a wider section of the trail overlooking ruins of an ancient city. Where stone structures once stood, only charred rubble remained. Jasce asked the consort about it.

"According to legend, Ishikan had been a beautiful city, advanced for its time until one day, it ceased to exist," Consort Lekov said.

"What happened?"

"Scribes tell of a blinding light followed by a fierce wind. But no one really knows." The consort gazed at the ruins and a moment of sadness flashed in her eyes.

They continued up the trail, zigzagging up the rocky ledge before leveling off at the edge of Fannar Forest. By late afternoon, they finally cleared the trees and emerged onto a snow-covered meadow separating them from the base of the Olwen Mountains. Frozen waterfalls carved through rocky crags and sheer cliffs as if the formidable mountain wept.

The consort held up a hand, signaling the group to stop. "We walk from here." She slid off her Ornix and tied it to a tree.

Jasce hopped off Bruiser but let him roam freely. "Stay close," he said, patting his neck. He removed his swords from the harness attached to the side of his horse and slid them into the scabbard along his back. The rest of the team dismounted and trekked through the heavy snow toward the mountain.

Conquering the Darkness

Caston rested his hands on his hips as he stared up at the sheer cliffs. "Where's this cave?"

"Behind there," Consort Lekov said, pointing to the waterfall. Streaks of water carved through the ice and flowed into a small pond where the ground was clear of snow and a pungent smell filled the air.

Prince Andrei removed his cloak and laid it on a nearby boulder. "There's a hot spring underneath. Keeps everything from freezing over. But unless you were looking, you'd never suspect anything hiding behind it."

Jasce craned his neck around the waterfall. He smiled when he saw an ancient-looking door concealed by vines and bushes.

Prince Andrei removed a brass key from his pocket and inserted it into the lock. His eyes glowed slightly, and he grunted as he pulled the door open. A loud creak sounded, followed by a puff of dust.

"But how do you know someone hasn't already taken the Stone?" Nicolaus asked, walking forward.

Prince Andrei yanked him back as a four-foot-long blade swung past the opening, lodging itself into the stone wall. Nicolaus swore, his eyes wide.

"That's how." The prince's eyes glowed again, and the muscles in his arms bulged as he pulled the rope and secured the lethal steel. "Plus, only a Balten's strength could reload that blade."

Jasce snuck a glance at Caston. An Amplifier would have the strength, but one still needed a key, and the lock didn't appear to be tampered with.

The prince continued, "If the trap is set, a chain-reaction of sounds alerts the compound."

"What compound?" Kenz asked, shielding her eyes from the sun.

Prince Andrei pointed toward the north. "It's along that ridge. You can't see it from here, but they have an unobstructed view of the meadow. We have soldiers stationed year-round."

The consort removed a small mirror from her pocket, and using the sunlight, signaled the guard station. Within seconds, another light shone back. "Not everyone needs to go into the cave. Matvey and my soldiers will remain here. I suggest some of your people stay, too." She looked between Jasce and Caston.

"You're commander," Jasce said to Caston, even though there was no way he wasn't going into that cave.

"I'll remain here, as will Jaida and Kord." Caston eyed Nicolaus.

Nicolaus slung his bow and a quiver of arrows across his chest. He also had a scimitar strapped to his back, and the hilts of throwing knives peeked out from the top of his boots.

"That's what I figured." Caston approached Jasce and called Kenz and Flynt over. "Be careful in there and don't take chances. That Stone isn't worth your lives." He gave Jasce a hard look.

"Understood," Jasce said, even though he didn't agree. Getting the Stone, having his magic returned, and keeping it out of Drexus's clutches was worth the risk.

Caston held Jasce's elbow and whispered, "I mean it, Jasce. We just got you back. Please, don't do anything stupid."

Jasce pulled back and frowned, still surprised the ex-Hunter cared about his well-being. As second in command, Jasce always had a target on his back. But to discover Caston genuinely cared about him? He shook his head. They must have become close friends, something he didn't know he needed until now.

Prince Andrei slipped off his pack and pulled torches out, handing one to Flynt and pointing to his ignitor switch. "If you'd be so kind."

Flynt clicked his wrist, and a green flame sprung to life in his palm. Soon, all the torches were lit. He peered into the mouth of the cave. "I suggest Kenz takes lead."

"Agreed. I'll cover the rear," the consort said, drawing her sword and taking a lit torch.

Jasce eyed the bracelets on Kenz's wrist and addressed the consort. "You're going to have her lead?"

Kenz crossed her arms. "Really?"

Flynt snorted while Nicolaus chuckled and shook his head.

"What? It's a valid question," Jasce said, glaring at the group.

"You had her take point all the time," Kord said with the hint of a smile.

"I did?"

Kenz rolled her eyes and ignited her shield.

Conquering the Darkness

Caston's eyes crinkled around the edges. "We'll be here when you come out."

"Let's go," Prince Andrei said, following Kenz and disappearing into the darkness.

Jasce sighed, removed the dagger from the scabbard on his thigh, and stepped into the gloom of the cave.

Chapter Twelve

Kenz's indigo shield coalesced with the flames from the torches to illuminate a stone walkway covered with dust. Stalagmites protruded along the solitary path, some taller than Jasce, while stalactites clung to the ceiling, forming what looked like massive stone teeth. Sounds of dripping water accompanied them down the narrow walkway, and if it weren't for the torches and the light glowing from Kenz's shield, they'd be plunged into absolute darkness.

Jasce pushed up his sleeves and wiped the sweat from his brow as the air grew warmer the deeper they descended. Wet stone, smoke from the torches, and the sickly smell of decay tickled his nose.

"Mind your step," Prince Andrei said, lighting another torch and throwing it over the side. Flynt swore and jumped back, pressing against the wall. The falling glow from the torch illuminated a steep drop into an enormous cavern below.

"What is that sound?" Nicolaus asked as he peered over the edge.

Steam rose from small pools of white mud that bubbled and splattered onto the cavern floor. More stalagmites surrounded the area like deadly spears, sharp enough to impale armor.

Jasce rubbed his chest and snuck his flask from his pocket, taking a quick swallow. The two-day ride in the cold had not been kind to his back. He was returning his flask when movement flickered along the peripheral of his vision. He lifted his torch and peered into the shadows.

"What is it?" the consort asked.

"I thought I saw something." He pointed to the other side of the cavern. Holes large enough to fit a person were carved into the cave wall.

"It was probably a bat. They live here because the hot springs keep the temperature warm." She gestured to the ceiling, which squirmed as if alive with thousands of bats clinging to the rocks and fissures.

Nicolaus swore, and his face drained of color.

Kenz turned and frowned. "What's wrong?"

He licked his lips. "I'm not a fan."

She smiled. "Are you afraid of a little bat?"

Nicolaus glared at her. "Just keep your shield above us, will you?"

Kenz laughed and continued down the path. Rocks skittered as the group followed, single file, until they reached the bottom. Pools of bubbling liquid, boulders, and stalagmites formed a natural, if not deadly, obstacle course. Tunnels of varying sizes were tucked into the cave's walls, splitting off in different directions. Jasce seriously hoped they wouldn't have to crawl through one of those to get to the Stone.

"Which way?" Kenz asked.

"Time for our Alturian friend to become useful," Prince Andrei said, summoning Nicolaus to the front of the line. "All my father knew, and his father before him, and so on, was that the Creator Stone was hidden in this cave. For safety precautions, the exact location was never passed down, nor a map drawn."

"I told you you'd need me." Nicolaus removed a leather pouch from his pocket. He unwrapped the Empower Stone sliver and closed his eyes. His nostrils widened as he breathed in the wet air. The shadows molded to him, and the outline of his body shimmered. He pivoted and his arm moved as if an invisible thread tugged on his hand. Finally, he opened his eyes and put the sliver back in its pouch. "That way," he said, pointing to the tunnel on the other side of the cavern.

"Very well," Prince Andrei said. "Oh, and don't fall into those bubbling pools. According to legend, they'll melt your flesh right off."

"Wonderful," Flynt said, his lips pursed as he gazed across the floor of the cavern.

Conquering the Darkness

Kenz ignited her shield, one in each hand, and put them between her and the bubbling pools.

"That's handy," Nicolaus said, nudging Jasce, who scowled. "I'll scout ahead." He Shade Walked into the shadows, reappearing on the other side of the treacherous route.

They maneuvered along the cavern floor, climbing boulders and leaping over the pools of bubbling mud. Jasce stumbled and inwardly swore at the pain radiating down his spine and leg. They cleared the lethal obstacle course to find Nicolaus waiting on the other side.

"Two more tunnels," he said, and pointed to the right. "That one should lead to the Creator Stone."

A scuttling sound made Jasce turn. Lifting his torch and retrieving his dagger, he scanned the area but only darkness stared back. Whatever made that noise sounded much larger than a bat.

Kenz's indigo light faded, along with the torches, as the group disappeared around a corner. He glanced once more into the cavern and jogged after them, memorizing any unique details so they wouldn't get lost. They traversed through the tunnel, having to hunch as the space grew smaller, and finally arrived in a large room with eleven columns carved into the walls. The largest column stood in the center and was at least twenty feet high, with a completely smooth surface. The diameter of its base was six feet and tapered off as it neared the ceiling.

Jasce crossed his arms and looked up. "I'm assuming the Stone is up there?"

The consort nodded. There were no handholds or rough edges to grab, so climbing it wasn't an option. "The question is, how do we get it?"

"These columns are definitely not manmade," Flynt said, walking around the room.

The others wandered around, looking for a way to scale the imposing structure. The consort shoved her dagger into the column and swore when the tip broke.

"Nicolaus, can you Shade Walk up there?" Kenz asked.

Nicolaus squinted and shook his head. "It's too narrow at the top."

"I have an idea," the Balten prince said. His eyes glowed, and everyone retreated as he tilted his head back and yelled. Within seconds,

Prince Andrei's Defender emerged, holding an enormous spear. The prince cupped his hand and the Defender mimicked him, allowing him to step onto the Defender's palm.

"Did you know they could do that?" Jasce asked Nicolaus.

"No, I did not."

Flynt snorted. "What happened to you knowing everything?"

Nicolaus scowled at Flynt. "I can see why Jasce never liked you."

Flynt's eyebrows disappeared underneath his auburn hair as he stared at Jasce, who shook his head and strode to the other side of the column.

The Defender lifted the prince to the top of the structure. "There's a chest, and it's anchored in," he said, retrieving his dagger from his belt. With a grunt, he slammed his blade into the metal attachments, breaking the bands and freeing the chest. He secured the box and returned to the ground, stumbling as he stepped off the Defender's palm. The chest fell to the ground as the Defender's apparition united with its host. Consort Lekov moved to the prince's side to steady him.

"I'm fine," he said, inhaling a deep breath. When he opened his eyes, they had returned to their normal ice-blue color.

Nicolaus picked up the wooden case. "I thought it'd be bigger." The chest was square, about six inches across, and a gold lock shimmered from the light of the flickering torches.

Prince Andrei cleared his throat and drew his sword. "Put it down."

"Only trying to help." Nicolaus placed the chest on the ground and retreated a step with his palms raised.

Kenz tucked a lock of hair behind her ear. "Does our magic react the way it did with the Empower Stone?"

Nicolaus's brows furrowed as he stared at the steel box. "Based on the information retrieved from the Vastanes, the Creator Stone only affects those without magic."

"Open it." Jasce's eyes remained fixed on the box. His pulse thudded and a line of sweat dripped down his spine.

"No, we need to get it back to my father," the prince said.

Jasce drew his sword and pointed it at the Balten prince. "I said, open it."

Prince Andrei widened his stance and glared at him. "No."

Conquering the Darkness

Consort Lekov, who'd been standing next to the prince, stepped forward and slid her blade free from its scabbard.

"Jasce, do you think now is the time—" Kenz stopped when he threw her a look.

"We need to know if the Stone is in there. I didn't come all this way for nothing." He scowled at the prince and tightened his grip on his sword.

"Lower your weapon, Commander," Consort Lekov said, her eyes as hard as the blade pointed at his chest.

Jasce tilted his head. He figured Kenz and Flynt would back him up if the situation turned violent, but he still needed the prince and consort as allies. He lowered his sword.

The consort rested a hand on the prince's arm. "Andrei, it's fine. Let him see it."

The prince swore under his breath but withdrew another key from his pocket. With a click, the box opened.

"Whoa," Flynt said, leaning forward. A clear, jagged rock about the size of Jasce's fist lay inside the box. The Stone contained some sort of black substance that had settled on the bottom.

"Now back away." Jasce's grip tightened on his sword, but he kept the weapon at his side.

Prince Andrei scowled but stood and took a step back. "You understand if you use the Stone, you must honor the bargain with my father."

Jasce slid a glance at Kenz. "I need my magic," he whispered to her.

The muscle in her jaw fluttered. "Nicolaus, is this safe?" she asked, her eyes darting between Jasce and the Stone.

"We're about to find out," the Shade Walker said.

"Seriously?" Kenz ignited her shield but didn't seem to know where to put it.

Jasce tore his gaze from the Stone and nodded. She sighed and enveloped him with purple light.

His breathing echoed off the protective walls of her shield. The liquid inside the stone rippled as his finger grazed it, shooting a tingle through his hand and arm. He tilted his head and focused on the hypnotizing movement of the substance. Caston had said their lives weren't worth it, but Jasce wanted—no, *needed*—his magic back. And his memories.

With a final glance at Kenz, he rested both palms on the Stone and removed it from the box. The liquid swirled faster and faster until the Stone turned black. Intense pain coursed through his arms and into his chest, but he gritted his teeth and focused on his breath as what felt like molten fire tore through his body.

A cold table and the sound of machines filled his mind.

The taste of blood as he bit down on a leather strap.

His body arching off the table, and Drexus telling him to hold on as he wished for death.

Magic thrumming through him and a strength like he'd never known.

Jasce yelled as his body turned rigid from the pain. The indigo light surrounding him disappeared and hands wrenched him away from the Stone. He fell on his back and his chest heaved. Sweat dripped down his temples.

"Jasce!" Kenz leaned over him.

He focused on her green eyes and breathed. Slowly, the pain subsided. Consort Lekov knelt, grabbed his elbow, and helped him sit. The swirling black liquid slowed and settled once more at the bottom. Prince Andrei used his tunic to pick it up, dropping it into the chest and slamming the lid shut.

"Serves you right," he mumbled, twisting the key in the lock.

Kenz placed her hands on Jasce's face with a hopeful look in her eyes. "Are you all right?" They both knew what she really meant: *Do you remember me?*

He recalled the memory that had flashed through his mind when he touched the Stone—the day he'd received the Amplifier serum, remembering the sounds, smells, even the pain. He stared at the freckles lining the bridge of Kenz's nose. The procedure was the only memory that had returned. He looked away, not wanting to see the disappointment on her face.

"Did your magic return?" Nicolaus asked.

Jasce slowly rose to his feet and focused on the humming pulsing

Conquering the Darkness

through his chest. If he was again a Vaulter, would he even know? "I feel a slight buzzing."

"Then it must have worked," Consort Lekov said.

"Can you vault?" Kenz asked, her voice tight.

Jasce shrugged. "I have no idea how."

"Last time, your hands just sort of disappeared," she said.

He lifted his hands and turned them palms up, concentrating. Nothing happened.

"We need to leave," Prince Andrei said. "You can play around with it later."

Jasce narrowed his eyes. He didn't want to hand over the Stone, not yet. Maybe if he held it longer, more memories would return. But the prince had secured the chest to a loop on his belt, his sword still unsheathed. Once they cleared the dreary walls of this cave, he and the prince would have a little chat.

Jasce waved him forward and returned his sword to its scabbard. Kenz gave him a worried look before taking the lead again. Flynt walked past Jasce and stared at his chest as if trying to see the magic.

Nicolaus leaned close. "What did you feel?"

"Pain. A lot of pain."

"But your magic has returned?"

"I think so. I might need to hold it longer."

"If you drain the Stone, it will need to recharge."

"How does it do that?"

"From the light of the moon."

Jasce sighed. "That's not convenient."

Nicolaus patted his back. "Nothing ever is."

Kenz led them through the tunnel toward the central cavern. As they maneuvered around the bubbling pools, the hairs on Jasce's neck tingled. He glanced over his shoulder. Consort Lekov caught his look and raised her torch.

A hiss rattled from the blackness as two massive pincers emerged from a hole in the cave wall. The consort yelled and fell back while swiping her torch at the creature. Jasce seized her arm before she stumbled into one of the molten pools. He held on to her and raised his dagger.

Claws, easily the length of a sword, snapped as a shiny red body slithered from its hiding place. A spiked tail raised in an arch, the sharp tip dripping a clear liquid. The round, flat head encased beady black eyes that swiveled between the consort and Jasce. He shoved the consort away from the edge of the pool toward Nicolaus.

The creature whipped its barbed tail at them. Jasce dodged to the side and stabbed it with his dagger. His blade bounced harmlessly off the crimson shell. The creature reared and snapped its claws. The cavern buzzed as more animals emerged from the holes in the cave's wall.

The creature lashed out again with its pincers. Jasce batted it with his torch and the animal scampered away.

"Flynt! Fire, now," Jasce said as he drove the beast back. A green fireball blasted by him, hitting the animal between its twitching eyes. A loud screech echoed off their stone surroundings.

Jasce turned and sprinted for the group.

"Quickly, to the other side," Prince Andrei said, waving everyone past him with one hand. They darted through the bubbling pools, leaping over the smaller ones. Flynt continued sending his fire while Kenz projected her shield to protect their retreat.

A scuttling sounded from above them. Before Jasce could raise his torch, his back hit the ground.

"Jasce!" Kenz yelled.

He wheezed as the air was knocked out of him. Holding on to each pincer, he twisted his head to avoid the snapping jaws.

The shadows shimmered and Nicolaus emerged with his scimitar drawn. With a quick slash, he removed the poisonous barbed tail. The creature roared. Jasce bucked his hips and threw the beast off him. Nicolaus drove the curved blade into the soft tissue behind the animal's head. It twitched and fell silent.

Jasce pushed to his feet and rested his hands on his knees. "Thanks."

"Anytime, Commander." Nicolaus grimaced and used the corner of his tunic to wipe the green blood off his sword. "Well, I'll never wear this again."

Kenz called their names, and they hurried across the cavern toward the waiting team. Flynt had killed the other two creatures while the remaining ones scurried back into their holes.

Conquering the Darkness

"What the hell were those things?" Jasce asked, still trying to get his breath. His hands shook as he removed his flask and took a quick drink. He offered it to Nicolaus, who frowned and shook his head. Jasce shrugged and drank a little more to ease the sensation of thousands of spiders crawling along his skin.

Prince Andrei glanced at Consort Lekov. "I thought they were extinct."

"So did I. If memory serves, they're called Scymids. But I've never heard of them being that big or aggressive."

"We need to go," Kenz said, pointing toward one of the larger tunnels where the sounds of claws scraping stone echoed through the cavern.

"Agreed," the prince said, and directed everyone up the narrow path.

The sound of clicking and hissing grew louder. Jasce raised his torch and swore as a hoard of Scymids emerged.

"Run!" He pushed the prince past him as one creature lashed out with its deadly tail.

Another one dropped from a hole above them, separating Jasce and the prince from the rest of the group. Jasce swung the torch while stabbing with his dagger. A massive claw swiped at him, he lost his balance, and emptiness engulfed him, the lethal spikes of stalagmites beckoning. His arms spiraled over thin air as he tried to regain his balance.

Prince Andrei gripped the straps of Jasce's armor and yanked him back.

Jasce got his feet under him and turned. "Watch out!"

The prince tried to dodge the sharp claws of the Scymid, but the walkway was too narrow. The sound of ripping fabric and flesh was followed by a yell.

Jasce kicked the creature into the cavern below. A sickening thunk sounded as a stalagmite pierced through the creature's armored shell, but the damage had been done. Blood poured from the prince's stomach. Jasce hauled him to his feet, practically dragging him up the path.

Flynt and Nicolaus fought a pair of Scymids while the consort used her speed and strength to fight the creatures obstructing the path. Kenz flicked her wrists, using her shields to block the creatures scurrying out of their holes.

Light glowed around the corner. They sprinted for the opening, Jasce's lungs burning, and he fought the pain in his back as the spasms grew worse. Half carrying the Balten prince wasn't helping, and the Scymids were catching up.

"Hurry," Flynt yelled over the deafening hissing sound.

"We need to barricade the entrance once we get out," Jasce said through clenched teeth. He glanced at the prince's pale face. Blood oozed through his fingers pressed against his stomach. "Almost there."

They needed Kord.

The air grew colder as they approached the cavern's exit. Consort Lekov sprinted toward the opening, followed by Nicolaus, Kenz, and Flynt. Finally, Jasce and Prince Andrei emerged. Jasce tried to shut the door behind him, but one creature blocked him.

"Move!" Flynt yelled.

Jasce lunged with the prince as a stream of fire blasted past them. The consort used her magical strength to pummel the side of the entrance, knocking stones loose. Melting snow and mud poured from above the cave, crushing any creature that tried to escape. With a final burst of flame, the Scymids' roars were silenced and the cave entrance sealed.

Jasce turned and froze. Kord, Jaida, Caston, and Matvey knelt in the snow with soldiers holding swords to their necks. And at the end of the line stood a man, a face from Jasce's nightmares made flesh.

"Hello, Jasce."

Chapter Thirteen

"Drexus," Jasce growled as shock and rage exploded through him at seeing his former commander flanked by a small squadron of soldiers.

Cold, dark eyes stared out of a gaunt face, and lips curled into a malevolent sneer. He was dressed in black, from his short hair streaked with gray to a long cloak, boots, and one leather glove. Where his other hand should have been, a metal claw opened and closed.

Even though Jasce couldn't physically remember the betrayal, the fact that Drexus had hidden his sister from him, used him to gain power, and ordered the Hunters to double-cross him made his heart pound. He squeezed his dagger while supporting Prince Andrei, who was losing an alarming amount of blood.

Everyone seemed unharmed except for the Balten guards, who lay unmoving in the snow. Caston brandished a bloody lip and Matvey was hunched over, gripping his side. Jasce's eyes met his sister's as she focused on her magic, her jaw set with strands of hair floating off her shoulders. A soldier with black veins swirling up his neck stood behind her and was the only one not wielding a weapon.

Jasce barely moved his hand, instructing her to wait. They were at a disadvantage, especially with Drexus's soldiers pointing swords at Kord's, Caston's, and Matvey's backs.

"I can see your mind plotting, but remember, I taught you everything you know." Drexus said to Jasce and then nodded to the wooden box hanging from Prince Andrei's bloodstained side. "Give me the Stone and no one dies."

The prince bared his teeth. "No."

Drexus drew his sword.

Jaida turned to plead with the man behind her. "Vale, please. Don't do this."

The man's eyes shifted to brown, and sorrow lined his face. Jasce didn't remember the Spectral, but Kord had told him he had betrayed them and then escaped with Jaida and Drexus. The Vastanes had experimented on him, and now he had Balten, Gemari, and Shade Walker magic inside him. It was a wonder he was still breathing. Currently, he was the most powerful Spectral alive, even if his magic was volatile and slowly killing him.

Drexus glared at Jaida, and when he shifted his focus to the Balten prince, Vale leaned down and whispered to her. Her eyes widened, and she fisted her hands. She glanced back at Drexus and then quickly faced Jasce.

The sky grew dark as a storm advanced from the east and a fierce wind blew, the ice crystals stinging Jasce's face. He hoped the Balten soldiers stationed at the mountain compound could see what was happening in the valley below and were on their way.

"Your Highness," Drexus said with a sneer. "You're in no shape to fight me. Hand over the chest and I'll let them live."

"I can't do that." Prince Andrei grimaced as he held his stomach. Blood dripped through his fingers, turning the snow crimson.

"Very well." Drexus approached Kord, who struggled to free himself from the guard holding him. Drexus shoved his blade through Kord's side.

Kenz screamed and ran toward her brother, but Nicolaus lunged, wrapping an arm around her waist and hauling her toward him.

"Kenz, no," he said, holding her while trying not to drop his bow.

Conquering the Darkness

Kord's eye widened as he gaped at the blood staining his sweater. Jasce's heart pounded as Kord groaned and slumped into the snow.

"Let me go," Kenz said, twisting out of Nicolaus's hold.

Drexus pushed the soldier guarding Caston out of his way. He yanked him by the hair and exposed his throat. "Your brother's alive, for now. But will he be able to heal your commander?"

She skidded to a stop.

"Smart move." Drexus tilted his head. "I remember you—the feisty sister. I could have used someone with sharper claws." He gave Jaida a disappointed look and then focused on the Balten prince. "Now, hand it over."

Caston swallowed and grunted. "Don't give it to him."

Jasce shoved the fear and anger down, forcing his body to remain still. He focused on the slight buzzing inside him and attempted to vault, but nothing happened. He scanned the area, needing a distraction, and noticed Consort Lekov taking a small step toward the prince. He caught her eye and then yanked Prince Andrei toward him.

Jasce stuck his dagger under his chin. "Give him the Stone."

The prince's eyes widened. "I knew we couldn't trust you."

"I'll not allow them to die. Hand it over, or I will make you."

Drexus chuckled. "Your compassion always made you weak. Best listen to the Angel of Death, Your Highness."

The prince glared at Jasce and then his eyes darted over his shoulder to where Consort Lekov stood. Jasce tilted his head ever so slightly.

A yell sounded behind him as the consort unleashed her Defender. Within seconds, the ancestral apparition formed, wielding an enormous dual-bladed ax.

"Now!" Jasce shouted. He shoved the prince behind him and charged at Drexus, drawing his sword.

He sprinted through the snow, forced to dodge the green fireballs and arrows whizzing through the air on his path toward Drexus, who ordered his men to attack. Mid-stride, Jasce flicked his dagger at the soldier behind Caston, who used the distraction to free himself and Matvey. He slid a glance at Kord, encased in Kenz's shield and struggling to get to his feet.

Jasce spun and sliced through another soldier.

"You're on the losing side, boy," Drexus said as Jasce hurdled over the body.

"Don't call me 'boy.'"

Jasce ignored the pain in his back and the sounds of battle behind him, and allowed every frustration, the lost memories, the deep well of his hate to empower his attack. He roared and drove Drexus back. Drexus barely raised his sword in time to block a strike aimed at his neck. The sting of betrayal had Jasce crashing his sword against Drexus's again and again, finally knocking the blade from Drexus's hand.

His knuckles whitened as he prepared to cut his former commander in half.

A yell sounded behind him, followed by an ear-piercing crack that reverberated through the blustering wind. Out of the corner of his eye, he saw Vale raising his hands. The ground shook, and Jasce stumbled, his body contorting as he tried to regain his balance. A bolt of pain shot down his spine, causing his back to arch and his leg to collapse.

Drexus laughed and retrieved his sword from the snow. With a flick of his ignitor switch, black fire sparked and traveled along the blade. "What do we have here? The Angel of Death kneeling before me. How fitting."

Panting and blinking away the sweat dripping into his eyes, Jasce groaned and used his other sword to help him stand. He staggered into his fighting stance and lifted his weapon.

Drexus advanced, and the snow hissed as the blazing sword skimmed along the surface.

Jasce attempted to move his feet, but his legs felt like they were encased in blocks of ice. His arms shook. He hadn't been prepared, and without magic he couldn't defeat Drexus. He tried again to tap into his reawakened power, but the buzzing had diminished as his body and mind weakened.

Drexus, as if sensing Jasce's vulnerability, intensified his attack.

Jasce barely lifted his weapon to block the fiery sword aimed at his chest. Drexus leapt forward, and Jasce parried, but he wasn't quick enough. Drexus brought his elbow around. A crack sounded through Jasce's head, and blood dripped from his nose and into his mouth.

Conquering the Darkness

Blinking away the tears caused by the blow and stumbling in the deep snow, he didn't see Drexus's foot until it collided with his chest.

Jasce landed in a heap and cried out as his back seized up again. Drexus stalked toward him, victory sparking in his cavernous eyes.

No, he thought, rolling over and trying to get his arms under him.

He yelled when Drexus's foot struck again, breaking ribs. Blood pooled in his mouth and ran down his chin. With a sidelong glance, he saw Jaida dragging Kord away from the fray while the rest of his team battled Vale and the remaining soldiers. Prince Andrei still had the box clutched to his chest while Matvey and the consort protected him.

Metal flashed. With a roar, Drexus jumped and, as he came down, his clawed fist connected with Jasce's temple. Stars exploded and he dropped to his side.

"Vale, get the chest. Now!" Drexus ordered as he pulled Jasce's hair, yanking him to his knees and whispering in his ear. "I will have that Stone and Jaida, and you'll die drenched in blood and failure."

Vale lurched across the blood-flecked snow toward Prince Andrei. Glowing daggers formed in Vale's hands. He flicked his wrists.

Matvey yelled and dove in front of the prince.

"No!" Prince Andrei said.

Matvey grunted, his eyes wide as he stared at the four glowing blades lodged in his chest. The prince crawled to his guard as Matvey collapsed in the snow with unseeing eyes. The consort fell to her knees, her Defender's magic spent.

Vale picked up the chest and stepped over Matvey and the prince, throwing more daggers at the rest of the group. Kenz blocked the lethal projectiles with her shield while Caston helped Nicolaus to his feet. The Shade Walker grimaced, holding his wounded shoulder.

Drexus placed his sword against Jasce's throat. He swallowed and felt the blood trickle down his neck.

"Drexus, no!" Jaida screamed, sprinting toward them. Everyone turned and froze as they stared at Jasce, kneeling in the snow and covered in blood. Kenz's eyes widened, and she shook her head, her hand covering her mouth.

Jaida skidded to a stop as Jasce hissed from the blade digging deeper into his skin, more blood spilling down his chest.

"Don't," Jaida sobbed. "Please. I'll do anything. Just let him live."

"No, Jaida," Jasce whispered.

"I'm so disappointed in you," Drexus said to her. "But you can still be of use to me. If you come with me, I'll spare him."

The shadows shimmered, and Nicolaus appeared. He lunged forward with his dagger aimed at Drexus's back. A glowing arrow zipped past Jasce's face. Nicolaus yelled and dropped his weapon, clutching his stomach where the arrow vibrated. Vale strode forward with the chest containing the Creator Stone tucked safely in the crook of his arm.

Drexus released Jasce and grabbed the Shade Walker's cloak. "You have something I need."

Nicolaus struggled against the metal claw while Drexus searched his pockets. A satisfied grin formed on Drexus's face as he pulled out the leather bag holding the sliver of the Empower Stone. He raised his sword and Nicolaus's eyes widened.

The blade stopped mid-strike.

Nicolaus stumbled back.

The muscles in Drexus's arm quivered as he tried to administer the killing blow.

Jaida's hair swirled, her arms raised, and her eyes narrowed.

"How dare you," Drexus said through gritted teeth. He twisted his clawed hand, ignited his fire, and launched a stream of fire at Jaida. She ducked just as indigo light enclosed Drexus and blocked the blast.

Vale hurled arrows at Kenz, who lowered her shield around Drexus, barely getting it up in time to protect the others.

Drexus gripped Jasce by the throat. "Jaida. Come here, now."

"Let him go," Jaida said, taking a step toward them. Her hand rested on her hip, where her dagger was hidden.

"Fine," Drexus said, sheathing his sword. Spit peppered Jasce's face as Drexus knelt over him. "Death is too easy for you. Live with your defeat, knowing you're worthless and a complete failure." He clicked his ignitor and formed a whip out of fire. "Let's add one more scar." Lifting his arm, he slashed the whip across Jasce's face. Flesh sizzled and blood boiled. Jasce yelled and collapsed to his side, holding his damaged jaw.

Jaida screamed and ran to him.

Conquering the Darkness

"Vale, grab Jaida. We got what we came for."

At Drexus's command, Vale strode toward Jaida, who withdrew her dagger. Vale grabbed her wrist and squeezed, causing her to cry out as her fingers opened and the blade fell into the snow.

Jasce groaned and extended a bloody hand toward his sister.

The pounding of hooves and shouts drifted through the storm and across the meadow, as the Balten soldiers from the mountain compound rode furiously toward their prince and consort.

Caston, his body a blur, sprinted toward them.

Vale handed Drexus the chest while clutching Drexus's arm, then yanked Jaida to his side as the shadows shimmered.

Just before they vanished, Caston launched himself at Vale, wrapping his arms around his waist and knocking him and Drexus away from Jaida.

Vale's eyes widened as darkness surrounded him, Drexus, and Caston. Drexus's yell was cut short as the three of them disappeared.

"Caston," Jasce whispered, before the fiery pain in his body dragged him into the abyss.

Chapter Fourteen

A red glow danced behind Jasce's eyelids and a scratchy wool blanket covered him from the chest down. Whispered voices originated from somewhere behind him. He slowly opened his eyes and tried to remember the last thing that happened: His sister and the others kneeling in the snow, Kord getting stabbed, Vale taking the Creator Stone, Drexus beating the ever-loving hell out of him. Failure squeezed his chest—Drexus had defeated him again, and the Stone was gone.

"How are you feeling?" a deep voice asked.

Jasce tore his eyes from the ceiling. Kord sat in a leather chair with his arms crossed. He'd removed his patch, and dark shadows shone under his eyes. The scar carving through half his face shimmered from the candlelight, partly hidden by the two-day scruff of his beard. He'd replaced his bloodstained sweater with a tan tunic.

Jasce groaned and sat up. "I wasn't the one stabbed."

"I'll be fine. If I hadn't had three other people needing healing, I'd already be better. Still, I can't believe that power-crazed maniac stabbed me."

Jasce sighed and raked his fingers through his tangled hair. They could have been killed, and for what? They had failed to protect the Creator Stone, and now Drexus had two pieces of the Heart.

His body tensed, and he looked up. "Caston?"

Kord unfolded his arms, and sadness flashed across his face. "We couldn't find him. Vale disappeared with Drexus, Caston, and the Stone."

Jasce bit back a curse. Drexus had commanded Vale to take Jaida, but Caston had sacrificed himself for his sister. Rage burned inside him. There were so many reasons to kill his former commander, and when he'd had the chance, he'd failed.

Jasce rubbed his side and looked around. "Where are we?"

"The Balten garrison. We needed to regroup and heal before returning to Nivia."

With our tails between our legs, Jasce thought bitterly.

The compound had two other rooms branching off from the main one where Jasce sat. Flynt stood in the small kitchen stirring something in a pot while Kenz slept in one of the worn chairs near the fireplace. Scorch marks scarred her chest piece, but otherwise she looked uninjured.

"Where's Jaida and everyone else?" Jasce asked.

"Jaida's with the consort, tending to Prince Andrei. Keeping him alive drained my magic, but he's at least stable. Nicolaus and the guards are patrolling the area." Kord pinched the bridge of his nose. "Unfortunately, we lost Matvey."

Jasce winced, remembering the warrior diving in front of his prince and being impaled by Vale's magical daggers.

Kord rubbed his jaw and glanced at his sleeping sister. "Kenz told me about the creatures in the cave. The prince is lucky he's alive."

Jaida and the consort emerged from the back room. "He's too stubborn to die," the consort said, and placed a hand on Jasce's shoulder. "Thank you for rescuing him."

He nodded and surveyed his sister. "Are you all right?"

Jaida wrapped her arms around her waist. "Yes."

Flynt leaned against the entryway to the kitchen. "Stew's ready, if anyone's hungry."

"You can cook?" Jaida asked, cracking a small smile.

Flynt rubbed the back of his neck. "I just heated it up. One of the soldiers made it."

Conquering the Darkness

"Ah. Well, it smells delicious." She turned to Jasce. "Coming?"

"In a minute." He rose and limped to where Kenz slept. He knelt in front of her and touched her leg.

She jerked and blinked her eyes open. Rubbing her neck, she glanced around groggily. "You're awake."

"As are you." Jasce smiled and pulled a chair over. The door opened and snow billowed in as Nicolaus and two soldiers entered.

"All clear and the Ornix are safe," Nicolaus said, placing his quiver of arrows and bow by the door before removing his hat and cloak.

"Bruiser?" Jasce asked, a stab of guilt coursing through him. He hadn't even thought of his horse with everything else going on.

Nicolaus raised his palms. "He's fine. Although I don't think he likes me very much."

"He has good taste."

Nicolaus huffed. "You're hilarious. Anyway, how are you doing?"

"I'll live."

"Well, that's a relief." Nicolaus smirked and looked at Kenz. "Your ability with that shield is quite impressive."

"Thank you," she said, sneaking a glance at Jasce.

Jasce ground his teeth at the slight flush brightening Kenz's cheeks and immediately swore from the jolt of pain through his jaw. He touched his beard, and his hand came away streaked with blood.

"That needs stitches," Kenz said.

Jasce arched his brow and glanced at Kord, who raised his hands. "My magic isn't ready yet, sorry. Stitches will stop the bleeding for now and keep it from getting infected."

Kenz stood and held Jasce's hand. "We'll do it the old-fashioned way." She addressed the consort. "Where's the medical kit?"

Jaida emerged from the kitchen with a bowl of steaming stew. "Do you know what you're doing?"

The glare Kenz shot Jasce's sister might make a man quiver in fear. Jaida, however, scowled back. The consort handed over the kit and a bottle of whiskey. "For medicinal purposes."

Kenz led Jasce to the washroom and pointed to a wooden stool. "Sit."

Jasce obeyed and watched her organize the supplies and fill a basin

117

with water. "I think Jaida asked a fair question. Do you know what you're doing?"

Kenz gave a small smile. "I stitched up your back last year. You would have died otherwise, so yes, I can handle the cut on your face."

He brought the bottle to his lips and swallowed the whiskey. "Duly noted." He savored the slow burn as Kenz lit a candle and held her knife over it. Watching the metal glow, Jasce asked, "What are we going to do about you and my sister? She's a part of my life, as are you. I don't want to lose her again."

Kenz sighed. "I know she didn't mean to kill Amycus. My head knows this, but my heart hurts. Kord keeps telling me to forgive her, but..."

"But what?"

"It's difficult, especially when I don't feel it. You know what I mean?" She lifted her eyes from the glowing steel and looked at him.

"I suppose." He took another long pull from the bottle. Amycus's journal entry floated to the forefront of his mind.

> *There is so much rage and bitterness in Jasce. It's drowning him and his full potential, not just as a Vaulter, but as a man. One day he'll have to learn, as I have, that these emotions will destroy his soul. One day, he'll have to learn to forgive.*

He had harbored anger and resentment for as long as he could remember. As a Hunter, he'd allowed his rage to empower him. If he let it go, then what? He feared he would be an empty shell. Or at least a powerless one.

Kenz sat across from him on a bench and raised her dagger. "I've been wanting to do this from the moment I saw you." He was about to protest when she scraped the edge of the blade against his uninjured cheek.

"Shaving off my beard was what you wanted to do?" Jasce asked.

"Among other things, yes."

Hair floated to the ground, and the scraping of the knife against his skin filled the silence. He swallowed and focused on her eyes, the color reminding him of an exquisite emerald. He counted the freckles across

Conquering the Darkness

her nose, which seemed familiar, like something he'd done many times. His eyes drifted down her face to her mouth, her bottom lip trapped by her teeth. He looked away and tried to ignore the desire heating through his loins.

"Look up," she said, gently tipping his chin. "And don't move. In fact . . ." Her words trailed off as she lifted the bottle and took a long pull.

"I'm not sure you should be drinking."

She chuckled and worked on his neck. Using small scissors, she cut the hair around the wound Drexus had given him and dabbed on ointment that temporarily numbed the skin. "Once Kord's magic returns, I'm sure there won't be too big of a scar."

"What's one more? And besides, I can grow the beard back. That way, you won't have to see it."

She looked into his eyes. "You're beautiful, with or without scars."

The sound of his swallow filled the silence.

She smiled and threaded a needle. "Better take another drink. This might hurt."

"Not remembering you hurts more," he said, his voice sounding like jagged steel. He had no idea where those words came from, but deep in his soul, he meant them.

She handed him the bottle and whispered, "Me too."

He took another long drink, shut his eyes, and breathed deeply through his nose as the needle pierced his skin. Starting at the top of his cheek, she methodically worked, her fingers confident and steady. He wished he remembered what they had been like together and a deep ache tightened his chest. Losing the Creator Stone and his chance for his memories to return had him digging his nails into his palms.

"Doing okay?" she asked.

He nodded and attempted to calm his raging thoughts. She sewed a few more stitches, just below his chin, and then dipped a rag in a bowl of water to wash the blood from his face.

"All done."

Jasce opened his eyes and blinked away the spinning room. Alcohol, exhaustion, and lack of food made him sway. He gingerly touched the sutures on the side of his face and suspected once the numbing cream wore off, the wound would sting like a beast.

He focused once again on Kenz's eyes and the dark circles below them. "My turn."

She quickly lifted her head. "What?"

He took the rag and gently cleaned her face, letting his thumb trace her bottom lip. His eyes drifted to her chest piece, scorched and scarred. "Let's get this charred armor off you."

"I can—"

"I know you can," he interrupted. "But I have a hunch you've taken care of me a lot, and I'd like to return the favor."

He held her hands and helped her stand, then began unstrapping her chest piece, one buckle at a time. His fingers stopped as an image of them standing in a stream flashed through his mind.

He lifted his gaze to meet hers. "We've done this before, haven't we?"

She licked her lips and nodded. He didn't take his eyes from hers as he unhooked the rest of the clips and lowered the damaged armor to the ground.

He cleared his throat. "In your world, do friends kiss?"

Her cheeks flushed, and she nodded again, seemingly unable to speak. He held her face as his heart hammered in his chest, his body immediately responding to her, the longing so intense he almost groaned.

A loud knock had them jumping apart. "Hey you two, some of us also need to clean up," Flynt said.

Kenz stepped away and glanced at the door.

Jasce's eyes narrowed. "I really can't believe I ever liked that Fire Spectral."

"I heard that." Flynt knocked again, louder.

"Almost done," Kenz said to Flynt as she retrieved her armor.

Jasce gathered the bloody bandages and bowl. "Thank you for taking care of me."

She blinked back the tears pooling in her eyes. "That's what friends do." She opened the door and slid past Flynt, who stood with his arms crossed and his brows raised.

Conquering the Darkness

"Don't you look dapper?" he said with an amused smile.

Jasce shook his head. "I'm positive I never liked you."

Flynt laughed and shut the door behind him.

When they returned to the living room, everyone was hunched over their dinner. Kord handed bowls of stew to Kenz and Jasce, and he gingerly took a bite, thankful for the numbing medicine Kenz had applied along his wound.

"I'll be with Andrei if anyone needs me," the consort said, taking her dinner to the other room.

"Oh, thank all that's magical," Nicolaus said. Jasce raised his brows, and the Alturian continued. "That ridiculous beard is finally gone. It really wasn't your best look."

"I agree," said Jaida, giving him a playful wink.

"Me too," Flynt said, returning to the room.

"Yeah, well, I didn't ask any of you, so shut it." Jasce studied the group. Dirt and dried blood covered their clothes and dark smudges marred the skin under their eyes. Between the Scymids and Drexus, they were lucky to be alive.

"How did Drexus even know where we were?" Kord asked.

"The Empower Stone led him right to the cave. It probably didn't help that I had the missing sliver. Which he now has." Nicolaus winced.

Jaida's face drained of color.

"What's wrong?" Flynt asked, grabbing her hand.

Jasce tapped his finger on his thigh as he frowned at the Fire Spectral. He was getting too cozy with his sister for his liking. Kord nudged his leg with his foot and shook his head. Kenz pressed her lips together and looked away to hide her smile.

Jaida stood and paced in front of the fire. She tugged on the strands of her hair and mumbled under her breath.

"Jaida, out with it," Jasce said. "What's going on?"

Fisting her hands, she spun around and faced the room. Her cheeks had reddened, and her gaze darted to every dark corner. "Vale said something to me before the battle. His eyes had turned brown, and he seemed to come back to himself."

"And?" Kenz said, waving her hand in a *get on with it* motion.

"He told me Drexus had implanted another sliver of the Empower Stone inside me, somewhere," Jaida said.

Jasce swore and then grimaced at the pain in his face. He couldn't believe Drexus would endanger his sister like that. Psyches were the most sensitive of Spectrals with Mental magic. Surely Drexus knew this. He obviously didn't care, though. Jasce and Jaida had been nothing more than his weapons, and he would do anything to make them sharp and lethal.

"Wouldn't you know if Drexus implanted a crystal inside of you?" Kenz asked.

Jaida frowned and thought for a moment, and then snapped her fingers. She looked at Jasce. "He must have found the Empower Stone and hidden it in his study, which was why he got so angry at me for being in there."

Jasce nodded. "And then you woke up in the infirmary and didn't know why. He must have sensed your power and saw an opportunity to embed the sliver inside you, with you none the wiser."

"That must be it." She shook her head as sadness flashed across her face.

Flynt swore and his fire sparked. "What a sick bastard." Jasce couldn't agree more.

Nicolaus crossed a leg over his knee and peered at Jaida. "The story only says one sliver was missing."

Jaida squirmed under everyone's stares and then focused on Jasce. "Remember when that Vastane hag wheeled out the Empower Stone?"

"Really?" Jasce said, crossing his arms.

She flicked her hand at him and sat. "Right. Anyway, I remember seeing two grooves cut into the Stone. Nicolaus must have had the original sliver."

"So Drexus found the Empower Stone years ago and hid it. But why? Why wouldn't he use it?" Kenz asked.

"Look what it did to Jasce. No offense," Flynt said.

"A little taken," Jasce mumbled.

Flynt continued, "Maybe he experienced something similar and hid it until he found the other three Stones."

Kord chewed on the side of his thumb as he stared at Jaida. "You having a sliver of the Empower Stone would explain the damage done during the battle in Orilyon."

"Yes. At one point, I had both the slivers, plus I was near the Stone." Relief flashed through her eyes. All that magic flowing through and around her explained the shockwave that had leveled a town block. Jasce snuck a glance at Kenz, who fiddled with her bracelets.

"It's also why my magic has returned. Your procedure didn't work," Jaida said to Kord, who arched a brow.

"Now it makes sense why Drexus didn't seem surprised by your magic. I was a little taken aback, I might add," Nicholas said.

"As was I." Hurt flashed through Flynt's amber eyes before quickly disappearing. Jaida bit her lip but said nothing.

"Wouldn't you have detected the magic if the sliver was inside her?" Kenz asked her brother, eyeing Jaida like she was some creepy bug.

Jasce nudged her with his knee, and the look on her face melted into indifference. "Kord, see if you can sense it," Jasce said.

"May I?" Kord asked Jaida, getting to his feet.

Jaida nodded. Kord ran a hand over her arms, legs, mumbling sorry when he touched her stomach and hips. Flynt cleared his throat. Kord had her turn around, and his eye closed as his hand stopped at the base of her head.

"It's here."

Jaida gasped and touched the back of her neck. "How could he do this to me?"

Jasce huffed out a disgusted laugh. "Because all he cares about is power and domination. I bet that's why you've been getting those headaches."

Jaida scanned the room. "Okay, everyone quit staring at me like I'm some monstrous experiment."

"Kord, can you remove it?" Flynt wove a flicker of green fire through his fingers, something Jasce found rather annoying.

"Yes. I need to get her to a medical facility and then figure out how to remove it. Otherwise, Drexus can track her, which we don't want."

"Maybe we do. I could be the bait," Jaida said.

"No way!" Jasce and Flynt said at the same time.

Jaida dipped her chin, hiding her smile while Jasce glared at Flynt, who glared right back.

"Okay, you two," Kenz said, shaking her head. "Let's table this for now and come up with a plan when we return to Nivia. We all need to rest."

Jasce placed his half-eaten stew on a side table and walked toward the kitchen to stare out the window, the cold floor on his bare feet making him shiver. The snow-covered land sparkled like gems with the light of the full moon. A Khioshka sprinted past, pursuing a white fox weaving through the snowbanks. Jasce empathized with that fox, running for its life. He just didn't know what he was fleeing from. His past? His future? Drexus? He absently rubbed his hand over the scar on his sternum where Drexus's blade had pierced muscle and bone.

He shook his head as he stared out the window and blocked the murmurs behind him. How could Drexus put that sliver inside his sister? He thought Drexus had at least cared about her, but she was nothing more than a pawn, an experiment, just like he had been.

Death is too easy for you. Live with your defeat, knowing you're worthless and a complete failure.

His heart pounded like it was going to beat out of his chest as he tried to rein in the anger stirring in his gut from Drexus's words. He flung open the cupboards and sighed. Soldiers always had alcohol on hand to keep them company during the long nights, making them not so dark. And he suspected tonight the darkness would be especially grim.

Chapter Fifteen

Jasce tossed and turned most of the night, until, with a groan, he finally relented. His mind circled between the battle with Drexus and how colossally he'd lost to the fear that had gripped him when Kord was stabbed. Vale's black eyes haunted him, too. When his thoughts drifted to Kenz and how he'd almost kissed her, how her touch felt so familiar and longing made his pulse race, he decided drinking would be more productive than trying to sleep. He retrieved Amycus's journal along with the bottle of whiskey by his bed, settled into a chair in the main room, and started where he'd left off.

> *Cerus and I finally crossed the Desert of Souls after a quick stop in Carhurst, where I met the son of Jedrek and Dwyn Haring We then used the ring to locate the Empower Stone. Kraig gave me a place to start*—"*where the Camden Mountains end and the shore begins." From there, it was just a matter of time and searching until we found the Stone, and find it we did.*
> *I've always wondered if Elemental Spectrals could control all four elements. I believe the power is in each of us, but over time, we tend to favor our dominant element. The Empower Stone was the key! I can now manipulate fire, water, and earth as well as air.*

Cassie Sanchez

Why didn't I listen to Cerus, who begged me to be careful, or Kraig's warning about the balance of magic? Why did I push it? I thought I could control the amount of magic flowing through me. Cerus tried to help me and, in a moment of weakness, I lost control and killed him.
Because of my hubris, I've buried a dear friend.
I've added murder to my list of wrongs and my hands are stained with blood.
I have to get rid of the Empower Stone. No one can have that kind of power. Imagine if someone acquired all four pieces of the Heart? I will find another way to unite the Spectrals. But why would they even follow me once they learn what I've done?

I'm out of time. Drexus and his Hunters have found me.

Jasce lifted the bottle to his lips to find it empty. Thankfully, the worst of his pain had dulled, but his body still ached everywhere. Pushing out of the chair, he limped to the kitchen, thinking about what Amycus had done. He had found the Empower Stone and used it to control all four elements. The consequences had been disastrous. And based on what Jasce had learned when he awoke from his injury, Amycus's magic had been slowly killing him.

He found another bottle of whiskey and uncorked it. He heard his sister's reproach about how drinking was not the way to solve one's problems, but he couldn't bring himself to care. Not in the dead of night, when the taste of defeat was still fresh on his tongue. Jasce leaned back in his chair and closed his eyes.

The chair creaked next to him. "Couldn't sleep, huh?" Kord asked, stretching his long legs in front of him.

"Very astute of you."

Kord's penetrating gaze made him grit his teeth. He focused on the mesmerizing flames dancing along the charred wood.

"You get more sarcastic, and meaner I might add, when you're drunk." Kord lifted the empty bottle and glanced at the one resting in Jasce's lap. "I'm worried about how much you're drinking."

"I have it handled. Besides, it takes the edge off," he said, tearing his eyes from the fire.

"Takes the edge off what?"

"Everything."

Kord sighed. "I see."

The fire crackled, and the fierce wind that had blown all night continued to harass the compound. Thunder rumbled off the peaks of the mountains as if competing with the wind for dominance.

"Did Amycus tell you he found the Empower Stone?" Jasce asked.

"The only time he mentioned it was during the Gathering, after stealing the sliver from you."

Jasce tapped the arm of his chair. He vaguely remembered Kord telling him this back in Orilyon. Amycus wanted to protect him from succumbing to the magic of the Empower Stone and had stolen the sliver, hoping to right his wrongs.

"We haven't talked about your magic. Did the Creator Stone work?" Kord asked, breaking the silence.

That was another reason he was awake. The faint buzzing inside him made it impossible to stay asleep. He supposed it was something he'd get used to. "I think so. Something feels different, but I don't know how to use it."

Kord pointed to the journal on Jasce's lap. "Does Amycus say anything about teaching you?"

"He mentions our time training, but no actual instruction."

"And your memories?"

"Only one, when I got the transfusion. Otherwise, just bits and pieces."

Kord leaned back in his chair. "Well, that's better than nothing."

Jasce placed the journal and the bottle on the side table. "Why aren't you sleeping?"

"Bad dreams. Plus, I never sleep well without Tillie beside me." He sighed. "I miss my wife. And my son."

Jasce stood and walked to the window, able to sympathize with the bad dreams. A soft, purplish glow illuminated the tops of the snow-covered mountains as dawn awoke from its slumber. His mother's words echoed in his mind. *The light chasing away the darkness.*

He had never properly grieved his mother's death and wasn't even sure how to. He hadn't thought it was important. When Drexus forced him into the Watch Guard, staying alive had been his sole purpose. As he grew stronger and more lethal, his mission evolved from survival to revenge.

"How did you get over Amycus's death?" Jasce asked, turning from the brightening sky.

Kord's brows lifted. "What makes you assume I'm over it?"

"You don't seem upset, I suppose."

"We all grieve in different ways. I miss him and catch myself wanting to talk to him, wishing he was here. But I also want to honor him and try to lead as he did. I still feel the pain of his loss. Here," he said, pointing to his chest. "Why do you ask?"

"Every sunrise reminds me of my mother. I haven't seen one in ages, but when I do, I'm gripped with a sorrow I don't know what to do with. So I block it. I train, I work in the forge." Jasce glanced at the empty bottle. "I drink."

"What about your father?"

He faced the window again and found his reflection frowning back at him with troubled eyes that looked clear instead of blue. Stitches carved through part of his face, and his hair was long and scraggly. Besides the color of his eyes and the stitches, the resemblance between him and his father was startling.

"I don't deserve to grieve over him. It's my fault he's dead."

"Hmm." Kord stifled a yawn and rose from the chair. "I need coffee."

Jasce pivoted and stared wide-eyed at the Healer. "Um, okay." That wasn't the reaction he was expecting. Based on the brief time he had known Kord, the man usually imparted some words of wisdom or a quirky saying. He limped back to the chair and shut his eyes to the swaying room.

He jerked awake when Kord nudged his arm.

"Want some?" Kord asked, holding a mug in front of him.

Conquering the Darkness

"Thanks."

"My magic is full strength. I'll heal you when I'm done with this," Kord said, lifting his mug in a toast. Jasce nodded and sipped the hot brew.

"Regarding you grieving your parents, as a Healer my job is to fix things, make things better. And I feel like a failure with you."

Jasce slowly turned his head. He struggled to find the connection, but figured Kord would get around to it eventually. "Why me?"

"One, because I couldn't heal the injury caused by Drexus. Those Snatchers blocked my magic, and the medical staff was too focused on keeping you alive. I wish there was something more I could do than temporarily relieve the pain."

"And two?" Jasce asked. Kord had already told him why he was unable to heal his back—too much time had passed, so the damage was permanent. It seemed time didn't mend all things.

"Most of your wounds aren't physical and are so deep, no one can touch them. You've buried them, having never dealt properly with your past."

He attempted not to squirm while Kord examined him as if he could peer into his soul. "I can't change the past."

"True. But you can learn from it."

"Is there a point to this conversation?"

Kord looked offended. "Of course. I always have a point."

"I mean, do you?"

Kord chuckled and punched him playfully in the arm. "My point is, you might be subconsciously suppressing your memories."

Jasce rubbed the spot where Kord hit him. "Why would I do that? I hate not knowing who I was, that I was a better man, someone people liked and respected." As the Angel of Death, the soldiers had feared him, and he'd thought that was enough. But based on what he'd learned after waking up without his magic or memories, it seemed people actually had enjoyed his company, looked up to him. It surprised him to discover he wanted to be that person again.

"I believe it's about forgiveness, starting with forgiving yourself." Kord gave him a small smile.

Jasce clenched his teeth at this notion of forgiveness. First Jaida, then the words from a dead man, and now Kord. Forgiveness wasn't an option for him. Besides, he needed to deal with more pressing matters. "I'm going back to Pandaren."

"Yeah, I figured. And *we're* going with you." The Healer crossed his ankles and stared into the fire. "Nice deflection, by the way."

Jasce grunted and closed his eyes, allowing the crackle of the burning logs to lull him to sleep.

A few hours later, everyone gathered in the living room. Consort Lekov joined them, followed by Prince Andrei, who was dressed in a clean tunic and leather pants. His color had returned, but shadows clung to the skin under his ice-blue eyes.

"How are you feeling?" Jasce asked.

"Better, thanks to Kord."

"Yes, he's quite handy to have around," Nicolaus said, rubbing his stomach where the arrow had struck. With Kord's magic recharging, he could heal everyone. He had removed the stitches in Jasce's face and healed the wound. There was a faint scar, but he didn't care, especially after what Kenz had said about scars, her words and touch still stirring inside him.

"So what's our next move?" Kenz asked, sitting beside Flynt, whose hair was rumpled and his eyelids half-closed. Jaida sat on the other side of the Fire Spectral while the consort and Kord occupied the couch. Nicolaus stood against the wall near the door the Balten guards had gone through to start their patrol.

Jasce leaned against the mantel. "I'm going to rescue Caston. Which means I won't be going back to Nivia." He looked at Prince Andrei. "Please explain this to your father, but I can't return."

The prince, who'd remained standing, crossed his muscular arms. "What about the deal you made—the Creator Stone for my sister's hand in marriage?"

"Technically, I don't have the Stone."

"But you did use it. He will expect you to keep your side of the bargain."

"You don't want me marrying your sister, so why are you pushing this?" Jasce asked, shoving away from the mantel. The prince automatically widened his feet as if expecting a fight.

Conquering the Darkness

Consort Lekov stepped between them. "We have bigger issues to deal with, Andrei." She turned her granite-like gaze onto Jasce. "And I will speak to the king."

Jasce and Prince Andrei glared at each other until Kenz cleared her throat. "Obviously we're going with you to save Caston."

"Here, here," Nicolaus said, smacking his knee.

Jasce severed the staring contest with the prince and faced the group. "Obviously," he said sarcastically as he addressed his sister. "I won't tell you what to do, but you'd be safer in Balten. Princess Irina has Healers that can remove the sliver."

Jaida shook her head. "I'm going."

Flynt's jaw pulsed as he stared at Jaida, then focused on Jasce. "We don't even know where Drexus took Caston."

"True. But I'd bet he's near Orilyon. Drexus has always wanted to rule, whether it was the Bastion, the palace, or Pandaren. My guess is he'll use the Creator Stone to build his army and then attack Orilyon. At least, that's what I would do."

Kord swore. "That's where the Inhibitor Stone is."

"Why did you send it there again?" Prince Andrei asked, an edge of steel lining his voice.

"We figured it was the safest place, and because Maera is developing a way to manipulate the Stone's magic to fight Drexus."

Nicolaus frowned. "It will take time for Drexus to create and train his troops. That's at least one positive thing. Plus, he doesn't know you found the Inhibitor Stone, right?"

Kenz shook her head. "Not that we're aware of. But what if he interrogates Caston?"

"Caston would never reveal the Stone's location. Drexus trained us too thoroughly to withstand torture," Jasce said, tapping his lip. "Drexus might search the desert or go after the Abolish Stone. Does anyone know where it is?"

"The king thinks it's somewhere near Terrenus," said Consort Lekov.

"Then we will send soldiers to Terrenus to warn the archduke," Prince Andrei said, and the consort agreed.

"So we just travel to Orilyon and wait?" Kenz asked.

Jasce sighed. "I haven't gotten that far with the plan yet. We'll need your spies," he said to Nicolaus, "to monitor the desert."

Flynt took hold of Jaida's hand. "We need to get the sliver out of her. We don't want Drexus knowing where she is."

"Agreed." Jasce paced along the mud-stained rug in front of the fire.

"One thing I don't understand is why did Drexus want the sliver Nicolaus had?" Consort Lekov asked. "He has the Empower Stone. Why does he need the sliver?"

Nicolaus lifted a finger. "Magic must have balance. I don't believe the Stone will work to its full capacity while the two slivers are missing. And now that he has the Creator Stone—well, magic is definitely out of balance. There are warnings of terrible storms and earthquakes, magic rebounding and not responding like normal." Nicolaus shrugged. "Those may just be stories, though."

Kord rubbed his hand down his face. "Great."

"One step at a time," the consort said. "For now, we need to protect the other two Stones."

Jasce continued pacing, aware of all eyes tracking him. He didn't like the idea of leading them into a potential war with Drexus and his magical army, but he also knew he couldn't defeat him alone.

"Kord, can you remove the sliver here?" he asked.

"I'd rather not. Where's the nearest town with a medical facility?"

He stopped pacing and faced Jaida, who bit her bottom lip.

"What?" Kenz asked, looking between them.

Jasce tilted his head back and sighed. Of all the towns in Opax, why this one? He had vowed years ago never to return to where his life had been forever changed. "Looks like we're going to Delmar."

Chapter Sixteen

The following day, Consort Lekov and Prince Andrei led them to Cardend, a small town on the northern edge of Balten where they would spend the night. In the morning, they would secure a boat to take them across Lake Chelan to Delmar.

Jasce leaned against the stable wall and watched the silhouettes of the consort and prince, with their team of Ornix, grow smaller in the waning light. Bruiser nudged his arm, and he wove his fingers through the horse's silky mane, relaxing in his calming presence. He wondered what the king would do now that he had decided not to return and fulfill his part of the bargain. Would King Morzov force him to marry Irina? Could he? He didn't want to cause diplomatic tension between Pandaren and Balten. Queen Valeri already wasn't a fan of his, and if his decision brought strife between the two countries, he'd never hear the end of it.

He exited the stable and headed to the Edge, a small tavern and inn on the outskirts of the town. He pulled his cloak tight around him and lowered his hood to block out the blowing snow as he strolled past the harbor and stone cottages lining the main road. Smoke billowed from the chimneys and the warm glow of candlelight illuminated the frost-covered windows.

Jasce kicked the snow off his boots as he entered the tavern and trudged upstairs to the bedrooms. Kord, Kenz, Flynt, Jaida, and Nicolaus stood in the middle of the hallway.

"What's going on?" Jasce asked.

Kord leaned against the doorjamb to an open room. "Because of the monthly winter market, there are only two rooms available."

Jasce arched a brow and peeked into a room with two small beds.

"The other room is even smaller, with only one bed," Kenz said, mimicking her brother's position against the wall.

"Ah, the dreaded one-bed scenario," Nicolaus said with a mischievous glint in his eye. "I'll stay with Jaida, for safety precautions."

Jasce opened his mouth, but Flynt interrupted him. "That's a no."

"For once we agree," Jasce said, crossing his arms.

"Well, what do you recommend?" Nicolaus asked.

After much debate, Flynt removed a deck of cards from his bag and each person drew a card to determine who would get the largest room. Kord and Kenz won, and Flynt opted to sleep on the floor since they were accustomed to traveling together.

Which left Jasce, Jaida, and Nicolaus standing in the narrow hallway, peering into the closet-sized room.

Nicolaus took the cards and shuffled the deck.

Jasce rolled his eyes at the Shade Walker. "Jaida, you sleep here."

Flynt glanced at the bed. "I'm more than happy to give up my spot on the floor and keep her company."

Jaida hid her grin and entered the tiny room.

"And I'm more than happy to kill you," Jasce said, tapping the hilt of his dagger.

Flynt's brows raised, and Jasce shut the door to his sister's protest. "Nicolaus and I will stay downstairs."

"I beg your pardon." A glass broke and a cacophony of laughter drifted up the stairs from the tavern below. Nicolaus pursed his lips. "I don't sleep in alehouses. I am a prince, remember?"

"How could I forget? Now let's go." Jasce tromped down the hallway, ignoring the snickers from Kenz and Kord. "The boat leaves at dawn, so sleep fast."

Conquering the Darkness

～

A dense fog blanketed the ground as the sun struggled to break free from the storm clouds clinging to the mountains.

Bruiser had whinnied and reared up on his back legs, almost knocking Jasce senseless as he tried to persuade the stubborn beast onto the boat. He placed a hood over the horse's head and, after many sugar cubes and lots of coaxing, managed to settle him into one of the makeshift stalls.

Kenz walked by and patted Bruiser's velvety nose. "I feel your pain."

Jasce hadn't had a moment alone with her since she'd stitched up his face. As he watched her walk toward the back of the boat where her brother and Flynt stood, he figured it was better this way. Their "friendship" was new and fragile, and one wrong move could ruin it. His old self normally wouldn't care, taking what he wanted and to hell with the consequences. But a nagging urge to protect their tenuous relationship had him showing the type of restraint that made his jaw ache.

Jaida stood next to him at the other end of the boat, leaning against the railing, her blonde hair blowing off her face as the sun finally punched through the clouds hovering on the horizon. Nicolaus chatted up the captain, who seemed at a loss for words as the Alturian wove a dramatic story while waving his hands and laughing.

"What if the queen throws me into the dungeon when we arrive in Orilyon?" Jaida asked, biting her lower lip.

"I'll get you out if she does." Jasce draped an arm around her. "I'm sure Queen Valeri has more important issues to deal with than one little Psyche."

She wiggled her fingers and ice particles twirled in the air, sparkling like diamonds. "Do you think Kord can remove the sliver safely?"

"He seems more than capable."

"I still can't believe he did this to me," Jaida said, sadness creeping into her voice as she rubbed the base of her neck.

"Neither can I." He tamped down on the rage. It wouldn't help his sister if he lost his temper, and besides, better to nurture the fire festering in him for when he confronted Drexus. "Kord will get it out, and you'll feel a lot better. I'm sure of it."

She gave him a weak smile and continued swirling the ice in the air. Her brow furrowed. "Are you nervous about returning to Delmar?"

He focused on the dancing crystals, ignoring her question as a sliver of envy spiked through him at how easily his sister used her magic. He'd found a few entries from Amycus of their time training, but there were no explicit instructions on how to use the magic. Kenz had told him that Amycus had instructed him to *will* himself to a certain spot. Whatever that meant. He'd tried in the tavern last night, even picking Nicolaus's brain, whose Shade Walking magic was similar, but he still couldn't vault.

His memories also hadn't returned, despite the one of him strapped to a table getting the Amplifier serum. Whenever Kenz saw him, an expectant look flashed across her face, replaced by disappointment.

Jaida tilted her head, waiting for an answer.

"Nervous? No. Dreading, yes." He ran his hand along the railing and stared out across the lake, small waves rocking the boat in a gentle rhythm. He longed for the same calmness but hadn't been able to unravel the knot in his stomach, even with the flask in his pocket. "I vowed never to return to Delmar. Even as a Hunter, I never went. Drexus didn't push me regarding my decision, which I always thought was strange. He obviously didn't want me discovering the depth of his treachery."

"I've never been back, either." She allowed the ice crystals to drift into the lake and disappear. "I was a lot younger than you, so I don't think it will be as painful. But if you need to talk, I'm here, okay?"

He pulled his sister close. "Thanks, Jai."

Jasce squinted into the distance toward Delmar Harbor. The town wasn't large, but the harbor had always bustled with fishermen and travelers. He lifted a trembling hand and brought his flask to his mouth, which had suddenly turned as dry as the desert.

They drifted past fishing vessels in search of their morning catch as they neared the shore and, as they drew closer, one sailor threw a rope to where a dockhand was waiting. The wood creaked as the boat bumped gently against the jetty. Jasce led Bruiser down the ramp and removed his cloak now that they were off the freezing water. Kenz, who had been mostly silent during the trip, walked beside him. He noticed her freckles were stark against her pale skin.

"You okay?" he asked.

She pressed her lips together. "Don't enjoy sailing."

Jasce glanced from her to the lake, where only a few small waves kissed the shore. "That wasn't really sailing."

"Don't care," Kenz said, and inhaled a deep breath.

They walked along the wharf behind the others, passing various vendor booths displaying their unique wares. Jasce scanned the area, automatically searching for threats. A few dockhands stopped what they were doing to gawk at the strangers. A man near one booth lowered his hat. He twisted around and strode down the nearest alley.

"So this is where you were born?" Kenz asked.

Jasce tore his gaze from the person hurrying from the boardwalk and shoved a hand into his pocket. The sound of Bruiser's hooves clomping against the wood filled the silence. He really didn't want to talk about his childhood, but Kenz nudged him and he finally answered, "Yes, this is where I grew up."

"Did you have a favorite place?"

"I helped a blacksmith, Braxium Sarrazen, from time to time. My way of escaping, I suppose."

She raised her brows. "Escaping?"

"Life at home wasn't always pleasant, and although I acted like the protective big brother, there were days I didn't want the responsibility."

"Ah." She looped her hand through his arm. "Can I see this forge?"

He smiled down at her. "I don't even know if the old curmudgeon is still alive." He felt her stiffen as Jaida approached with Kord and Flynt trailing behind.

Jasce slid a look at Kenz from the corner of his eye. "I need you to try harder at being nice," he whispered.

"Sorry, knee-jerk reaction," she whispered back, and released his arm.

"I'll take you to the medical facility. It isn't much, but should have everything you need," Jasce said to Kord.

"I remember where it is," Jaida said.

Jasce frowned. "Don't you want me there?"

Kord arched a brow. "I'll send Flynt if there's any issue, but I'm not worried."

"Easy for you to say. That's not your sister you'll be digging around in."

"Digging around in?" Kord shook his head. "I'll try not to be offended by that remark."

Jaida kissed Jasce on the cheek. "It'll be fine. We'll catch up with you later."

He watched Jaida, Kord, and Flynt until they turned down a side street. Nicolaus led Bruiser toward the area of town where a few inns were located, saying he'd take care of the accommodations, clearly still irritated about having to sleep in a tavern. They weren't sure how long they would be staying in Delmar, having agreed to wait until Nicolaus received word from his spy network. Jasce was certain Queen Valeri wouldn't appreciate the number of Shade Walkers sneaking around her kingdom, but for now, they were necessary.

The muscles in Jasce's back loosened as he strolled with Kenz down the main street. The cold, humid air did nothing for the chronic pain, and walking seemed to relieve the ache. They passed the center of town, where the weekly market took place. Many shops hadn't opened yet, except for the bakery where the smell of fresh bread wafted through the air. As a child, he had loved visiting first thing, after dawn had broken. The old baker always saved him one of her mouthwatering cinnamon rolls.

They stopped at the bakery and bought some pastries and two cups of coffee. A rock skittered in the nearby alley, and the hairs on his neck stood to attention. Jasce peered down the narrow pathway and thought he saw a flicker of movement.

"I miss Tillie," Kenz said, nibbling on the sugary confection.

"I hear she's very talented." Jasce sipped his coffee and angled his body to have a clear view of the side streets.

"She really is." Kenz stared into the distance. "I hope they're okay."

"Kord said they were in Carhurst, right?" She nodded. "They should be far enough away from whatever Drexus is planning. But I wouldn't blame you or Kord if you wanted to go back."

Conquering the Darkness

Kenz gave him a sad smile. "A part of me wants to, but if we don't stop Drexus in Opax, what will prevent him from invading Paxton?"

"True." Except now that he had the two Stones, could anyone defeat Drexus? He hoped whatever Maera was concocting in the Sanctuary would give them a fighting chance.

Kenz finished her pastry, and he had to clear his throat as the tip of her tongue licked the sugar off her fingers. The visual put images in his head that were beyond those of friendship. She talked about Carhurst as she drank her coffee, but he filtered out her words and focused on the subtle noises coming from the alley behind the bakery. Whoever was following them had horrible stalking skills. Kenz frowned as he edged away from her.

With a sudden lunge, he reached behind a stack of wooden crates, fingers clutching onto a wool cloak, and yanked the man from his hiding spot.

"What the hell?" the man said as Jasce rammed him against the stone wall.

Kenz dropped her coffee and ignited her bracelets. Indigo light flickered.

"Why are you following us?" Jasce shoved the man again, causing his hat to fall off. Brown eyes, framed with wrinkles, glared back, and scraggly gray hair lined a familiar face. One Jasce hadn't seen in years.

"Braxium?"

The blacksmith pushed Jasce off him. "What's the matter with you? Shoving an innocent man into a wall."

"You were following us. Poorly, I might add."

Braxium straightened his cloak, frowned at Kenz, and then focused on Jasce. "I thought I recognized you on the dock but wanted to be sure."

"Wait," Kenz said, lowering her hands, her bracelets extinguishing their glow. "This is the blacksmith who let you escape into his forge?"

Jasce rested his hands on his hips. "Seems so. Though why he's sneaking around in alleyways, I can't tell you."

"Isn't this fortuitous?" Kenz winked at him.

"Or just bad luck," Jasce muttered.

Braxium huffed. "You know, I am standing right here." His eyes darted to Kenz's bracelets and his brow arched. "No reason to be standing out here in the cold. Come on." He turned and ambled down the road.

Jasce pinched the bridge of his nose. He wasn't in the mood for a stroll down memory lane. Besides, the memories of his childhood weren't the ones he needed—or wanted—to remember.

Kenz interlaced her fingers with his and dragged him after the blacksmith. "It'll be fun."

"You and I have very different definitions of fun."

They stopped at a small fence with a stone pathway leading to a familiar cottage. A hammer and anvil sign hung over the wooden door.

Kenz stared up at the insignia and whispered, "Reminds me of Amycus."

An urge to draw her close had him reaching out, but he quickly lowered his hand.

"Are you going to stand around like idiots or come in?" Braxium's gruff voice sounded as he reemerged from the cottage. He had removed his cloak, revealing a tan tunic and pants smudged with dirt.

Jasce sighed and led Kenz down the path and into a cottage brimming with memories.

Chapter Seventeen

"I wasn't sure if you were still alive," Jasce said, removing his cloak and knapsack and laying them on a table in the entryway.

"Hell, boy. I'm not that old." Braxium watched Kenz remove her cloak and place it on top of Jasce's. "Who's she?"

Kenz covered her mouth to hide her smile.

Jasce shook his head. "This is my friend, Kenz Haring."

"Haring, huh? I'm familiar with that name."

"You are?" She followed the blacksmith down a hallway to a set of closed double doors. As a kid, Braxium snuck Jasce through the back door, so he had rarely used the main entrance unless Jaida was with him.

The doors opened, and the smell of metal and smoke assaulted his nose. Braxium's forge was just as he remembered. He strolled past a large wooden table with tools scattered on the scarred surface. Soot-covered stone lined the wall, and a fire crackled in the hearth occupying one corner of the room. Two anvils stood on either side and blades of varying sizes decorated the wall and filled baskets. His hands itched to organize the cluttered room.

He ran a finger through a layer of dust on a small worktable, smiling when he saw his initials carved into the wood. He had spent hours in this spot, learning the craft, discovering how metal would bend to his will with enough heat and patience.

"Nothing has changed." Jasce felt the blacksmith's eyes on him as he examined a chisel.

"Why would it?" Braxium asked, settling on a stool and surveying the forge. Kenz joined him at the table.

Burning wood popped as logs shifted, and a tree limb scratched on the window from the breeze blowing off the lake. Jasce finished his perusal of the space and leaned against the cluttered worktable.

Kenz cleared her throat, breaking the silence. "You said my name was familiar. Did you know my parents?"

Braxium tore his gaze from Jasce to stare at her. "Yes."

She shifted on her stool. "How?"

The blacksmith sighed, as if resigning himself to a lengthy conversation. "From the war. Your mother was a powerful Water Spectral. It's no wonder you and your brother's magic is so strong. Your dad being an Amp helped, too."

"How do you know about our magic?" Kenz asked at the same time Jasce asked, "You fought in the war?"

Braxium rose to his feet, waving them to follow as he left the forge and walked down another narrow hallway that opened into the living room. "Might as well make yourselves comfortable," he said, pointing to a worn-looking couch with a low table separating it from two mismatched chairs. Books and papers were piled on every flat surface, along with a dirty set of horseshoes, a hammer, and some nails.

"Tea?" Braxium asked, disappearing into the kitchen.

"You have anything stronger?" Jasce called over his shoulder while reading the titles of the books on the bookshelf. Kenz squeaked as she fell into the deep cushions of the worn couch. He lifted a brow and smiled.

Braxium brought in a tray with three teacups, a small pitcher of cream, and a glass bowl full of sugar cubes and placed them on the table. A spicy aroma drifted up through the steam. "I wasn't sure how you took it."

Jasce removed his flask and poured some whiskey into his cup. He sighed as the woodsy flavor of the tea and the burn of the whiskey warmed his throat and belly. Kenz frowned at him.

"What?" Jasce asked.

"Pretty sure she's thinking it's a little early for that," Braxium said.

"It's for medicinal purposes."

"Uh huh," the blacksmith said, and lowered himself into a dark green chair, the lines around his mouth deepening as he observed him.

Jasce winced when he sat, his back stinging from the cold and the long ride from the compound the day before. Sleeping on a wooden bench in the tavern hadn't helped, either. "About the war. Were you part of the Watch Guard?"

"It wasn't called the Watch Guard in my day. But no, I'm just a simple blacksmith." He stared out the window, sipping from his teacup.

"So you had no military training, and yet you still fought?" Jasce drained his tea. Something wasn't adding up, but he couldn't figure out what.

"I had a little training. From Amycus."

Kenz wriggled out of the couch and sat on the edge. "You knew Amycus, too?"

"Yes. That's how I learned about you and your brother. He'd send letters from Carhurst from time to time. Interesting man, that one. How is he?"

She lowered her gaze. "He died a few months ago."

Jasce let his mind wander while she filled Braxium in on the highlights of their time in Orilyon with the Gathering and Queen Siryn's betrayal.

It didn't make sense. Amycus had been battling the Vastanes. Why would he train a blacksmith to fight?

Kenz was talking about what Drexus was planning when Jasce interrupted her.

"Why would Amycus train you?"

Braxium tapped his lip, his brown eyes narrow. "We were about to lose the war when the king sent a call for help, asking Spectrals to fight. At the time, I was living on the outskirts of Delmar. I abandoned my family to join the cause."

"You're a Spectral?" Jasce couldn't recall the blacksmith using any magic when he'd worked in the forge.

Braxium nodded. "I'm a Vaulter."

The teacup slipped from Jasce's hand, but he caught it before it crashed onto the rug.

"And before you ask, yes, Amycus wrote to me about you as well," the blacksmith said, his eyes searching Jasce's face.

Jasce relaxed his hands and placed the cup on the table. "You kept your magic hidden."

"It was safer that way, once they started hunting us."

"What else did Amycus tell you?"

"Only what I needed to know." Jasce tilted his head at the vague answer. "Anyway, the last letter I received was another call for help when he was planning an attack on the Bastion."

"I didn't see you there," Kenz said.

"That's because I wasn't."

Jasce rested his forearms on his thighs. "If that's the last you heard from Amycus, then you aren't aware that Jaida's alive."

It was Braxium's turn to almost drop his cup. "What? No, that's not... she died that night."

Jasce shook his head. "That's what we all thought. But Drexus had taken her. She's a Psyche, like Mom."

"How did you learn Lisia was a Psyche?" Braxium asked, his eyes wide.

"Amycus."

Braxium hands trembled as he placed his cup on the table. "Where is she?"

"Here, at the medical facility." Braxium opened his mouth, but Jasce raised a hand. "She's fine. Just gathering supplies." He didn't need to tell the old man about the sliver of the Empower Stone.

Braxium released a tremulous breath and leaned back into his chair. "After all this time, she's been alive. If only Barnet would have known."

Jasce huffed. "He wouldn't have cared." He stood and walked to the window, gazing out at the villagers making their way into town. His father always had a soft spot for Jaida—daddy's little girl, he supposed.

Conquering the Darkness

But as the drinking got worse, so did the paranoia. Soon, even his sister couldn't make the man smile.

"Jasce, your father had his faults, but deep down he was a good man," Braxium said.

He spun around and pointed at the blacksmith. "Don't you dare. He betrayed my mother, got her killed, and did nothing when Drexus captured Jaida and me." He lowered his hand. "Why would you even defend him?"

Braxium's eyes shone, and he slowly rose to his feet. "Because he's my brother."

Jasce's mouth dropped open. He blinked and shook his head. "What did you say?" he asked in a whisper, stepping closer to the blacksmith.

Kenz stood and twisted her wrists, triggering her bracelets.

Braxium raised his hands, a look of pleading crossing his face. "Barnet was my younger brother. I'm your uncle."

The blood rushed through his ears, and his fists trembled. Secrets and lies seemed to be his family's curse, whether self-inflicted or at the mercy of others. His mother keeping her magic a secret, his father's betrayal, Drexus capturing Jaida when Jasce had thought she was dead. And now this. His temper snapped.

He strode forward, only to crash into a wall of indigo light. Taking a step back, he glared at Kenz. Braxium's mouth gaped as his eyes darted between them.

With her hand raised, she approached him like he was a trapped animal. "I need you to calm down."

Jasce pressed his hand to the shield. "You've done this before, haven't you?" he asked, the sound of his voice echoing off the enclosure.

"You don't always take secrets from your childhood well."

Digging his nails into his palms, the sting of pain settling his mind, he practiced his breathing, willing his heart to slow down. Braxium inched closer and lifted Kenz's other hand, inspecting the bracelets.

"Did Amycus make these?"

"Yes." She allowed Braxium to remove her bracelet and examine it further.

Now that Jasce really looked at the blacksmith, he saw a resemblance through the nose and chin. Braxium was taller than his father had been, but they shared the same hair color, build, and face shape. The last time he had seen his father, Barnet had been gaunt and weak, and so drunk he couldn't defend himself against the assassin there to kill him, against his very own son.

He rubbed his hand over his mouth. "Why wasn't I told? Why would you or my father keep this a secret?"

"We were estranged. My family wasn't pleased when I joined the war, so I left the Farone name behind and became Braxium Sarrazen. Barnet didn't like magic. You were just a baby when he discovered Lisia was a Psyche. He wasn't thrilled." He reattached Kenz's bracelet to her wrist. "Anyway, I moved back to Delmar and tried to reconcile with him. He swore me to secrecy, not wanting me to influence you or Jaida. It seemed better, and safer, for you not to know who I was, but I couldn't stay out of your lives. I felt it was my responsibility to look out for you as your dad's drinking got worse."

"And what a fabulous job you did." His entire body vibrated with fury. "Will you lower your shield?"

"Once you calm down," Kenz said, her bracelets glowing brighter.

He turned his back on the room and drained his flask to subdue his anger. Inhaling deeply, he sat in a chair and raised his brows expectantly at her. The indigo light disappeared but her bracelets continued to glow.

"And where were you the night your brother betrayed his wife and children?" Jasce asked.

"Drinking runs in the family," Braxium said, his voice strained. "Barnet had come here that night, but I was . . ." He looked away, pressing his lips together as a tear trickled down his cheek. "I was passed out in the tavern. By the time I came to, Lisia was dead and there was no sign of you or Jaida. We thought Drexus had killed both of you. And then Barnet got word that someone saw Drexus's men throw you into a carriage. He wanted my help to rescue you, but he wouldn't wait for me to sober up." Braxium collapsed into the chair, as if his confession sapped the last of his strength.

"Your father loved you, Jasce. He made mistakes, but . . . he tried to get you back. He tried to right his wrongs."

"Stop." Jasce fisted his hands, not wanting to hear any more as shame and regret assailed him, emotions he wasn't equipped to deal with. He held his head, unable to bear the thought of Barnet traveling to the Bastion to rescue him from the hell that had been his life. Bile rose to the back of his throat, the tea and whiskey swirling in his gut along with a wretchedness he'd never experienced.

Braxium continued as if Jasce hadn't spoken, his eyes glazed, lost in the past. "He returned from Orilyon broken and started drinking again. Disgraced and tormented by his actions, he fled the village. I found out years later he'd been killed."

Jasce shot to his feet, stumbled, and rested a hand on the shelves to keep from collapsing. He had justified the murder of his father for more than thirteen years, for what he did to his wife and children. But to hear Barnet had attempted to get him back? The last thing his father ever saw was Jasce's face and a dagger aimed at his heart.

He moaned and trudged toward the door. "I can't . . ."

"Jasce, wait," Kenz said.

He yanked open the door to find Kord, his fist raised and about to knock, with Flynt and Jaida standing behind him.

"The lady at the bakery . . . Whoa. You okay?" Kord asked.

Jasce's eyes darted to his sister's. She'd never forgive him now, not after she learned her father had regretted his mistake and had tried to save him. He'd murdered his father in cold blood. He was a monster, unworthy of forgiveness.

"Oh, Jaida," he groaned. He shoved past them and sprinted down the dirt-covered street. If only he could outrun his past, his failures, his choices. But it seemed no matter what he did, the consequences of his mistakes continued to drag him under like a millstone around his neck. He ran until he neared the land where their cottage had been.

Black flames circled his mother, Jaida's screams echoed through the night. Terror paralyzed him as Drexus sliced a dagger across his mother's throat.

The weight of the images of his past, the guilt suffocating him, dropped him to his knees. His fingers dug into the coarse sand, and a sob escaped his lips. Lifting his head, he roared as grief crushed him from all sides to where he couldn't breathe.

He jolted when a large hand rested on his arm.

"I've got you," Kord said, and wrapped his arms around him.

His spine stiffened. Jasce had never known sorrow or remorse like this.

A different image flitted through his mind of Kenz, lying on a beach covered in blood. The scene shifted to a rooftop, with him holding her as Kord tried to heal her.

It was a memory of another time, and pain like he'd never experienced had brought him to his knees.

He peered past Kord to where Kenz stood in the distance, her arms folded tightly.

"She told me," Kord said, seeing where Jasce looked.

"He wanted me back, and I killed him," he whispered.

Kord knelt with him in the dirt. "I know."

Jasce turned from Kord's sympathetic face and was met by wide, gray eyes.

"What happened?" Jaida asked.

Braxium gently took hold of her arm and whispered to her. Jaida's face twisted as the truth about her father was revealed to her, too. She covered her mouth and shook her head. Jasce flinched when she directed her gaze at him. A different type of pain cracked through his chest as disgust filled her eyes. She turned on her heel and walked away. If she hadn't despised him before, she would now.

Revulsion from his sister. Kenz's disappointment with him being unable to remember her. Pity from Kord, who had practically said he was unfixable. The emotions threatening to drown him were too much.

If there was one thing he'd learned as a Hunter, one thing he was thankful to Drexus for, it was having the skill to bury these feelings. "Worthless emotions," Drexus had called them. And right now, he agreed with his former commander. To hell with who he'd been for the last year. If all his memories were like the ones he just recalled, he didn't want them. The despair and guilt served no purpose and wouldn't alter his path. He still had a job to do, and wallowing in self-pity would only get him killed.

Jasce focused on his training and, bit by bit, hardened his heart, shoving the emotions into the darkest part of his soul and locking them away.

Conquering the Darkness

He wiped his face and rose to his feet. With one last look at the charred remains of his childhood, he turned and walked past Kord and Kenz, not sparing them or his uncle another glance. He wasn't even sure if Braxium knew how his brother had died, that the Angel of Death had ended Barnet Farone's life. He couldn't tell him, not now, maybe not ever. Braxium would just be one more person to look at him with either disgust or disappointment.

"Jasce, please, let us help you," Kenz said, taking a step to follow him. Her foot skidded in the dirt when he raised his hand.

"Just . . . leave me alone."

Chapter Eighteen

Jasce tromped through the Nisene Forest as his thoughts hammered inside his skull, flexing and relaxing his hands to rein in his fury. His feet automatically trekked along the trail his mother had used when she took them on adventures to protect them from their father. He stalked through the trees toward town, listening to the sounds of the creek nearby, until his anger subsided into self-loathing.

The path dumped him out ironically in front of the Broody Cauldron, the tavern his father had frequented. He blamed the cold for the shiver trailing down his spine since, in his haste to leave Braxium's, he'd forgotten his cloak. The surge of warm air relaxed his shoulders as he inhaled the scent of burning wood, ale, and roasting meat. He strode past the bar, his stomach rumbling, and ignored the stares of the patrons. He doubted anyone recognized him. It had been years since he'd had to plead with his dad to come home, practically dragging him out the door.

Jasce chose a table tucked into the corner and observed a group of older men drinking and playing a card game. It felt like days ago when he first stepped onto the docks in his hometown, so much had happened. His life, once again, had been flipped upside down.

The many glasses of whiskey he drank finally did the job, effectively numbing all the places that hurt, at least physically. Unfortunately, the alcohol couldn't erase the expression he'd seen on Jaida's face.

He hoped she was all right, and for a fleeting moment was thankful Flynt was so protective of her. He assumed Braxium had told her he was her uncle and wondered if having another family member besides him comforted her. They were no longer the last of the Farones, even if Braxium had taken a different surname.

He also couldn't erase the fuzzy image of Kenz bleeding out on the beach or the scene on the rooftop. Profound grief clung to that snippet of memory, one he didn't understand. Obviously Kord had healed her, but there was something more, a piece of knowledge that slipped through his grasp.

He tapped his finger on the table as he watched two men argue over their card game. The room fell silent when the front door opened and his uncle crossed the threshold. He removed his hat and scanned the tables and barstools until his eyes found Jasce's. He muttered hellos to a few villagers as he passed, stopped at the bar to talk to the bartender, and approached Jasce's table.

"I asked your friends, who are waiting for you at the Misty Lodge, if I might talk with you first. May I sit?"

Jasce sipped from his glass and gestured to the empty chair. Braxium twisted his hat through his hands and glanced around the room, which had returned to its normal cacophony of noise. Glasses clinked, dice were thrown, and cards shuffled. An older woman placed a cup of coffee in front of Braxium along with a loaf of bread.

"Thank you, Janelle," he said, pushing the bread toward Jasce.

"It's been ages since I've seen you in my tavern," Janelle said, and glanced at Jasce, tucking a strand of grayish-blonde hair behind her ear. "Who's your friend?"

"This is my nephew, Jasce Farone."

Her mouth opened in surprise. "Jasce Farone? I didn't know he was your nephew." Heads turned from the men at the nearby table.

"That makes two of us," Jasce said, keeping his face free of emotion but unable to hide the slur in his words.

Braxium rubbed the back of his neck. "I have a niece, too."

"Aren't you full of surprises? I've known you all these years, and I'm just learning this secret." She rested her hands on her hips. Her gaze drifted toward Jasce, and a flash of sadness flickered through her kind blue eyes. "Well, either way, it's good to see you. Both of you. Let me know if you boys need anything else."

His uncle nodded and blew on his coffee. Janelle smiled at Jasce, wove through the tables, and slipped behind the bar.

Jasce had no words, so he picked up the whiskey bottle and topped off his glass. They sat in silence while the sounds of normal life surrounded them. He envied the patrons' carefree socializing. The last time he'd sat with friends and laughed had been in Balten with Princess Irina and Nicolaus, the night Kenz and Kord had returned to his life. But that felt more like a wishful dream than a reality.

"Amycus mentioned you'd become a skilled blacksmith," Braxium finally said. His eyes drifted to the bottle and the muscle in his jaw ticked.

Jasce flopped back in his chair, his body and mind hazy. "Are we going to engage in small talk now?"

Hurt flashed through Braxium's eyes, quickly replaced by anger. "It's better than watching you get sloppy drunk."

Slowly, Jasce brought his drink to his lips and drained it in one gulp, then slammed the empty glass on the table.

Braxium huffed. "If you think I'm afraid of you, think again."

He leaned forward. "Do you know who I am? I'm the Angel of Death, a Hunter, an assassin. You definitely should be afraid."

"You *were* the Angel of Death. Amycus told me all about you." He pointed his finger. "So drop the tough act. You wouldn't hurt family, no matter how drunk you are."

Jasce scowled at the blacksmith. He'd obviously lost his touch if he couldn't intimidate an old man.

Wanting to be left alone, he went for the throat. "And do you know who killed your brother?"

Braxium swallowed, and tears lined his eyes. "I do."

He gritted his teeth. "Good. Now, don't let the door hit you on your way out."

"I just got you and your sister back." He reached across the table and grabbed Jasce's arm. Scars marred his skin from years of working with fire and molten steel.

Jasce yanked his hand away. "What makes you think you have me back?"

"I'd like a relationship with you, Jasce. I failed your family, and I'd like a second chance."

He shook his head. "How can you tolerate my presence? I murdered your brother in cold blood."

"I forgave you the moment I saw you. I can't imagine what you experienced from the time you were twelve under Drexus's command. You may have been the one to wield the blade, but I blame Drexus for Barnet's death."

How could his uncle forgive him? That would be like him forgiving Drexus for murdering his mother—it was ludicrous.

Jasce shook his head. "You don't know who I am. Hell, *I* don't even know who I am."

"You found yourself once, based on Amycus's letters. And I believe you can do it again."

Jasce's knuckles whitened as he squeezed his glass. "That person disappeared the minute they removed my magic and my memories."

"Kenz said your magic is coming back. And I can reteach you how to vault. The question is, do you need your memories to become the man you want to be, assuming that's what you truly desire?"

He narrowed his eyes, his brain too addled by alcohol to contemplate what the blacksmith was implying.

Braxium chewed the inside of his cheek. "If you'll let me help you, I believe we can get you on the right path."

"And how do you suppose we do that?"

He pointed to the bottle. "We start there."

∽

A citrusy smell tickled his nose, and a warm body pressed against his. He slowly opened his eyes, immediately slamming them shut as fingers of morning light drifted through the curtains, flinging daggers through his skull.

Conquering the Darkness

He focused on the woman's rhythmic breathing instead of the pain and nausea coursing through him. The last thing he remembered before the alcohol escorted him into oblivion was Braxium half carrying him to the Misty Lodge.

His mind slogged through the haze and caught up to his body. His hand cupped Kenz's breast, and he'd grown uncomfortably hard. They were both dressed, which was a shame, even though he was in no shape to do anything but let his mind drift to images that didn't fall into the "friend" category.

Why was she here, in his bed?

He inched away from her, hoping not to wake her. The pain in his head returned with a vengeance and his stomach rolled. Lurching from the bed and tripping over his boots, he barely made it to the washbasin.

Within seconds, gentle hands were holding his hair and rubbing his back while he heaved. Embarrassment might kill him if the headache didn't do the job first. He wiped his mouth and struggled to his feet. His fingers shook as he dug in the pockets of his cloak and removed his flask.

"Not sure that's the best idea," Kenz said quietly.

"It's the only one I have right now." He brought the flask to his mouth and swore. The bloody thing was empty.

She handed him a cup of water. "You really are a mess, aren't you?" There was no judgment in her voice, just concern.

He frowned and sipped slowly, not wanting to throw up again. Returning to the bed, he rested his elbows on his knees and held his head.

The bed creaked next to him. "Chew on this. It'll help with your nausea."

He eyed the small green leaf in her palm and took it, sniffing the minty aroma.

"I didn't mean to wake you," he said, chewing on the herb.

"It's okay."

"I don't want to sound rude, and believe me, before I puked up my guts I was extremely happy to wake up next to you, but . . ."

"Why am I here?"

Jasce lifted his head and eyed her. A shadow of a smile tugged at her mouth as she tucked his hair behind his ear. He nodded.

"Braxium didn't want you to be alone. Naturally, I volunteered."

"Naturally." He fell back on the bed and closed his eyes. He really was a mess. What must Kord think? Or his sister? He peeked open one eye. "Is Jaida okay?"

Kenz fiddled with her bracelet. "Physically, yes. Kord removed the sliver Drexus had implanted into her, which is just sick, by the way."

"Physically?"

Her gaze drifted over his face. "I don't know Jaida well, but she seems furious and upset." She huffed out a breath. "She has your temper."

"Did you put a shield around her, too?"

"No. That might've caused a scene." Kenz smiled and stared out the window. "Sorry about that. You had your 'mean Jasce' look."

"My 'mean Jasce' look?" He could only imagine what his facial expression had been when Braxium had revealed his secrets. "You've done that before, haven't you? Put your shield around me?"

She nodded.

He pushed up onto his elbows and examined her profile. "Why did Kord have to heal you?" The memory lurking in the corners of his mind filled him with unexplainable sorrow.

She slowly turned toward him. "What do you mean?"

"I remembered you lying on a beach, and then on a rooftop. There was so much blood." His voice gave way to an onslaught of fear, grief, anger, and hopelessness.

She lay next to him, their arms touching. "Snatcher attack."

He gave her a sidelong glance. She was holding something back. He wasn't sure how he knew that, but he did.

"Have more memories returned?" she whispered.

"Not really, just a few vague images. I'm sorry."

Her smile didn't reach her eyes. The corner of her tunic had slid off her shoulder and a star-shaped scar marred her pale skin. The image of waking up next to her with his hand cupping her breast sent a jolt to his loins.

He rolled to his side and traced the scar with his finger. "What happened here?"

Her breath caught, and the sound ignited a fire inside him.

"Arrow," she whispered, and then cleared her throat, avoiding his gaze. "You and I were on a mission, and I got shot, protecting you . . ." Her voice trailed off as his lips pressed against the mark.

He raised his brows. "Why did you have to protect me?"

She swiveled her head to face him. "You were preoccupied with killing another Hunter."

"We must have not been together yet."

"Why do you say that?"

He kissed the spot again and smiled at the vein pulsating in her neck. "Because why would I be preoccupied with anyone besides you?" He licked a trail from the scar along her collarbone to the hollow of her throat. Her citrusy scent and the softness of her skin made his heart beat in time with hers.

She closed her eyes as he slowly undid the laces of her tunic, running his knuckles across the exposed skin. He moved closer, needing to feel her. Her mouth parted in pleasure as he opened her shirt and marveled at the bare skin. Her nipples hardened and he couldn't resist tasting them. She moaned and arched into his touch, and the desire to worship every inch of her drowned out any rational thought.

She shook her head. "I can't . . . I can't do this." Pushing against his chest, she slid out from underneath him and scooted to the end of the bed.

He dropped his face onto the sheets, still warm and smelling like her. Dammit, why did he do that? They were supposed to be working on their friendship, and he'd acted like a lust-filled teenager.

She sniffed, and when he lifted his head, he caught her wiping a tear off her cheek. He swore and got to his feet, wincing as he adjusted himself while she tied her tunic together with shaking fingers. Being near her made him lose himself.

He leaned against the dresser. The distance between them felt cavernous as her very essence drew him toward her like a lone candle in the darkest of nights. He was a ship lost at sea and she was the lighthouse guiding him home. "Kenz, I'm sorry. I find you so alluring and my body knows you. I . . ." He lifted his hands and then let them drop to his side.

She looked up, her green eyes sparkling like emeralds. She opened her mouth, but a knock made both of them flinch.

"Can I come in?" Kord asked, his voice muffled.

Jasce sighed and walked to the door.

Kord's penetrating gaze traveled along his face, down his body, and back up again. Jasce tried not to squirm under the evaluation. "Wanted to check on you." Kord's eyes slid to his sister and narrowed. "Kenz, give us a minute, will you?"

Kenz narrowed her gaze. "Why?"

"Man talk."

Jasce dropped his face into his palm and muttered under his breath.

"What was that?" Kord asked.

"Nothing," Jasce said, pushing off the door.

"Fine, I'll meet you downstairs," she said, frowning at her brother before slipping out the door.

Kord wandered through the small room and paused at the soiled washbasin. "Rough night?"

"Rough morning." Jasce walked to the bed and flopped down on it. "Look, I know what you're going to say, and you're right."

Kord's brow arched. "Oh really? And what am I going to say?"

Jasce twirled his hand in the air. "Something to the effect of 'stay away from my sister until you figure yourself out.' Am I wrong?"

Kord sat in the chair, stretched out his legs, and crossed his ankles. "No, you're right. But I would have said it more eloquently."

Jasce huffed out a laugh. "I'm sure you would have." He raked his fingers through his hair. "I find myself drawn to her in ways I can't explain."

"I understand. I'm just asking you to be careful. Please. She hasn't been the same since you lost your memories." He raised a hand when Jasce opened his mouth. "And yes, I know that's my fault. But she is hurting and desperate for you to remember her and what you both had. So I'll ask you again to please be careful."

"I will." He didn't want to hurt her. He couldn't control whether his memories returned, but he could control his reaction to her. Well, based on the last few minutes, he couldn't. But if he wanted to protect her, then he'd have to put distance between them. The thought made him shake his head and sigh.

"Thank you." Kord stood, held out a hand, which Jasce took, and the Healer pulled him to his feet. "Now, let's go downstairs and talk about your treatment plan."

Jasce's eyes widened and he tried to pull out of his friend's grasp. "My what?"

Chapter Nineteen

The smells of roasting meats and baked bread permeated the small private dining room in the tavern. A fire sparked in the hearth on one side of the room, nestled between two windows, with a view of the lake and the forest beyond. Snow had fallen during the night and the sun, reflecting off the brilliant white landscape, shot arrows into Jasce's skull. He raised his hand to block the light and stumbled for a chair. He mumbled his thanks when someone closed the curtain.

The cook placed a sizzling platter of sausages on the table, which he pushed away for fear of throwing up again.

"Here." Kord set a cup of coffee in front of him. "As you can see, we are all worried about you."

Seated around the table were Braxium, Kenz, and Kord. Nicolaus lounged in one of two overstuffed chairs by the fireplace with Flynt taking the other. Jaida leaned against the wall with her arms crossed, and when their eyes met, she looked away.

Jasce lifted a hand. "Before we start whatever this is, Jaida are you—?"

"I'm fine." Her gray eyes sparked and wisps of hair floated off her shoulders as the painting behind her rattled.

Kenz had told him his sister was angry, but anger didn't cover it.

Any progress they had made the last few months evaporated in a blink of an eye. He would need to reconcile with her eventually, but it seemed he had other matters to contend with. "So what's this all about?"

"You're sick," Braxium said in his gruff voice.

"Excuse me?" he said with his mug halfway to his mouth.

Kord cleared his throat. "What Braxium is trying to say is that—"

"Don't soften my words, Kord. Jasce has an illness, and until he faces that fact he'll never get better." Braxium leaned forward and glared at them, his brown eyes resembling granite. "You lot have let this go on long enough."

The room erupted from his accusation, and the noise threatened to explode Jasce's head. He swore when a loud whistle sounded.

"Sit down and shut up." Nicolaus had risen to his feet. "You too," he said, pointing at Jaida, whose eyes widened. She pulled up a chair and sat next to Kenz. "Obviously, Braxium's communication skills are lacking, but you've all turned a blind eye or been too worried about how the Angel of Death would react."

"My communication skills are fine," Braxium said.

"They really aren't." Kord rubbed his forehead.

"What are you guys talking about?" Jasce asked, massaging his temples. "I'm not sick."

Nicolaus approached the table, ignoring Jasce as if he wasn't there. "Helping Jasce break his addiction will need to be a team effort."

Addiction.

Jasce contemplated that word while the Shade Walker talked. He wasn't addicted. He could handle his drinking and stop any time he wanted to. Who could blame him for getting drunk when he'd discovered his father had regretted what had happened and tried to get him back? Guilt threatened to swamp him, haunted by the empty bottles, the blood splattered on the wall, the feel of it dripping down his face.

He tore his eyes from his fisted hands and glanced around the table to find everyone staring at him. "Look, last night was a bad night. That's all. I've got it under control."

"I don't think you do." Kenz reached for his hand, but he leaned away. He resented the compassion in her eyes. He also couldn't stomach the pity emulating from everyone in the room.

His uncle rested his arms on the table. "You have a problem with alcohol, just like your father and me."

His temper spiked. Why wouldn't people give him a break? "I don't have a problem."

"Keep telling yourself that." Braxium drummed his fingers and held Jasce's stare. "When was the last time you haven't had a drink?"

He scowled at the blacksmith and forced himself not to fidget. He honestly couldn't remember. "There's not a lot to do in Balten in the middle of winter."

"So all the Baltens are addicted to whiskey?" Braxium asked with a smirk.

"Of course not." He huffed, and then inwardly swore.

"Jasce, I say this out of love and, unfortunately, experience. I've lost so much because of my addiction. My wife, my brother, you and Jaida. If it wasn't for Amycus and my forge, I doubt I'd be sitting here today." Braxium lowered his gaze and swallowed. "I don't want to see you lose your friends. And it sounds like if you go up against Drexus without a clear head, you might forfeit your life. Is what's in that flask more important?"

Jasce didn't want to admit that during his last fight with Drexus outside the cave, his reaction time had been slower. He'd blamed his injury, which was partly true. But he had been drinking to dull the pain. If it hadn't been for Jaida, he might be dead. He couldn't suffer another defeat to his former commander.

"How about you give us one week without drinking? If you truly have it under control, then we'll back off," Kord said.

"How about one day?" Jaida asked, lifting her chin. "Could you go an entire day without having one teeny little sip?"

Jasce straightened in his chair. The sting of betrayal hurt more than he wanted to admit. None of them understood the demons he battled, the darkness threatening to consume him.

"Jasce," Nicolaus said softly. "They all love you and want what's best. They aren't teaming up against you or betraying you."

He spun and frowned at the Shade Walker. It was as if the man had read his mind. He forced down the anger that longed to ignite and burn everything to the ground. He'd prove them all wrong, starting with his sister. Going one day without drinking would be easy. All he had to do was stay occupied with something else, not let his thoughts or his past overtake him. And he knew just what that was.

"Fine. You're on," he said, glaring at Jaida.

"Fine." She glared back.

"Kord, give me the sliver so I can train with Braxium. I don't have time to wait for my magic to strengthen on its own." He held out his hand, his brows raised.

Kord's eyes darted around the table. His mouth opened and closed and then he said, "Don't we need to talk about this? Dealing with a drinking problem is not an inconsequential matter."

"There's nothing to discuss. One day without drinking, starting now. Give me the sliver. Please," he added through gritted teeth.

Kord glanced at Braxium, who waved as if saying *go ahead*. He reached into his pocket and brought out a bundle of fabric.

Jasce snatched it out of his palm. "Braxium, meet me at your cottage in five minutes." He held the sliver tightly to hide the tremor in his hands and marched through the dining room and out the door. The cool air slapped him in the face, effectively clearing his head. Closing his eyes, he breathed in the scent of pine and snow while listening to the gentle lap of water on the shore of the lake. He wasn't sure how much longer he could have sat at that table, having to endure the disappointment on everyone's face. He'd rather see loathing than pity.

The door opened behind him, and Kenz touched his arm, turning him gently. "I'm sorry about all of that. I know you're angry."

Jasce peered through the window into the dining room. Flynt spoke with Jaida near the fireplace, while Nicolaus sat at the table and loaded his plate with sausages. Of course he was mad. Who wouldn't be? They had obviously planned this meeting while he'd been passed out, talking about what a drunk he was, too weak to handle the misery of his life.

He shook his head, dispelling those thoughts. He knew they cared for him. Even though he'd only spent a short amount of time with them, their concern for his well-being was genuine.

Swallowing his pride, he walked down the cobblestone path onto the main street. "I do feel a bit ambushed."

Conquering the Darkness

"I can understand that. But it was the only way we could talk to you. Even if it wasn't much of a discussion."

"I got the gist of it. Plus, I have more important things to do than debate my drinking habits."

Kenz frowned as if she wanted to continue that conversation, then sighed and threaded her arm through his. "So what did my brother and you talk about? Or is it a secret?" She squinted up at him, the sun shining on her face, illuminating the dusting of freckles and the green in her eyes. A pink flush filled her cheeks and her full lips curved into a half smile.

A breath lodged in his throat. "You're exquisite."

"That's what you talked about? My looks?"

Jasce laughed. "No." Should he tell her what he and Kord discussed? For some strange reason, he wanted to be completely honest with her. "He asked me to be careful with your feelings, which I agree with. What happened back there won't happen again."

"Oh," Kenz said, staring at the road.

He lifted her chin. "Please understand that I want to explore every curve of your body, kiss every inch of you. But I don't want to hurt you, and I can see the sorrow in your eyes when you realize my memories haven't returned."

A blush darkened her cheeks. "What if I don't care if you remember?"

He continued down the street. "I'd like our friendship to be built on the truth. And right now, I think you do care." He looked at her out of the corner of his eye to catch her fiddling with her bracelet, something she seemed to do when she was feeling guilty. He remembered her conversation with Caston about how she was hiding something from him. She obviously feared his reaction.

They stopped outside the gate leading to Braxium's cottage. She gazed down the road toward the end of town. "I want us to be honest with each other, too."

He trailed his thumb along her bottom lip. "That's all I ask."

Footsteps clunked as Braxium trudged out of an alleyway. He marched up to Jasce and poked him in the chest. "Don't ever boss me around again. I'm your uncle, and if you want my help you'll show some respect."

Jasce bit back a response since he still didn't know how to vault, and his uncle was the only Vaulter he knew. It would be foolish not to take advantage of this opportunity.

Once again, he swallowed his ego and dipped his chin. If this day continued the way it started, he'd soon be choking on his pride—if he had any left.

Braxium grunted, nodded to Kenz, and shoved the gate open.

"Good luck," Kenz said, and gave him a quick kiss on the cheek.

"Let's go, lover boy. I don't have all day," his uncle shouted from the entryway of his cottage.

Jasce rolled his eyes. "Yes, sir."

Chapter Twenty

The clear sliver of the Empower Stone lay in Jasce's palm. That Drexus had embedded this crystal in his sister made him seethe, but he harnessed his anger and focused on his magic. He released a sigh as the thrumming ignited inside him, spreading from his chest to his arms and legs. Closing his eyes, he willed his power to grow stronger.

Braxium yanked the sliver from his hand and dropped it on the table. He bent at the waist to examine the crystal. "That thing has quite the punch."

"Why did you take it?"

"Because your hand started to disappear. I don't want parts of you ending up all over Delmar." His uncle straightened and walked toward the back door. He glanced over his shoulder. "You just gonna stand there?"

Jasce wiggled his fingers. Everything looked solid to him, and he hadn't sensed his hand disappearing. Shrugging, he followed Braxium into a small courtyard. Neatly trimmed hedges lined one side of the enclosure, and across from the bushes was freshly tilled earth, where he imagined fruits and vegetables growing. He wouldn't have guessed the surly blacksmith had a knack for gardening.

"Do you remember anything from Amycus's training?" his uncle asked.

"No. Supposedly, Amycus told me to *will* myself to a certain spot. Whatever that means."

His uncle tipped his head from side to side. "That's one way to look at it."

Jasce crossed his arms. "And how do you look at it?"

"I'm getting to that part." Braxium mumbled something about impatient kids, and Jasce suppressed a smile. He certainly wasn't a kid anymore. The minute he had stepped through the gate of the Bastion, his childhood had ended.

"Imagine a door. Open it and walk through. For now, picture a large door. As you become more comfortable, the opening will get smaller." Braxium walked five feet away. "Now, vault to me."

Jasce closed his eyes. He imagined a barn door and envisioned himself walking through it.

Nothing happened.

He cracked his neck and shook out his hands, tuning out the sounds of wagon wheels clattering over cobblestones and the smell of rain. Once again, he pictured the door, even reaching out with his hand to open it. His magic spiked. A pressure filling his chest grew into a tug and darkness engulfed him.

A loud oomph greeted him, followed by a sharp pain in his knees.

"I said to me, not on me." Braxium shoved him off and got to his feet, wiping the dirt off his trousers.

Jasce grunted and stood with a smile on his face. He'd vaulted, and the sensation was exhilarating.

"Not bad for your first try. I bet you'll learn quicker this time around." Braxium tapped his forehead. "It's in there, somewhere. Give it time."

Time was something he didn't have. Drexus was building his army, and the Abolish Stone needed to be found. At least the Inhibitor Stone was safe, and hopefully Caston was still alive. But the passage of time was like a spirit lurking in the gloom, its ghostly fingers grasping, its sole purpose to drag him into the murkiness.

Jasce closed his eyes and focused on the buzzing inside him. He vaulted quicker this time but appeared half the distance between himself and the blacksmith.

"Again," Braxium said, backing up a few more steps.

They practiced throughout the morning, with his uncle offering tips and encouragement. Though Braxium had some rough edges, he was an excellent teacher. Jasce focused on his magic, trying to ignore the tremor in his hands and the sweat sliding down his back and temples. Braxium had suggested they take a break for lunch, but he'd declined.

The sky darkened and the clouds emptied. He swiped at the freezing rain dripping down his face while he vaulted, testing his power and going farther each time. Lightning sizzled through the air as he finally collapsed to his knees, panting.

"That's enough. You've drained your magic." Braxium helped him to his feet.

Jasce stumbled, grabbing his back. Bracing his hands on his knees, he breathed in the frigid air and tried not to throw up. The nausea had worsened the longer the day progressed and, with his magic drained, his body and mind had no defense for the craving raging inside him. The longing for a drink made it difficult to focus on anything but the feel of a glass in his hand, the smoky flavor biting his tongue and warming his throat.

His heart threatened to beat out of his chest as he groaned and lurched toward the side of the building. Resting a hand on the wall to keep from falling, he dry-heaved.

Brown boots slid into his periphery, and embarrassment, along with a sharp pain in his head and back, made him wish for the ground to swallow him whole.

"By my calculation, you've gone about twelve hours without a drink," Braxium said, leading him by the elbow into his cottage. He pointed to the table, disappeared down the hallway, and returned with a towel.

The sound of cupboards opening and closing and the tread of boots on the wooden floor made Jasce wince and lay his head on the table.

Was he so far gone that he couldn't make it half a day without his body responding violently to not having a drink? He pushed the thought away. He'd drained his magic, nothing more.

His uncle tapped his arm. "Wake up, son. You need to eat."

He slowly lifted his head and eyed the steaming cup of broth in front of him. He pressed his lips together and pushed the mug away. "Not hungry."

"It's important to keep up your strength. This will help. Trust me."

"It's just my magic, that's all. Once it recharges, I'll feel better."

Braxium crossed his arms. "Let's test that." He placed the sliver of the Empower Stone on the table and raised his brows expectantly.

Scowling at his uncle, he grabbed the crystal. His body stiffened as the crystal ignited the embers of his magic into a roaring flame. He gasped at the power flowing through him. Releasing the crystal, he reached for the cup. His hands shook. Two daggers impaled his eyes, piercing his skull. The nausea returned so violently he barely made it to the bucket his uncle had placed at his feet.

He wiped his mouth and glared at Braxium, who drummed his knuckles on the table and stared at him, a look of sadness filling his eyes.

"Not that this helps, but I've been in your position, years ago. It's a sickness, Jasce, but your body can heal and learn how to function without the alcohol."

Jasce fell back into the chair, focusing on the wood planks in the ceiling. He couldn't be this weak. He was an assassin, a trained warrior who had endured more than most people his age. Surely he was strong enough to overcome this insatiable craving. Anger replaced the denial. Who cared if he had a sip of whiskey from time to time to dull the pain or quiet the demons prowling in his head?

But Braxium's words from this morning came back to him. *I don't want to see you lose your friends. And it sounds like if you go up against Drexus without a clear head, you might forfeit your life. Is what's in that flask more important?*

His purpose was defeating Drexus once and for all. So he forced down the broth, little by little, willing himself not to throw it back up.

A knock thumped on the door. Braxium pushed away from the table and opened it. Kord's muffled voice, along with Kenz's and Jaida's, sounded from outside.

Braxium mumbled something and pulled the door closed. "You have visitors. Can they come in?"

Conquering the Darkness

"Kord only. I don't want Kenz or Jaida to see me like this." *Especially Jaida*, he thought, not wanting to acknowledge the expression of *I told you so* he might see on her face. A shiver snaked along his body despite the extra logs on the fire.

Braxium nodded and allowed Kord inside. Jasce couldn't hear what was said to Kenz and Jaida and was relieved when the door clicked shut.

Kord strode in and sat across from him while Braxium disappeared into the kitchen.

"If you're here to gloat, don't bother," Jasce said.

"Looks like you're in enough turmoil."

"I'm sure Kenz and Jaida weren't thrilled with being turned away."

"At least now they have a common enemy," Kord said with a small smile.

"True." Jasce rubbed his temples while the blacksmith returned with three mugs. Coffee filled two of them but from the third wafted peppermint and ginger.

Braxium placed the fragrant concoction in front of him. "This will help with the nausea." Jasce took a sip and grimaced. His uncle cleared his throat. "I'm not one to mince words, as you know. You're in for a rough time. There are two theories. You can stop drinking immediately and suffer through the side effects, which will be extreme. Or you can taper off. You'll have the same issues, just not as intense and spread out over a longer time. There are risks with both, but with Kord here, at least quitting won't kill you."

Jasce stared between Kord and Braxium. With Drexus building his army and doing who knew what to Caston, he didn't have the time or luxury to taper off. He knew he was in for a couple of grueling days based on his recent reaction. Better to purge the alcohol from his system and learn to live without it. He'd never shrunk from a challenge or engaged in a battle without complete commitment. Why start now?

"Let's just get this over with."

"I figured you'd say that." Braxium rose to his feet and pointed to the cup. "Drink up. I'll be in the forge if you need me."

Jasce narrowed his eyes and watched him leave the room. He winced as he rose from the table and plopped down into the chair closest to the fire.

Kord sat next to him, his one green eye focused on the dancing flames in the hearth. "At what age did you start drinking?"

Jasce scratched the back of his neck. "Probably when I began training to become a Hunter. Sixteen, I suppose."

"And what were the main reasons you drank?"

He tapped his finger on the arm of the chair and examined the Healer. "Why do you want to know?"

Kord turned to him. "Because we need to discover the root cause. I have some theories, but this is your journey. It's time to get very honest."

He'd rather take the whip any day than bare his innermost being, hacking open the scars that had formed around his heart. Physical pain he could handle. But to delve into the place where he'd buried his emotions since he'd witnessed the death of his mother and was forced into the Watch Guard? The thought made his head pound. What Kord was asking him to do, to reveal all the evil things he had done, the darkness residing in him—he wasn't sure he had the courage. In his mind, his world, he hadn't known Kord long enough to relinquish his tainted soul. And deep down, he secretly hoped the Healer wouldn't run the opposite direction.

As if Kord read his thoughts, he said, "I realize this is hard. But please hear me when I say you can trust me. You can trust Kenz and Braxium, too. And I know your sister and you don't have the strongest relationship, but I believe she wants what's best for you."

"I don't understand why any of you are willing to help me. After all the people I've killed. I'm a heartless murderer . . ."

Kord knelt in front of him. "You may have been that, Jasce. But you changed, and you need to believe that you are worth the recovery, beating this addiction, and not using alcohol as a vice." He placed his hand on Jasce's shoulder. "You are worth every second we spend with you to get you back."

He chewed on the side of his thumb. When did he last feel worthy? He'd advanced in the ranks of the Watch Guard and the Hunters until he was second in command. But had those accomplishments given him a sense of worth? There was only one person in his life, who he remembered, that had made him feel worthy—his mother. Sure, his sister had admired and loved him when they were children, but that wasn't the

Conquering the Darkness

same thing. And his father? Jasce couldn't recall ever feeling close to Barnet, especially when his drinking and paranoia had driven him away.

He thought about the trajectory of his life and recognized the path he traveled—a path of destruction. He knew he couldn't change the past, the mistakes he'd made, the people he'd hurt. But he could choose an alternate course, one that might lead to hope and maybe even love. Those two words were as foreign as the vulnerability Kord was asking of him.

How many times did Drexus teach his recruits that love and compassion were weak emotions? Anger, rage, hostility—those had been the foundations of Jasce's existence since the age of twelve. He had tried clinging to the goodness instilled by his mother, but once he'd committed his first kill, some of that virtue slipped away. And with every job thereafter, the darkness grew stronger and stronger, snuffing out any light, any morality. He hadn't known that with every person he destroyed, he killed a piece of his mother again and again.

In his core, even without memories, he sensed Kord, Kenz, and Amycus had shed light into the deepest recesses of his soul. Reuniting with his sister, even if they were on shaky ground, continued chipping away at his heart of stone. And now, meeting his uncle, another member of his family? He owed it to himself and to those who continued to stand by him to conquer the darkness once and for all.

Chapter Twenty-One

Jasce recalled a time when he lay facedown on a cot in the medical facility at the Bastion, unable to roll over, where simply breathing hurt. He had only been a member of the Watch Guard for a few years and had advanced through the ranks. He'd endured another brutal whipping from Drexus for sneaking food to a soldier. When the doctor cleaned the bloody stripes crisscrossing his back, Jasce remembered thinking death would be better.

He thought the same during the hours and days of purging the alcohol from his system.

His entire body felt like a battered punching dummy. His bones burned, as if liquid steel coursed through every joint and muscle. He'd be shivering one moment, unable to get warm, and then sweating profusely. At one point, rage had erupted from him as he demanded a drink, forcing Jaida to give him a sleeping tonic.

"I can't heal you while your body is learning to function without alcohol," Kord had explained on the first day. "Otherwise, I'll just be delaying the process. But we're here to ride out the storm with you."

Kenz, Jaida, Kord, and Braxium had all taken turns tending to him. Later, Jasce would be embarrassed to have Kenz and Jaida there, stroking his back as he vomited his guts up or as he curled into a ball, shivering near the fire.

On the fourth day, he woke in the middle of the night on the floor in the living room, the flames dancing in the hearth emitting a comforting glow. Jaida hummed a tune their mother used to sing to them during their many escapes into the forest. His head lay in her lap, and she ran her fingers through his hair, just like his mother had done.

He gazed into the fire. A log shifted and sparks fluttered into the air as he thought about what his uncle said that first night. They had sat at the table while Jasce sipped broth, his trembling hands making what should have been a simple task challenging.

"If you can accept responsibility for your actions and embrace the part of you that is broken, then you will become a man of humility and wisdom. You will have a chance at a different life. Keep thinking on this when the desire for a drink brings you to your knees. And believe me, it will."

Jasce hadn't understood what his uncle meant until he was in the throes of ridding his body of the poison that had become such an integral part of his life. In between bouts of sickness and fitful sleep, he'd had a lot of time to think.

He had first started drinking to relieve his stress and unwind, but eventually the pleasure and relief diminished. It wasn't long until his motivation became a way to avoid guilt and shame, to obscure the pain.

Braxium said to take responsibility for his actions, and he might as well start now. Thankfully, the shivers had finally stopped, and he could speak a full sentence without his teeth chattering. "Jaida," he whispered.

The humming ceased, and her fingers stilled.

He needed to apologize before he lost the courage. "I'm so sorry. Those words fix nothing, but I want you to know—"

She continued combing through his hair. "Shh. You don't need—"

"But I do need to." He winced as he pushed off her lap and gripped her hand with the little strength he had. "My arrogance and obsession for vengeance blinded me."

Jaida squeezed his hand. "Drexus played a part in this. Some of the blame lies with him."

He held both her hands as if they were a pillar of strength. "I'm sorry for k . . ." Closing his eyes, he inhaled through his nose and tried again. "I'm sorry for killing our father."

Tears streamed down his sister's face. She folded in on him, wrapped her arms around his waist, and sobbed. He gathered her in his lap and rocked her while she cried, saying over and over how sorry he was. For their father, for not fighting harder for her, for his behavior in Balten and keeping her at arm's length. Finally, her body stilled and her breathing leveled out. He wiped the tears from her cheeks.

Her gray eyes sparkled beneath wet lashes and her cheeks were flushed, but a shadow of a smile lined her face. Resting a hand on his jaw, she said, "We're good."

Her words soothed him like a healing balm to an open wound. When they were young and needed to apologize for hurting each other, the sibling who'd been wronged made a choice—to forgive or harbor a grudge. They'd always answer each other with a *we're good*, meaning all was forgiven.

The pressure on his chest lessened, allowing him to take a full breath, something he didn't realize he hadn't been able to do. His eyes drooped, and he yawned as exhaustion threatened to overtake him.

"Do you remember the story Mom told us about the Heart of Pandaren?" Jaida asked, taking a pillow from the couch and laying it across her lap. She patted it and he rested his head. Her fingers wove through his hair again.

"Which one? She had a few."

"She talked about the magical beings that created the Stone—Theran and Cerulea. I remember wanting to be like Cerulea with all that mental power." A gentle laugh escaped her lips.

"That's right. And Theran had a sword of lightning and fire, I think." He fiddled with a loose thread on the worn rug. "Amycus actually found information about them when he traveled to Alturia."

Her fingers stilled. "Wait, they're real? I thought they were just a myth."

"I guess not. His journal is in my knapsack if you want to read it." He yawned again as the flames from the fire continued their hypnotic dance.

"Maybe later. You need to rest."

His eyes slowly closed. "Thank you for being here," he whispered, before falling into a dreamless sleep.

∼

The temperature dropped and snow fell the morning of the sixth day, creating a blanket of white—clean and unmarked. Jasce sat on the couch with a quilt tucked tightly around him. Kenz had read to him last night and fallen asleep on the chair next to him. He stared at her for what seemed like hours, memorizing every detail of her face.

Braxium walked into the main room, and when he met Jasce's gaze, he smiled.

"There you are," he said, sneaking a glance at Kenz. "You're through the storm. I can tell by your eyes."

He had to admit, his mind seemed clearer. He hadn't realized he'd been functioning in a fog while living in Balten. His temperature had finally leveled out to where he was no longer sweating or shivering, and the nausea was gone. He'd chipped a tooth from grinding his teeth so hard, and his body ached all over, but he felt better, healthier.

"I bet you'd like some coffee," his uncle said.

He sighed. "Yes, I would."

Just then, the door opened, and Kord and Jaida entered the cottage. They both stopped when they saw him sitting up on the couch. He rubbed the back of his neck and gave them a small smile.

"Jaida, come help me with the coffee," Braxium said.

"Sure." She blew Jasce a kiss and followed her uncle into the kitchen.

Kord strode across the room and plopped down next to him on the couch. He glanced at Kenz, who was still fast asleep. "That girl could sleep through a stampede."

Jasce chuckled. "Yeah, she hates mornings."

Kord snapped his head toward him. "What did you say?"

"She hates mornings." He frowned. How did he know that?

"Have your memories returned?" Kord asked, hope shining in his eye, while resting a hand on Jasce's arm. A tingly warmth ran through his body, taking away the aches and pains. A spark of energy flowed

Conquering the Darkness

through him, causing his magic to stretch its arms wide as if saying, *finally*.

Kord kicked Kenz's chair. "Wake up."

She jostled and glared at her brother. "What?"

Kord nodded to Jasce, who was transfixed on the fireplace, staring at nothing, as he realized his memories were no longer lost to him. He remembered getting the serum, the dungeon in Bradwick, Kord and Kenz rescuing him, and traveling to Carhurst where he met Amycus. He vividly pictured the blacksmith's forge.

Kenz tumbled from the chair, causing one of her throwing knives to fall out of her boot and skid along the floor. He stopped it with his foot and picked it up.

She knelt in front of him and placed her hands on his legs. "Jasce?"

He examined the markings on the blade. "I made this for you. In Amycus's forge." He tilted his head. "You threw one at me."

She laughed and wrapped her arms around his neck, pressing her mouth against his. Her citrus scent filled his nose and more images flooded his memories: Learning his mother was a Spectral, Kenz saving his life, the attack on Edgefield Prison and discovering Drexus was the one who killed his mother.

"What's going on?" Jaida asked as she and Braxium returned. She carried a tray with cups of steaming coffee.

Jasce spun around and stared at his sister. The quilt puddled onto the floor as he slowly rose to his feet. The Battle of the Bastian flashed before his eyes. He steadied himself on the back of the couch. "You almost killed me. And Kenz." He remembered his sister's eyes hardening with loathing as she raised him into the air, attempting to tear his body apart. He could practically feel her hatred for him when she had lifted her arms and hurled every fallen weapon at him.

The tray shook, and coffee sloshed over the side of the mugs. "Jasce," she whispered. Braxium steadied her, his eyes darting between the siblings.

He collapsed to his knees and heard the couch creak as Kord rose to his feet. Everything from the last year came rushing back—the Gathering, the Snatcher attack and Kord losing his eye, Queen Siryn and the Empower Stone.

Cassie Sanchez

A beach soaked with blood.

A rooftop filled with pain.

He lifted his face and stared at Kenz. "Our child." His voice was barely a whisper.

She covered her mouth and shook her head. "I . . ."

That's what she'd been hiding from him, what she'd spoken to Caston about in Balten. She had been afraid to tell him. A sense of urgency replaced the sadness as he rose to his feet and walked toward her. She winced and shied away. Kord took a small step toward his sister.

Jasce glanced at Jaida. "I'll talk with you later, but right now, I need a word with my fiancée." He wrapped his arm around her waist and vaulted. Within seconds, they reappeared in his room at the Misty Lodge.

Kenz bent over and rested her hands on her knees. "You really need to give a girl some warning."

He leaned against the door, unable to speak from shock and utter dismay. Relief at his restored memories battled with the misery of losing so much. He had lost himself to the lure of the Empower Stone and abandoned the man he'd worked so hard to become. The loss of his child and Amycus's death squeezed his chest like a vise. The growing list of failures and the carnage surrounding him made him slide to the floor. Wrapping his arms around his legs, he rested his head against the door and closed his eyes.

He hadn't protected the woman he loved or their unborn baby. He'd allowed the darkness inside him to win.

It had been six days since his last drink, and the desire to deaden the pain made him lurch to his feet and reach for the doorknob. The tavern was only steps away and the temptation for the familiar taste of whiskey made his mouth water. He fisted his hands to control the trembling and bowed his head. Drinking had governed his life, but no more. He hadn't spent the last few days in hell to cave so easily.

Arms wrapped around his waist. "I'm sorry I didn't tell you about the baby. Please know I was trying to protect you from more heartache."

"I understand why you did." He turned in her arms and rested his forehead against hers. "I want a drink so desperately right now, and it's taking every ounce of willpower to stay in this room."

"Maybe I can give you a reason not to leave." She slowly removed her tunic and slid down her pants, revealing lacy black undergarments. "I've missed you so much."

Desire ignited inside him, and his body immediately reacted until he noticed the scars carving across her ribs—the place where the Snatcher had sunk its lethal claws. He remembered her blood oozing through his fingers, the alarmingly slow beat of her heart, followed by a hopelessness that had threatened to drown him.

"Kenz." He traced a finger along the jagged skin.

She lifted his chin. "I'm okay."

He swallowed. "I'm the one meant to have scars. Not you."

"Well, that's just silly." She untied the laces of his tunic and slipped his shirt over his head. Her hands caressed his chest and his stomach quivered at her touch.

He ran a thumb along her jaw and bottom lip. Her eyes shone as a tear escaped down her cheek.

He pulled her into his arms and rested his chin on the top of her head. "I'm so sorry for the past couple of months. I would have lost my mind had the tables been turned."

"I'm pretty sure I did," she mumbled into his chest. "I was so afraid I'd never get you back."

He lifted her face. "I have a feeling we'd always find one another. Even when I didn't have my memories, my body, my heart, knew you." He pressed his lips gently to hers and savored the softness.

She deepened the kiss and he moaned, turning them and pressing her against the door. She opened her mouth, giving him full access as his tongue danced with hers. He nipped her lip, trying to restrain the urge to take her where they stood, bodies flush against one another—the perfect fit. The need to drown in her overcame him. He'd never get enough of her, and an explosive urgency made his breath catch.

He trailed kisses down her throat. "I'd love to take my time, but if I don't have you now, I might burst into flames."

Kenz let out a husky laugh. "We can't have that, can we?"

He lifted her off her feet and, as she wrapped her legs around his waist, carried her to the bed. She sat on the end while he knelt in front of her. He removed her camisole and stared in wonder.

"I've desperately missed these," he said, grazing his thumbs along the tips of her breasts. She closed her eyes and her lips parted. He gathered her in his mouth, swirling his tongue around the sensitive skin while her fingers ran through his hair, pressing him closer. His hand skimmed down the smooth skin of her stomach until he slid his fingers beneath the lace, drifting lower and lower until she gasped and arched her back. The silky wetness waiting for him made him groan. The need to taste her, ravage her, had him pressing her onto her back and shredding the lace covering her. He gripped her hips and made her writhe until his name erupted from her lips and her body shuddered.

Lifting his head, he stared at her naked body, her rising chest, toned legs, midnight hair fanned out around her. She was exquisite in every way, and she was his. And he was finally hers again.

She lifted to her elbows. "Do you need help?" she asked, eyeing his pants.

"Nope." He untied the laces and let his trousers slide to the floor, his body springing free from the clothing binding him.

She bit her lip as her eyes traveled from his waist to his bare feet and back up again. "Make love to me, Jasce."

He crawled onto the bed and pressed himself against her. Her wet heat and the softness of her skin drove him mad. He kissed her as their bodies joined, a familiar and rhythmic dance that felt like home. Desire and need built inside him as he moved faster.

"Look at me," he said as she groaned his name, wrapping her legs around his waist, matching him with every thrust. Getting lost in the hypnotic green of her eyes, he lifted her hips, needing to be deeper, to not know where he ended and she began. The bed squeaked and rocked beneath them. With a cry, she threw her head back, which was his undoing. He surrendered and fell over the edge with her.

Chapter Twenty-Two

Jasce kept his promise to Kenz and worshiped her throughout the day. When they weren't making love, they talked about their time apart. She spoke about their mission to find Drexus and how they ended up in the Desert of Souls with the Inhibitor Stone. He held her close as she cried over the death of their child, of discovering he didn't remember her, of what they had. He kissed her tears away, until they both fell asleep in each other's arms.

He woke while it was dark with her naked body flush against his. He hated to get up, but the pain in his back and leg made lying still impossible. His hand thumped the edge of the nightstand where his flask normally waited. He sighed. If that wasn't confirmation he had a problem, he didn't know what was.

He quickly dressed and strode to the edge of town, where a rocky beach sloped into Lake Chelan. The sky to the north shone with streaks of green and pink. He frowned, having never seen that before, and wondered if the imbalance of magic was causing the strange phenomenon. A dense fog covered the ground, parting with each step, and his breath puffed in the cold air. He dreaded what he was about to do, but based on the times he'd tried the ice treatment in Balten, the results were impressive.

"First things first," he said, gathering wood and starting a fire. He would need its warmth when he emerged from the freezing water. He placed his dagger on a nearby rock and, removing his boots and clothing, he stepped into the small ripples lapping against the rocky beach. His feet burned as the cold settled in. Not wanting to be a coward, he dove into the lake. The initial shock took his breath away and as he surfaced, he remembered the four-count breathing technique Irina had taught him. Soon, his heartbeat slowed and his body relaxed.

While he swam to a nearby rock, he thought about his and Jaida's relationship and the baggage accompanying it. He needed to speak to her, not liking how he'd left her at Braxium's. Drexus had used them both, twisting their minds and altering their behavior. Both of them had experienced their own personal hell after their family was torn apart. She had forgiven him for his atrocities, so how could he not forgive her? The weight on his chest lightened as he returned to the shore.

He squinted into the fog, barely able to see the man standing on the beach, his silhouette shimmering in front of the fire. As Jasce neared, he could make out the deep purple traveling cloak and silver hair.

Nicolaus watched him with his brows raised. "What a miserable way to start your day."

Jasce carefully traversed across the rocky beach to where he'd left his clothes. Goosebumps covered his red skin, but thankfully the pain had diminished. He quickly dressed, securing the scabbard holding his dagger onto his thigh while eyeing the Alturian.

"You have your memories back. That's good," Nicolaus said, resting his hands on his hips.

"How can you tell?" The last memory he had of the Shade Walker was on the streets of Orilyon, battling the Vastanes. The prince had trusted him, even when he'd lost his mind and thought he was Azrael.

"I can see the distrust in your eyes." Nicolaus chuckled and continued. "Actually, I ran into your sister last night and she told me. Congratulations, I'm sure you're relieved."

Relieved? Overwhelmed was probably a better word. He glanced toward the forest on the other end of town. The sky had shifted from a midnight blue to a light purple and the strange lights had disappeared.

Conquering the Darkness

"How did you find me?" Jasce asked, sitting on a rock and lacing up his boots.

"I saw you leave the inn."

Jasce looked up with his brow arched.

Nicolaus rubbed the back of his neck. "Yes, well, it seems I slept in the wrong room last night. Or the right one, depending on your point of view." The man gave a sheepish grin and pointed to a field behind him. "Since you're up, let's do some training so you're not such a liability."

"Excuse me?" Even with the injury to his back, he wasn't a liability, ever.

"Just joking, Commander. Come on."

He followed Nicolaus to the clearing, wondering what the Alturian could teach him. He'd witnessed the man fight during the Gathering and knew he was a competent warrior, but not as skilled as Jasce. Or at least, not how he'd been before Drexus had stabbed him through the back with his sword.

"I've seen you warm up before you train. I think this technique will help with your pain, your flexibility, and your balance." Nicolaus removed his cloak. "Do what I do."

He observed the Shade Walker for a few minutes. The man's sculpted muscles rippled as he extended his arms while performing a deep lunge, all the while focusing on his breathing. He pivoted and continued moving, combining the practice into a fluid dance.

The sun emerged over the treetops and the sky turned a brilliant blue without a cloud in sight. Both men had removed their tunics and sweat glistened across their carved bodies.

Soon Kenz arrived with Flynt and Kord, who carried a bag of pastries and cups of coffee. A sadness tightened the skin around Kord's good eye as he placed the items on a flat stone. The absence of Tillie and Mal made Jasce's chest hurt, and he couldn't imagine what his friend was feeling without his wife and son.

His friend.

Immense relief had Jasce striding toward Kord and gripping his forearm. "Thank you."

"For what?"

He squeezed Kord's arm. "For not giving up on me."

Kord smiled and pulled him into a bone-crushing hug.

"Can't breathe, buddy."

Tears lined Kord's eye, and he quickly swiped them away and cleared his throat.

Flynt walked past and nodded at Jasce. "Good to have you back." He gathered some more wood and clicked his wrists together, igniting green sparks. The fire quickly blazed to life and everyone scooted closer.

He mumbled a thanks while he gathered his emotions. Jaida hung back with her arms crossed and eyes darting around the field as if she was unsure where to look. Jasce slowly approached her. He reached for her hand, wondering if she'd pull away. When she didn't, he leaned down and whispered in her ear. "We're good, right?"

The doubt on her face morphed into a beautiful smile. "We're good." She wrapped her arms around his waist. He rested his chin on the top of her head, closed his eyes, and smiled. All was forgiven between them. The past would stay where it belonged as brother and sister chose to press on, move forward, and strive for a better life.

They walked toward the fire, arm in arm, and any awkwardness in the group disappeared. A group of women lingered on the far side of the field, giggling and pointing at Jasce and Nicolaus, who were both still shirtless.

"Why are you two half-naked?" Kenz asked, throwing a look toward the women.

"Training," Nicolaus said, using his tunic to wipe the sweat off his chest. "I found your man swimming in the lake, at the crack of dawn, I might add."

"What? That water is freezing. I mean, there's literal ice floating on it," Kenz said, pointing at the lake.

Kord sipped his coffee. "Interesting."

"What's interesting?" Flynt asked, digging into the bag of pastries.

"Ice is therapeutic and can help heal minor injuries. But I've never thought of throwing you into the lake," Kord said.

Jasce laughed. "I'm sure you have."

"How is your back?" Kenz asked.

"Better, for now." He ran his fingers through his hair. "Normally, I'd have a drink to numb the pain. I learned this technique in Balten."

"Well, it's definitely a healthier option," Jaida said, who sat next to Kenz by the fire. They whispered as they watched Nicolaus meander to where the other women loitered.

During his detox, Jasce remembered Kenz and Jaida forging a truce as they talked about Amycus. He'd wanted to get up, to confess he needed them both in his life, but his body wouldn't cooperate.

Relief filled him now as he watched them making fun of the Alturian prince. Gratitude for both of them being willing to lay their differences aside made him smile.

Nicolaus sauntered back to the group with a smug grin on his face.

"You're such a flirt," Kenz said.

"That is true," Nicolaus said. "My fabulous charm and dashing good looks secured horses to take us to Orilyon."

"You didn't tell them where we were going, did you?" Jasce asked, crossing his arms.

"Do I look stupid?"

Jasce arched a brow and tapped his bicep.

"I'll take your silence as a no." Nicolaus threw on his cloak. "But regarding your question, no, I didn't tell them." A flicker of worry drifted across his face. He still hadn't heard from his spies, so the group had decided to return to the kingdom city. He forced a smile. "Now open your pockets. I'm not the only one paying for our ride."

His team spent the rest of the day gathering supplies while Jasce and Jaida strolled to Braxium's cottage after receiving word he wanted to see them.

When they entered the forge, their uncle stopped digging through a dust-covered chest and gave Jaida a hug. She smiled and tucked a piece of hair behind her ear.

"I'm proud of both of you." Braxium focused on Jasce while he sat on the stool. "You'll need a new coping skill for when you're stressed or angry. Why do you think there's so many blades in this room?"

Jasce chuckled. "Not sure I can manage a traveling forge, but I'll figure something out." Stress and anger would definitely accompany him on his journey toward Drexus and the Stones, making the desire to drink more tempting.

"I have an idea to help your back. I created a brace about a year ago for a villager when he fell off his horse and busted up his leg," Braxium said.

Jasce eyed the materials on the table, and his mind instantly started creating an interlocking system, similar to his armor, that would give him more support. "Weren't you the one who taught Amycus that new type of chest piece?"

Braxium's eyes crinkled around the edges. "He told me you'd perfected it."

"Unfortunately, it's in Orilyon."

"Right," he said, smacking his thighs and getting to his feet. "No time to lose. Let's get to work."

Jasce and his uncle worked on the brace while Jaida listened to stories of when they were young. Working with Braxium reminded him of his time with Amycus, and an influx of grief swirled with the fond memories. He excused himself in the early evening and strode to the edge of his uncle's property. Leaning his arms on the wooden fence, he marveled at the sunset.

The creak of the door sounded, and he knew who it was based on the tread of heavy steps along the stone pathway.

"How are you feeling?" Braxium asked.

"Thirsty," Jasce said.

"The desire will lessen as time goes on, but will never truly go away." His uncle picked at a piece of splintered wood. "When do you leave?"

"Tomorrow." It was a three-day ride to Orilyon, and they had agreed to travel through the Nisene Forest to avoid the towns. The route was longer but safer, since they didn't know who was loyal to Drexus. Without any news on Drexus's whereabouts or on Caston, the sinking sensation in his gut intensified as he thought about his friend and the sacrifice he'd made to protect his sister.

Jasce watched a flock of birds dart through the darkening sky. "Do you want to come with us?" Ever since meeting Kenz and Kord, he had longed for a family, even though he hadn't reacted that way when Kenz told him she was pregnant. Another stab of grief shot through his heart.

Conquering the Darkness

A part of him wanted to be angry with her for not staying out of the battle, but he would have done the same thing. She was a Shield and her job was to protect. He couldn't hold it against her.

"I'm too old to go gallivanting across the countryside," Braxium said, resting his forearms on the fence. "But you know where to find me."

He stared into his uncle's brown eyes, eyes just like his father's. "I wish we had more time."

"Me too."

Jasce cleared his throat. "Thank you for helping me."

His uncle sniffed and together they stood in silence and watched the sun dip below the horizon. Jasce turned and rested a hand on Braxium's shoulder. "Gather all the Spectrals who are loyal to Queen Valeri, from here and Havelock. War is coming. Tell them to be ready."

Braxium pulled his nephew into a hug. "I'm proud of you, son."

Jasce swallowed the lump in his throat and returned his uncle's embrace.

Chapter Twenty-Three

"Why always dawn?" Kenz asked, yawning as she and Jasce arrived at the stable. They'd all stayed up late telling stories, and besides drinking coffee instead of whiskey, it had reminded him of old times. Even Nicolaus had joined in, and Jasce had to admit, the more time he spent with the Shade Walker, the more he grew on him. Of course, he'd never tell the prince that.

Braxium waited for them as he double-checked Bruiser's saddle. "I agree with Kenz. It's bloody early." Bruiser snorted and bobbed his head as if in agreement. "Good horse." The blacksmith patted Bruiser's neck and removed the leather brace from his satchel. He handed it to Jasce. "Finished last night."

Jasce held up the brace and admired the craftsmanship as Jaida, Flynt, and Kord arrived, all wearing their riding leathers. He wrapped the contraption around his waist and tightened the buckles. The effect was immediate, giving him the support he didn't realize he needed. Metal hinges, lined with canvas, secured the sides and allowed him the freedom to move.

"This is excellent work," Jasce said, adjusting the straps on his side.

"Not to mention it looks rather intimidating," Kord said, patting his back.

Braxium tapped his lip. "Check to see if your chest piece fits over it. You might have to make some adjustments."

Jasce slid on his armor. The fit was snug, but he could fix that later. "Thank you."

His uncle grunted and resumed readying the other horses for their journey north. While Jasce fiddled with the straps, Kord pulled Braxium aside. They spoke for a minute and then Kord handed him a piece of paper. Jasce assumed it was a letter for Tillie.

"Where's Nicolaus?" Jaida asked, braiding her hair and looking toward town.

The shadows shimmered and he appeared, his silver hair messier than usual.

Flynt chuckled. "Rough night?"

"Why dawn?" the Shade Walker mumbled.

Jasce's laugh was cut short when a village boy sprinted into the stable. His chest heaved as he tried to speak. "Riders from the west, about to cross the Camlen Bridge."

Jasce and Braxium glanced at each other and vaulted to the edge of town. They crawled through the bushes to where they had an unobstructed view of the road.

Braxium removed a spyglass from his pocket. "Looks like five of them, all wearing cloaks with hoods." He handed Jasce the glass.

"They certainly don't look friendly." He handed the scope to his uncle, but he waved him off.

"Keep it." Braxium edged back behind the trees. "You're going to need it more than me."

Jasce held the ornate glass in his palm and then placed it in his knapsack. "Alert the soldiers, just in case."

"Just in case what?"

"They get past me."

Braxium held his hand, giving him the sliver of the Empower Stone. "I will see you again," and then disappeared. Jasce stared at the spot where his uncle had stood and hoped that wasn't the last memory he'd have of the man.

The crystal sent a shiver through him. He'd been so preoccupied with breaking his addiction and his memories returning that he'd completely forgotten about the sliver.

Jasce vaulted to the stables where the others had already mounted their horses. He swung himself onto Bruiser. "We need to leave. Now."

"What's going on?" Kord asked.

Jasce explained the situation. "Nicolaus, you're with me. You four split up. We'll meet at the rendezvous point."

"What do you plan to do?" Kenz asked, bringing her horse alongside his.

"Welcome them to my town, of course," he said with a wink. "Now go." Jasce kicked Bruiser, who took off at a gallop to intercept the riders with Nicolaus on his heels. He glanced back once as his team left Delmar behind.

Nicolaus unhooked his bow and strapped a quiver of arrows across his chest. "I'm assuming you have a plan?"

"I always have a plan," Jasce said. They wove through the alleys and stopped on the edge of the forest clinging to the far end of town.

"Stay hidden until I give the signal," Jasce said, pulling his hood over his head.

"What's the signal?" Nicolaus asked, and then mumbled a curse as Jasce rode Bruiser through the trees toward the main road.

The five men skidded to a halt. The one in the center removed his leather hood and glared at him.

"What's the hurry, boys?" Jasce asked.

"We're searching for fugitives. Now out of the way."

"Maybe I can help? Some strangers passed through last night."

The leader glanced at the riders on his right and left. "Was there a female Psyche in the group?"

Jasce scratched his jaw. "Well, I'm not really sure. What does she look like?"

The man reached into his cloak and removed a rolled piece of paper. It took all of his training not to react when he saw a drawing of his sister with a large bounty. A sense of relief washed over him when he read the words "Wanted Alive."

"It takes five bounty hunters to find one woman?" Jasce asked.

"She's with rogue Spectrals, some dangerous. Have you seen her?"

The four other men dismounted and fanned out around him. He hid a smile as he asked, "Who ordered this bounty?"

"Commander Zoldac. She has something he wants." The leader leaned forward. "I'll ask you one more time—"

"Is the bounty only for the Psyche?"

The man narrowed his eyes. "Yes."

"Well, that's rather insulting." Jasce slid off his horse and removed his hood. Giving Bruiser a slap on the rear, he drew one of his swords. "I'm sorry, but you aren't welcome in my town."

"Wrong choice. Men, kill him."

The four mercenaries, each holding a sword, advanced.

Jasce focused on the man closest to him while he breathed, calming his heart and his mind, allowing years of training to trigger the lethal warrior inside of him.

The ground trembled suddenly, and he widened his stance to keep his balance. The Earth Spectral lifted his hands and created a dust cyclone. Jasce dodged the flying rocks, but one got through, hitting him in the temple. He retrieved the throwing knife from his boot, flicked his wrist, and launched it through the air. Dirt and rocks toppled to the ground.

He vaulted and appeared next to the Earth Spectral and snapped his neck. Jasce wheezed as his lungs tightened. Not only was there an Earth Spectral, but also apparently an Air. He recalled Amycus's lessons and disappeared before passing out. He materialized behind the Air, spun on a knee, and sliced through the man's legs. Screams of pain accompanied the yells from the other soldiers.

Jasce glanced over his shoulder, wondering where Nicolaus was, when a burning pain ripped through his upper arm. Swearing, he tossed his sword to his uninjured hand and crossed blades with the bounty hunter who'd cut him. Jasce grabbed him and yanked him close, using his elbow to crack his nose. Blood poured down the man's face and his groan was silenced as Jasce brought his sword around, slashing through flesh and bone.

An arrow whooshed by his face. Spinning around, he stared into the wide eyes of the fourth soldier, his sword raised for the killing blow. The bounty hunter dropped to his knees while clutching the arrow lodged in his chest. Jasce's shadow shimmered, and Nicolaus emerged with another arrow notched and ready to fire.

"Glad you could show up," Jasce said, wiping the blood from his temple and wincing at the pain in his right arm.

"Next time be clear on what the signal is," Nicolaus said, his eyes resembling diamonds as he glared at the remaining bounty hunter.

The leader, still sitting on his horse, trained his crossbow at them. "That was impressive, but futile."

Jasce and Nicolaus disappeared at the same time. The man swore as a dagger impaled his chest and an arrow lodged into his shoulder, knocking him from his horse. They walked up on either side, and grabbing him by his cloak, Jasce yanked him to his feet. "What does Drexus want from Jaida Farone?"

"Go to hell," the bounty hunter said through gritted teeth.

Jasce twisted the hilt of his dagger. The man yelled and his knees buckled. "What. Does. Drexus. Want?" he asked, his jaw muscle throbbing from grinding his teeth. He had a pretty good idea, as the sliver of the Empower Stone lay inside his pocket like a lead weight. But was there more to Drexus's sick plan?

"I know who you are. There are only so many Vaulters who can fight like that," the soldier said with pure hatred in his eyes. "The Commander will kill everyone you know, starting with that ridiculous queen. He'll take his rightful spot on the throne, and there's nothing you can do to stop him."

Fury coursed through Jasce. With teeth clenched, he yanked his dagger free from the soldier's chest. Nicolaus lunged for him but was too late. Blood splattered their faces as Jasce's knife slashed across the man's throat. The bounty hunter slumped to the ground, his mouth open in a silent scream.

"Why did you do that?" Nicolaus asked, grabbing Jasce's arm. The Shade Walker's usual smiling eyes narrowed in rage. "He could have given us Drexus's location."

"We'll have to trust your spy network for that information. Besides, we don't have time to torture the truth out of him." He used the man's cloak to wipe the blood off his dagger.

Nicolaus swore and glanced down the abandoned road. "The lack of news from my spies is unsettling." He adjusted his tunic and lifted his chin. "Drexus plans to kill Queen Valeri, doesn't he?"

"Looks that way." Not only had Drexus placed a bounty on Jaida, but a death warrant on his entire team. He peered northwest toward Orilyon and his stomach twisted into a knot. "We need to hurry."

Chapter Twenty-Four

Jasce and Nicolaus convened with the others near the Galinas River in the Nisene Forest on the outskirts of Delmar and explained the situation with the mercenaries and the bounty on Jaida. Jasce had gone back and forth about whether to tell her, but he didn't want to keep secrets. Nicolaus added the part of Drexus's plans to steal the throne and the threat against the queen. After receiving a scolding from Kenz about being more careful, Kord healed Jasce's arm and temple.

They rode hard all day, finally slowing down as the sun disappeared behind the tall pines. Finding a place to camp for the night, they dismounted from their horses. Jaida rubbed her lower back and winced.

"You okay?" Jasce hadn't had the opportunity to talk with her during the ride. She had handled the news regarding the bounty on her well, simply saying, "Drexus doesn't enjoy losing what he thinks belongs to him."

She stretched her arms above her. "I'm not used to riding all day like that. My backside is out of shape."

"I think it's in great shape," Flynt said, chuckling as he walked by carrying their bedrolls to the center of the camp.

Jasce clenched his fists, but Jaida touched his arm. "He's trying to get under your skin. I can handle him."

He patted his horse's neck while glaring at Flynt, who had started a fire. *At least he's good for something*, he thought. "What are your feelings toward him?"

Jaida's brow furrowed. "I'm still getting to know him, but I like what I've discovered so far."

He sighed, needing to remember she was almost twenty-two years old and not the little girl he'd protected when they were growing up. "Okay. I still might punch him. Just saying." With a final pat on Bruiser's neck, he secured the remaining horses.

That night, they took turns standing watch. Jasce sharpened his dagger while leaning against a pine tree on the outskirts of camp. The sound of night filtered through the brush—small animals scurrying among the dead leaves, an owl hooting in a tree, the gurgle of the river. A branch snapped, but he stayed focused on his blade. He'd smelled Kenz's citrus scent the minute she slipped out of her sleeping roll.

"Your stealth is awful," he said, eyeing her as she emerged from behind a tree.

She rolled her eyes. "Sneaking up on you is a goal I do not wish to attain."

He returned his dagger to its scabbard. "Can't sleep?"

"Kord's snoring is making it difficult." She sat next to him, stretched out her legs, and tilted her head back to gaze at the stars peeking through the branches of the tree.

She gave him a sidelong look. "What?"

"I love the way you smell. Have I ever told you that?"

She arched a brow. "I'd say the same, but . . ."

He frowned. "But what?" She opened her mouth, but he pressed a finger to her lips. "Don't answer that. Not all of us can smell so dainty." He slowly lowered his hand.

Kenz smirked. "Dainty? Just because I'm a warrior doesn't mean I need to stink. You boys really should try bathing every once in a while."

Jasce pulled her next to him and closed his eyes, content to listen to the steady rhythm of her heart. "Why do you think our magic doesn't respond the same anymore?" He'd been wondering about this ever since his memories returned. In the past, he'd always been able to sense her, but now he couldn't. He also couldn't discern anyone's emotions. That part, he didn't miss.

"It must have had something to do with having two types of magic."

He fiddled with a lock of her hair. "That's the only thing that makes sense. I miss it, though—feeling you and your magic. Granted, it was distracting at times."

"I miss it, too. But I can sacrifice that to have Jasce instead of Azrael." She played with a loose thread on the hem of her cloak. "When I woke up after losing the baby and you weren't there, and then seeing you standing next to Queen Siryn with only a street separating us." She inhaled a quavering breath. "I thought I lost you to Azrael forever and my heart broke."

He cringed and thought of the mercenaries he'd killed without a second thought. "Kenz, a part of Azrael will always be there, just like the need for a drink. I'm not sure if I'll ever be able to completely destroy the darkness inside of me." He looked deeply into her beautiful green eyes. "But I will try. For you, for us."

She rested her palm on his cheek where the scar Drexus gave him now lay. "You don't have to try alone. I'm here and always will be." She kissed him, bringing her cloak around them to ward off the chill. He was anything but cold as her body pressed against his.

He ran his hands down her side, his thumbs grazing the edge of her breasts. He wasn't worthy of her love or acceptance. And if she kept kissing him like this, he'd take her against the tree and to hell with keeping watch.

He bunched her tunic in his hands and took a deep breath. "You need to stop, otherwise I'll be shirking my duty."

She gave a husky chuckle. Her swollen lips and flushed cheeks made him want to bury himself inside her, losing himself to her silky softness. Her smile melted from her face when a wolf howled in the distance, followed by an answering call.

"They're getting closer," Jasce said. "I heard them after we left Delmar."

"What? Are they tracking us?" She sat straighter against the tree and peered into the night.

"Not sure, but I'm not concerned. Yet."

"First bounty hunters and now wolves," Kenz mumbled, and rested her head on his shoulder.

A muffled cry pierced through the darkness. Jasce shot to his feet and immediately pulled Kenz behind him while grabbing his dagger. Kord yelled and sat up with wide, unseeing eyes.

Kenz ran toward him. "Shh. It's all right. Just a dream."

Kord thrashed, and Jasce grabbed his arms. "It's okay. You're safe."

Kord blinked and swallowed, glancing around the campsite. He stared from Jasce to Kenz. "Sorry. I hope I didn't wake you."

Kenz shook her head.

Jasce sat on his heels. "What was that about?"

Kord rubbed his forehead. "Just a bad dream."

"Do you get them a lot?" Jasce asked.

"As much as anyone, I suppose."

The wolves howled again, this time much closer than before. They looked toward the east, where the sky turned from black to a midnight blue with only a few stubborn stars clinging to the night.

"Wake the others," Jasce told Kenz. "We need to go."

～

The wolves' howls shadowed them as they rode alongside the river. They neared the outskirts of Bradwick and then headed northwest toward Orilyon. The forest thinned, and the landscape turned into the familiar grassy plains Jasce had ridden through when he implemented the raids as a Hunter.

The wolves maintained their distance but were definitely tracking them. His team kept close to the tree line, but with every howl, they grew more anxious. By late afternoon, the ragged breathing of their horses forced them to stop.

"Flynt, I want small fires surrounding our campsite," Jasce said once they set up camp. Most animals were afraid of fire, so hopefully the wolves would keep their distance, but he kept the horses saddled just in case. Dark clouds swirled overhead, and the trees bent with the wind. Thunder sounded in the distance.

Conquering the Darkness

Jasce strapped on his swords and slid a dagger into each boot. "Kenz, you and Nicolaus with me. Kord, stay here with Flynt and Jaida."

Jaida wrapped her arms around her waist. "Where are you going?"

"And don't you think we should stick together?" Flynt asked.

Jasce released a breath and attempted to rein in his frustration. He'd been on edge since seeing Kord wake up from his nightmare, and he was tired of being stalked by the wolves. And even though his body had purged itself from the alcohol, the need for a drink nagged at him, an ever-present temptation chipping away his resolve.

"We're going into the forest to hunt some wolves, and Kenz and Nicolaus are the most skilled with the bow." He added, "And I really don't need to explain my orders."

Jaida narrowed her eyes. "You're my brother, not my commanding officer."

Flynt's brows disappeared behind his auburn hair while Kord sighed.

Jasce stalked toward Jaida. "As your brother, I should've never let you come with us. And now you're in more danger than ever, so don't push me, Jai." He turned to stride into the forest when a sharp object struck the back of his head. His shoulders stiffened as he slowly faced his sister.

Small pebbles floated over Jaida's hand. "You're an ass, you know that?"

"Yes, I'm aware. I've actually been called one quite a few times." He gestured to Kenz, who chuckled in agreement. "We'll be back soon."

Kenz gave Kord a kiss on the cheek, while Nicolaus strapped on his bow and a quiver of arrows. "Anyone want to kiss me goodbye?" He scanned the blank faces and shrugged. "You have no idea what you're missing."

Jaida snorted as the three jogged into the forest toward the howling wolves. Jasce didn't like leaving his sister behind, but he trusted Kord and Flynt to keep her safe. And deep down, he knew she could hold her own. He reached into his pocket for the sliver of the Empower Stone, wondering if he should have left it with her, just in case, but he didn't have time to return to the campsite as a howl echoed from the east. Besides, the crystal might come in handy if the wolves attacked.

Jasce paused as they approached a clearing and stared into the darkening forest. A sheen of sweat glistened on Kenz's forehead, and Nicolaus rested his hands on his hips and breathed deeply.

"Are we really going to kill a wolf?" Kenz asked.

"I'd like not to, but we need to establish some boundaries. Plus, I want to know how large the pack is," Jasce said. Wolves were territorial, but he'd never heard of a pack being this dedicated to tracking humans.

They walked a little longer, stopping when a growl sounded from their left. Jasce held up his hand but didn't draw his sword. Kenz and Nicolaus had arrows nocked. Another growl sounded behind them.

A large white wolf emerged through the bush, snarling and revealing sharp teeth. Six more appeared, three behind, one on each side, with the last standing next to the white one.

"Now what?" Kenz whispered.

"Stay still. They're wondering if we're a threat," Jasce said.

"Are we?" Nicolaus asked, keeping his bow lowered but ready to fire.

Jasce hoped the wolves were simply being curious. He had little experience with them and most of the information he'd learned from his mother since they had spent so many nights in the woods.

A russet-colored wolf to his left snarled and prowled forward. Jasce shifted his stance, putting himself between the wolf and Kenz. The white one, he assumed the alpha, gave an answering growl and lifted its nose. All seven wolves spun and looked in the same direction with their ears back.

The sound of chirping birds stopped.

A branch snapped.

The hairs on the back of Jasce's neck stood at attention. He remembered this sensation.

"Kenz, shield," he whispered.

A black blur shot through the woods. A yip sounded behind him. Claws, snapping jaws, and fur tumbled into the bushes.

He swore and drew his swords. Pine needles crunched and twigs snapped as five Snatchers burst through the foliage, their white eyes scanning the wolves and humans.

"These beasts are loathsome," Nicolaus said, raising his bow, aiming at the leader of the group. The Snatchers, created by the Vastane queen,

Conquering the Darkness

resisted magic, yet could also track it. The sliver of the Empower Stone, plus Kenz's, Nicolaus's, and Jasce's magic were like blood in the water to these beasts.

One the size of a pony shifted its attention to Jasce, scraping its three-inch claws into the soil. Large, yellow teeth snapped as it stalked toward him.

The Snatchers shifted their weight to their haunches. The wolves charged forward and attacked the beasts head-on. They wouldn't last long against such lethal creatures.

"Kenz, raise your shield." Jasce twirled his swords as a Snatcher locked eyes on him.

An arrow whizzed by. Nicolaus disappeared in the shadows, reappearing and letting loose another arrow, stopping a Snatcher from burying its teeth into the white wolf's throat. The snarls and roars were deafening. Another wolf yipped as a Snatcher landed on it, bloody jaws targeting the jugular. Jasce vaulted and kicked the creature off the wolf. He sliced his sword through the Snatcher's neck. The wolf lumbered to its feet, shaking its head, and regarded Jasce with its golden eyes. It dipped its head and ran toward the members of his pack who fought against two other Snatchers.

Jasce looked over his shoulder as a creature prowled toward Kenz. "Kenz! Shield!"

She stood frozen, her eyes wide and face pale. With shaking arms, she raised her hands but her indigo light only fluttered. The creature reared back. Jasce tapped into his magic, disappeared, and slashed his sword in one fluid movement. The Snatcher's head fell to the ground and black blood splashed across Kenz's face. Her body jerked, and she stumbled back.

"Nicolaus. Get her out of here," Jasce ordered.

Shadows rippled and the Shade Walker reappeared next to Kenz. He wrapped an arm around her waist and disappeared. A Snatcher landed with claws outstretched at the exact location where they would have been. Jasce knelt and spun. The beast roared as his sword sliced through its middle. The white wolf locked its jaws around the fallen Snatcher's neck.

Jasce fought alongside the remaining wolves until the only sound was his harsh breathing. Sweat and blood ran down his face, and his back twinged, but the brace held.

One wolf lay near the bushes, its soft coat matted with blood. The russet one limped over to it and sniffed. He released a howl that sent a shiver down Jasce's spine. The alpha held Jasce's gaze while it walked to its fallen pack member.

Jasce tipped his chin toward the white wolf, gripped the sliver of the Empower Stone, and visualized their campsite. Concentrating on the magic flowing through him, he felt the tug and disappeared.

Jaida squeaked and Kord drew his sword as Jasce reappeared on the edge of their campsite. He scanned the area, looking for Nicolaus and Kenz.

"Where's my sister?" Kord lowered his sword, his brow furrowed.

"They should be here. Nicolaus Shade Walked Kenz out." His heart pounded in his ears as he looked around, searching the shadows.

"What happened?" Jaida asked.

"Snatchers attacked us and the wolves."

Flynt spit onto the ground. "I hate those things."

Jasce paced the edge of the forest, not wanting to talk until his fiancée was safe. He'd never seen her so frightened before.

Finally, Nicolaus arrived with Kenz tucked to his side, his bow across his chest and his knuckles white around the hilt of his sword. Kord swore when she staggered, and Nicolaus tightened his grip to keep her from falling.

Jasce rushed to her, held her shoulders, and peered into her eyes. "Are you all right?"

Her hands shook as she clutched his wrists. "I'm okay." Her voice trembled.

"Let me look at her," Kord said, and led her toward the fire. He settled her on a bedroll and wiped the blood off her face.

Jasce pulled Nicolaus aside. "What took you so long?"

Nicolaus stared at his hands as if the answer lay in his palms. "I don't know. My magic kept failing me, only allowing me to disappear for a few seconds. We had to run most of the way."

Jasce crossed his arms. Nicolaus's Shade Walking was powerful. He should have been able to handle that distance easily, just as Jasce had.

"How many Snatchers were there?" Jaida asked, as she and Flynt joined them.

"Five," Jasce said. He had heard some Snatchers escaped during the last battle with Queen Siryn and had hoped the Paladin Guard killed them all. But it seemed there were still some rogue ones left. The wolves hadn't been tracking Jasce and his team. Instead, they'd been hunting the Snatchers, who must have trespassed into their territory.

Nicolaus wiped the dirt off his leather pants. "There are packs of them wandering through Pandaren. Some even crossed the desert into Paxton."

"How do you know that?" Flynt asked.

Nicolaus arched a brow and stared at Flynt like he was an idiot.

"Right. Spy," Flynt said.

Jasce peered into the forest. Who knew how many more Snatchers were out there? He would not endanger his team by waiting to find out. "Mount up. We're leaving for Orilyon. Now."

Chapter Twenty-Five

The horses ran through fields shining like liquid gold as the sun continued its descent. A muscle in Kenz's jaw ticked and her knuckles whitened as she gripped the reins. Jasce was relieved when the fear in her eyes morphed into anger and color crept back into her cheeks.

Hours later, they finally stopped at a military compound a few miles outside of Orilyon. Torches lit up the stone walls, and shouts sounded from the watchtower as they approached.

"I better handle this," Kord said to Jasce, with a quick glance at his sister. Worry flashed across his face as he dismounted. "It might help to have the Alturian prince, too."

Nicolaus hopped off his horse and raked his fingers through his silver hair. "It's all in who you know."

Jasce rolled his eyes as Jaida sided up next to him. She pulled her cloak tight around her, her breath creating white puffs of clouds. "I hope this isn't a bad idea."

"Me too." He could tell his sister was nervous by the way she kept biting her lip, but there was no avoiding coming to Orilyon or meeting with the queen. He had a mission to complete, and the queen's banishment of his sister would not stand in his way.

Jasce slid off his horse and signaled for Kenz to follow him. They stood in the open field with the garrison on one side and the walls of Orilyon on the other. The moon hung like a silver orb among black velvet. "Are you okay?"

She crossed her arms and stared after Kord and Nicolaus. "I don't want to talk about it. Not now."

He gently turned her chin to face him. "I can understand that. But we're a team."

"Yeah, and I just became the weakest link." Tears of anger filled her eyes.

"You are one of the most courageous warriors I've ever known."

She fisted her hands. "I froze back there and could have gotten you or Nicolaus killed. I was a coward."

"Courage is not the absence of fear." She stared out over the fields, her lips pressed into a flat line, but he continued, "Considering what happened to you and our . . ." Jasce swallowed. "Our child, I don't blame you for your reaction."

"A captain of the Guard can't act that way, and you know it."

If there was one thing he understood about Kenz, she didn't like to be coddled. "True. But how about I give my fiancée a break?" He pulled her into his arms. "Just this once."

She would eventually have to overcome her fear because he suspected they hadn't seen the last of the Snatchers. But for now, he simply held her, becoming a safe refuge where she had nothing to prove.

She leaned into his hug and sighed. "I'm sorry," she mumbled against his chest.

He tightened his embrace. "Nothing to apologize for."

Kord whistled and waved them over.

"Here goes nothing." Jasce led their horses toward the compound. Jaida and Flynt dismounted and followed while Kord and Nicolaus waited at the guard tower with two soldiers behind them. Jasce recognized one of them.

Darin nodded when he approached. "Commander Farone. Good to see you again." Darin wore his brown hair short, and the black uniform hugged the muscles in his chest and arms. A gold "N" was stitched above his heart.

Conquering the Darkness

"Darin," he said, grabbing the man's forearm. "Good to see you, too."

The soldier scanned the group, his eyes pausing on Jaida. "You all must be hungry."

Kord's stomach rumbled. "Famished."

Darin chuckled. "The kitchen is closed, but I'm sure we can rummage up something."

They followed him past the towers guarding the entrance to the garrison. The portcullis clanked shut once they entered, and after leaving the horses at the stable, Darin escorted them to the dining hall.

The layout of the southern compound was like the Bastion, but smaller. Torches lit the corridor and their boots reverberated off the stone walls. They entered the dining hall and walked past rows of wooden tables, stopping at one near the hearth. Flynt gathered wood stacked against the wall and, using his magic, started a fire while Kord and Darin disappeared into the kitchen.

Jaida leaned close to the flames, rubbing her hands together, while Nicolaus and Kenz sat across from her. Jasce removed his armor and brace and winced from the pain running down his spine and leg. The leather and metal support had definitely helped, but after the fight with the Snatchers and hours of riding, he needed a reprieve. The desire for a drink coursed through him and he automatically reached for his flask. His fingers brushed against the sliver of the Empower Stone.

He hadn't thought much of the power he'd experienced when he held the crystal as he vaulted, except that his magic reacted differently from the last time he used the sliver. With only his Vaulter magic, his power seemed stronger and purer without the Amplifier mixed in. The way it was supposed to be, he figured. Magic and its rule of balance.

The sound of the crackling fire filled the silence as Jaida snuck glances at Kenz.

"What?" Kenz finally asked, glaring at her.

"I was just wondering if you were okay."

"I'm fine," she said through gritted teeth.

"I can tell."

Jasce scowled at his sister. "Knock it off."

Jaida wrinkled her nose at him and then focused on Kenz. "We're all afraid of something. And sometimes that fear wins. It doesn't make you weak."

Kenz leaned forward and rested her arms on the table. "And what are you afraid of?"

Jaida trailed her fingernail through a groove in the table, her eyes unfocused. "Sometimes I'm afraid to close my eyes at night because of the nightmares. Other times, I fear Drexus capturing me again and turning me into a monster."

Jasce tapped his finger and waited, unsure what his fiancée might do. Kenz and Jaida's relationship was still on shaky ground, and he was too tired to break up a fight between them.

Finally, Kenz nodded. "I've never frozen like that. It's a sensation I don't want to experience again."

Jaida reached across the table, hesitated for a second, and then squeezed her hand. Kenz pursed her lips as if she was touching something sticky, but her shoulders relaxed, and Jasce exhaled a breath he hadn't realized he'd been holding.

"Relax, brother. Did you expect us to brawl right here?"

He arched a brow. "Actually . . ."

Darin and Kord brought over a platter of dried meats and cheeses with a few bowls of cold porridge. They hadn't eaten since that morning and all conversation stopped as they shoveled in their food.

After settling his immediate hunger, Jasce addressed Darin. "Any news regarding Drexus's location?"

Darin straddled the bench and strummed his fingers. "We've received mixed reports. Some say he's north near Wilholm and others say he's south. We aren't sure what information to trust."

"He has the Creator Stone, and I think his next target is Queen Valeri." Jasce stabbed at a slice of meat more aggressively than was warranted. He didn't mention the bounty on Jaida, not wanting that knowledge to get out in case Drexus had spies within the Pandaren Guard.

Darin's eyes widened. "He has two of the Stones?"

Kord wiped his mouth. "He also took Caston. We have no idea where he is or if he's still alive."

Darin cursed and shoved back from the table. Addressing Jasce, he said, "You remember where the barracks are. Numbers eighteen through twenty are available. I need to report to the queen."

"She won't be pleased at being woken up at this hour."

Darin rested his hands on his hips and sighed. "True, but not telling her until the morning would be worse for me."

They finally made it to the barracks, dirty and exhausted, but at least warm and full. Each room contained two beds, and once again the issue of sleeping partners reared its inconvenient head. Everyone was too tired and sore from their journey, and Jasce didn't have the energy to argue with Jaida over who slept in her room, but he did pull Flynt aside.

"I don't know what your intentions are with my sister, but I expect you to be honorable."

Flynt scowled at the hand gripping his arm. "I had a younger sister, once. But eventually, big brother needs to back off." He pulled Jasce's fingers free. "However, until this whole mess is over, I'll keep my hands to myself."

Jasce stared at him for a few heartbeats. "You *had* a younger sister? What happened?"

Sorrow filled the Fire Spectral's amber eyes. "That's a story for another time. Just know I understand the protective brother instincts."

Jasce hesitated, questions begging to be asked to a man he realized he'd never known all that well. But he nodded and then walked across the hall. He knocked on Kord and Nicolaus's door. The Shade Walker opened it, dressed only in silk undergarments. Despite his royal background, Nicolaus had seen his fair share of battles based on the scars along his arms, chest, and thighs.

"Did you need something, Commander?"

"Just making sure everyone's settled."

Nicolaus glanced at a snoring Kord. "I'm looking forward to arriving at the palace. I'm desperate for my own room."

Jasce leaned against the doorjamb. "You know, for a spy, you really are a prince."

Nicolaus pressed a palm to his chest. "You wound me."

He laughed as the door shut. When he arrived at his and Kenz's room, she was already asleep, having slid the two beds together and leaving the candles burning. Even though he was exhausted, his thoughts bounced around inside his skull, making his head hurt. Was Drexus already in Orilyon? Was he strong enough to defeat his former commander? And what about Caston? He hoped he wasn't too late to save his friend.

Sweat dampened the hair on his neck, and his hands trembled. He remembered where the soldiers kept their stash of alcohol, and the desire for a drink had him moving toward the door. Everyone was asleep. No one would know.

Just a sip, he thought. He reached for his cloak, and Amycus's journal fell out of the inside pocket and landed with a thunk on the floor. It had been a while since he'd read through the worn pages. He plopped down in the only chair in the room and listened to the rhythmic sounds of Kenz's breathing.

It's been two months of hell since my last entry. I needed time to heal and then had to retrace my steps to locate my journal. Thankfully, it was still in the cave where I'd hidden it. This book has become a reprieve for me, a way to purge my soul. My emotions are battling each other—the need for vengeance against what Drexus did and gratitude for the person who helped me escape. (I cannot mention her name, otherwise her life would be forfeit if this journal fell into the wrong hands). I am alive because of her. I desperately want to kill Drexus for what he did to me in that dungeon. I'm ashamed of succumbing to the torture and revealing where I'd thrown the Empower Stone. Hopefully, the sea currents have sent it down the coast where he will never find it. At least he isn't aware of my ability to use all four elements.

The magic-suppressing collar he developed is brilliant, yet terrible. The sensation of having all my magic smothered was an experience I don't wish to repeat. When Drexus and I first experimented with the Brymagus plant all those years ago, I never thought he'd take it to this extreme. Why is he persecuting his own kind? His need for control and power have blinded him. I feel partly responsible for his success with the collar, but maybe I could use his ideas for good instead of evil. Something to ponder later, I suppose.

Conquering the Darkness

~~~~~

Every time I look at my ruined hands, bitterness and revenge consume me. The scars Drexus left are a constant reminder of the torture I experienced. However, I've found a light, someone whose gray eyes and kind smile make me want to be a better man, a man not defined by anger or hate.
Delmar is a small village, its people welcoming. I've even met a blacksmith who allows me to work in his forge to earn a little money while I'm still on the run. I fear I will forever have a bounty on my head. Drexus has seen to that. But thankfully, Braxium has no love for the Watch Guard. He does, however, have a love of whiskey. I can see he's trying to numb his pain, but I fear he may lose himself in the bottle.

Jasce sighed and stared at the ceiling, his need for a drink extinguished for now. How had Braxium not only fought the battle of his addiction, but won? Same with Amycus and his desire for revenge. He understood firsthand the addicting lure of vengeance and could only imagine the torture Amycus went through at Drexus's hands. Jasce had given in to the lust for revenge, but Amycus had somehow resisted the temptation.

Meeting his mother—Jasce figured that's who Amycus had meant with the gray eyes and kind smile—had made him want to be better, to not let destructive thoughts and behaviors define him. He glanced at Kenz. She had become a beacon of light to his blackened soul and made him strive to be worthy of her acceptance and love. One way to do that was to honor his promise about drinking. He had to believe he was stronger than his addiction and would prevail. If not for himself, then for the woman he loved.

He returned the journal to his pocket and slid into bed. Kenz whimpered when he gathered her in his arms. He'd never seen her freeze like she had when the Snatchers attacked in the forest, obviously still traumatized from almost dying and the death of their baby. He couldn't imagine what she felt, and then waking up without him by her side.

Guilt swamped him, and he held her tighter. He hadn't been there when she'd needed him most, having surrendered to the effects of the Stone and the seductive presence of the Angel of Death. But he meant what he said. He would always struggle to resist the temptation to resort to his old ways. And now he'd be battling the ever-present desire to drink. It was one thing to contend with a living, breathing enemy and quite another to wage war with his baser self. His thoughts continued to circle until exhaustion and the comfort of Kenz's body pressing against his finally coaxed him to sleep.

Chapter Twenty-Six

A knock had him wrenching his dagger from under his pillow. He could have sworn he'd just shut his eyes, but fingers of light drifted through the small window. The knock sounded again, this time louder. Jasce sighed and slid on a pair of linen pants.

He yanked open the door and scowled at Kord. "What?"

"Sorry for the early wake-up call, but Queen Valeri wants to speak to you at once."

Jasce peeked over his shoulder to find Kenz sitting on the edge of the bed with black circles darkening the skin under her eyes. He faced Kord. "After breakfast and coffee."

Kord opened his mouth to argue and then glanced at his sister. "Is she all right?" he whispered.

"She will be. We'll meet you in the dining hall." Jasce shut the door and leaned against it. Kenz had awakened screaming once during the night, but he'd been able to soothe her back to sleep.

She stood and slid into her leather pants and top. He walked across the room and picked up her armored chest piece. "I still hate taking orders from that woman."

She chuckled, slipped her armor over her head, and reached for her boots. "I'm not surprised."

He crossed his arms and watched her hands, relieved to see her fingers were steady. When she rose to her feet, his heart lodged in his throat. She was such a fierce warrior and had won the battle for his heart. The vulnerability of that thought used to scare him, but not anymore. He believed his heart was in trustworthy hands and yearned to provide the same level of comfort and dependability.

Jasce secured his brace, quickly got dressed, and together they entered the crowded dining hall. He bit back a groan and rubbed his temple at the overwhelming din of voices and scraping forks. It seemed every soldier stationed at the command post was eating breakfast at the same time.

The loud voices turned into murmurs and whispers as Jasce and Kenz walked toward the far side of the room where the rest of his team sat, plates loaded with eggs, bacon, and toast.

News always traveled fast among soldiers, and he wondered what they had been told regarding their overnight guests. The guards on the watchtower the night before must have recognized him. He noticed a few soldiers salute or nod their heads even though he was no longer their commander, despite Nicolaus and Darin using the title. Jasce had no authority over them.

Kenz settled next to her brother and rested her head on his shoulder. She looked like she could fall asleep sitting up. Jasce straddled a chair and eyed his sister. Her hair hung loosely down her back and she white-knuckled her cup of tea, staring at nothing.

"How did you sleep?" he asked her, sliding a look at Flynt.

"Okay, except this guy talks in his sleep and kept me up part of the night," Jaida said, pointing at the Fire Spectral.

Flynt sputtered through his coffee, causing Nicolaus to swear and jump back. Flynt's cheeks reddened. "No, I don't."

Both Kord and Kenz answered at the same time. "Yes, you do."

His amber eyes widened as he glanced around the group, stopping at Jaida. "What did I say?"

She dabbed at her mouth with a napkin. "Most of it was just gibberish."

"Most of it?" He leaned forward and rested his arms on the table.

A flush ran up Jaida's neck. "The rest is for another time and place."

Conquering the Darkness

Flynt scowled at her and shoveled eggs into his mouth, mumbling about women being impossible.

Jasce hid his smile behind his mug until he caught Kord staring at him with that penetrating gaze he hated.

"Why aren't you eating?" the Healer asked, his green eye narrowed.

Jasce pressed his lips together. "Not hungry." Between the lack of sleep, the noise emanating around the room, and the nausea swirling in his stomach, he was very close to retching. He was barely keeping the coffee down, but he didn't need a caffeine headache on top of everything else.

"I'm sure you'll still experience side effects of withdrawal, but I can help you with those." Kord reached across the table and placed his hand on Jasce's forehead. Immediately, warmth flooded his body, and his churning gut settled.

"Thanks." He didn't have a clue what was in store for them at the palace, and just in case he and his sister ended up in the dungeon, it would be wise to eat something. He took a piece of dry toast and choked it down.

Darin marched toward their table. "Your horses are ready. We need to go." He winced as Jasce glared at him. "All of you," he said, glancing at Jaida.

Jaida, who'd been smiling and laughing at Flynt, lowered her fork. All emotion melted from her face, turning her youthful features hard and unyielding. Jasce recognized the tactic—Drexus had taught him the same thing.

They rode silently through the southern gate of Orilyon and up the cobblestone road toward the palace. The crashing of waves and the smell of brine wrapped around Jasce like a soft blanket as he lifted his face and relished the warmth on his skin. Palm trees swayed in the breeze, and the rising sun melted away the crisp morning mist. Spring was quickly approaching on the coast, leaving the bleakness of winter behind.

He was not looking forward to this meeting with the queen, and wondered if the council would be present. The last time he'd been in the War Room, he'd killed one of the members, Larkin Haldren. Granted, Queen Siryn had been controlling him with her magic, but he couldn't deny that the desire festering inside his soul to be rid of the man had already existed.

The Bastion loomed in the distance with a sense of foreboding. He had thought returning to the compound he'd called home for so many years was what he wanted. But now he wasn't so sure. What once felt familiar sent a shiver down his spine as if hundreds of spiders crawled over his skin.

The palace windows sparkled from the sun and the white stone of the turrets practically glowed. They rode through the large wooden gates toward the courtyard. Handing off their horses to the stable boy, they followed Darin up the steps and through the ornately carved doors.

He could have walked these corridors blindfolded as they passed tapestries and paintings of the royal family, yet Jasce found himself stopping in front of a painting he'd never paid attention to before. A woman with long red hair and harsh features glared at him. On her neck lay a gold pendant with a clear gem. The placard indicated this was Queen Namaha d'Adreci.

He remembered the story his mother told of the girl who had stolen the sliver of the Empower Stone, which had been passed down through the ages. The crystal ended up in King Valeri's possession until the night Drexus killed him and started the war between Naturals and Spectrals.

He fisted his hands. Now his former commander had both the Empower and Creator Stones. *He can't get the other two*, Jasce thought.

Kord cleared his throat.

"Right." Jasce marched down the hall, his boots thumping on the black and white marbled floors.

Two soldiers stood guard outside the entrance to the War Room. They saluted Darin and opened the doors.

"Leave your weapons," one guard said, pointing to the table in the hallway. The man's expression was almost comical as his eyes grew wider and wider, and Darin coughed to cover his laugh. Daggers, swords, crossbows, even an ax thudded onto the table as his team unloaded their blades.

Jasce swallowed the bile surging up his throat and stepped into the War Room. The last time he'd been in this room, Queen Siryn had violated his will, forcing him to do the unthinkable. He breathed through his nose, digging into his Hunter training and squashing the dread making his heart race. Straightening to his full height, he faced the Queen of Pandaren.

Queen Valeri sat at the head of the large oval table, with General Alyssa Nadja at her side. The queen's brown eyes narrowed slightly when they entered. The light from the chandelier reflected off her crown, making the rubies and sapphires glow. She wore an ivory gown with embroidered purple vines trailing down the bodice. She looked elegant yet formidable.

The council members turned toward him: Lady Wuhl from Wilholm, Lady Darbry from Torrine, and Lord Rollant from Carhurst with Captain Reed standing behind him, leaning casually against the wall. A new face stared at him, and it was one he recognized immediately.

The smug expression on Phillip Gallet's face had Jasce reaching for his dagger. He bit back a curse as his hand brushed against his empty sheath. He couldn't comprehend why the warden of Bradwick Prison, the man who had tortured him for three days, sat at the table with his pudgy fingers drumming on the polished wood.

"What the hell is he doing here?" Jasce asked, pulling against Kord's hand, which tightened on his arm.

"Hello, Azrael. Or should I call you Mr. Farone? So much has happened since we were last in each other's presence," Lord Gallet said with a smirk.

Jasce gritted his teeth. "I ought to kill you where you sit."

"Mr. Farone, stand down." Queen Valeri's eyes cut like the edge of a knife, penetrating and sharp. "The council voted in Lord Gallet to represent Bradwick."

He counted to ten before tearing his gaze from the ex-warden. Now was not the time to lose his temper, especially when his sister's future hung in the balance. He couldn't give the queen any reason to reinforce Jaida's banishment—or worse, imprisonment.

Jasce bowed his head. "Your Majesty." His team followed suit, except for Nicolaus, who plopped down in the chair across from the queen, giving her a catlike grin.

Queen Valeri arched a sculpted brow. "Prince Jazari, welcome back."

"Good to be back." Nicolaus adjusted his tunic and nodded to the council members.

She scanned the rest of the group, finally landing on Jaida. "I thought I told you to never return." The queen lifted a finger, silencing both Jaida and Jasce. "I'll deal with you in a minute. Mr. Haring, report."

Kord stepped forward and updated the council of the events since arriving in Balten. When he informed them of Caston, Jasce winced. Queen Valeri's eyes flicked to him, but she quickly returned her attention to Kord. Lord Rollant swore when Kord mentioned Drexus escaping with the Creator Stone.

The steady rhythm of the queen's strumming fingers filled the silence as everyone processed the information. "General Nadja, I want the Guard ready. Nicolaus, what news from your spies? And yes, I know you have quite a few roaming my lands."

Nicolaus's eyes widened briefly before hardening. "They have been uncharacteristically quiet."

"I want you to find out why." The queen folded her arms on the table and glared at Jaida. "Why are you here?"

Jasce opened his mouth to answer, but Jaida touched his arm. She dipped into a curtsey. "Your Majesty, I know Drexus better than anyone, and I am here to help."

"How do we know you can be trusted?" Lady Torrine asked.

Jaida lifted her chin. "You don't, but I will do whatever needs to be done to stop Drexus."

"It's my understanding that both Mr. Farone and his sister were in league with Commander Zoldac," Lord Gallet said. "I don't think we can trust either of them."

"And we're supposed to trust you?" Jasce asked, the blood rushing in his ears. "You wanted magic and were desperate to learn how Drexus had performed the transfusion. For all we know, you're working with him, especially now that he has the Creator Stone."

The council members gawked at Lord Gallet, whose face had turned crimson with sweat beading on his forehead.

"Enough," the queen said. "We've all done things we are not proud of, but to defeat Drexus once and for all, we need to be united."

Conquering the Darkness

"But he killed Larkin," Lady Wuhl interjected, pointing at Jasce. "He betrayed us all."

Kord stood alongside Jasce. "Queen Siryn manipulated him and his magic, forcing him to attack Lord Haldron."

"Or so he claims," Lady Wuhl said. "Where's the proof?"

Lord Rollant placed his palms on the table. "Serena, we all know the two magics impacted Jasce's mental fortitude, and those magics have been removed. He never attacked the queen and only defended Jaida's life or his own."

"Yes, but there are consequences," Lady Wuhl said.

Jasce cleared his throat in the attempt to choke down his pride. "Lady Wuhl, and members of the council, saying I'm sorry doesn't right the wrongs, and those deaths will always be on my hands and mine alone." He scanned the faces in the room. "Yet I still ask that you accept my apology for my actions as commander during the Gathering."

Surprise flashed across the council member's faces. The queen raised her chin, a hint of a smile tugging on the corner of her mouth. She glanced at Lord Rollant, who tapped his lip as he observed Jasce.

"That's all very touching. Good on you, Commander," Nicolaus said. "But I suggest moving the Inhibitor Stone immediately. Once Drexus realizes it's no longer in the desert, he will come here. I've seen him wield the Empower Stone, and Vale is practically invincible. Added to this misery, Drexus is creating more Spectrals, loyal to him alone."

"We will discuss this further. Mr. Haring, please sit," the queen said to Kord. "The rest of you are excused."

Jasce glanced at Kenz, who shrugged and followed Flynt and Jaida into the hallway.

"Oh, and Miss Farone, I'm trusting you. Don't make me regret it."

Jaida turned. "You won't, Your Majesty."

As they exited the room, Lady Torrine's voice drifted through the closing doors. "Are you sure he's ready, Lorella?"

Jasce spun on his heel, but the door to the War Room snapped shut. Was she talking about him? And if so, ready for what?

Chapter Twenty-Seven

General Alyssa Nadja found Jasce and his team, who had been joined by Aura and Delmira, in the dining hall after the meeting. She dropped her sword on the bench, snagged a slice of bread off Jasce's plate, and mumbled, "Starving." She'd slicked her brown hair into a tight braid, and an armored chest piece covered her uniform. Her ranking and the letter "N" peeked out near her collarbone.

"Help yourself," Jasce said, sliding the plate toward her, unable to eat since his stomach had twisted into knots. The War Room had evoked unwanted memories. He vividly remembered Queen Siryn controlling him as he tried to restrain Azrael and stop the momentum of his sword slicing through Tobias de Sille, a Gemari. Thankfully, the general had survived. Lord Haldron, on the other hand, hadn't. Queen Valeri had been lenient with him, considering he was guilty of treason and murder. He owed a lot to his friends and Nicolaus for vouching for him.

Alyssa glanced at Jaida and held out her hand. "We didn't meet last time. I'm General Nadja."

Jaida shook Alyssa's hand. "Nice to meet you."

"Alyssa is one of my finest generals," Jasce said to his sister. He'd trained alongside her before he became a Hunter, and even at a young age, her skills had been impressive. They'd never talked about how she ended up in the Watch Guard. A conversation for another time, he supposed.

Jasce observed a group of fourth-year recruits. A girl with the Water symbol on her tunic gave him a shy smile.

"When did the Spectrals get emblems?" he asked, recognizing a few Amps and Fires sitting with the young girl. A teenage boy he didn't know sat with the group, his white eyes constantly scanning the dining hall. Jasce had never seen a Tracker so young before. As with Psyches and Vaulters, that mental magic was rare.

"After you left. Caston and I wanted to know who had magic and what kind. They still train together, so don't give me that look. Some sixth-years came up with the symbols. Even the Naturals wear one." She pointed to the "N."

Jasce was hesitant about singling out anyone, magic user or not, but he wouldn't argue if the new system was effective. "How have things been the last couple of months?"

"A little tense. You and Caston are missed. Seb and I have it under control, and Aura and Delmira are a huge help, but there are a few soldiers who push the boundaries."

Jasce wondered about Caston. He didn't expect Drexus to kill him since Caston was a valuable hostage, even though he wouldn't willingly give Drexus any information.

Hold on, he thought.

Alyssa touched his hand. "We'll get him back, sir."

He sighed, hoping she was right. "You don't need to call me 'sir' anymore. I'm not your commanding officer."

A look flashed in her eyes, but quickly disappeared.

"What?" Jasce asked.

"It's just good to have you back." She scanned the dining hall and then leaned in close. "You'll find out soon enough, but there are rumors of people going missing from the towns."

"Which towns?" Jasce asked.

"All of them, at least in Opax."

Conquering the Darkness

Kenz, Flynt, Jaida, Aura, and Delmira stopped eating and scooted closer. Alyssa regarded them and then continued, "I'm waiting for reports from a few garrisons. I've heard from Ferox, but not the others, possibly because of the weather."

"The weather?" Aura raised her brows.

"A dust storm was reported near Ironbark Garrison, and there's a buildup of ice in the south. You probably just missed it."

Flynt fiddled with his ignitor switch. "Do you think it's because Drexus has the two Stones?"

Alyssa flashed Flynt a warning look, but Jasce waved her off. "They already know," he said, pointing to Aura and Delmira.

Jasce and Kenz had told them of their exploits from finding the Creator Stone to arriving in Orilyon. Having his team united and together again felt right, which made the absence of Caston even more distressing.

"It has to be." Jasce tapped his finger on the table. "Let me know when the other garrisons report in."

"Will do." Alyssa glanced at Kenz and Flynt. "I realize you've both just returned, but Queen Valeri told me to inform you that you still have a job to do."

Flynt leaned back in his chair and draped his arm behind Jaida. "When does my next class start?"

Flynt sounded tired. They all did, but the queen was right. They had responsibilities to attend to. Except Jasce. For once, he didn't know what to do. His presence wasn't required at the meetings, and he didn't have recruits to train. Tillie and Mal were safe in Carhurst, he hoped, so he couldn't visit them.

"In about ten minutes," Alyssa said, tearing into a piece of chicken.

"Don't they feed you?" Kenz asked, smiling.

"I skipped breakfast because of the queen's early morning council meeting. By the way, keep an eye out for Lord Gallet. He doesn't like you," she said to Jasce.

He snorted. "I'm not surprised." He still couldn't understand why the council voted that weasel in. They probably weren't aware of all that happened in the Bradwick dungeon. But it was also not his problem anymore. Once Drexus was defeated, he'd never work under the queen again, nor sit in meetings with nobles.

"Yes, but if it wasn't for him, I wouldn't have rescued you." Kenz nudged him playfully.

"Is that how you two met? In a dungeon?" Jaida asked, smiling.

"Yep. He was helpless and filthy, I might add," Kenz said.

"I was not helpless," Jasce muttered. "Don't you need to go to work?" He directed his stare at Kenz, who laughed along with Flynt. She kissed his cheek as the two pushed away from the table.

"Sounds like quite the story," Jaida said.

"It's good to have you back, Commander," Aura said as she and Delmira excused themselves, also having recruits to train.

Alyssa wiped her mouth with the back of her hand. "The queen wants you to join her tonight for dinner."

He rubbed his temples. "Why?"

"You'll have to ask her. Your old rooms are available, and I'll make sure Jaida is set up next door." She picked up her sword and addressed Jaida. "If you need anything while you're here and big brother isn't accommodating, let me know."

"Thanks." Jaida watched the general stride across the dining hall. "I like her."

"Me too."

He finished his coffee and glanced around the room. He nodded to a few soldiers, but most kept their distance. It wasn't fear he saw in their eyes, more like confusion, as if they weren't sure what to do. He could relate.

"So now what?" Jaida asked.

"I honestly have no idea. I've never been just a civilian."

"Hmm. How about a tour of Orilyon? I'd love to see where 'big brother' likes to go."

He smiled. "Sounds like a plan."

"But no vaulting. I don't want to puke all over you."

"Horse it is." He laughed and led his sister out of the dining hall toward the stables.

They visited the various markets of Orilyon. He showed Jaida the bakery where Tillie had worked and the tavern he had frequented as a

Conquering the Darkness

Hunter. They spent most of their time near the docks, shopping at the vendor booths along the Navalia Boardwalk. The air grew chilly with the breeze drifting off the ocean, and he was about to suggest they return to the palace when he overheard some sailors talking.

"No luck today, either," one man said, spitting onto the docks. "It's like the fish have all gone somewhere else."

"Well, the waves are rougher than normal," the other sailor said. "Did you hear about the flooding near Wilholm?"

A flock of birds drew his attention, the noise of their squawking almost deafening.

Jaida shielded her eyes from the sun. "That seems odd, doesn't it?"

"Very odd."

More people on the docks stopped what they were doing to observe the birds flying north along the beach.

"Do you think it has something to do with the Stones?" Jaida asked, keeping her voice low as her gaze shifted between the sailors and vendors.

"Nicolaus said the magic imbalance could affect the weather, and animals can sense anomalies before we do." Flooding, dust storms, ice, plus the unusual fog and strangely colored sky he'd seen in Delmar. What was Drexus doing with those Stones? And people missing from towns suggested he was recruiting, but where could he be hiding?

Jasce led his sister off the boardwalk toward the palace. The sun sank lower on the horizon, and he needed to clean up before he had the privilege of dining with the queen. He pinched the bridge of his nose. He'd been in Orilyon for less than twenty-four hours and she was already ordering him around.

"Thanks for today," Jaida said, as they entered the Bastion. "I'm going to visit the Sanctuary. Have fun at your dinner." She winked and strolled down the hall, disappearing around the corner.

He quickly changed and tied back his hair. Holding his dagger, he contemplated whether to bring the weapon. *I'm just a civilian*, he thought, and exited the room, his body feeling uncomfortably light without the familiar weight of his dagger on his thigh.

When he arrived, Lady Wuhl and Lord Gallet were seated at the large table. They spoke in hushed whispers and immediately stopped when he entered the room. Lord Rollant and Lady Darbry, both holding a glass of wine, talked with Kord in the corner.

Queen Valeri emerged from a discrete door on the other side of the room, followed by Alyssa. The crimson carpet lining the expansive space muffled their steps while chandeliers flickered.

Jasce's gaze landed on a scowling Lord Gallet. "At least the atmosphere is welcoming," he mumbled.

"Good, everyone's here," the queen said, gathering her skirts and sitting at the head of the table. She signaled to the guards to shut the doors.

Jasce eyed the council members suspiciously as he walked to an open chair and caught Kord staring at him. The lines around his mouth deepened and his eye narrowed. That look meant Jasce was about to hear something he wouldn't like, and he immediately wondered if they had received news on Caston.

"Mr. Farone, thank you for joining us," the queen said as servants brought glasses of wine to the table. Jasce waved it off, asking for coffee. Queen Valeri arched a brow. Once everyone was served, she continued, "I called this meeting to address some concerns the council has regarding my decision."

Lord Gallet crossed his arms over his extended stomach and glared at him.

Lady Wuhl ran a finger around the rim of her wineglass. "Not every town is represented. Thorel got caught in an ice storm. Since he acts on behalf of both Havelock and Delmar, he should get a say."

"And what about Lady Sandel? Shouldn't the town of Rochdale express its opinion?" Lord Gallet asked.

Lord Rollant lifted his chin. "Rochdale and Hillsford report to me. And Thorel's territory, as well as Dunstead, has been accounted for."

"Why do you run three territories?" Lord Gallet's face turned red.

"Because I'm special." The muscle in Lord Rollant's jaw ticked as he held the ex-warden's stare.

Jasce frowned. What were they talking about? The smaller villages had representatives, but they didn't attend council sessions. And what did they have to do with him, anyway? This was why he hated meetings.

Conquering the Darkness

Nobles and their pettiness made his eye twitch. He lifted a finger. "Excuse me. But do I need to be here for this?"

Kord rubbed his forehead. The queen opened her mouth but snapped it shut at the sounds of stomping boots and yelling. Warning bells sounded just as the doors flew open. Queen Valeri shot to her feet.

"A group of Spectrals have infiltrated the palace," Darin said, rushing to her side. "We need to get you out of here."

Chapter Twenty-Eight

Jasce pushed back from the table. "It's Drexus. He's after the Inhibitor Stone." He inwardly cursed for leaving his weapons and armor in his room, and based on the noise in the corridor, there was no time to collect them.

Another set of bells rang, this time from the Bastion.

The queen gathered her skirts and marched past the council members. "All of you, get to the safe room."

Alyssa blocked her path. "You too."

"I'm not letting that bastard get the Stone. Besides, I'm the only one who can retrieve it."

A soldier ran in and whispered to Darin, whose jaw pulsed. "Your Majesty, guards spotted Vale in the corridor." Darin gave the queen a knowing look.

Queen Valeri's face paled. "The Stone isn't safe, not with his magic."

Kenz pushed past the guards with Captain Reed on her heels. "A group of Spectrals have broken into the Sanctuary. They're capturing Healers." Kenz looked at Jasce. "Caston is with them."

A lead ball dropped in his stomach. Jaida had gone to the Sanctuary. He needed to get there now to protect his sister and save Caston, but he also needed to secure the Stone. He breathed a sigh of relief when Nicolaus emerged from the shadows.

"How can I help?" the Shade Walker asked, his bow already slung across his chest.

"General Nadja, Nicolaus, Darin, and Kenz, guard the queen. Kord, go with the council members. Reed, you're with me," Jasce ordered.

"No. I'm going to the Sanctuary," Kord said, retrieving his sword.

"If they're after Healers, I don't want you near that place."

"I agree with Mr. Farone." Kord opened his mouth to protest, but Queen Valeri held up her hand. "That's an order, Mr. Haring."

Kenz took hold of her brother's hand and squeezed.

"Be careful," he said, and then peered at the remaining group. "All of you."

"You too." Kenz rushed over to Jasce and kissed him, giving him one last look before she followed Darin, Queen Valeri, and Nicolaus from the room. Soldiers filed in behind them while Kord and the rest of the council evacuated through the side exit.

Jasce grabbed Alyssa's hand. "Protect my fiancée, please."

Alyssa saluted and sprinted after the queen.

Reed strode toward the hallway, but Jasce stopped him. "We're vaulting to the Sanctuary. Hold on."

Reed's eyes widened. "Wait, I can just run."

"No time." Jasce reached deep into his magic, felt the tug at his chest, and darkness swallowed them. In less than a heartbeat, they appeared, surrounded by chaos. Members of the medical staff lay dead on the floor, and smoke billowed from the back room. Jaida fought alongside Delmira, who used her yellow shield to protect a group of Healers. Aura battled three soldiers, wielding her air shield to block their swords while drawing the breath from their lungs.

"Watch out!" Maera yelled.

Jasce and Reed ducked. Heat sizzled over their heads as a blue fireball blazed past. The Fire Spectral who threw it sneered and disappeared into the shadows.

"Did you see that?" Reed asked.

"Yes, I did." How many types of magic did Drexus's soldiers possess? And how did he get more Shade Walker magic?

Conquering the Darkness

The Fire Spectral reappeared on the outskirts of the fray next to Caston.

"No," Jasce whispered.

Black lines swirled up Caston's neck and his brown eyes were as black as pitch. A strange collar wrapped around his neck, different than the one Queen Siryn had invented. Caston's jaw ticked when he saw Jasce.

"He's like Vale now, isn't he?" Reed asked.

Jasce wanted to scream in rage at what Drexus had done to his friend.

A second man stood next to Caston. His silver shield split in two, protecting them and another soldier, whose sword pointed at two Healers, their arms bound. The other half of the shield blocked the main door, keeping members of the Paladin Guard out.

The Fire Spectral held a blade to Caston's throat. "Drexus said you'd come. Stand down or your friend dies." The muscles in Caston's neck corded and his eyes shifted to brown. Caston snapped his head back, connecting with the Fire's nose. Blood dripped down his lips and his face twisted with fury. Caston lunged away from the Spectral, who removed a familiar-looking device from his pocket and pressed a button. Caston's back arched and he fell to his knees, gripping the collar at his throat. The Fire smashed the hilt of his dagger against Caston's temple.

Jasce stepped forward as his friend crumpled to the ground. Reed yanked him to the side as a blade of ice flashed past him, nicking his cheek. A Water Spectral laughed and resumed her attack on Delmira and Jaida. Two other soldiers joined her.

Maera ran in a crouch toward Jasce, tendrils of blonde hair falling loose at her shoulders and a smear of blood lined her cheek. "I need to get to my office. I have something that can stop them."

Fire and debris blocked the door. He held Maera's arm. "Reed, help Jaida and Delmira and get those Healers out of here."

Maera stumbled and her hazel eyes widened as they vaulted from the main room to her office. "Your magic's returned?"

"Jaida's too, as well as Drexus's. It seems your procedure needs some work."

She mumbled under her breath and rushed toward a locked chest.

"Get the crossbow." She pointed to a cabinet across the room while opening the chest and shoving glass vials of green liquid into a satchel.

Jasce jogged to the corner of the office and retrieved the weapon. "What's your plan?"

She held a vial in her palm. The glass tube was notched at one end to fit the bowstring while the tip of a needle protruded from the other. "Long story, but this should nullify their magic, and hopefully help Caston."

Anger and sadness swirled inside him at what Drexus had done to Caston. "I'll get him back. I promise."

Grief pinched the corner of her eyes. She and Caston had grown close during the Gathering and seeing him like this must have been heartbreaking for her as well. He swung the satchel over his shoulder and placed the vial against the string of the crossbow. "Hold on."

Maera gripped his waist, squeezed her eyes shut, and within seconds they materialized into the main room of the Sanctuary. Blue fire blazed throughout the building and the sound of crashing swords was deafening. A few soldiers from the Paladin Guard had slipped through a side entrance, which was now blocked by a solid wall of ice.

"How did that get there?" Maera asked.

"Looks like Drexus has been busy," Jasce said. The maniac had given a Fire Spectral Shade Walking magic and combined Water and Air magic—the result was a soldier who created weapons of ice. These new Spectrals were more powerful than he could fathom.

The Water Spectral twirled her hands, forming frozen daggers, and thrust her arms forward. Aura barely raised her air shield in time to block the lethal projectiles.

He aimed and released the vial. The Water flicked her wrist and more blades of ice flew before the woman jerked, her eyes wide as the needle stabbed into her neck. Her mouth twisted in rage, and she raised her hands. Confusion flitted across her face before a floating cabinet struck her in the head. Jaida lowered her arms.

"Jasce," Aura said. Her hands, covered in blood, gripped a melting dagger lodged in her chest.

He vaulted to her, catching her before her legs gave out. "Aura, hold on." The ice melted in his hands and blood oozed through his fingers as he frantically searched for a Healer.

Jaida and Reed fought against an Amp while the Fire hurled fireballs at Delmira's shield. Blood dripped from her nose and her arms shook. Maera dropped to her knees next to Aura and pressed against the wound where the blade of ice had been. Blood pooled on the ground.

Delmira's shield sputtered under the intense fire.

Jasce released Aura and dug through the satchel for another vial-tipped arrow. He lifted the crossbow, let out a breath, and released the bolt. The Fire Spectral spun around, his fire snuffed out, but he still managed to disappear into the shadows.

"Dammit," Jasce said. The delay in the suppression of magic had given the Spectral time to Shade Walk.

Delmira nodded her thanks. Her eyes widened when she noticed Aura on the floor. She looked behind her to the Healers in the back room. Yelling something at them, she lowered her shield. One Healer, a young man, opened the door and ran after her.

"Jasce," Aura whispered, blood dripping from the corner of her lip into her white hair. She coughed and cried out. Her hand tightened around his.

"Shhh," Maera said, trying to mop up the blood seeping through her tunic. "Help is coming."

Aura shook her head.

"Aura, no!" Delmira dropped, her knees splashing in a puddle of blood and water, while she encircled Aura, Maera, and the Healer with her shield. The yellow light, paler than normal, flickered. Jasce stood and stationed himself in front of the group, his bow loaded with another vial.

The Healer pressed his hands to Aura's chest. "Come on," he said, his jaw clenched.

Maera touched her fingers to the Air Spectral's neck as tears dripped down her cheeks.

Aura's eyes stared blankly at the ceiling.

Jasce bit back a curse and scanned the room. Caston struggled to his feet, his teeth bared as he held his head. The Shield continued blocking the door while the other soldier had forced the two captured Healers to their knees.

The ice wall obstructing the side entrance shattered as Kord smashed his way through. His face contorted from sadness to rage as he took in the scene of destruction, blood, and bodies.

"Jasce!" Jaida pointed behind him.

The Amp sprinted for him and he tried to dodge, but she was too fast. She shoved him, and glass shattered as his body careened through a window. He crashed into an exam table and fell to the floor. His back and leg burned with pain and blood dripped from the lacerations on his arms. He yanked a shard of glass from his shoulder.

Kord ran to him and helped him to his feet.

"What are you doing here?" Jasce asked, unable to mask the anger in his voice.

"These are my people, my staff. I refuse to hide in the safe room while they fight." Kord's eye narrowed, and a muscle ticked in his jaw.

Movement flickered in the corner of Jasce's vision.

Vale, blood staining his tunic and pants, materialized in the middle of the room. His black eyes examined the scene and found the Healer next to Aura. Disappearing into the shadows, he reappeared, backhanded Delmira, and vanished with the young man.

He resurfaced behind the Spectral with the silver shield and seized the other two Healers.

"He's picking them off one by one," Kord said.

Jasce limped out of the exam room. With Vale showing up, he needed his magic at full strength. Unwrapping the sliver they'd removed from Jaida, he tucked it into the side of his mouth. The magic from the Empower Stone coursed through him, igniting his power.

"What are you doing?" Kord asked.

"I need both hands. And I need you to leave, now." He searched for the crossbow he dropped when the Amp had launched him across the room.

Kord was about to argue when a scream sounded. The Amp stalked toward the door Delmira had guarded and ripped it off its hinges. Jasce didn't have time to retrieve his weapon. He vaulted while reaching into his satchel and tackled her to the ground.

She elbowed him in the jaw, causing the sliver to fly out of his mouth while stars exploded in his vision.

Shoving him off, she stood. "I'm going to rip you in two."

"I don't think so." Jasce pointed to the vial lodged in her side.

The Amp yanked it out and lunged toward him. He swept his leg and knocked her feet out from underneath her before he pounced on top of her, wrapped his hands around her neck, and twisted. She fell limply to the floor.

He winced as he struggled to his feet. Kord shot past him to check on his Healers. Jaida's hair swirled as she lifted her hands, bombarding the silver barrier protecting the Shield and blocking the door. The shield flickered as more and more objects flew across the room.

"Jaida!" Jasce threw one of the vial-tipped arrows halfway between her and the Shield. She flicked her wrist and changed the trajectory of the vial. Normally, any weapon bounced off, but the vial smashed against the silver barrier. The Shield's eyes widened when his protective wall disintegrated. Jaida lifted the Spectral into the air and threw him into the wall, where he slumped to the ground.

Pandaren soldiers stormed into the room as Vale reappeared. He tilted his head and the earth shook. Jasce stumbled and gripped an overturned table to maintain his balance. Chunks of ceiling near the door collapsed, crushing the guards who had finally broken through. Screams sounded from the men and women under the wreckage.

Jasce picked up a fallen sword and stalked toward Vale. If he could distract him, he might have a chance to vault Caston to safety.

Black lines swirled over Vale's body as his eyes drifted from Caston to where Kord was running to help the crushed soldiers. His lips curled as he disappeared.

Jasce didn't have a second to decide. Vale could not get his hands on Kord. There'd be no stopping Drexus with his experiments if he did. He focused on Kord and vaulted.

"Oof." Kord raised his fist.

Jasce pushed him away, ready to stab Vale with the last vial.

Vale lurched back and sneered. "Too bad about your Shield." He trailed a finger through the blood spattered on his clothing. A glowing sword emerged from thin air while the ground continued to shake.

Bile surged up Jasce's throat. *No*, he thought. That couldn't be Kenz's blood.

"We have three Stones. When Drexus chose me over you, he obviously picked the better warrior." Vale's voice sounded like many as he inched closer to Caston, who struggled to his knees. He angled the glowing sword at Caston but yelled when his wrist twisted and cracked. The weapon clattered to the floor and disappeared.

Jaida walked toward him with her arms lifted. "Vale, stop this. Please."

Vale grimaced as she lifted him off his feet. He used his other hand and flicked a magical dagger at her. She stopped it midair, but with her focus on the blade, Vale dropped to the ground.

He staggered toward Caston and held a knife to his throat. "I'll kill him if you come any closer."

Maera shuffled from under the table and ran toward him, but Caston grimaced as the blade dug into his neck, forcing her to stop. She covered her mouth and shook her head. "Caston."

"Fight it," Jasce said to Caston. He tapped into his magic. Could he vault Caston away without Vale slicing his neck open?

Caston slowly turned toward Maera. His eyes shifted and the lines stilled. "I'm so sorry."

Vale glared at Jasce. "You will lose."

Jasce lunged forward, his hand grabbing thin air as Vale and Caston disappeared.

Chapter Twenty-Nine

Jasce lowered his hand and attempted to rein in his fear. The fresh blood on Vale's tunic, plus the words he'd said, twisted his insides into knots. He needed to find Kenz. Now.

He yanked Kord by the collar. "Do you know where the queen hid the Stone?"

Kord's eye darted over the carnage in the Sanctuary. Tables overthrown, shelves toppled with tonics and salves dripping onto the cracked floor. Scorch marks from the fire marred the walls and broken glass surrounded the dead. Reed held his head and struggled to his feet while Jaida used her magic to lift the section of ceiling off the guards so Maera could check on them.

Jasce gave Kord a shake. "Do you know?"

Kord removed Jasce's hand from his tunic. "No, but I have an idea where to look."

"You've done enough. If you'd just stayed in the safe room, I could've rescued Caston instead of having to protect you from Vale."

"You would have done the same."

"I don't have time to argue. Kenz may be hurt. Now where is the bloody Stone?"

"Follow me." Kord's back was rigid as he left the Sanctuary.

Jasce ran past Jaida. "Help Maera and Reed. I'll be back."

Jaida nodded. She'd used her magic well and fought bravely, even against Vale, which must have torn her already broken heart over what Drexus had done to the Earth Spectral. And Caston. Jasce clenched his teeth. Drexus had put more than one type of magic in his friend, evident by the black swirling lines and the emptiness of his eyes. But where Vale had embraced the new power, Caston seemed able to fight it, but how long could he resist the magic's lure?

Jasce scowled at Kord's back as they ran through the halls, his anger with the Healer tangible. Kord led him down the main corridor, swerving around soldiers helping the wounded, and past the grand staircase. They skidded to a stop near two bodies. One was a soldier Jasce recognized, a sixth-year if he remembered correctly, her neck twisted at an unnatural angle.

He turned the other one over and stared into the face of Indago, a Tracker he'd brought in for the Gathering. Blood covered his robe and eyes that were normally white had turned blue. Jasce felt for a pulse even though he already knew the man was dead.

Kord shut the blank eyes of the recruit and stood. "I believe it's down here." A toppled vase lay next to a tapestry with scorch marks.

They yanked the tapestry from the wall, where a small door to a secret passageway had been forced open. Torches lit the cobweb-infested corridor, and voices echoed off the damp stone walls. Jasce picked up his pace, trying hard to breathe past the ache in his chest. Visions of Kenz's broken body lying in the blood-soaked sand flashed through his mind, causing him to stumble. He didn't think he could go through that again.

They finally rounded a corner emptying into a small room. Someone had blasted apart the wooden door and an empty chest lay on the ground. He slowed as his eyes found Kenz, then rested a hand against the wall to keep from collapsing to his knees.

She limped toward him, holding her side. Blood ran down her hip and leg, and her face was the color of parchment, making her freckles stand out.

He gathered her in his arms and nuzzled his face in the crook of her neck. "I feared the worst."

Conquering the Darkness

"I'm okay." She pulled back from him. Sadness etched through her eyes. She looked over her shoulder and Jasce's stomach clenched.

Kord, who had been standing next to his sister, saw where Jasce stared.

"Oh no," Kord whispered, and ran toward the queen.

Queen Valeri lay on the ground, her eyes vacantly staring at the ceiling. Next to her lay her crown, the metal twisted and broken. Alyssa knelt near her, shaking her head and biting her knuckles.

Jasce squeezed Kenz's hand and approached Nicolaus. "What happened?" he asked, watching Kord run his hand over the queen.

Nicolaus pressed against a gash on his arm. "Vale had a Psyche and he . . . well, I'm not sure what he did, but I think he killed the queen from the inside out."

Kord sat back on his heels and shook his head.

Jasce swore and took in the damaged room. Slumped against the wall were two of Drexus's soldiers, both with arrows piercing their chests. The box that had contained the Inhibitor Stone lay open amid a stream of blood coming from a body facing the wall. He knelt next to the man and turned him over. Darin's empty eyes stared back.

Kenz wrapped her arms around herself. "I'm so sorry. I should have protected them both."

Nicolaus spun, his silver eyes piercing like diamonds. "This wasn't your fault. The blame lies with Drexus and that abomination."

Alyssa, face covered in blood from a wound on her forehead, gently closed the queen's eyes and struggled to her feet. She grimaced and pressed a hand against a gash across her leg.

"General." Kord stood and touched her, healing her wounds. The physical pain etched across her face lessened, but the emotional turmoil remained locked in her troubled eyes. Kord turned his attention to his sister.

Nicolaus stared at Jasce. "You need to have an emergency meeting with the council."

Jasce rose to his feet, trying to ignore the crimson warmth soaking into the leather on his knee. He pointed at Alyssa. "General Nadja is—"

"We need someone with more experience, especially against Drexus." Nicolaus winced at Alyssa. "Sorry."

She lifted her hand as if to wave him off. "It's fine. Besides, with the queen dead . . ." Her sentence trailed off as she pressed her lips together, blinking back tears.

Nicolaus was right. They didn't have time to mourn. They needed a plan.

"Nicolaus, bring the council members to the command room in the Bastion. Kord, check on Maera, Jaida, and Reed, and then join us. Alyssa, I need the Paladin Guard at their battle stations. If I know Drexus, this isn't over."

～

An eerie silence filled the room as the council learned their queen was dead. Tears slid down Lady Darbry's cheeks while Lord Rollant wrapped an arm around Lady Wuhl. Lord Gallet stared at his intertwined fingers, the corner of his lips turned downward.

Jasce's eyes flicked to the table near the hearth where bottles of alcohol glowed from the fire. The need for a drink made his hands shake. He clenched his teeth and focused on the flickering flames engulfing the wood and sending sparks into the air. Besides the queen, he'd lost Aura and Darin, and six Healers had been taken, along with the Inhibitor Stone. Plus, he'd failed to rescue Caston.

He paced along the wall with the map of Pandaren behind him. *What would Amycus do?* he thought as he walked past the table. Kord spoke quietly with Lord Rollant and Alyssa, while Kenz and Captain Reed leaned against the wall.

"How did they know where the Stone was?" Lord Rollant asked. Sadness etched along the corners of his eyes. Of all the council members, he seemed to have the closest relationship with the queen.

"And how did they get in?" Captain Reed asked, dabbing a rag to the cut on his head.

Jasce glanced at Nicolaus, who nodded in agreement. They must have both been thinking the same thing. "Best guess—Vale's been lurking in the shadows. The attack on the Sanctuary was a distraction, though they need Healers for what Drexus is doing."

Nicolaus leaned forward and interlaced his fingers. "I believe Vale used Shade Walking magic to bring his Spectrals into the Bastion and palace and then simply waited for the queen to retrieve the Stone." His eyes turned hard as anger marred his normally jovial face. "We walked right into their trap."

"I didn't realize Shade Walkers could transport that many people at once," Lord Gallet said, his brow furrowed.

"With the Empower Stone, he can. Even a sliver of it would give him the strength," Jasce said. "Do we know where Vale went?"

"Unclear, sir," Alyssa said, her back straight and eyes forward.

"Send word to our outposts and garrisons. I want the Paladin Guard ready—"

"I'm sorry," Lord Gallet interjected. "But who put you in charge?"

Jasce pinched the bridge of his nose. They didn't have time for politics.

Lord Rollant stood and cleared his throat. "Queen Valeri put Mr. Farone in charge."

Jasce spun to face the man. He couldn't have heard Lord Rollant correctly.

Lord Gallet shook his head. "The entire council did not agree to this."

"He has more than proved himself loyal to Pandaren and the queen," Kenz said, her cheeks warmed by the anger in her tone.

Lord Gallet narrowed his gaze. "I wonder if you'd be so swayed if he wasn't warming your bed every night."

Within seconds, Jasce yanked the man from his chair. "Mind what you say."

"Mr. Farone, stop," Lady Wuhl said.

"See! This is what I mean. He's not fit to rule," Lord Gallet said, his watery eyes bulging.

Jasce's grip loosened. Fit to rule?

Kord crossed his arms. "Lord Gallet, that's my sister. I'd rethink how you address her."

The ex-warden swallowed. His gaze darted between Jasce and Kord, then he gave a shallow nod.

Jasce released him and wiped his mouth. He glanced around the table at the wide-eyed stares from the council members. Kenz's eyes sparked as she glared at Lord Gallet.

Lord Rollant retrieved a scroll from his inside pocket. "As you're aware, the queen assigned Kord Haring as the Spectral Liaison and me as her head advisor. Before the events of the Gathering, she had named Commander Farone as the King Regent of Pandaren in the event anything happened to her, until the governing body voted on her replacement." Lord Rollant's eyes softened when he looked at Jasce. "Why do you think she was so hard on you? She was preparing you to lead, to put Pandaren before everything and"—his gaze flicked to Kenz—"everyone."

King Regent?

His blood rushed in his ears as he gaped at Lord Rollant. The queen had loathed him during the best of times, and he actually agreed with the slimy ex-warden. He wasn't fit to rule, barely able to handle the demons of his own life. Sure, he could command armies, but a kingdom?

He rested his hands on his hips and focused on the stone floor. The room had fallen silent as everyone stared at him. So this is what the council members were discussing at dinner before all hell had broken loose. Now he understood what Lady Darbry had meant when she'd asked the queen if he was ready.

He sighed, lifted his head, and faced Kord. Even though he was still furious with him, the tension in his body lessened when Kord nodded as if to say, *You can do this.*

Jasce surveyed the room until he found Kenz. She pushed off from the wall and laced her fingers with his, giving them an encouraging squeeze.

"I won't do this without you."

Kenz inhaled a quavering breath. "I'll be here every step of the way."

His heart rate settled. She was his anchor in this storm, the light leading him down the correct path. He'd never consider ruling Pandaren without her by his side.

Swallowing, he faced Lord Rollant and said, "Now what?"

"Before we go any further, this formality must take place." Lord Rollant motioned to Kord, who crossed the space to stand next to him.

Conquering the Darkness

Jasce's spine stiffened as Lord Gallet opened his mouth, but Nicolaus intervened. "Surely you aren't challenging your queen's orders. I believe that's considered treason."

The man snapped his mouth shut as his eyes darted to the other council members. He sagged in his chair and indicated for Lord Rollant to continue.

"On behalf of Pandaren's Council, Spectral Liaison, and myself, I promote you, Jasce Farone, to King Regent of Pandaren. Do you solemnly swear to protect your kingdom and your people with your life?"

He straightened to his full height. "I swear."

Chapter Thirty

The room broke out into a smattering of applause, some more enthusiastic than others. A knock on the door had everyone turning. Alyssa opened it and let Jaida, Flynt, and Maera inside.

Jaida tilted her head as she glanced at the standing council members. "What did we miss?"

"Your brother has been named King Regent," Lord Rollant said, returning the scroll to his pocket.

Jaida's mouth dropped open and Maera's brows lifted. Flynt's shoulders sagged. "We don't have to bow, do we?"

Jasce chuckled. "You, maybe. Everyone else, no."

Lord Rollant approached him and Kenz. "We'll have a proper ceremony when this is over."

"I don't need a ceremony. But we will have one for Queen Valeri, Aura, Darin, and the other soldiers and Spectrals we lost today."

Nicolaus, who'd been surprisingly quiet, stepped forward. "I'd suggest we keep Queen Valeri's death a secret, for now. People are nervous enough without having lost their beloved queen."

"Agreed," Jasce said. "No one knows of her death except those in this room. If anyone lets this leak, you will answer to me. And if that doesn't secure your tongue, you'll answer to my fiancée."

Kenz snorted and crossed the room to talk with Reed, Flynt, and Jaida.

Maera approached and gave a slight bow with her head. "Congratulations, I think."

Jasce pinched the bridge of his nose. He needed to strategize their next move, not receive accolades for a position he didn't want. But for now, he would do what was necessary to protect those he loved from Drexus, and if that meant assuming the role of King Regent, then so be it.

He walked to the table and sat, surprised when everyone else followed suit. "My first order of business is to promote General Nadja to Commander."

Alyssa's eyes widened for a split second, then she pulled back her shoulders. "Sir, I won't let you down."

"You never have. Find out where Vale went, and make sure the Guard is ready."

She saluted and marched out of the room.

"So, now what?" Lady Darbry asked.

"We must attack. Drexus cannot get away with this." Lady Wuhl slammed her fist into her other hand.

"He won't, not if I have anything to say about it," Jasce said. "Nicolaus, does your knowledge of the Creator Stone give us any kind of timeline before Drexus will have his army?"

"Based on my information, the Creator Stone, once drained of magic, can only recharge by the light of the moon. Obviously, the fuller the moon, the quicker it can restore its power."

"And how many people can use the Stone before it's drained?" Kenz asked. She'd taken the seat next to Jasce and rested her hand on his knee, stilling his bouncing leg.

Nicolaus pondered the ceiling. "Considering what I witnessed when Jasce used the Stone, five people, at the most ten. That's just a guess, though."

"Are you saying Jasce has his magic back?" Lord Gallet asked.

"It's King Regent," Lord Rollant said, giving the man an admonishing look.

Lord Gallet's face reddened. "King Regent," he choked out, "is your magic back?"

Jasce tapped a finger on the table and held the man's stare. He needed to come up with a better title, since being called King Regent would get very old, very soon. "Yes."

Lady Wuhl glanced at Maera. "I thought you removed his magic."

"I did," Maera said.

Jasce tried not to bristle at the council's reaction to having his magic returned. They seemed to forget he was still a lethal warrior, with or without magic. "I used the Creator Stone. However, Jaida's and Drexus's magic have also returned, which means the procedure the Vastanes and Maera performed wasn't perfect." He shot a look at Maera. "No offense."

"Some taken," she mumbled.

"The primary concern," Lord Rollant interjected, "is that Drexus has his magic and, I assume, is using the Empower Stone to make himself more powerful."

Jasce nodded. "Drexus has also put more than one type of magic into his Spectrals, including Caston, which is why they needed Healers."

"What do you think is Drexus's next move?" Lady Darbry asked.

"He'll create his army while trying to locate the Abolish Stone."

Captain Reed pushed off the wall. "If he gets all four, he controls all the magic, isn't that right?"

"And becomes invincible," Flynt muttered from the corner of the room.

"Then we can't let him get that Stone," Lord Rollant said.

Nicolaus lifted a finger. "If I may, Kraig Carnelian was last seen leaving Terrenus, and I assume he's coming here. King Morzov is also preparing his army and will wait near the Arcane Garrison until further instruction."

"And how do you know that?" Lord Gallet asked.

The Shade Walker shook his head. "I simply don't understand why people keep asking me that."

"I thought you hadn't heard from your spies," Lord Rollant said, his eyes narrowed.

"I have a few in Paxton," was all Nicolaus said. Jasce figured he'd have a chat soon with the Alturian about the number of Shade Walkers in his kingdom.

His kingdom.

The idea, the responsibility, made his chest tighten. He had to focus on breathing to slow his heart rate.

He stared at the map while the council members debated options. The Paladin Guard would be no match for Drexus's army if his Spectrals had more than one type of magic. And now that he had three of the Stones? Who knew the repercussions? He needed to meet with Archduke Carnelian. The Gemari had more knowledge about the Heart of Pandaren than anyone else, if he could trust Amycus's journal.

"Captain Reed, how many Spectrals do we have in the Guard?" Jasce asked.

"Not enough. And the Naturals won't stand a chance against Drexus's magical army," he said.

"Then we need to even the playing field." He addressed Maera. "How many of those vials do you have?"

"Around thirty," she said, getting to her feet.

"Can you make more?" Jasce asked.

"Yes, but without the Inhibitor Stone I'll have to use Brymagus, which will take time. Thankfully, the room where we are growing the plant was untouched."

Nicolaus raised his finger again, and Jasce had the strong desire to cut it off. "Would you two like to fill the rest of us in?"

Jasce gestured to Maera, who explained the weapon she'd created using the Inhibitor Stone while he strategized their next move. He had a decision to make. Go after Caston or retrieve the Abolish Stone. The Stone might be the only way to defeat Drexus, but the thought of abandoning his friend made his gut clench, the knot growing bigger with every sacrifice he had to make.

Further plans were discussed, with each lord and lady agreeing to return to their lands after the memorial service to recruit all able-bodied Spectrals and soldiers, and to warn against joining Drexus's army. Traitors would be shown zero leniency. At one point, Jasce reached under the table for Kenz's hand. The task ahead of them seemed insurmount-

Conquering the Darkness

able, and what Drexus had done to Caston weighed on his soul. What if Caston couldn't be saved?

He shook his head. He wouldn't think like that. Everyone was, once again, looking to him to lead. All he had was his training as a Hunter, his team, and the woman sitting next to him. He hoped it would be enough.

Jasce returned to the Sanctuary after the meeting and knelt next to Aura's body. Delmira sat in a chair nearby, holding her head, giving him some privacy to say goodbye. The medical staff and remaining Healers buzzed around the demolished facility, putting things back in order. Kord and Maera worked tirelessly by their side, and even Jaida stepped in as if she'd always belonged.

Aura had been a powerful Air, but an even more loyal soldier and friend. She had been part of his inner team, and her death would be felt by the entire Guard. "Rest easy now, friend."

He stood and walked over to Delmira. She lifted her head, blood matting her short white hair and dried tear tracks lining her face. A bruise darkened her cheek and jaw.

"When you're ready, I'm going to need you." Jasce squeezed her hand before leaving the Sanctuary. How many more friends would he lose in this war against Drexus? How many more loyal soldiers would die at the hands of those in league with tyranny?

∽

Silver banners hung from the walls in the Bastion, and flags flew from the turrets. The Paladin Guard surrounded pyres ascending from the middle of the grassy field like ominous grave markers. Jasce, comforted by the familiar weight of his armor, stood at the base of the pyres, with Kenz on one side and Lord Rollant on the other. Commander Alyssa Nadja guarded the remaining council members. Jasce and Alyssa had spread a rumor that the queen had been called away to a diplomatic mission to the Far Lands and therefore couldn't attend the funerals. The council had agreed that no one could know about her death or who the new King Regent was until they defeated Drexus.

With the loss of Caston, Lord Rollant reinstated Jasce as

Commander to keep up the ruse. He'd already given his speech, highlighting the bravery and dedication of Aura, Darin, and the other soldiers they had lost. He'd never spoken at a funeral, and the longing for a drink to settle his nerves set his teeth on edge. Knowing this was his knee-jerk response, his weakness, made him want to lash out in a rage. His uncle was correct about needing to find a healthier coping device.

He glanced behind him and spotted Kord with his arm wrapped around Delmira. Jaida, Maera, and Nicolaus stood next to them while Flynt and two other Fire Spectrals took their spots near the pyres.

He signaled to the Fire Spectrals, who ignited their different-colored fires. The whoosh of the flames was soon accompanied by the crackle of wood as the pyres, along with the bodies, burned.

As was tradition, soldiers knelt by the pyres to leave a tribute, and then returned to the Bastion.

Jasce clenched his fists and focused on the smoke merging with the clouds. The image of Amycus wrapped in white linen, flames snaking up the wood, and smoke darkening the blue sky pierced through his heart. He hadn't remembered the man during the funeral, but he recalled every detail of that day. The death of his friend and mentor seeped like an infected wound that wouldn't heal. And now he had to watch more lives—friends, members of the Guard, people he'd fought side by side with—turn to ash.

A shape emerged through the darkened sky. Squinting into the distance, he noticed the strange shadow heading their way, and there was more than one.

He nudged Kenz. "Do you see that?"

She looked to where he pointed. "What is it?"

"Not sure." His soldiers were easy targets in the open field, and if someone wanted to attack, this would be the perfect time. Not wanting to cause a panic, he whispered to Lord Rollant, who jerked his head and gazed into the sky. Soon, Alyssa was escorting the council members toward the Bastion.

The shapes grew closer, still obscured by the clouds and smoke, and clearing the field was taking too long. He needed his Guard inside the safety of the compound.

Conquering the Darkness

He grabbed Kenz's arm. "You and Delmira gather the Shields and have them ready."

Delmira stepped away from Kord and wiped her eyes. "What's going on?"

"We may have uninvited visitors," Jasce said, signaling toward the sky.

Kenz focused on the clouds, her eyes widening. Without a word, she and Delmira walked among the Guard to find the other Shields.

Nicolaus appeared on Jasce's right. "Problem?"

"Possibly." He searched for Jaida and found her talking with two soldiers, both wearing Psyche insignias on their uniforms.

A murmur went through the lingering crowd as the smoke parted on an unnatural breeze. A black wyvern broke through the clouds and headed straight for the field. The horns on its head glimmered from the watery light, and its scales shimmered with each beat of its massive wings.

Relief, with a hint of trepidation, flowed through Jasce. It seemed the archduke of Terrenus, Kraig Carnelian, received the message from the Balten prince regarding the Creator Stone. He had made good time flying across the Culmen Range, Paxton, and the Desert of Souls.

And by the scowl on the Gemari's bearded face, he was not happy.

Jasce ordered the remaining guard to stand down. "Be ready," he whispered to Nicolaus and Kord. Alyssa jogged back onto the field with her sword drawn. The ground shook and the stone walls reverberated with the roars of the winged beasts as the archduke's wyvern landed near the entrance to the Bastion. Four more wyverns with their riders followed suit.

"He looks really put out," Kenz said, her bracelets glowing blue.

Jasce sighed. "Yes, he does."

Archduke Carnelian slid off his wyvern, wincing and rubbing his chest. He spoke to his soldiers before marching across the field to where Jasce waited. The Gemari glanced at the burning pyres and a flicker of sorrow filled his eyes. His long brown hair was windblown from his travels and his leather and steel pants had a layer of dirt on them. A dual-bladed ax peeked over his shoulder.

Jasce met him halfway. "Archduke Carnelian, you have a lot of nerve flying your wyverns into my compound."

The archduke's eyes narrowed. "Is it true Drexus has the Creator Stone?"

Nicolaus approached and dipped his head. "Your Grace."

Archduke Carnelian pointed his finger. "What are you still doing here?"

"Trying to protect the Stones," he said with his chin raised.

"And what an outstanding job you've done."

Nicolaus bristled but Jasce stepped between them. "Let's talk somewhere a little more private, shall we?"

The archduke opened his mouth to argue, but then glanced at the smoldering pyres and wide-eyed soldiers. He dipped his chin. "I need to speak with Lorella."

Jasce rubbed his face. Not only did he have to tell the archduke that Drexus possessed three of the four Stones, but also that Queen Valeri was dead. His first day as the leader of Pandaren was off to a fabulous start.

Chapter Thirty-One

The tension vibrating off the archduke's body had Jasce digging his nails into his palms as he led him, his general, Tobias de Sille, and Nicolaus down the narrow hallway toward the command room. Recruits, excited to see the wyverns, pressed against the stone walls when the four strode by.

"I do not envy your new role," Nicolaus whispered, and patted Jasce's back before taking a seat at the table.

"Makes two of us," Jasce mumbled as Archduke Carnelian strode for the corner of the room and poured himself a drink while Tobias stood guard near the door. The last time he'd seen Tobias, he had cut him down with his sword under the influence of Queen Siryn.

"General, it's good to see you," Jasce said.

"Not sure I share that sentiment." Tobias crossed his muscular arms. Wisps of black hair had escaped from where he'd tied it back. He wore his beard short, unlike the archduke, and his dark eyes narrowed slightly. The general carried no weapons since Gemaris created them out of thin air thanks to the gems in their chests, Tobias's glowing through the leather and steel latticework of his armor.

"I don't doubt that." Jasce glanced over his shoulder toward the archduke. He'd removed his cloak, revealing a solid leather chest piece, different from what the Gemaris normally wore. "How angry is he?"

Tobias huffed out a laugh. "Let's just say I've never heard such colorful language when he found out about the Stone."

"Super."

Kord and Lord Rollant entered, followed by Alyssa. Tobias smiled at her, and Jasce's brows rose when she blushed.

The archduke drained his glass, poured another, and offered one to Jasce. Saliva pooled in his mouth with the temptation to savor the soothing burn cascading down his throat.

He shook his head and chose the middle chair at the table. "Please, sit."

Archduke Carnelian shrugged, removed his ax from the scabbard on his back, and sat across from him, with Tobias taking the chair on his left. "Where's Lorella?" the archduke asked.

Jasce glanced at Lord Rollant, not sure who should take the lead in this awkward conversation. Thankfully, Lord Rollant spoke first.

"Your Grace, it is with a heavy heart I must inform you that Queen Valeri is dead."

Archduke Carnelian had lifted his glass to his mouth but stopped mid-drink. He spluttered and pounded his chest. "Excuse me?"

Jasce rested his arms on the table. "Vale and Drexus's Spectrals attacked, and in defending the Inhibitor Stone, the queen perished. We have spread the rumor that she is out of the country. There's no need to cause panic."

A vein throbbed in the middle of the archduke's forehead. "Are you telling me the leader of Pandaren is dead *and* Drexus has three of the Stones?"

Kord cleared his throat. "Part of that is true."

"I knew I shouldn't have left the Stones where they were," the archduke said, his voice mimicking the growl of his wyvern.

"Wait," Tobias said. "Which part is true?"

Lord Rollant leaned forward. "Queen Valeri had named Commander Farone as King Regent, before he . . ." He glanced at Jasce.

"Lost my mind?" he provided.

Lord Rollant winced. "Precisely. Because Jasce chose to go to Balten, she elected Mr. Haring as the Spectral Liaison and me as the crown's advisor until either Jasce returned or the threat of Drexus had been neutralized."

The archduke's brows disappeared into his shaggy brown hair. "Lorella chose Jasce as King Regent?"

"It's shocking, I know," Jasce said.

The Gemari tilted his head. "Not entirely."

"It's a bit shocking," Tobias said, smirking. Alyssa giggled behind her hand.

Jasce turned slowly toward his new commander. "I don't think I've ever heard that sound come out of you before." She threw him a dirty look. "Anyway, we think Drexus is going after the Abolish Stone next."

"Of course he is. With him having three Stones, magic is already affected. If he gets the fourth . . ." He shook his head.

"Do you know the Stone's location?" Nicolaus asked.

The archduke's granite-like eyes slid to the Alturian. "Yes. And no, I will not tell you. We had agreed you would protect the Creator Stone. What the hell happened?"

Jasce tapped his finger on the table. "What exactly is going on between you two?" The archduke seemed irate with Nicolaus for something that wasn't his fault.

"It's none of your concern," Archduke Carnelian said.

"As King Regent, I beg to differ."

"You can beg all you want. It makes no difference to me."

Nicolaus sighed and slid an uneasy glance at Jasce. "Kraig and my father have an understanding. An alliance, if you will. My job was to secure the Creator and the Inhibitor Stones."

Kord's eye narrowed as he stared at both men. "What sort of alliance?"

"You and King Jazari made a deal regarding the Stones? Was Queen Valeri aware of this arrangement?" Jasce slid a sidelong glance at Lord Rollant, who shook his head.

The archduke crossed his muscular arms. "The Alturians and Gemaris have detailed information about the Heart. Once Drexus disappeared with the Empower Stone, we felt it was no longer safe to leave the remaining pieces where they were."

"For the record, I did not agree to this plan," Nicolaus said.

"Yes, but you were aware of it. You've had ulterior motives this entire time," Jasce said.

Nicolaus's shoulders slumped. "Jasce, I wasn't going to take the Stones without first speaking with Queen Valeri. Or you, for that matter. Please believe me."

He glared at the Shade Walker. Why should he expect anything different from a spy?

"It doesn't matter since Drexus has the Stones," Archduke Carnelian said, crossing his arms.

Jasce pointed to the archduke. "You and I will have a very serious conversation when this is all over." The Gemari lifted his brows and the corner of his mouth curved.

"I don't mean to interrupt, but you said something about magic being affected. How?" Alyssa asked.

"Magic will respond erratically, though to what degree, I'm not sure. This is unprecedented." He shot a look at Nicolaus, whose eyes narrowed. "Nature will also be impacted."

"How?" Kord asked.

"Storms, earthquakes, the tides. I'm sure you've already seen some strange weather." The archduke addressed Jasce. "Your people will need to be warned."

Jasce's leg bobbed under the table while an unpleasant thought filtered through his mind. One he should have contemplated earlier, but with the death of the queen, being named King Regent, and the arrival of the archduke, he hadn't had the margin to process it. Drexus had somehow learned the Inhibitor Stone was no longer in the desert. How did he discover it was at the palace? Members of the old Watch Guard who had served under Drexus still resided at the Bastion. Or was there a spy, somewhere higher up, maybe even in the council? He glanced at Lord Rollant. The man wanted power but had also been loyal to the late queen. Surely, he hadn't orchestrated this. Jasce thought about the ex-warden, Lord Gallet. The weasel had tortured him for information about Drexus's transfusion of the Amplifier serum. The man certainly was ambitious, but was he brazen enough to commit treason?

One thing Jasce was sure of—he was tired of reacting. He needed to take the fight to Drexus before he created any more Spectrals. Time was still on their side since the Creator Stone required moonlight to recharge, and the last time he looked, the moon was a mere sliver of light dangling in the night sky.

A large hand pressed down on his leg. "You're shaking the entire table," Kord said.

He pushed out of his chair and paced.

"What's on your mind?" Archduke Carnelian asked.

"I want to find Drexus, take a small contingent of soldiers, and retrieve the Stones. It's time we took the fight to him."

"I must point out that fighting on the front lines is not the role of King Regent," Lord Rollant said.

"I'm more useful out there than sitting behind a table or, magic forbid, on a throne."

"I figured you'd say that."

Jasce pondered the map, wondering where Drexus might hide—somewhere safe, where he could protect himself while also creating his army. One of the garrisons would be the ideal spot, especially if there were soldiers loyal to him. Up north was the Ferox Garrison, but that didn't seem likely as it was too out of the way, as was the Eremus Garrison, which hopefully the Baltens would soon occupy. He would have heard if Drexus had attacked the Arcane, as it was now an orphanage. His eyes traveled across Opax, finally landing on the Desert Garrison where Edgefield Prison once stood. His team had burned a section of it to the ground, but the compound had been rebuilt. When he was a Hunter, the prison, which was now barracks, had held one hundred prisoners. Before the Gathering, the garrison was minimally staffed, but if Drexus had been recruiting these past few months, there was no telling how many soldiers were there now.

"Commander Nadja, have you received a report from the Desert Garrison?"

"No sir, I haven't."

"Hiding in plain sight," Jasce whispered.

"What did you say?" Kord turned to stare at him.

"I'm wondering if Drexus is hiding in plain sight at the Desert

Garrison." He rested his hands on the back of his chair and addressed the archduke. "Where is the Abolish Stone?"

"Safe," Archduke Carnelian answered, his eyes hard and unyielding, like the mountains he lived in.

Jasce sighed. "Very well. Your wyverns will get us to the compound quicker than horses. I assume you'll want to tag along."

"You assume correctly."

⁓

That evening, Jasce met with his team to discuss strategy for their next mission. Of course, Kenz and Kord were going, along with the archduke and Tobias. As there were only five wyverns, the team would be small. He decided having a Shade Walker would be convenient as well as a Fire Spectral. What he hadn't expected was to be cornered in the dining hall by both Jaida and Maera.

"I'm going with you," Jaida said, her arms folded and eyes like steel.

"As am I," Maera said, mirroring his sister.

He lowered his fork to the table and glared at them. "What value do either of you bring to this mission?"

Flynt, who was sitting next to Jasce, spewed his drink, forcing Kenz and Kord to jump out of the way. He wiped his mouth and mumbled, "Harsh."

Jaida raised her hand and Jasce's body lifted off the bench and smacked into the back wall.

"Hey!" Kenz flicked her wrist, and an indigo shield wrapped around Jaida, releasing Jasce from her paralyzing hold.

"How's that for value?" Jaida asked behind Kenz's wall of light.

He gritted his teeth and straightened his tunic. The dining hall had gone silent. Walking around the table, he signaled to Kenz to lower her shield. He grabbed Jaida's arm, and within seconds they reappeared inside his living quarters.

"What the hell's the matter with you?" he asked. "You will not challenge me like that in front of my soldiers or use magic against other members of the Guard. Is that clear?"

"You've wanted to leave me behind from the beginning, and I'm sick of it. I'm just as capable as you, Jasce. I'm not some weak little girl who needs your protection."

"No, you are my sister, and it's my job to protect those I love. I'm also your King Regent. If you wish to be a member of the Paladin Guard, you will obey orders."

Jaida's face turned red. "Are you seriously pulling rank?"

"Damn straight, I am. And if I know Drexus, he still wants you back, which makes you a target, and I will not allow that!" His anger boiled to the surface. The desire to lash out had his blood pulsing through his ears.

Sadness filled Jaida's eyes. "Everyone you care about is a target for Drexus. You can't protect all of us."

He rested his hands on the mantel, breathing and counting until his pulse settled. She was right. If Drexus wanted him to suffer, he knew exactly where to strike. The leather couch shifted as Jaida sat, and wood crackled in the fireplace.

They remained silent until the door squeaked open, and Kenz entered. "Can I have a minute with your sister?"

"I don't think that's a good idea," Jasce said, turning.

She lifted her palms. "Just girl talk. It'll be fine."

Jaida crossed her arms, her eyes bouncing back and forth between them.

He sighed. "Sure." The two left him staring at the glowing embers in the fire. A fierce wind rattled the window, and he pictured the sea, an angry churning of foam and waves crashing on the shore, beating the sand into submission.

Why couldn't Jaida understand? He'd lost her twice, once when she was only a child and again, when she'd chosen Vale and Drexus over him. The wound still ached, never fully healed. The warrior in him knew she would be a valuable addition to his team, and possibly an effective distraction for Drexus and Vale. But as a brother?

Jasce swore. He couldn't use his sister as bait. What kind of monster was he?

The kind that killed his own father.

He fell back into a chair and closed his eyes. Images of empty bottles splattered with blood infiltrated his mind, along with the screams of a dying man. He glanced to the bookshelf where a bottle of whiskey was hidden. When he'd first returned to his rooms at the Bastion, he and Kenz had thrown all the alcohol away, but he'd forgotten the one lurking behind some dusty books, knowledge that seemed to have been waiting for his resolve to weaken.

His hands shook, and the need for a drink had him rising to his feet.

A knock sounded on the door.

Jasce licked his lips, his eyes darting to the bookcase.

The door opened and Kord entered, worry immediately washing over his face as he stared at him. All Jasce could do was lift a trembling finger to the temptation that was about to make him break a promise.

Kord strode across the room and shifted the books aside. He retrieved the bottle, opened it on his way to the kitchen, and poured it down the sink.

Jasce groaned as the smell of the whiskey wafted through the air. He imagined the taste, the burn down his throat, the uncoiling of his shoulders. The escape.

"Come on," Kord said, grabbing him by the elbow and leading him out the door. They didn't speak until they entered the training yard. Kord picked up two practice swords, handing him one, and stepped into the sparring ring. "I'm not as good as Caston, but fighting helps you relieve stress. And you, my friend, are stressed."

An ache punched through Jasce's chest as he thought about Caston. He had become such a valuable friend, someone who understood the assassin skulking inside him. He cracked his neck and twirled the blade.

After what felt like hours, sweat ran down Jasce's face and chest and his back ached, but his mind had settled, and his shoulders had unattached themselves from his ears. He ran his fingers through his damp hair and returned the practice blade to the rack. It was then he noticed Kenz, Jaida, Maera, and Flynt sitting on benches.

Kenz rose and approached the ring. "That was very entertaining."

"Glad you enjoyed it."

"Feel better?" Kenz asked.

"Much." Jasce looked at Kord. "Thank you."

"Anytime," Kord said, panting, resting his hands on his knees. "But tell me, how much were you holding back?"

Jasce chuckled. "Not that much."

"Humph." Kord returned his sword, and his one green eye penetrated into Jasce's soul. "Anytime you need to do that"—he pointed to the weapons rack—"I'm here. And remember, the struggles you face today will make you stronger in the future. When we are uncomfortable, that's where genuine change begins."

"Okay . . ." Jasce glanced at Kenz, who pressed her lips together to keep from laughing.

Kord left him in the ring, mumbling about getting something to eat.

Jasce tied back his hair while Maera and Jaida strolled over. Three strong-willed women—he didn't like his odds.

"Did you two have a pleasant chat?" he asked Kenz.

"We did. Thanks for asking," she said, and gave him a kiss on the cheek. "I'll see you back in our room."

"Wait—" Jasce tried to grab her, but she evaded him, her body quaking with laughter.

He crossed his arms and stared at Maera and Jaida. "Out with it."

Jaida bit her lip, glancing at Maera, who smiled encouragingly. "We understand you're in charge, but we'd like to go on this mission. I realize Drexus wants me, and probably Maera, but we can use that. And we will follow your orders and stay out of the way, if necessary."

Maera stepped close and whispered. "I know you're going after Caston. You can't ask me to stay behind." Jasce stared into hazel eyes full of resolve. He wouldn't stay behind if it was Kenz captured by that madman. She moved back and spoke louder. "Plus, I have the Inhibitor vials."

"And you know what I can do." Jaida folded her arms and then released them. "Please."

He wanted to laugh as his sister tried desperately for diplomacy, but he managed some self-control and kept his face expressionless. He circled the two women, tapping his chin, and finally stopped in front of them.

"I want you both suited up with armor. I'll see you at dawn." He strode past Flynt, who simply shrugged and then laughed out loud when Jaida said, "Wait. Dawn?"

Chapter Thirty-Two

J asce returned to his room to find it lit with candles and articles of Kenz's clothing leading him to the bedroom like a silky trail showing him the way home. His heart, which had finally settled after his sparring match, threatened to thump out of his chest as he ran a lacey camisole through his fingers. Desire sent a shiver down his spine, and molten heat burned through his core.

He walked into their room, and his mouth dropped. Kenz sat against the headboard, her toned legs stretched out in front and her midnight hair cascading over her naked breasts. His gaze traveled the length of her, taking in every bare curve before returning to her face.

Her green eyes sparkled with mischief. "Took you long enough."

"If I knew you were waiting for me like that"—he waved at her naked body—"I would have told them both to shove off." He leaned against the wall and crossed his arms. "You are achingly beautiful."

"And I need you," she said huskily, trailing a finger between her breasts and down her stomach.

His gut clenched and an insatiable hunger took his breath away. "The feeling is mutual."

"Prove it." She maneuvered to her knees and crawled across the bed, beckoning him with her finger, and his mind imagined all the things he could do with her in that position.

He stalked toward her, his eyes capturing every sultry detail—the swell of her breasts, her peaked nipples, the apex of her thighs. His hunger to devour her made his mouth water. He yearned to touch her, wanting to lick every part of her, to explore and immerse himself in her until she was screaming his name.

She straightened and untied the laces of his tunic. Her knuckles scraped against his skin when she removed his shirt, and his body trembled as goosebumps formed along his arms and legs. Her hands traveled across the muscles of his chest and stomach. Untying his pants, she slid her tantalizing fingers inside. His head fell back, and he groaned as she stroked him.

She gestured to his boots. "Those need to go."

He leaned forward and kissed her softly. "Indeed, they do." Within seconds, he'd unlaced his boots and removed his remaining clothing. He pressed his lips to hers and pulled her against him. Her body fit perfectly with his, as if she'd been made just for him. He skimmed his hands along the sides of her breasts, swirling his thumb over her nipples, smiling when she moaned into his mouth. Deepening the kiss, he trailed his hand past her stomach.

"Kenz," he said, feeling how much she wanted him.

Pulling him onto the bed, she straddled him, their lips never breaking from each other, the exploration of his fingers causing her hips to jerk. A wave of pleasure crashed through him as she lowered herself onto him, her hot silkiness surrounding him.

She finally broke their kiss and arched her back—slowly, methodically riding him. He let her set the pace, control the movement, and when she smiled down at him, he froze, his hands gripping her hips.

"I lose myself when I look into your eyes," he said, enamored by her fierce beauty and strength. Her loyalty and courage to do what was right, even when it was difficult. She brought out the best in him, and as they continued to move together, consumed by love and passion, he vowed to never let her go.

He focused on her rolling hips, the way he felt when he was inside her instead of thinking this may be the last time they made love. He

Conquering the Darkness

shoved the fear down and sat up, wrapping his arms around her, needing her as close as two people could get.

~

Jasce's cheeks ached from smiling as he sailed through the air on the back of a wyvern with Kenz riding behind him. Rays of sunshine glistened off the wyvern's red scales and the beat of its powerful wings set a relaxing rhythm as they flew toward the Desert Garrison. His eyes watered from the coolness of the winter wind, and he was thankful for the Balten fur-lined cloak he'd brought with him.

"We need one of these," Kenz yelled in his ear.

He nodded in agreement. Bruiser wouldn't approve, but having a wyvern around made traveling so much quicker. A four-hour horse ride turned into a much shorter flight. They had left Orilyon in the afternoon—Jasce had been kidding when he told Jaida they'd leave at dawn—and would arrive near the garrison in time to finalize their plans. Lord Rollant had again scolded him for going, but there was no way he could send others into Drexus's clutches without him. Plus, there was another part of the mission he was determined to finish.

Kord rode a golden wyvern with Maera holding on for dear life. Jasce hadn't realized she was afraid of heights, which explained why she kept her face tucked behind Kord's back with her eyes pinched closed.

Tobias and his midnight-blue wyvern carried Nicolaus, whose teeth sparkled with his infectious grin. He'd missed the opportunity to ride a wyvern during the Gathering and acted like a giddy teenager when they had saddled up. Flynt and Jaida rode a light green one, while the archduke and his black wyvern led the procession.

Alyssa and Delmira had watched with longing as they'd flown away, but Jasce needed them to stay with General Seb and Captain Reed to prepare the Guard. Too many unknown variables made him nervous. He hadn't heard from the Eremus compound whether the Baltens had arrived, nor did he know the number of Spectrals the lords and ladies of the towns had recruited.

They landed on the edge of the forest to provide cover for the wyverns. The garrison hugged the Desert of Souls, which in the past was a disadvantage for Spectrals. With the Inhibitor Stone removed and most of the Brymagus plant destroyed or taken, the desert no longer posed a threat by suppressing their magic. Both the front and side entrances were now vulnerable.

Jasce knelt behind a boulder, squinting into the distance and observing the guards' rotation. He'd been in this spot for what seemed like hours and his back cramped. He'd sent Tobias and Flynt to the north gate to scout the area while Nicolaus and Kord explored the desert entrance. Jaida, Maera, and the archduke remained at the campsite, preparing the power-suppressing vials. Flynt had created a few bombs containing the leftover magic from the Inhibitor Stone but hadn't had the time to make as many as Jasce would have liked. Still, something was better than nothing.

Kenz yawned. "I never realized how boring this was."

Jasce turned and rested his back against the boulder to relieve the ache. "Spy work can be pretty tedious. It's not all chopping off heads, you know."

She rolled her eyes. Raising her arms above her head, she arched her back and stretched.

His stomach clenched at the outline of her curves, and he thought about last night. A part of him wanted to vault her out of harm's way and never let her out of his sight. To simply escape this land and the threat of Drexus and live their life in peace. But as a warrior and now the King Regent, he couldn't do that. And he wouldn't abandon his family or Caston.

She lifted a brow, catching him gawking. "Focus on the mission, oh mighty assassin."

"You're making it very difficult." He tugged her toward him. Her citrus scent comforted him as he kissed her, sliding his tongue along the seam of her lips. She wrapped her arms around his neck while straddling him and deepened the kiss.

Images of taking her behind the boulder on the soft grass made his body throb with need.

"Ahem."

Jasce peered over Kenz's shoulder to see Nicolaus leaning against a tree with a catlike grin on his face. A stuffed bag was draped across his chest.

Kenz adjusted her clothing and slid off him. The heat gathered between them cooled and left him with a different sort of ache. She folded her arms. "How long have you been standing there?"

"Long enough to know that my idea of reconnaissance differs greatly from yours. I like yours better."

"Why haven't I killed you yet?" Jasce asked, getting to his feet and securing his weapons.

Nicolaus chuckled. "Because deep down, you love me."

"Abysmally deep." Jasce marched past him. "Did you get the uniforms?"

"Of course I did." Nicolaus patted the bulging bag.

Jasce thought about Nicolaus and his deception as they walked the short distance through the woods to the clearing where everyone waited. The agreement his father and the archduke had made regarding the Heart of Pandaren grated along his nerves. A part of him understood why the Shade Walker kept that information to himself: The man was a spy and that behavior was ingrained in him, just like the assassin dwelling inside Jasce. But he also couldn't help feeling betrayed. He kept reminding himself that Nicolaus wasn't Bronn or the other Hunters who'd left him to die. Nicolaus had proven himself loyal more times than not.

At the campsite, they talked strategy, with Jasce and Tobias finalizing the plan. Jasce, Kenz, Flynt, and Kord, dressed as Drexus's soldiers, would enter the garrison through the north entrance, the one used for supplies, and search for the Stones. If everything went as planned, they'd be in and out with no one the wiser. But just in case all hell broke loose, the archduke would fly his wyvern to the main gate and destroy it, attempting to barricade the soldiers inside the compound, while Nicolaus and Tobias eliminated the guards on the balustrade.

Nicolaus removed four uniforms from his bag and handed them to Kenz, Flynt, and Kord. "If you need help changing, I'd be more than happy to assist you," he said to Kenz, who arched a brow. He winked at Jasce as he handed him the last uniform.

"If you need help keeping your mouth shut, I'm more than happy to oblige." Jasce yanked the uniform out of Nicolaus's hands.

Kord held his disguise in front of him and tilted his head. "Really?"

Nicolaus shrugged. "There aren't a lot of men your size. It'll be a tight squeeze."

Jasce had considered replacing Kord with Nicolaus to infiltrate the garrison due to how recognizable the Healer was, especially with the eye patch. But he had a hunch Kord's magic would be useful. And knowing Kord, he wouldn't have stayed behind anyway.

Kord mumbled as he maneuvered the uniform over his head. The seams stretched so far Jasce thought the buttons might fly off if Kord sneezed. Flynt and Kenz had already changed, and Jasce was relieved to see the outline of Kenz's chest piece. His uniform was a snug fit, too, with his back brace and armor, but at least they'd blend in with the other soldiers.

Across the campsite, the archduke pulled his general aside. Tobias shook his head and waved an arm, upset about something.

Jasce frowned at the Gemaris, then returned his attention to the map he'd drawn of the garrison. After the Battle of the Bastion, when the queen had promoted him to commander, he and Caston had visited the compound while it was still under construction. Hopefully, the main areas hadn't changed too much from the original design.

Tobias returned to where Jasce stood, his mouth downturned.

"Everything okay?" Jasce asked.

"Yes," Tobias said, examining the map, his keen eyes seeing everything.

"I never apologized for almost killing you," Jasce said, quietly, staring at the glowing gem shining through the man's chest piece. He'd liked and respected the Gemari warrior and remembered trying to stop his blade from swinging, but the Vastane queen's power had been too strong.

Tobias looked up, his brows inching up his forehead. After a moment, he said, "Apology accepted."

Jasce scanned the campsite, locating the archduke talking with Nicolaus and Jaida. "Is he all right? I noticed him wincing earlier when he got off his wyvern."

Conquering the Darkness

Tobias focused on the map. "Just an old injury. Nothing to worry about."

Jasce frowned and glanced again at the archduke. Tobias was hiding something. He just wasn't sure what. But now wasn't the time. Once the moon dipped below the horizon and before the sun illuminated the eastern sky, they would hopefully have the Stones in their possession.

Chapter Thirty-Three

The grass whispered with the sound of running footsteps. Guards' voices floated down from the parapets, their silhouettes visible from the flickering torches. Jasce, Kenz, Kord, and Flynt hid in the shadows, sprinting in a crouch toward the side entrance. Two soldiers leaned against the wall with crossbows resting on their shoulders.

A tug and Jasce reappeared with his dagger drawn, swearing as he crashed into the stone surface. One soldier's mouth opened but with two quick slashes from his blade, both guards fell silently to the ground. He dragged them from their posts while the others caught up.

Kenz's bracelets glowed while Flynt melted the lock. "Just like old times, huh," he said, his eyes fixed on the molten door.

Jasce arched a brow. The last time they'd all been at the Desert Garrison was when he'd learned Drexus was the Fire Spectral who had killed his mother. He hoped this mission would be more successful. They had lost one of their own—Slater, an Earth Spectral—during their attack.

Once again, the responsibility of potentially leading people to their death weighed heavily on him, making it difficult to take in a deep breath.

He shoved the thoughts away and focused on the job. If everything went according to plan, they'd be in and out with no casualties, at least on their side. He'd show no mercy for the men and women who aligned themselves with Drexus.

The door finally opened into an empty supply room. Kenz entered first with her shield raised. Kord and Flynt followed. Jasce glanced once more upon the open field and slinked inside, quietly shutting the door behind them. If memory served correctly, the connecting corridor should take them to the command room and training grounds. From there, the hallways jutted out like spokes on a wagon wheel.

"We don't have much time. You three start at the command center and work your way to the medical facility," Jasce said.

"That wasn't part of the plan. Where are you going?" Kord glanced at Kenz, who shrugged.

"To the dungeon to get Caston."

Kenz rested her hands on her hips. "Why are we just learning this now?"

"Because the archduke never would've gone along with it. Besides, it doesn't take four of us to search for the Stones."

"You're right," Kenz said.

Jasce opened his mouth to argue and then snapped it shut. "I am?"

"It only takes two. I'm going with you to find Caston."

Kord narrowed his eye. "What makes you think he's in the dungeon?"

"A hunch." Jasce had thought a lot about Caston's location because he couldn't afford to be wrong. He didn't have time to be. During the attack on the Sanctuary, the Spectrals had treated Caston like a prisoner, not a comrade, especially as he continued to fight the effects of the multiple magics. The safest place to leave him would be in a cell.

Flynt ran a hand through his hair, peeking nervously into the hallway. The sound of marching boots echoed off the stone walls. "We don't have time to discuss this."

"For the record, I don't like this plan." Kord crossed his arms. "Don't do anything stupid."

The corner of Jasce's lip lifted. "Who, me?"

With a huff, Kord and Flynt disappeared down the corridor. Jasce and Kenz strode toward the dungeons, keeping their heads down. He held his breath as they passed a group of soldiers. No one looked at them twice.

"You gave in pretty easily to me joining you," Kenz whispered as they edged along the wall.

"I knew you'd come with me," was all he said as he peered around the corner. The door to the dungeon was thirty feet away.

"Am I that predictable?" A hint of playfulness marked her voice.

"Just faithful, sweetheart." He approached a wooden door with a viewing slot lined with iron bars. Kenz wrinkled her nose at the smell of blood and waste seeping through the hole.

He knelt and pulled two silver lockpicks from his pocket.

"Hey, those are mine."

"I know." He wriggled them into the lock while ignoring Kenz's tapping boot.

"Oh, move aside." She nudged him out of the way. Within seconds, she had the door unlocked. She shoved the picks into the top of her braid. "All you had to do was ask."

Jasce frowned, realizing she was right. Of course, she also would have peppered him with questions. Sometimes he forgot how capable she was and that they were a team. Years of working alone was a hard habit to break. "Noted."

They silently descended the stairs, where the air grew colder and more foul. They slowed when they neared the bottom, and he held up his hand. Two guards were hunched over a table playing cards.

"I don't think that Stone is working right," a guard said, shuffling the deck.

"Why do you say that?"

"Because Federick never came back. People are saying that Drexus is using it too quickly and some aren't surviving."

The soldier frowned and examined his cards. "Do you think we made a mistake joining his army?"

The man shrugged. "Queen Valeri should have offered land, money, and power like Drexus did."

The guard rubbed the back of his neck, a look of unease flitting across his face. "My brother, who was in Wilholm, was discovered and convicted of treason. Drexus might not have the upper hand anymore."

"He's smart. It'll work out and we'll get our magic soon. Then we'll get what's rightfully ours." The man placed three coins on the table.

Jasce pointed to the farthest guard and tapped Kenz's bracelet. She nodded. An indigo light filled the room as her shield wrapped around the soldier.

"Hey!" The other guard drew his sword but wasn't fast enough. Jasce had his hands on his head and neck and twisted. A loud crack sounded, followed by the man slumping onto the table.

"Keys," Jasce said to the soldier trapped inside Kenz's shield.

His eyes, wide with fear, stared at his fallen compatriot. He swallowed and shook his head.

"Kenz, convince him, will you?"

"Happily." She fisted her hand, and the wall of indigo light shrank. The man yelled and tried to push against it. His face twisted in pain, and he immediately grabbed his shoulder. Kenz withdrew the shield from around his head.

"I didn't know you could do that." Jasce waved to the section of her shield parting around the guard's head. She wiggled her eyebrows as he leaned a hip on the table, giving an air of casualness despite the clock ticking in his mind. "Shall we try again? Keys."

The guard's eyes darted to his uniform jacket. The shield parted and the man inhaled. Jasce held him by the throat while reaching into his pocket and wrapped his fingers around the iron keys.

He handed them to Kenz. "Find Caston. I've got this." She grabbed a torch and jogged down the dark corridor. "Where is Drexus keeping the Stones?"

"If I tell you, I'm dead," the guard said.

Jasce drew his dagger and twirled it. "You know who I am?" The soldier nodded while his eyes fixated on the spinning steel. The assassin in him savored the power fueled by anger and revenge. He could practically smell the fear seeping through the man's pores.

"Tell me where they are, and I'll kill you fast. Keep the Stones hidden, and well . . . you'll only wish Drexus was the one killing you."

Conquering the Darkness

"Jasce! Get down here." Kenz's voice echoed off the stone walls.

He picked up his pace, using his borrowed uniform to wipe the blood off his dagger. Moaning drifted from the dark recesses of the cells he passed. An iron door stood ajar, and he had to tamp down the rage threatening to explode when he saw Caston shackled from the ceiling. Blood covered most of his body and black lines swirled through the skin he could actually see. Kenz worked her picks into the metal cuffs around his wrists, her eyes narrowed in concentration.

Jasce pressed his fingers to Caston's neck and sighed in relief when he felt a pulse. It was there, faint and erratic, but at least he wasn't dead, only unconscious.

"Hang on, buddy. We're getting you out." He fumbled through his pocket until he found a vial with the magic from the Inhibitor Stone.

The cuffs sprung open and Jasce used one arm to keep Caston from falling. "Hold him steady," he said to Kenz as he jammed the needlelike tip into Caston's leg.

"What's that?" Kenz asked.

"This should temporarily block the magic."

"Let me guess. You stole that from Maera, too?"

He ignored the comment. Once the vial was empty, he removed it from Caston's thigh. The swirling lines slowly receded, but his eyes remained closed and his pulse fluttered at an alarmingly slow rate.

Jasce grabbed Caston's arm and threw him over his shoulder. He grunted as his spine compressed under the weight. "We need to get him to Kord."

Fear flickered across Kenz's face, but she lifted her chin and drew her sword. As they hurried down the corridor, other prisoners cried out. Jasce recognized a few Healers from the Sanctuary. The rest were members of the Paladin Guard.

Kenz handed one of them the keys. "Get everyone out," she said, and continued down the hallway. The sound of warning bells rang on the other end of the compound.

He stumbled on the last step as they emerged from the dungeon. Even with his brace, his back spasmed and a shot of burning fire blasted down his leg. He fell to one knee and tried to breathe through the pain.

He'd forgotten how heavy Caston was. Kenz pushed him behind the door as the stomp of boots permeated the hallway.

"Quickly, to the main gate!" a soldier yelled.

Something must have happened to cause the archduke to enact Plan B by destroying the entrance to the soldiers' barracks.

Another wave of guards sprinted past them. There was no way he could carry Caston without looking suspicious while soldiers ran through the hallways. And the pain in his back made vaulting three people to their campsite impossible. If he'd had the sliver of the Empower Stone, vaulting would be easy. He cursed himself for dropping the crystal in the Sanctuary. No one had seen it since.

Kenz seemed to come to the same conclusion. "Vault Caston out. I'll stay and help the prisoners."

"There's no way in hell I'm leaving you here."

The clank of chains and shouts emerged from the bottom of the stairs. He figured at least fifteen prisoners were heading their way.

Kenz yanked him to his feet. "There's no time. Go."

Jasce swore and kissed her hard. "Don't do anything stupid. And if you can, wait here. I'm coming back."

She opened her mouth to say something, but he'd already disappeared, his mind telling him she was correct, but his heart screaming in defiance for leaving her.

Hissing in pain, his back and leg throbbing, he reappeared in the middle of the field. Wyverns flew overhead, and the violet sky lit up with fireballs launched from the turrets of the garrison.

Why hadn't he appeared at their campsite? Maybe the pain caused him to be short on his landing. Caston moaned, and Jasce scanned the field. He limped toward a cluster of boulders lying nearby.

"Put me down," Caston said, his voice weak and gravelly.

Jasce grimaced as he lowered him onto the wet grass and examined his friend's face. The black lines had disappeared and Caston's eyes had returned to their normal brown color.

"You look like hell," Jasce said.

Caston chuckled, then groaned in pain, grabbing his side. "Don't make me laugh."

Jasce tore the hem of his uniform and used it to wipe the blood off the ex-Hunter's face. "I need to go back for Kenz. Stay here." He removed a sword from the scabbard on his back and laid it on Caston's lap.

"I'm not going anywhere." Caston rested his head on the boulder. Jasce stood, but Caston reached for his hand. "Thanks for coming for me."

Jasce squeezed his hand, focused on the dungeon, and vaulted.

The heat of fire washed across his face. "What the hell?"

He had reappeared inside the supply closet, now engulfed in flames. Withdrawing his sword, he vaulted again and appeared in front of the dungeon. Someone had ripped the door from its hinges, and a prisoner lay dead at the entrance, his face frozen in an anguished cry.

"Kenz, where are you?" he whispered. The fire blocked the exit she would have taken, which meant she needed to find another way out. He pictured his drawing of the map and remembered the other entrances into the compound. The closest one was through the dining hall and kitchen. From there, he wasn't sure which corridor led outside. Since he didn't trust himself vaulting to that exact spot, he took off in a sprint, heading into the depths of the garrison. He rounded a corner and froze as the tip of a blade lodged into his chest piece.

"Dammit, Jasce. I almost impaled you." Kord lowered his sword and stepped back. Fire danced through Flynt's fingertips, and scorch marks scarred his uniform, but otherwise they both looked uninjured.

"Have you seen Kenz?" Jasce asked.

Kord narrowed his eyes. "She's supposed to be with you."

Jasce growled in frustration. "She was helping the prisoners escape while I vaulted Caston out." He pushed past them, but Flynt stopped him.

"It's a dead end."

Jasce led them back down the corridor. "Did you find the Stones?"

"No. But we did run into some members of Drexus's elite squad," Kord said.

"His what?"

Flynt frowned at his ignitor switch when only green sparks sprung to life. "Spectrals with more than one type of magic. The minute the alarm sounded, they rushed to the command room. There was no way to get past them."

There was still one more place the Stones could be—the medical facility. At least the Creator Stone might be there, based on what the guard in the dungeon had said. And if memory served, there was also a way out.

"This way," Jasce said.

Two soldiers stood guard outside the facility. "What are you doing down here?" One asked, his hand hovering near the hilt of his weapon. "You're supposed to report to the courtyard."

Jasce strode forward, twirling his sword, but Kord pushed him out of the way, grabbed the two men, and crashed their heads together. They slid down the wall, unconscious.

"We don't have to kill everyone, you know." Kord shoved open the door and gasped. "What in all that's magical?"

Jasce edged past him and froze. In the middle of the room stood a pedestal with tubes snaking along the stone floor next to empty cots or still embedded inside people. A woman with bronze skin and silver hair lay chained against the wall, dead, her body punctured with open wounds.

Kord ran toward an occupied cot and felt for a pulse. He pursed his lips and went to another bed.

Flynt neared the pedestal and examined the hoses. "What was he up to?"

Jasce approached a woman with a tube lodged in the center of her chest. "A guard said Drexus was using the Creator Stone too quickly. But how did he transfer the magic? I thought you had to touch the Stone."

A faint pulse thumped under Jasce's fingertips. "Kord, over here." He examined where the tube attached to her skin, similar to how Drexus had performed the transfusion with his Hunters. A dark, congealed substance lined the tubing.

Kord ran over and placed his hand on the woman's forehead. She moaned and her arms jerked. "It's okay. We're here to help."

"Can you remove it?" Jasce asked.

Kord unhooked the fastenings and, with a sickening squelch, the

Conquering the Darkness

tube sprung free, plopping onto the ground. Flynt swore and jumped back as the gelatinous liquid splashed onto his boots.

Kord closed his eye and pressed his hand to the open wound. The woman's pulse beat stronger under Jasce's fingertips.

Sounds of breaking glass came from down the corridor.

"Flynt, bar the door," Jasce said, observing Kord, whose brow furrowed as he used his magic.

The woman's eyes shot open. Her entire body shook, forcing Jasce to hold her down to keep her from falling off the bed. "What's happening?"

Kord yanked his hands away as if they'd been burned. The skin around her wound blistered and turned black.

"No, no, *no*." Kord returned his hands to her shoulders. The woman screamed and her body stiffened. The blackness spread from the center of her chest and the blisters burst open, pus and blood oozing over skin resembling torched paper.

Jasce yanked Kord away while the woman writhed on the bed. Her back arched and mouth opened in a silent scream. She collapsed onto the cot, her blank eyes staring at the ceiling.

Kord gaped at his trembling hands. He swallowed and looked at Jasce. "I . . . I think I killed her."

Shouts came from outside the door.

"We need to go," Flynt said, striding to the far side of the room.

Jasce took hold of Kord's elbow. "Come on."

Kord moved as if in a trance.

Banging fists struck the outer door of the medical facility.

Flynt ran ahead and through a storage room, aiming for the door at the other end. "Yes!" He slowly opened the door and peeked out. "All clear."

Jasce dragged Kord toward the exit, knocking over a cabinet to block their retreat. "Flynt, seal it."

Flynt ignited his fire and cursed when it sputtered out. He tried again, sighing when green flames sparked to life. He pressed his hand to the doorjamb and melted the lock.

Jasce held Kord by the shoulders. "I need you to put whatever happened behind you. Only for now. We have to find Kenz and get out of here."

Kord's darting eye finally focused on Jasce's face. He licked his lips and nodded.

Jasce examined him, satisfied with what he saw, and scanned the clearing. The roar of wyverns sounded from the other side of the compound. A blast of fire exploded from the turret, and a silhouette he'd recognize anywhere sprinted through the darkened field with a group of prisoners behind her.

"There." He pointed and sighed with relief.

"That seal won't last for long," Flynt said, his gaze drifting to where Jasce indicated.

"Run," Jasce said. They'd only gone a little ways when a crash sounded behind him. He had to try to vault them out, since he didn't want to lead the soldiers to Kenz and the prisoners. He grabbed Kord's and Flynt's arms, gritted his teeth, and focused on the direction Kenz was running, hoping he'd appear in the right spot. The tug pulled at his chest and darkness engulfed them.

Chapter Thirty-Four

"Oomph."

Jasce, Kord, and Flynt, a tangle of limbs and swords, crashed into the retreating prisoners. Kord toppled into his sister, while Flynt dropped to his knees and immediately threw up, making a few prisoners curse and jump out of the way.

"I hate it when you do that," the Fire Spectral said, gagging.

A squirming body lay under Jasce, letting loose a multitude of swear words.

"Easy." Jasce winced as he pushed off the man. The pain in his back was becoming a problem, one he couldn't afford right now. He'd aimed for landing in front of Kenz but had come up short, again.

He held out his hand to help the prisoner up. A teenager with familiar hazel eyes glared at him. His blond hair, slicked with dirt and grime, hung limply on his shoulders, his uniform was torn, and a cut on his cheekbone had scabbed over.

"Rowan?"

Maera's son's face paled. "Commander. I'm . . . sorry. I didn't know it was you."

Jasce grabbed his forearm. "That was an impressive display of swearing."

"Jasce!" Kenz said as Kord helped her up. She ran and threw her arms around him.

He held her tight and buried his nose against her neck. "You're all right?"

She pulled away, her eyes darting along his face. "Fine. You?"

"I'm never leaving you in a dungeon again." He drew her against him, and she chuckled and pressed her cheek into his chest.

Flynt rose to his feet and wiped his mouth. "This isn't the best time, you know. We need to get out of here."

"Right," Jasce said, giving Kenz one last squeeze. Twelve prisoners circled them, all wide-eyed and filthy, most wearing Paladin Guard uniforms or the clothing worn by the Sanctuary staff. A foreign-looking woman, her auburn hair sheared short, wore silk pants gathered at the ankles and a torn tunic. She folded her arms around her middle and lifted her chin, revealing a gray collar around her neck.

"Who are you?" Jasce asked.

Kenz led him out of earshot. "She's from Vastane. I'm not sure why Drexus took her."

He stared at the woman, who kept her distance from the group. He'd figure that out later. Right now, he needed to get the rest of the team out of here. "Have you seen the others?"

"I think they're on the north side."

He stared at the compound. Burning torches made the structure look like a monster of darkness surging up from the deep.

Tightening his brace, he said, "Get them to the campsite, then take Kord to help Caston. I left him by some boulders on the other side of the field. Flynt and I will find the others."

He hated leaving her behind again, but the prisoners and Caston needed their help. Kenz and Kord were more than capable. Besides, Maera and Jaida would be waiting for them.

Kenz rested her hands on her hips. "Why did you leave Caston by some random boulders?"

"Long story," he muttered.

"I'm going with you," Rowan said, wiping the dirt from his already soiled pants.

Conquering the Darkness

Jasce turned, not realizing Maera's son stood behind him. "You're in no condition."

"You'd be surprised. Anyway, I'll simply follow you."

He arched his brow. "Very well. Flynt, let's go."

He looked at Kord, whose face was pinched and his hands fisted. It wasn't like the Healer to back down from a fight, but what happened in the medical facility shook him more than Jasce realized. Kenz led the prisoners and her brother through the darkened field as storm clouds formed above them and balls of lightning erupted in the sky.

The three of them ran toward the sounds of roaring wyverns. Vaulting would have been quicker, but he wasn't confident of where they'd end up. He didn't know if his inconsistent vaulting was because of the burning pain down his spine and leg or if it had to do with magic being out of balance. He suspected the latter based on Flynt's flickering fire and what happened when Kord tried to heal that woman. If that was the case, then they were in deeper trouble than he'd originally thought.

As they ran, he glanced at Rowan. "I thought I'd stationed you at the Ferox Garrison."

The young man's jaw twitched. "You did, but after you left, I requested a transfer to the Desert Garrison. Bad move on my part."

Flynt cleared his throat. "Sorry, but who are you?"

"This is Maera's son," Jasce answered as they slowed, nearing the corner of the compound.

"Ah." Flynt peered around the wall and his eyes widened.

Jasce wanted to borrow some of Rowan's unique swear words as he evaluated the scene.

Streams of black fire shot through the sky while the archduke's wyvern swerved to avoid the blasts. Drexus had positioned himself between the desert and the collapsed entrance of the compound. Flanking him were ten soldiers plus Vale. On Drexus's left was a Tracker, her white eyes scanning the field.

Tobias flew low and released a glowing bolt from his crossbow. The Tracker lifted her hand and a red shield ignited, blocking the arrow. The wall of light flickered and disappeared.

Dust cyclones twisted across the field while daggers of ice flew through the air. More fire spewed from the balustrade.

Nicolaus shot an arrow from the back of his wyvern, and a body toppled from the parapet.

Rocks skittered behind them, and Jasce, Flynt, and Rowan all spun. Caston limped over, his face pale and his jaw set while he gripped Jasce's sword.

"What the hell are you doing?" Jasce asked.

"The prison . . ." Caston rested a hand against the wall. "Drexus's soldiers are breaking through the barricade."

"Dammit." He glanced at the burning field. "How much time?"

"Maybe ten minutes."

He glared at Caston. "You're backup only, you hear me?"

Caston huffed. "Pretty sure I'm *your* commanding officer." His gaze darted to Rowan, who stared between him and Jasce.

Jasce withdrew his other sword and gave it to Rowan. "Rowan, this is Commander Narr. Caston, Rowan—Maera's son."

Caston's eyes widened, and he held out his hand. "Good to finally meet you."

Rowan shifted his gaze from Jasce's sword to Caston's hand then shook it. "You too, Commander."

Jasce addressed Rowan, pointing to the sword in his hand. "Don't lose that. Flynt, buy us some time and stop those soldiers. Burn the whole bloody place to the ground for all I care."

"You got it." Flynt ran in a crouch toward the barracks.

"What do you want me to do?" Rowan asked.

Jasce unsheathed his dagger. He needed another weapon and a clear path to Drexus. "See if you can lead some of his Spectrals away. Caston, go with him." Rowan saluted and disappeared into the field with Caston limping behind him.

A green fireball exploded into a pile of wood near Drexus's Spectrals. A few of them leapt out of the way, while others chased Flynt through the field.

"Nicely done, Flynt," Jasce said, and sprinted for Drexus.

The beat of a wyvern's powerful wings and ear-piercing roar sounded overhead. Tobias and his wyvern dove at the other Spectrals, causing them to scatter. Vale strode to the middle of the field and lifted his hands. A glowing crossbow appeared.

"Tobias!" Jasce shouted, still running toward Drexus. The Gemari tried to maneuver out of the way of the arrow, but it caught him in the shoulder, flinging him off his wyvern.

Drexus spun toward Jasce, and his mouth curled into an evil grin.

Jasce caught movement out of the corner of his eye. He tried to dodge the man sprinting for him, but the Amp was too fast. His dagger flew out of his hand as the Spectral tackled him to the ground.

"I'm going to crush you," the Amp said, wrapping his arms around Jasce.

A sharp pain stabbed Jasce in the ribs, and he couldn't breathe. He focused on vaulting but the throbbing in his side was too intense. Without warning, the Amp's mouth dropped open and his magical strength weakened, allowing Jasce to suck in a breath. He bucked his hips and thrust his elbow into the Amp's throat. With his other hand, he removed his knife from his boot and stabbed the man in the stomach. The Spectral released a roar and tried to get to his feet. Jasce swiped at his legs and pounced on him. With a yell, he jammed his blade into the man's heart.

He wiped the blood off his face and scanned the ground for his dagger. He picked it up along with the dead Amp's sword.

"You just don't know when to quit, do you?" Drexus's jagged voice called out through the smoke and ash.

Jasce grimaced through the pain in his back and ribs as he trudged toward his former commander. A silver chain hung around his neck, and dangling from it was the Empower Stone. The Tracker moved between them and lifted her hand. She frowned and flicked her wrist but nothing happened.

"Because of you," Jasce said to Drexus, "magic is broken." He twirled the sword and stepped into his fighting stance.

Drexus tapped the crystal. "Not mine."

An arrow whizzed past Jasce's face and struck the Tracker in the chest. The Spectral cried out and dropped to her knees. Drexus scowled as the archduke flew overhead, nocking another arrow.

The corner of Drexus's lip curved. Black fire emerged in his palm, and with a shout, he thrust both hands forward.

A wall of fire pierced the sky, followed by a roar that made Jasce's heart stop. The wyvern tilted, taking the full force of the blast in its underbelly. The wyvern plummeted, and the archduke jumped off before smashing into the ground. The earth quaked, dust filled the air, and tendrils of smoke drifted from the wyvern's midnight-colored scales. Staggering to his feet, the archduke ran toward the beast.

Vale and another soldier blocked Jasce's path to Drexus. Two more Spectrals appeared behind him, both holding swords. Jasce tightened his grip on his weapon, twisted his head, and cracked his neck. Four versus one wasn't horrible odds. He just hoped their magic was as unreliable as his. He pivoted to keep one eye on Drexus while surveying the Spectrals inching closer.

Drexus prowled toward the archduke. "Not even your wyverns are immune to my power. Now, where is it?" A fireball blasted at the Gemari, who leapt out of the way.

The archduke rose to his feet and withdrew his double-headed ax. Drexus sneered and unsheathed his sword.

Jasce pivoted to see Vale twist his wrists, and two swords appeared in his hands. "Do you think you can fight me and live?" The eerie sound of many voices in one sent a chill down Jasce's spine. The black lines swirled faster, distorting Vale's face.

Another arrow whizzed by and struck Vale in the chest.

"No!" Vale screamed, removing one of Maera's vials and throwing it to the ground as if a snake had bitten him. The black lines slowly stilled.

Nicolaus flew overhead, reaching into his satchel for more vials. He shot two at a time, both vials hitting two of the three Spectrals behind Jasce. He used the distraction, slashed his sword, and forever silenced the soldiers.

Vale stumbled and stared at his hands. With a glare at Jasce, he ran toward the side entrance of the compound.

"You coward!" Jasce yelled, about to pursue him when he noticed Drexus standing over the archduke.

"No!" Tobias held his shoulder and limped toward them.

But he was too late. Drexus sliced his sword through the archduke's

Conquering the Darkness

leather chest piece, and the archduke screamed as Drexus carved his blade through skin, muscle, and bone. The wyvern lifted his head, golden eyes glazed while he attempted to crawl to his master.

Drexus punched his fist into the archduke's chest and tugged, making the Gemari's back arch. The wyvern roared, flapping his wings and trying to get his legs under him. A grin of victory lined Drexus's face as he discarded the archduke's body like a rag doll. He tipped his head back and yelled, raising the Abolish Stone into the air.

Jasce froze mid-stride. He clenched his jaw so hard a tooth cracked. Archduke Carnelian had the Abolish Stone on him this entire time and didn't tell anyone?

The sky split, and torrents of rain drenched him in seconds.

The ground rumbled as two wyverns landed on either side of him. They tucked their wings, and Maera and Kenz slid off one while Kord helped Jaida down from the other. Rain drops splattered the wyverns' scales, making them shimmer like molten metal.

"Mom?" Rowan trudged through the smoky field with Caston at his side. Maera covered her mouth as her eyes danced between her son and Caston.

Nicolaus had picked up Flynt, and they both dismounted as shouts from Drexus's soldiers echoed off the stone walls of the garrison.

Drexus stared at the bloodstained Stone clutched in his metal claw. "Finally." The round crystal was amber-colored and about three inches in diameter. One could walk right by it and never realize it had the power to destroy magic.

The Empower Stone around Drexus's neck glowed. Thunder rumbled and lightning struck a tree near the forest.

Drexus tilted his head, surveying Jasce's team. "I will only offer this once. Surrender now and join my army." He looked pointedly at Jasce. "That doesn't apply to you. It's time for you to die. But I know you'd willingly sacrifice yourself for the ones you love." His gravelly voice dripped with sarcasm.

Kenz twisted her wrists, and her bracelets glowed. Kord twirled his sword, and Flynt's green fire wove through his fingers.

Jasce's mind whirled. He needed to buy his team time so they could escape. They were no match for Drexus now, especially not with the soldiers headed their way. The thought of abandoning the Stones made him seethe, but he needed to protect the lives of his friends.

He surveyed the field where four wyverns gathered near the black one, who had finally risen to his feet. His long nose nudged the archduke's body, and he snarled as he lifted his head and glared at Drexus.

Jaida stepped forward. "Drexus, why are you doing this?"

Flynt scooted closer to Maera.

The skin around Drexus's eyes softened. "You know why. The Spectrals must be united, made stronger, and led by someone who isn't afraid to make the hard choices. There are other kingdoms, other magical creatures, who will destroy us. This was a cause you once believed in, until him." He pointed his silver claw at Jasce.

Drexus wrapped the Abolish Stone in leather, slid it into his inside pocket, and ignited a black fireball. "Last chance. Surrender or die."

"Now!" Maera yelled and threw a metal ball at Drexus's feet. The bomb exploded, sending green smoke into the air and knocking Drexus onto his back. His fire disappeared.

Jasce grabbed Kenz's hand and shoved everyone toward the wyverns. Flynt and Maera's bomb was an effective weapon, but the wall of smoke would suppress anyone's magic, including his team's.

Flynt dragged Jaida, practically throwing her onto a wyvern's back, while Kord and Nicolaus helped Tobias. Caston took hold of Maera, leading her toward a wyvern, with Rowan on their heels.

Maera looked behind her as Drexus growled and lurched to his feet, and her eyes widened in fear.

Drexus flicked his wrist.

Rowan yelled as his mother shoved him out of the way.

Jasce pivoted and watched in horror. Silver flashed. Caston and Maera fell to the ground.

Indigo light surrounded them as Kenz lifted her arms. Wings flapped overhead, stirring up dust and smoke as the two wyverns took off, one carrying Flynt and Jaida, the other carrying Nicolaus and Tobias.

Kenz enlarged her shield to encompass the other three wyverns. Jasce lunged for Caston and Maera at the same time Rowan did. They rolled Maera off Caston.

"Caston, let go. Please," Jasce said.

A sob of grief escaped from Rowan. "Mom, no." Drexus's blade was lodged in her chest, and blood dripped from the corner of her mouth, her eyes unfocused. Rowan shook her gently. "Mom?"

Caston maneuvered to his knees. "Maera."

Boots pounded and the swish of swords being drawn sounded around them. Drexus ordered his soldiers to attack. Arrows shot through the air.

Kenz winced with the impact, and her eyes widened as a few arrows slipped through her shield. "We have to go, now!"

"Get to the wyverns," Jasce said to Kenz and Rowan while he and Kord helped Caston lift Maera. She groaned as Caston struggled onto the wyvern.

Kenz's shield flickered as more arrows passed through, landing in the mud with a splash.

Drexus stalked through the field, the rain splattering against his sword and hatred sparking in his black eyes.

"Jasce, come on!" Kenz wrapped her free arm around Rowan's waist and kicked the wyvern in its side, her shield flickering.

The soldiers closed in.

Jasce and Kord ran toward the black wyvern, slipping on the wet grass and mud as the rain continued pelting them mercilessly. "Please," Jasce whispered to the wyvern, who still hadn't left the archduke's side.

Gold eyes swiveled toward him. The creature's wide nostrils twitched and then he lowered his body. Jasce and Kord hopped on just as Kenz's shield disintegrated.

Chapter Thirty-Five

Wind and rain pummeled them as the wyverns landed in a field on the outskirts of Bradwick. Jasce dismounted and ran toward Caston, whose grip tightened as Jasce gently lifted Maera out of his arms. Her face was too pale and her breathing shallow.

"I got her. Meet me at the Raven." Jasce vaulted in short bursts, no longer confident his magic would get him to his precise destination. He hoped Gaeline still worked at the tavern and could provide them a refuge for the night. He also needed to inform Captain Dacier that their wyverns were in a farmer's field and a few of Drexus's prisoners would arrive soon.

Gaeline was wiping down a table when he threw open the door. Lightning flashed behind him, the patrons turned, and the room fell completely silent. He winced and trudged toward her, unable to imagine what he looked like, dripping water and covered in filth and blood. Of course, she'd seen him in a worse state after the Snatcher attack six months ago.

"Not you again," she said, eyeing him up and down, frowning when she saw Maera in his arms.

"We need help."

She tapped her toe as if contemplating her options. "Follow me," she said with a sigh, and marched toward a back room.

Jasce readjusted Maera and limped after her. As he passed a group of men, he noticed one of Captain Dacier's soldiers based on the uniform. "Get your captain. Please," he added as an afterthought. The man scowled, but pushed back from the table and left the tavern.

"And what sort of trouble have you brought my way this time?" Gaeline asked. Her husband, Rolfe, who Jasce had briefly met the last time he was in town, rushed in, wiping his hands on his apron, his brow furrowing when he saw Maera.

"What's going on?" he asked, as Jasce laid Maera on the table. Pain was etched into her face and her chest hitched up and down at a rapid rate.

He removed his stained uniform, bundled it, and placed it under Maera's head. "Long story. Let's just say we are in a lot of trouble." He ripped a section from his tunic and wrapped it around the hilt of the dagger still lodged in her chest.

Rolfe offered the towel draped over his shoulder. It probably wasn't clean, but right now Maera had bigger concerns than infection.

The curtain separating the main room parted and Rowan sprinted inside. A muscle in his jaw pulsed as he examined the wound. "Can't we remove it?"

"She may bleed out if we do." Jasce released his hold on the blade to let Rowan wrap the rag around the hilt and apply pressure.

Kord lumbered in with Caston, trailed by the rest of his team. Tobias collapsed in the chair closest to the fire. Rolfe removed his apron and pressed it against the wound on Tobias's shoulder.

Kenz approached Jasce while Jaida, Flynt, and Nicolaus stood near the entryway. Flynt had his arm tucked protectively around Jaida, and Nicolaus stared at his mud-covered boots. Jaida whispered to Flynt, and then leaned down next to Maera to examine the wound. She pressed two fingers to Maera's neck. Her gaze found Jasce's, confirming what he already assumed. Maera was dying.

Jasce held Maera's bloody hand. "Hang on, you hear me?"

Her hazel eyes, just like her son's, darted to his. She swallowed and whispered, "My son."

Conquering the Darkness

"I'm here." Rowan reached for her other hand.

Caston stood at the foot of the table, his face pale and jaw set. "Kord, heal her."

Kord peered at his hands. "I . . . I don't know if I can."

"What do you mean?" Caston asked.

"Our magic isn't working properly," Jasce said.

Caston grabbed Kord's arm. "She isn't going to survive."

"What if . . . ?" Kord, unable to finish his sentence, held out his palms, a man desperate for assurance.

Jaida touched Kord's arm. "You won't know unless you try, but first we need to get that blade out of her."

Kord tore his gaze from Jaida's and inhaled a fortifying breath. To Gaeline, he said, "We need boiling water and clean rags. And any medical supplies you have."

Gaeline fixated on Rowan's hand holding the dagger, the rag rapidly turning crimson. Rolfe touched her arm. "We'll get what you need," he said, steering her from the room.

Jaida gently led Rowan to the end of the table near Maera's head. "We need space to work."

Kord approached Maera, his green eye stark against his pale face. He flexed his hands and spoke to Jaida. "Once I remove the blade, you need to provide immediate pressure."

Gaeline entered with a bowl of steaming water and a pile of rags, while Rolfe placed a bag on the table along with a bottle of alcohol. "To clean the wound," he said.

Jasce forced his gaze from the whiskey to the bag and emptied it, sorting through the supplies and listening to Rowan whisper to his mother while wiping the sweat off her brow. Jaida poured the alcohol over her hands and dried them with a towel. Jasce retreated a step, breathing through his mouth, and swallowed the urge to drink straight from the bottle.

Kord lowered a trembling hand onto Maera's shoulder. He closed his eye, as if in prayer, wrapped his fingers around the hilt, and slid the blade free. Maera screamed. Jasce and Rowan held her still while Jaida pressed a clean rag to the wound.

"Mom!" Rowan wiped away the blood dripping from the corner of her mouth.

"Please," Caston said, rushing to Kord's side, his eyes fixed on the soaked rag and Jaida's bloody fingers.

Kord bowed his head. With his jaw set, he rested a hand on Maera's chest, his face intent and focused.

Maera whimpered, but her breathing settled. Jaida continued applying pressure to the wound while she pressed against her neck, silently counting.

"Her pulse is getting stronger."

Jasce breathed a sigh of relief. Caston glanced at Rowan, who gave a small smile.

Kord hissed through his teeth and jerked his hand away as if he'd been burned.

"Kord?" Kenz said, grabbing his elbow.

The skin around Maera's wound darkened and bubbled. She yelled and her back arched.

Kord recoiled from Kenz and backed into the wall. "Don't touch me! I don't want to hurt you." He fell to his knees and shook his head.

Jasce closed his eyes and clenched his jaw to keep the fear at bay. Magic was truly broken if Kord's power worked the opposite from the way it should, harming instead of healing.

"Jasce!" Jaida beckoned him to her side. "We have to stop the bleeding. Hold the wound closed while I suture it."

Jasce placed his hand on the soiled rag while she rifled through the supplies on the table. She quickly threaded a needle and poured alcohol over Maera's chest. His breath hitched as the smell of liquor wafted to his nose. Thirst and disgust flowed through him. His friend was dying and it was the need for a drink that almost brought him to his knees.

Maera's face scrunched in pain, and her muscles spasmed.

Jaida pushed the needle through the ravaged skin, mindful of the black boils that had thankfully stopped spreading. Hopefully Kord had pulled away fast enough to not cause more damage.

Jasce dabbed at the blood and pushed the folds of skin together while Jaida worked, her hands steady and methodical.

"Kenz, see if they have something to help Maera sleep," Jaida said, the needle tugging at the damaged skin, the hole slowly closing. Maera whimpered. "Almost done."

Kenz returned from the tavern with a small bottle and uncorked it. "Sleeping tonic."

Jaida tied off the last stitch.

Kenz gently lifted Maera's head and whispered, "Drink this."

Maera's eyelids fluttered open. Her lips parted as Kenz poured the sleeping tonic into her mouth.

Jasce led his sister away from the table, allowing Rowan time with his mother. "Is she going to be okay?"

Jaida wiped the blood from her hands and then handed the rag to Jasce. "It's too early to say. She lost a lot of blood." She peeked to where Kord sat on the floor, holding his head. "I'm honestly not sure what he did to her, how much damage his magic might have caused."

Jasce squeezed the bloody rag in his hands. "I can't lose another one," he whispered.

She rested a hand on his arm. "You were smart to leave the blade in, otherwise she wouldn't have made it to town."

As a young recruit in the Watch Guard, a fellow soldier had been stabbed in the leg. Jasce, in a panic, had removed the dagger. He could still see the blood pouring from the wound, feel the warm heat drenching his hands as he tried to stop the flow. The boy had bled out in front of him.

His eyes darted to his friends, unsure of what to do now. Kenz led Caston from the table, whispering to him, while Tobias rested his arms on his knees and held his head, mumbling to himself. Rolfe pulled Kord to his feet and guided him to the chair near the fire.

So much pain and despair. It filled the room like a noxious gas, slowly suffocating him. The mission to the garrison had been his plan, and it had failed. They hadn't retrieved the Stones, and now his friends were hurting, physically and emotionally.

Gaeline entered, carrying a tray. Teacups rattled and a bottle of whiskey teetered as she placed it on another table. "The captain is here," she said to Jasce.

He nodded his thanks and shoved his emotions aside. They still had a job to do, and he couldn't afford to fall apart. Not now.

Jasce strode to where Nicolaus leaned against the wall, repeatedly running his fingers through his hair. "I think I know why you haven't heard from your spies."

Nicolaus's hand froze and his eyes narrowed.

"I found one in the medical facility. Drexus is capturing them and draining their magic."

"That bastard," Nicolaus said through gritted teeth. "He can't get away with this."

"He won't. But we have to regroup. I need you to inform Captain Dacier of our situation, then fly to the Eremus Garrison. Hopefully King Morzov and his army have arrived. You said you had spies in Paxton. See if they can alert the Gemari, and if your father can send aid, then so be it."

Nicolaus held his stare, his silver eyes brimming with sorrow and determination. He stared around the room as if contemplating the situation. Straightening his back, he dipped his chin. "It will be done." He took hold of Jasce's forearm and leaned close. "Do not lose hope. You are stronger than the darkest night. We both are."

He squeezed Jasce's arm and left the room. The curtain closed as Jasce thought about the Alturian's words. He wasn't sure if he was strong enough to overcome the trials ahead, but he didn't have a choice. As King Regent, as a warrior, as the protector of those he loved, he would find the intestinal fortitude or die trying.

He turned to Flynt. "Get to Orilyon and inform Lord Rollant and the council of what happened. Tell them to prepare for an attack."

Flynt's amber eyes hardened. He saluted and then veered to Jaida, held her face, and kissed her. Her surprised look was almost comical.

Jasce glared at Flynt. He now empathized with how Kord had felt all those times Jasce had kissed Kenz in front of her brother. He wanted to, at the very least, punch the Fire Spectral in the nose.

Flynt glanced once more at Jaida before disappearing through the curtain.

Jasce hoped the Paladin Guard was prepared, and that help would come to Orilyon. He'd wager his two swords the kingdom city was Drexus's next destination now that he had all four Stones.

Four Stones. Jasce allowed the anger to emerge through the other

Conquering the Darkness

emotions he'd buried as he stalked toward Tobias. Yanking him to his feet, he gripped the general's collar. "Were you aware the archduke had the Abolish Stone?"

Tobias's eyes narrowed. "Back off."

Jasce shook him. "Did you know?"

The Gemari shoved him and widened his feet. The corner of Jasce's lip lifted as he stepped into his fighting stance.

Immediately Kenz was between them, resting her hands on their chests. "No. We are not doing this now."

The blood pounded in Jasce's ears as he glared at Tobias. "Why would he bring the Abolish Stone here? He practically gift-wrapped it for Drexus." That was why the archduke wasn't wearing the traditional chest piece and why he'd brought an ax. The Gemari produced weapons out of thin air—unless they removed their magical gem.

Caston limped over to stand by Jasce, and Kenz still stood between them, her bracelets glowing. Jaida had inched closer but remained near Maera and Rowan.

The general raised his palms and retreated a step. "Archduke Carnelian had his reasons."

Jasce crossed his arms. "Well I'd like to hear them."

Tobias glanced toward the curtain as if hoping the archduke would walk in. He shook his head. "If we weren't able to use the Abolish Stone to nullify Drexus's power or retrieve the three Stones, then this was the only way."

Kenz lowered her arms. "What do you mean, the only way?"

"Magic is broken." Tobias jutted his chin at Kord, who rested his head in his hands. "The only way to fix it now is to mend the Heart."

Jasce paced the room. "Mend the Heart. As in, put it back together?"

Tobias nodded.

"But wouldn't that make Drexus invincible?" Caston asked.

"If we are to have a fighting chance at stopping him, then we will need our magic restored. The only way for that to happen is for the Heart to be put back together," Tobias said.

Jasce stopped pacing. "Why didn't he tell us?"

Tobias pointed to Caston. "For the same reason you didn't divulge your rescue mission. Do you think I wanted the archduke in that battle? He was supposed to stay on his wyvern, out of harm's range." The general pushed past him and unstoppered the whiskey bottle. He filled a teacup and drank it down in one gulp.

Jasce closed his eyes and bit back a groan as the buttery aroma of whiskey wafted through the room. He didn't know what to do, what his next steps were. He wasn't sure Maera would make it through the night, and he didn't want to witness losing another friend or see the anguish on her son's or Caston's faces.

The whiskey bottle beckoned him like a demanding lover and all he wanted to do was succumb to her embrace.

Chapter Thirty-Six

A full glass of whiskey perched on the scarred bar top, the gold liquid shimmering from the candles—a siren tempting a fated sailor to the deep. Jasce's fingers wrapped around the drink like a lifeline while he focused on the anger that had been his constant companion these past fourteen years. He wasn't one to wallow in self-pity, at least not for long. The anger was as familiar as the drink in his hand, so he clung to both.

The last few hours circled through his head over and over, on a never-ending loop of sorrow: Rowan's cries as his mother exhaled her last breath, a chair flying across the room and breaking into pieces as Caston yelled, Kord retreating to the corner, his magic betraying him when he'd needed it most.

Caston's grief and pain were tangible, not only for the loss of Maera but also for his queen. Hours before Maera died, Jasce had told Caston about the death of Queen Valeri. Rage had filled Caston's eyes, followed by the heavy weight of failure. Jasce imagined what his friend was thinking. If he'd been with the queen instead of Drexus's prisoner, might he have protected her? If he hadn't been weak and hurting from being held in that dungeon, could he have stopped Drexus's blade from striking Maera?

Jasce had empathized, but selfishly he didn't possess the strength to carry Caston's burdens. He'd stared at his team, all grieving in their own way, and realized they didn't need him, not at the moment. His eyes had drifted to the center of the room where Rowan sat near his mother, dried tear tracks lining his cheeks. Maera's covered body reminded him too much of the last time he'd seen Amycus, before his mentor had turned to ash.

He had quietly slipped into the cool air laced with wind and rain. Lightning carved a jagged line through the sky. He breathed deeply, counted to ten and then to ten again, but his heart threatened to pound through his chest and his hands shook. Needing some sort of release, he'd let his head fall back and roared. His knuckles cracked and bled from punching the wall.

He didn't know how to handle the emotions raging through him, and the desire for a drink had him returning to the Raven. The comfort of drowning all thoughts and feelings in a bottle had made him quicken his pace. Shoving through the door and marching to the bar, he grabbed a bottle of whiskey, intending to disappear, if only for a while.

The stool next to him squeaked, bringing him back to the tavern, the whiskey, the escape. The sky had lightened, claiming victory over the night. Kenz's green eyes, bloodshot and laden with sorrow, scanned his face. She stared at the glass clutched in his hands, his knuckles white with the strain.

"I was thinking about Caston," he said in a gruff voice. "He finally found love, a chance at a normal life. Did you know he wanted to be a carpenter?" Kenz shook her head. "Yeah, he told me that one night when we were working with some recruits. 'Settle down with a good woman who has a healer's heart.' That's what he said." He huffed. What would Caston do now? Keep going and move forward, he supposed, but would his heart ever be whole?

Kenz rested her hand on his arm. "We will all miss her."

He returned his gaze to the golden contents of his glass. "How's everyone else?"

"Rowan fell asleep a little while ago. Gaeline brought in a cot and blankets. Jaida and I got Tobias all sewed up, and he's checking on the wyverns."

Conquering the Darkness

"Good. That's good to hear." He waited a beat. "And Kord?"

She traced a vein of lighter wood on the bar. "He's pretty upset. This is unfamiliar territory, obviously. Jaida talked with him. Even convinced him to heal a cut on her leg."

Jasce's head shot around. "What?"

"She's fine. And Kord's magic worked like it was supposed to. He said he can now sense the difference and knows what to look for, but he's still afraid to use his power on anyone." She played with the bracelets that controlled her shield, one that usually protected her without fail. The laceration across her arm where an arrow had slipped through made him grind his teeth.

He released the glass and cracked his aching knuckles. "Are you all right?" He scanned her body for more wounds.

"I'm fine. Just scratches." She swallowed and looked at the full glass on the bar. "How much have you drank?" Her whispered words were laced with sadness and disappointment.

"None."

She slowly turned to face him. "None?"

Jasce inhaled deeply. "I wanted to, Kenz. I wanted to drown all this misery away. Before I even sat down, the whiskey was in my hand. But I couldn't bring myself to even taste it."

She gripped his hand. "Why? I mean, not that I'm happy you didn't, but what made you stop?"

"You, mostly." He kissed her palm, his eyes never leaving hers. "I've failed in so many areas." He touched her lips with a finger, silencing whatever she'd been about to say. "My need to manage everything and everyone puts a weight on my shoulders I'm unable to bear. At least without that." He gestured to the whiskey. "The control I have is an illusion, something I convinced myself of until I saw Maeia lying on that table, none of us able to save her. There's only one thing I can control, and that's myself. I've let alcohol have power over me, but not anymore. That is something I can overcome. With help, at times, from those I love."

He wiped a rogue tear from Kenz's cheek.

"I'm so proud of you," she said.

"I have a long road ahead of me, and hopefully we'll survive this war and travel down it together."

She wrapped her arms around his neck. "There's no other person I'd want to travel with." She kissed him tenderly.

"I don't deserve you. But I'm never letting you go."

"I'm not letting you go, either," she said with a smile.

"Good. Because I'd like you to do something with me."

Kenz's brow furrowed. "Um?"

He led her from the tavern, the full glass of whiskey abandoned and forgotten.

∼

What he had done was frivolous, and they didn't have time for such sentimental actions. But as he'd sat alone at that bar, he'd thought about his life and the events and trials that had led him to this moment. He couldn't erase his past like he'd removed the tattoo his mother had given him. Granted, the reason Amycus burned it off was to release his magic, but a part of him had thought he could plow forward and not deal with his mother's death or the ruin of his life before he'd met Kenz, Kord, and Amycus. Before he found his true self. And he wanted a reminder of his mother and the fierce protector she was inked permanently on his arm. He also wanted the tattoo to honor Amycus, Aura, Queen Valeri, Darin, and Maera. Even his father.

So he dragged Kenz to the local tattooist, who'd been irritated at being woken up until Jasce offered to pay double. The woman followed Jasce's instructions and recreated the two triangles with a sword in between. The original design had blocked magic, but this one resembled his life, with the top triangle depicting his past, the bottom his future. The sword represented his present. Although he was no longer a Hunter, he was a warrior and a blacksmith. Both wielded swords and were an integral part of his identity.

The image wasn't finished, just a rough outline, and he'd have it completed when the war was over. It was a start at least, a step in a new direction. And one he was proud of.

Jasce held Kenz's hand and led her back to the Raven and to their friends. He hoped they'd all rested because they needed to fly to Orilyon before Drexus regrouped and attacked.

Drexus's prisoners arrived while he and Kenz were with the tattooist. They made themselves comfortable in the tavern, and Gaeline, Rolfe, and another barmaid tended to their wounds and provided them with food and drink. Jasce winced at the look Gaeline gave him, one of exasperation, but her nurturing spirit would never turn away those in need. He'd make sure, as King Regent, to compensate her and her husband for their kindness.

He noticed the Vastane woman sitting in the corner near the fire. Dirt and filth covered her and her cheeks were sunken. He wondered when she'd last had a full meal.

"I'll meet you in there," Jasce said to Kenz, squeezing her hand. He walked across the tavern, briefly talking to a few prisoners, before making his way to the foreign woman with a loaf of bread he grabbed from the bar.

"Do you need anything else?" he asked, placing the food next to her.

She stopped rubbing her short hair and gazed up at him with startling blue eyes. "No."

"We didn't meet beforehand—"

"I know who you are," she interrupted. "You're the one who killed my queen."

Jasce narrowed his eyes. He detected no resentment or hatred in her voice, but she didn't seem overly thrilled, either. "It was her or me. I obviously chose me."

The corner of her lip quirked. "Obviously."

"What's your name?" He sat next to her, attempting to make her feel at ease.

"Kiana Hale."

"You!" Caston strode across the room, dark circles under eyes that brimmed with malice.

Both Jasce and Kiana stood. Caston towered over her, but she held her ground, tipping up her chin.

"What's this about?" Jasce asked, struggling with the need to step between his friend and Kiana.

Caston's lips pulled back in a snarl. "She helped Drexus. She did this to me." He waved to his body. The black lines that, thanks to Maera and her magic-suppressing vials, had temporarily faded, but for how long, Jasce didn't know.

Kiana fisted her hands. "I wasn't given a choice. And because I wouldn't help him anymore, he shaved my head, tortured me, and left me in that dungeon. So although I'm sorry for what happened, you aren't the only one who's suffered."

Caston's face reddened, and he lunged forward. Jasce pressed a hand against his chest and pushed him away. He looked over his shoulder. Kiana's eyes were wide, and she'd taken a small step back. "Will you excuse us for a moment?" He didn't wait for an answer as he dragged Caston outside.

Caston shoved Jasce and turned away. He mumbled under his breath and tore at his hair like a madman. Jasce touched Caston's arm. He spun and lifted his fists as if ready to fight off an attack.

Jasce raised his palms. "Whoa. You're okay."

Caston's eyes darted around, his lips moving but emitting no sound. Jasce had never seen his friend like this where fear seemed to have taken hold of his mind.

"Caston, look at me." Jasce waited while he paced and shook his head, finally yelling, "Commander Narr!"

Caston's spine stiffened. He slowly turned, the lines on his face deeper, his cheeks hollow.

Jasce approached him and held his stare. "Do you remember what you told me after I woke up without my memories?"

Caston frowned and shook his head.

"You said, 'I need you to remember your Hunter training.'" He looked hard into his friend's eyes. "You're going to need that training now. We both are."

Caston inhaled a calming breath and nodded.

"We'll figure this out. Together." Jasce examined his friend's eyes, no longer drowning in panic but full of resolve. "Now go clean up. Pigs smell better than you."

Caston arched a brow. "You don't smell so hot, either."

Worry still tied Jasce's stomach into knots, but Caston was strong and would recover. As commander of the Paladin Guard, he had to.

Conquering the Darkness

Jasce returned to the room at the back of the tavern while Caston walked upstairs. Rolfe had removed Maera's body and Gaeline had scrubbed the table clean, but blood stained the cracks in the stone floor. Maera's blood. He couldn't believe she was dead. The list of reasons to kill Drexus continued to grow longer.

Jaida checked on Tobias, while Kord and Rowan sipped from mugs of steaming coffee. Kenz busied herself packing a satchel with supplies and gave him a quick smile before her eyes darted to her brother and Rowan. The smile slipped.

Jasce approached the two men, both opposite in appearance in every way. He dragged a chair over, spun it, and sat with his arms resting on the back. "We're going to fly back to Orilyon within the hour." He waited until Rowan looked at him. "I want you to remain here with the wounded soldiers."

The muscle in Rowan's jaw ticked. "I'm going to kill that bastard. You can't ask me to stay out of it."

"I'm not asking you. It's an order."

Kord's green eye shifted between Jasce and Rowan, but he remained quiet.

Jasce leaned forward, making the chair creak. "You and I will talk soon about revenge and what it can do to your soul. You need time to grieve your mom, and I need you to trust me." Rowan looked away, his eyes lined with the tears of his grief. "Please," Jasce added.

Rowan stared at his boots and nodded.

Jasce would speak to Gaeline and Rolfe to ensure the boy stayed in Bradwick. They'd have a proper ceremony of his mother's life when the war was over, if they all survived.

"How are you doing?" Jasce asked Kord, taking his mug and drinking deeply, allowing the coffee to warm his belly.

"Better until you did that." Kord snatched the mug out of Jasce's hand. "Is your magic working properly?"

He shook his head. "My vaulting is definitely off. I'm not appearing where I want."

Kord stared blankly at the wall. "I wonder what will happen when he puts all four Stones together?"

"I honestly can't believe I'm saying this, but I wish Nicolaus were here. He'd know a little something about this."

Tobias limped over, with Jaida holding his arm.

Jasce tapped his finger on the back of the chair. Frustration with the archduke and his general for not telling them the location of the Abolish Stone still grated on his nerves. "Do you know what will happen when Drexus combines the Stones?"

Tobias winced as he sat. Kord instinctively reached out but yanked his hand away as if a flame scorched his fingers.

"I'm all right, just sore," Tobias said, waving him off as he settled into the chair. "My understanding is you need fire to merge the Stones together. Obviously not a problem for Drexus. And he needs to touch the Heart to use its power."

"And what will that power look like?" Kenz asked, leaning against the wall next to her brother.

"Based on legend, Drexus will have the ability to wield all ten types of magic."

"Great," Jasce said and stood, unable to sit still. Kenz sat in his unoccupied chair while he paced in front of the hearth.

"But will magic still not work properly?" Kord asked. He told Tobias about the medical facility in the garrison where Drexus had used the Creator Stone, and the dead bodies they'd found.

Tobias frowned. "Drexus should know better. He's not respecting the power."

"Of course he's not. He thinks he's above that," Jasce said.

Tobias rubbed his wounded shoulder. "But, again according to legend, our magic should be restored."

"Let's hope so," Kord said as Caston walked in, his damp hair clinging to the tops of his shoulders. He'd found a razor and shaved his face, keeping his goatee. A hollowness filled his eyes, from grief and, Jasce assumed, the violation of Drexus infusing him with different types of magic. He just made out the tip of a black line squirming on his neck.

Caston acknowledged the rest of the team. "Thanks for coming to get me."

"It's good to have you back, but you need a collar. The Inhibitor Stone magic is wearing off," Jasce said.

Caston pulled up the sleeve of one arm and sighed. "Do we even have any?"

"At the Bastion."

"I'll wear a collar for the rest of my life to not feel the way I did. How Vale can stand it, I don't know. But the number of Healers Drexus used to keep us alive . . ." He glanced at Kord. Many of those Healers had worked under Kord at the Sanctuary and were most likely dead or close to after having their magic drained constantly.

"Are you able to travel? We need to return to Orilyon." And Jasce needed to plan and prepare his soldiers.

Caston crossed his arms. "I'm fine, but I'm not going alone."

Jasce released a sigh. "You sure that's a good idea?"

"What are you two talking about?" Kenz asked, eyeing them with confusion.

"That Vastane witch is coming to Orilyon and answering for what she did to me," Caston said.

Jasce scrubbed a hand down his face. *One more thing to deal with*, he thought. If just managing his team made his eye twitch, he couldn't imagine ruling an entire land. No wonder Queen Valeri was so unyielding and callous.

Gaeline entered the room with more coffee, which Kord instantly drank. Grabbing a piece of paper, Jasce jotted a quick note and gave it to her. "Please deliver this to Braxium Sarrazen in Delmar." She raised her brows as she held the paper. He dipped his chin. "Thank you, and your husband, for your help. I'll compensate you for any expenses."

They shook hands, and she returned to the main room of the tavern.

Caston crossed his arms. "You'll compensate them?"

Kenz strolled over. "Didn't he tell you? Say hello to Pandaren's King Regent."

"Oh hell." Caston shook his head. "Don't think I'm bowing to you."

Jasce snorted. He wouldn't be in the position of King Regent long enough for anyone to worry about bowing to him. He retrieved his bag, slinging it over his shoulder, and strode for the door. "Time to go."

Chapter Thirty-Seven

They tethered the wyverns in the open field behind the Bastion instead of the paddock that was built during the Gathering. Jasce suspected they'd be needing them again soon. When Caston had dismounted with Kiana, he'd bound her wrists and sent her to the dungeon. Jasce had argued with him that her skills may be necessary to help remove the magic Drexus had put inside him.

"I'd rather wear a collar for the rest of my miserable life than have that woman touch me again," Caston had said through gritted teeth.

Jasce wanted to point out that wearing a collar and suppressing magic for extended periods, especially powerful magic, might drive him insane. But he figured that conversation could wait. Besides, there were more pressing matters to deal with.

Tobias had sent one of his soldiers to fly back to Terrenus, just in case Nicolaus's spies were unable to deliver his request. Jasce hoped more Gemari and their wyverns arrived in time. So far, he hadn't heard from Nicolaus or the Baltens. The lead ball in his stomach grew with each unknown.

He figured Braxium should receive his message by the following day. Not wanting to be caught unaware, he'd asked his uncle to travel to the

Desert Garrison. Once Drexus's army moved out, Braxium would then vault to Orilyon as quickly as possible.

Jasce stood in the middle of the Bastion training area in front of his soldiers and recruits. Both his commanders, Caston and Alyssa, flanked him with his generals behind him, including Kenz, who he'd promoted on their way into the compound. Being King Regent did have its advantages, and he'd loved how her face had brightened.

They agreed to continue keeping Queen Valeri's death and Jasce's promotion to King Regent a secret, explaining dangerous weather in the Far Lands delayed the queen's arrival. It was a flimsy excuse, but their hands were tied. As far as anyone was concerned, both Jasce and Caston were commanders, along with Alyssa. She offered to return to the rank of general, but Jasce wouldn't even contemplate the notion. The Naturals admired her and having her as their commander was strategically wise. It was unprecedented to have two commanders, let alone three, but these were unprecedented times.

"Paladin Guard, we have an unknown threat. Drexus Zoldac has acquired the four pieces of the Heart of Pandaren." Jasce waited for the gasps and murmurs to die down. "Spectrals, your magic might behave differently, so do not rely on it. Instead, your weapons training will keep you alive and give you an advantage over Drexus's soldiers. All of you, fight as a team, have each other's back whether you're a Natural or a Spectral. The time for petty differences ends now. For us to survive, we have to appreciate and respect our differences." The bridge between the two was shorter after months of working together, and maybe having a common enemy would unite them further.

"Commander Narr and Commander Nadja will give you your instructions. I want everyone battle ready." He walked in front of them, eyeing the men and women he'd helped train, and a surge of pride lifted his chest. "We are stronger, we are better, and we are smarter. Together we will conquer Drexus and his tyranny!" He nodded to his leaders and walked toward the Sanctuary, leaving a thunderous applause in his wake.

"Quite the speech," Kord said, leaning against the doorway. He'd changed out of his bloody fighting leathers and into the Healers' uniform.

Jasce huffed out a breath. "I really hate doing those. Anyway, I

Conquering the Darkness

wanted to see if you needed anything." He looked past Kord into the medical facility where the staff and Healers scurried around like a colony of ants. He was pleased to see Jaida among them. "Are they doing okay?"

Kord glanced to where Jasce indicated. "Telling them about Maera was rough, but they're rallying. I've got a group working on the Inhibitor vials and Flynt making more of those magic-snuffing bombs."

Jasce leaned against the wall. He had met earlier with Kord and Flynt in a storage room to inventory the Brymagus plant. They'd shivered as their magic disappeared upon entering the large space containing shelves of plants in various stages of maturation. Maera had been busy using the Inhibitor Stone, creating an elixir from the crystal and growing the plant. Hopefully, the Brymagus would be self-sustaining with the Stone gone, at least until Drexus was defeated.

"I've been meaning to ask how your back is." Kord watched Kenz speak to a group of recruits.

He shrugged. "I made some adjustments to the brace, thickened the leather on the sides. That sort of thing. It'll hold up."

"The brace or your back?"

"Hopefully both." He raked his fingers through his hair. "I'm going to try to keep her off the front lines."

Kord turned slowly toward him and tilted his head.

"I don't want Kenz in this war any more than you do. I just got her back." Fear squeezed his heart like a vise. Having her on the battlefield was bad enough, but now with her shield not working consistently? If he could vault her to safety, he would. "You're fortunate Tillie and Maleous are safe in Carhurst."

Kord rubbed his neck. "Yeah, about that." He waved to a spot down the corridor.

"Jasce!" Emile called out and ran toward him.

His mouth dropped open. He hadn't seen the young girl since the Gathering. She'd been one of Drexus's first successful experiments with combining magic, which Maera and Kord had to remove as the three types began killing her. Jasce wondered if her Earth magic had returned as well.

Jasce snapped his mouth shut, knowing he looked like a gaping fish.

"Kord," he growled as Emile plowed into him. He recalled the letter Kord had given to Braxium before they left Delmar.

Tillie, Maleous, and Lander, Emile's older brother, jogged toward them. The lead ball of worry in his gut doubled in size.

Emile peeled herself away from him, and the vanilla and cinnamon scent clinging to Tillie filled his senses as her arms wrapped around him.

"Don't be mad at Kord," she whispered in his ear. "It was mostly my idea."

He gazed into her ocean-blue eyes. "Mostly your idea, huh?"

She patted his cheek and walked into her husband's outstretched arms. The strain pulling at Kord's mouth lessened the minute they embraced.

"I needed to see my family," Kord said to him, a plea for understanding shimmering in his eye.

Jasce could only imagine how the separation had been slowly tearing his friend apart. He'd much prefer Tillie and the kids to have stayed in Carhurst where it was safe. But he also understood the need to have loved ones close by.

Lander approached Jasce and saluted. "Commander, it's good to see you again."

He cleared his throat. "You too, soldier." The kid had grown taller and filled out, his body resembling a man's instead of a teenager's.

Maleous's green eyes flickered with doubt as he stood on the outside of the circle. His black hair was longer, the tips brushing his collar. The last time he had seen his future nephew, Jasce hadn't remembered him, but he recalled the heartache that had altered the boy's face at hearing the news.

Jasce knelt. "Hey, kid."

"Do you remember me now?" His eyes hardened as he jutted out his chin.

"Maleous," Kord said, reproach lining his voice.

Jasce waved Kord off. "It's okay. And yes, I remember everything." He reached into his pocket and pulled out a leather band. "I made this for you. We can add the Healer symbol later." During his time in Delmar in his uncle's forge, he had tinkered with the band while working on his back brace. He handed it to Maleous, who at first eyed it warily until a grin formed, and his entire countenance changed.

Within seconds, the boy was in Jasce's arms. "I'm so sorry, buddy. I really am."

"It's okay," Maleous said, his voice muffled against his chest.

Boots clunked down the hall as Kenz ran toward her family. Hugs and laughter were exchanged, and even though having everyone together filled the hole in his heart, something alcohol had never accomplished, fear and worry gnawed at him like relentless waves eroding the shoreline.

―

"I look like an idiot." Jasce glared at his image in the mirror and tugged on the white and gold doublet. He had never felt this nervous with all the battles he'd fought, training under Drexus, or going before the queen after the Battle of the Bastion.

Kord stood beside him. "No, you don't. You look respectable."

Caston, who lounged in a chair with his legs stretched out before him, snorted into his tankard.

Jasce turned and frowned. "You're supposed to be on my side."

Caston wiped the ale off his goatee. "I am on your side. I've never seen you so uptight. It's just a wedding."

He faced the mirror, tugged on the doublet again, and sighed. "Am I doing the right thing?" Kord arched a brow, and he quickly continued, "Not in marrying your sister. I'm certain of that to the very core of my being. But the timing is a little . . ."

"Odd?" Caston said.

Jasce nodded and glanced at Kord, whose gaze softened.

"The minute I figured out I wanted to marry Tillie, I couldn't wait. So even though we're headed into a war of magical proportions, you marrying Kenz now is a wonderful idea. Now quit fussing and let's do this."

Kord squeezed Jasce's shoulder and left the room. Caston rose from his chair, but Jasce stopped him.

"I really appreciate you standing by me. I know this can't be easy with Maera."

The skin around Caston's eyes tightened. "You deserve happiness more than anyone I know, Jasce. Yeah, it's hard, but she would have been thrilled for both of you."

He gripped Caston's forearm. "Thanks."

Caston returned the gesture. "Come on, Mr. Respectable."

The sound of pounding waves drifted up the cliffside and through the open windows of the small chapel on the edge of the palace's courtyard. The glow from the sun kissing the horizon turned the sea into a canvas of blue, pink, and gold.

Jasce waited at the end of the aisle with Caston by his side. Tillie stood across from him and smiled warmly. Maleous, Lander, and Emile sat in the front next to Jaida, Flynt, and Delmira while Alyssa and Tobias occupied the row behind them. Before the Gathering, Kenz had wanted a large wedding, but in his opinion, this was perfect. His friends and family were here to witness him joining his life with a woman he was not worthy of, but he would spend the remainder of his days striving to become the man she deserved.

He lifted his head as the door squeaked open. Kenz entered on Kord's arm, and his stomach dropped, along with his mouth. He suddenly forgot how to breathe.

Her midnight hair hung loosely in waves of silk, and the glow in her cheeks as she smiled at him compelled him to take a step toward her, until Caston grabbed his elbow. She wore a simple ivory dress with one of her custom belts cinched around her waist. As she walked down the aisle, he noticed the tips of her black boots peeking out.

She was so beautiful it made his heart ache. And she was his, and he was hers. Why had he waited so long to marry her? If they'd been married, would he have surrendered to Azrael? Would he have lost his mind? Perhaps, but it served no purpose to fixate on the what-ifs. The tattoo still stinging on his arm was a reminder to not dwell on the past but to learn from it and press on, which was why he was marrying Kenz now. He wanted to be her husband for as long as he possibly could.

Kord led his sister down the aisle, something Amycus would have done if he'd been alive, and the thought sent a wave of sorrow to Jasce's heart. Kord placed a kiss on his sister's cheek, handed her over to Jasce, and sat next to his son.

Conquering the Darkness

"You're stunning," Jasce said.

She beamed up at him. "So are you."

Lord Rollant cleared his throat. Jasce hadn't been sure if he'd agree to marrying them with everything else going on, but he'd seemed happy to do it, especially since it was custom to have the lord or lady of the town perform the service.

"Thank you all for gathering here to witness the union of King Regent Jasce Farone and General Kenz Haring." He signaled to Jasce to say the words he'd practiced all afternoon.

Jasce took hold of Kenz's hands, her calluses lining up with his, and gazed into her eyes, the freckles dusting her nose, her flushed cheeks, the fullness of her lips.

"You've captivated me from the first moment I saw you when you rescued me. And you've been saving me ever since—from a dungeon, from death, from myself." He swallowed past the lump in his throat. "I regret not marrying you sooner. I regret the months we were apart, and I regret the times I've hurt you. But know that I will strive with every breath I have to become the man you deserve. You've taught me forgiveness and acceptance. You are my lighthouse in every storm, and without you, I cease to exist. My heart, my mind, my soul belongs to you and you alone." He squeezed her hands, feeling her heartbeat matching his. "Kenz Haring, I will love, protect, and honor you all the days of my life and beyond."

He exhaled as a weight lifted off his chest. A sniff sounded to his left, and he arched a brow as Kord swiped the tear escaping from under his eyepatch.

Kenz's eyes shone as she smiled up at him. "I didn't realize how empty I was until I met you. Although our start was a little rough—"

Jasce chuckled. "You wanted to kill me."

"That's a common reaction from most," Caston whispered behind him.

She shrugged. "That is true. A few times, actually." She cleared her throat and took a deep breath. He rubbed his thumbs over the soft skin of her hands. "You peered into the depths of my soul, a place few are brave enough to go. You sparked a fire inside me and brought me to life. You've shown me the meaning of courage and sacrifice. You believed in me, even when I didn't believe in myself, and you challenged me to become better. Because of you, I'm stronger, braver." She paused for a beat. "Nicer."

Flynt snorted and then grunted when Jaida elbowed him in the ribs.

Kenz laughed. "I am honored to fight by your side and to be called your wife. Jasce Farone, I will love you, protect you, and honor you all the days of my life and beyond."

His cheeks hurt. He couldn't hold back his grin even if he wanted to.

"Do you have rings?" Lord Rollant asked.

Caston handed him the silver ring Jasce had made from the steel taken from his armor. One day, when life settled down, he'd buy her a ring fit for a queen, but for now, this would have to do.

He slid the ring onto her finger. "This metal has protected my heart, which I now give to you."

Kenz ran a finger over the band and smiled. She turned toward Tillie, who handed her a bronze ring. Jasce recognized the metal as having come from the original gauntlets Amycus made. "I have put so much trust and faith in my magic, which I now put in you."

Jasce marveled at the band circling his ring finger, a symbol showing the world he belonged to someone else: heart, body, and soul.

"I now pronounce you husband and wife. You may kiss the bride." Lord Rollant smiled at Jasce.

He spun her in his arms, dipped her low, and pressed his lips to hers. The guests laughed and cheered. He finally brought her up, and they both turned toward their family.

Jaida ran toward them and embraced him. "I'm so happy for you," she said, wiping tears off her cheek. She hugged Kenz. "I've always wanted a sister. We might have started off rough as well, but I'm hoping you and I will become good friends."

Kenz laughed. "Seems a common thing with the Farone kids. But yes, I hope so, too." She hugged her back and then hugged Flynt and Delmira.

Kord approached Jasce. "Brothers at last."

"Were you crying?"

Conquering the Darkness

Kord sniffed and wiped his eye. "The dust in this room is miserable."

He chuckled. "Come here, you big lug." He'd never hugged Kord before, but today it seemed the most natural thing in the world.

Everyone took turns congratulating the bride and groom as they made their way to a reception room off the chapel. Champagne flutes clinked and cake was devoured. Tillie had outdone herself with a three-tiered chocolate cake with chocolate frosting. How she'd baked it so quickly, he'd never know. It was the most decadent cake he had ever tasted.

One server brought Jasce a mug of coffee, which he lifted into the air. Holding his new wife's hand, content to never let it go, he said, "Kenz and I want to thank you all for being here, for your support and love."

"Here, here," they shouted.

Jasce was about to kiss her again when hundreds of birds out the window caught his eye. Frowning, he walked toward the open door and peered outside. Birds of every size and species flew over the ocean. The room behind him fell silent as the roars of the wyverns blocked out the squawking.

Caston stood next to him and stared out over the beach. They both reached for the doorjamb as the ground trembled.

Kenz came out, followed by Kord. "What's going on?" she asked.

The ground lurched again. Thunder sounded and a fierce wind blew, followed by a shockwave that exploded the glass from the windows and knocked Jasce, Kenz, and Caston off their feet. Kord gripped the door to keep himself upright. Delmira had ignited her shield, protecting those inside from the shards of broken glass.

Jasce pulled Kenz to her feet. His magic thrummed inside him, chaotic yet powerful. He glanced at Kenz.

"I feel it, too," she said.

Jasce directed his gaze to the east, toward the Desert Garrison, toward the dreaded unknown. "He's restored the Heart."

Chapter Thirty-Eight

Jasce immediately called a meeting to discuss their next steps. As King Regent, he could have simply given orders, but as he'd told Kord over a year ago, a good leader isn't afraid to hear others' opinions.

Weariness pulled at his bones and a headache brewed behind his eyes as he strode down the corridor to his room at the Bastion. He'd sent Kenz ahead as he'd wanted to check on Flynt and the status of his bombs.

He rubbed his forehead and opened the door to darkness except for one candle sputtering on the table. Underneath was a note from Kenz saying she'd gone to the beach.

The tide had come in with a vengeance, and the sound of crashing waves was deafening. He scanned the beach and found her, wrapped in a blanket and sitting on a large boulder.

He strode across the sand and climbed beside her, pulling the blanket around him to ward off the chilly air. The breeze blew her hair away from her face and the moonlight made her seem almost ethereal.

"Husband," she said with a glint in her eye.

"Wife." His smile melted. "Not quite how I pictured our wedding night."

"Yeah, me neither, but then again, we've never had it normal or easy."

"I'd give my left arm to have some semblance of normal."

"Well, I happen to like your left arm." She entwined her fingers with his. "Are we ready for Drexus?"

The sea churned, and a wave crashed and gobbled up the sand, leaving foam in its wake. "We have a solid plan, but without knowing exactly what the restored Heart will do, we are at a considerable disadvantage." His thoughts matched the raging surf, and the what-ifs threatened to drown him if he focused on them for too long.

She drew her knees up and rested her chin in her hand. "What are you thinking?"

"That I should have knocked you out and thrown your sumptuous ass on the boat with Tillie."

She chuckled. "Sumptuous?"

He tore his gaze from the waves. "Very sumptuous."

Plans to evacuate the city were to begin in the morning, but Jasce used his King Regent powers to load Tillie and the kids onto a boat heading toward Alturia. Watching them sail away into the night had been rough, and he couldn't imagine how Kord had felt. Of course, Jasce had half a mind to throw him on the boat as well. Kord was too valuable to not be in this war, but having one more person to protect, one more way to fail made his stomach tighten into knots.

Kenz leaned toward him, her eyes never leaving his, and kissed him. Her soft mouth teased, and the tip of her tongue traced his bottom lip. Wrapping an arm around her, he deepened the kiss. Tongues danced and teeth scraped, but he wanted more, needing her as close as humanly possible.

Grabbing her waist, he lifted her and settled her on his lap. He groaned as her body moved against his. She ignited a fire deep in his core, one that threatened to burn out of control. Sliding a hand under her tunic, he cupped her breast and trailed his thumb over her nipple. He licked up the column of her neck, enjoying the sounds of her quickened breath.

She dug her hands under his shirt, running them along his back.

Conquering the Darkness

He'd always marveled at how she never shied away from the scars that carved across his skin.

"Kenz." He crushed his mouth to hers. She rolled her hips, and he moaned at the friction.

Even though it was tempting to take her right there on the beach, he wanted her shivering from his touch, not from the cold. Within seconds, he vaulted them to their bedroom.

She closed her eyes and rested her head on his shoulder while he held her close.

"What if this is our last night together, like this?" she whispered.

His hands stilled. So he wasn't the only one plagued by what-ifs. He tucked a lock of hair behind her ear. "It won't be."

"You can't promise that."

He pressed his forehead against hers and breathed in her scent. He gripped her hips. "If you knew this was your last moment, what would you do?"

She removed his tunic and ran her fingers through his hair. "A part of me would want to be doing exactly this. Another part would be us spending time with Kord, Tillie, and the kids."

He gathered her shirt and lifted it over her head. His hands cupped her breasts as her hips slowly moved. "Me too." He gently pressed his lips to hers.

She rode him until his desire left him undone. The need to be inside his wife, his best friend, his warrior, overcame him. He lifted her and laid her flat on the bed, then untied her boots and slid down her pants, arching a brow at her bare skin.

"My, my." He trailed his fingers down her center, satisfied that her desire matched his. If this was their last night together, then he planned to take his time—licking, kissing, tasting until she screamed his name, taking her over the edge again and again. He knelt before her, savoring each moan and shuddering breath until she came undone.

"Jasce, please." She arched underneath him and gripped the sheets until her knuckles whitened. "You. I want you inside of me." She opened her eyes and watched him remove his boots and pants, biting her bottom lip.

Cassie Sanchez

He ached for her as his eyes traveled up her glistening body. Lying on top of her and sliding in one glorious inch at a time, he filled her. She reached over her head, gripping the headboard, and lifted her hips, wanting more, taking him deeper. He moved slowly at first until the intensity drove him harder, faster. She matched his pace, her breathy moans sending shivers across his body until she cried out and clamped down around him. His muscles stiffened and his toes curled as he yelled her name, collapsing on top of her. Her heart pounded against his chest, as rapid as his own.

"This is how I want to spend every night with you, my beautiful, fierce wife." He rolled to his side, bringing her with him and holding her close. "Every night for the rest of my life." He wasn't sure how many he had left, but then again, no one ever knew when they'd breathe their last breath. He'd learned quite a few things from his wife, one of those being to cherish every moment they were together.

~

The Valeri Coat of Arms hung on the wall behind him, an intricate lattice pattern of gold, purple, and black with a white horse standing majestically on its hind legs. He'd only been in Queen Valeri's study once when she'd appointed him commander. Floor-to-ceiling windows overlooked the Merrigan Sea churning with whitecaps as far as the eye could see. Even though the Heart was restored, his magic seemed off, unsettled like the waves below. Jasce had a suspicion it had to do with the sliver he'd lost in the Sanctuary.

He sat behind a large mahogany desk carved with ornate designs and wondered fleetingly if Kord and Kenz had created it. The furniture had their level of craftsmanship and detail. Leaning back in the chair, he put his feet on the desk, contemplating Carhurst and a life without war, assassins, the constant battle of good and evil. After his night of making love to Kenz and holding her in his arms—he wanted that life more than ever.

The door swished open, and Lord Gallet entered. "Are you aware of the time?"

Jasce slid him a look out of the corner of his eye but remained silent.

Conquering the Darkness

He spun his dagger on the desk, watching the light from the chandelier sparkle on the steel.

"I don't care what your title is. I don't appreciate being summoned." The ex-warden glanced over his shoulder when Lord Rollant, Kord, and Caston entered.

"Perfect timing." Jasce lowered his feet and returned his dagger to the scabbard on his thigh.

"What is this about?" Lord Gallet asked, adjusting his blue doublet.

In between meetings and spending time with Kenz, Jasce had visited the dungeon. He wanted to check on his Vastane guest to see if she had any information that might help them fight Drexus. To help persuade her to talk, he offered to move her to the Sanctuary, where she might be of some use. Caston wouldn't be pleased, but his commander would be too busy to worry about Kiana.

What Kiana had told Jasce made it difficult for him to remain calm as Lord Gallet scowled at him. Jasce stalked around the desk, leaned on it, and crossed his arms.

"I'll ask you once, Phillip. Did you tell Drexus the Inhibitor Stone was in the palace?" He took satisfaction in watching the color drain from the man's face.

Jasce had wondered how Drexus had known the location of the Stone, suspecting there was a spy in the council. He wasn't shocked it had been Lord Gallet. Once a weasel, always a weasel.

Lord Gallet licked his thick lips while his eyes darted to the exit.

Caston drew his sword. "Don't even think about it."

"I have an eyewitness account of you informing Drexus of the Stone's location. Do you deny it?" Jasce asked.

The man lowered his head. "I do not."

Lord Rollant gasped. "Phillip, why? Lorella trusted you."

"The plan was she'd be in the safe room with us, not personally protecting the Stone." Sweat lined his upper lip and his hands shook. "She wasn't supposed to be harmed."

"Queen Valeri and my Healers are dead because of you!" Kord lunged forward and wrapped his fingers around the man's neck.

Lord Gallet's toes scraped the ground. When his face turned a lovely shade of purple, Jasce said, "Kord, release him."

Kord gave him a sidelong glance and then let go. Lord Gallet fell to the floor, gasping for breath.

Jasce gestured to Caston, who yanked the man to his feet. "You are a traitor to the crown and all of Pandaren, and therefore deserve death." He paced around him, satisfied to see the ex-warden tremble in fear. "But, as I'm trying to be a better person, I'll let you live out your days in the dungeon."

Lord Gallet's eyes widened as he stared up at Jasce.

Kord crossed his arms and glared with his one good eye. "He doesn't deserve it."

"I find myself agreeing with Kord," Lord Rollant said.

Jasce's fingers itched to draw his sword and remove the traitor's head. He owed him for the three days of torture and for his betrayal. But he had made a promise to Kenz to fight the darkness inside him, to quell his natural desire for revenge.

"Do any of us deserve leniency?" Jasce asked, returning to the desk.

Lord Gallet shook his head rapidly, and his breathing hitched. Panic flooded his eyes, which darted to the dagger on Caston's hip. Lord Gallet shoved Caston and grabbed the dagger's hilt.

"No!" Jasce leapt forward.

With a crazed sense of victory in his eyes, Lord Gallet dragged the dagger across his own neck.

Both Kord and Lord Rollant swore. Kord knelt and was about to place his hand across the man's torn and bloody throat when Jasce stopped him.

"Don't."

"You don't want me to heal him?"

Lord Gallet's eyes drifted to Jasce as he said, "I want to be the last thing he sees before he dies."

With a rattling breath, Lord Gallet's body seized and then fell limp, his head lolling to the side.

"Death is too good for him." Caston retrieved his dagger and used Lord Gallet's cloak to clean off the blood.

Jasce stood. "Yes, it is."

One problem solved. He needed to talk to Lord Rollant but didn't want to do it with the growing puddle of blood spreading across the floor. They moved to the room next door while Caston and Kord dealt with the body. Jasce handed Lord Rollant a scroll.

"What's this?"

"If I don't survive, I've named you as King Regent. My final wish is to dissolve the monarchy and create a democracy. I believe a few of the other council members and town leaders are in favor of this idea. It won't be easy and will take time, but I think it's best for Pandaren."

Lord Rollant stared at the paper in his hands. "Why me?"

Jasce paused, wondering how to phrase his answer. He chuckled. "You know, I thought you were the bad guy when I met you in Carhurst."

"I thought the same about you."

"Well, in my case, you were correct." He chose a chair by the fireplace and glanced around the room. Another one he'd only visited a few times. Lord Rollant sat across from him. "You've made mistakes, but haven't we all? In the end, you've shown yourself loyal to the queen and to Pandaren. Despite our past, I believe you'd make a just and fair King Regent until new leadership is voted in. Which wouldn't surprise me if you won."

Lord Rollant rubbed his jaw. "Thank you for your vote of confidence. And I like your idea of a new government."

"You'll need to find a replacement for Lord Gallet, and I'd recommend bringing in a few more representatives."

Lord Rollant crossed his ankle over his knee. "I still can't believe Phillip was so foolish."

Jasce snorted. "I can."

"Not to sound condescending, but I'm proud of you for not killing him."

He put his thumb and first finger together and said, "I was this close."

They talked for a few more minutes and then Jasce met Caston on the wall of the Bastion, satisfied to see soldiers at their posts. He tapped his finger on the balustrade as he overlooked Orilyon. Wagons, horses, and people on foot evacuated the city through the northern and southern gates. Lightning zigzagged across the storm clouds and raindrops splattered onto the stone wall.

Caston rested his forearms on the ledge. His body had the air of being relaxed, though Jasce sensed he was anything but.

"You sure you're okay?" Jasce asked. When he'd told Caston about his agreement with Kiana, his friend hadn't been pleased.

The muscle in Caston's jaw ticked. "I don't understand why you wouldn't send her away with the rest of the prisoners. She's dangerous."

"Kiana was forced to work for Drexus, just as Maera was. Yet you forgave her."

Caston fisted his hands. Jasce didn't think he would comment until he released a pent-up breath. "The images in my head haunt me. I wake up screaming, clutching my dagger, thinking I'm strapped to that table again. But the pain was so much worse than in my dreams. It was like my body wasn't my own, even though I kept fighting it. But I couldn't. The magic eventually took over, and all I could see during that torment was her face." He gazed into the courtyard as the soldiers continued to train. "I honestly don't know where I'd be if you hadn't rescued me."

Jasce was quiet for a while, letting Caston's words sink in.

Drexus and his experiments. When Jasce and his fellow Hunters had received the Amplifier serum, they had volunteered for it. But what Drexus did to Caston was a violation he couldn't imagine.

"I'm sorry that happened to you." He laid a hand on Caston's shoulder. "You're one of the strongest men I know. This won't break you. We'll destroy Drexus and win this war, and then—"

"Then what?" Caston's eyes searched Jasce's face for an answer he didn't have.

"Hell, I don't know. But we'll move forward together." He squinted into the distance. A fire sparked from the tower of the outpost. "Is that the southern outpost's signal?"

Caston looked to where Jasce pointed. "It is. Someone is coming."

Jasce immediately scanned the skies. "Archers, be ready!" he ordered as a dark shape took form.

"Is that Tobias's man? Surely he couldn't get to Terrenus and back that quickly?"

Jasce had to agree. Even flying on a wyvern, there was no way the Gemari could have made that trip in so little time.

Silver hair and tawny skin finally became visible. "It's Nicolaus,"

Jasce said. "But he's not alone." Someone was riding behind him. They dipped low over the Bastion. The person with Nicolaus disappeared and within a second reappeared next to Jasce.

Braxium held up his hand as Jasce drew his dagger. "Easy. It's me."

He sighed in relief. "You really shouldn't just appear out of nowhere like that."

Caston huffed out a laugh. "Pot, meet kettle."

Jasce brushed him off and focused on his uncle. "You got my message, then?"

"That was amazing. I could die a happy man after riding one of those." Braxium straightened his tunic while he gazed after the wyvern and Nicolaus. "And yes, I got your message. I was vaulting over here from Bradwick and ending up in all sorts of strange places. But then that shockwave hit, and I vaulted like normal. I ran into your Alturian friend outside the city, and he offered to give me a ride."

Caston frowned. "Want to fill me in?"

"Right. Braxium Sarrazen, meet Commander Narr. Caston, this is my uncle."

"He's your uncle?" Caston's brows inched up his forehead.

"*He* is standing right here." Braxium narrowed his eyes at Caston.

Jasce shook his head and led Braxium and Caston down the stairs, toward the field where Nicolaus secured his wyvern. "I had my uncle doing a little reconnaissance on Drexus with instructions to return if things got interesting."

"Yeah, about that." Braxium pointed at Jasce. "Not sure what constitutes 'interesting.' Drexus is organizing his army, and based on what I heard, my guess is they will set out for Orilyon within the next few hours."

They left the Bastion and stepped onto the field. Nicolaus finished speaking to one of the Terrenian handlers and then approached Jasce.

"What did you find out?" Jasce asked, shaking Nicolaus's hand.

"The Baltens are on their way, but I'm not sure they'll get here in time."

"What? Why?" He needed King Morzov's army if his plan was going to work.

"Because of the imbalance of magic, Balten experienced a series of avalanches. They were able to get two squadrons out of the worst part, but last I heard, the king still hadn't crossed Lake Chelan."

"Dammit." Jasce frowned out over the field where the memorial service had recently been held, the charred grass the only remnant of the pyres and the bodies that had rested on them. "We'll have to assume they won't make it. Caston, gather all the officers and meet me in the command room. Drexus and his army will be here in less than three days." Caston nodded and jogged back to the Bastion. Jasce needed to inform Lord Rollant and Kord of the newest development. He hoped he was correct about the timing of Drexus's arrival. "Anything else?" he asked as he and Nicolaus walked toward the palace, leaving Braxium to help feed the wyverns.

"I found two of my spies near the Eremus Garrison. They'll be arriving by nightfall, so let your archers know, will you?" Nicolaus laced his fingers behind his back. "And another thing. Couldn't you and Kenz have waited to get married until I was here? She would've preferred a prince walk her down the aisle. I'm sure of it."

"How did you know we got married?"

Nicolaus arched a sculpted brow and then shook his head. "Really? Why would you even ask that?"

Jasce almost stumbled. "You have spies at the Bastion?"

Nicolaus laughed. "Of course not. Tobias told me." He nodded over his shoulder to where the Gemari spoke with Braxium.

Jasce was about to give the prince a piece of his mind when lightning struck the top of the palace, sending sparks into the air. The pole on top shook, teetered, and plummeted to the ground. He and the prince disappeared, materializing in the courtyard to take stock of the damage. A few recruits were pressed to the wall, but thankfully no one was injured. The remains of the pole lay scattered on the shattered cobblestones. A visual reminder of the destruction heading their way, an omen of what was to come. With the Baltens delayed and no news from Terrenus, was he leading his soldiers to their deaths?

At the thought, any levity in his heart at seeing his uncle and Nicolaus again vanished.

Chapter Thirty-Nine

The candles flickered and the fire in the hearth sputtered as it made its last stand. Immediately, the air chilled and every dark corner threatened malevolence. With a shiver, Jasce stacked more logs onto the grate. As he stoked the flames back to life, he contemplated the decisions he'd made during the last strategy meeting. Every order jeopardized the lives of his men and women.

He returned to the map and pressed his palms to the table, double-checking the battle plans for what seemed like the hundredth time. He just couldn't see another way.

Three-quarters of the Paladin Guard were stationed at the southern outpost, where he currently was, while the remaining were at the northern compound under Caston's and Alyssa's command. Nicolaus and his two spies shade-walked between the outposts to deliver messages. Jasce hoped the Baltens and Terrenians arrived in time, but with each passing hour, that hope diminished.

He tapped the map where fields separated Orilyon from the forests surrounding the Desert Garrison. This was where he expected Drexus to come through on his way to the palace. But Drexus had to know that Jasce would assume this. What was he missing? His eyes felt like they were full of grit since he hadn't slept for more than a few hours in between meetings and patrols.

Kenz, who had remained diligently by his side, slept on the couch in the outpost's command room. He drew closer and monitored her breathing. It didn't seem like only a day had passed since he'd married her and held her in his arms. He hadn't been joking when he said he should have knocked her out and sent her with Tillie and the kids to Alturia, but he kept reminding himself she was a competent fighter and, with her shield now working correctly, she'd be invaluable to the plans he'd set forth.

The logical part of his brain knew this, but his heart was another matter as the silver ring around her finger shimmered from the flames engulfing the wood. His gaze shifted to the bronze band on his left hand. What if they didn't make it? What if she died during the battle? The thought shot pain through his stomach, forcing him to double over. He breathed through his nose and rested his hands on his knees. A bead of sweat trickled down his back.

The door opened and Braxium entered, pausing when he noticed Jasce, who stood quickly and raised a hand to fend off his concern. "I'm fine."

Braxium arched a brow and pulled the door shut, glancing at Kenz asleep on the couch. "That didn't look fine," he whispered. "By the way, congratulations on your nuptials. I'm sorry I missed it."

Jasce gave a weak smile. "Me too."

"You should get some sleep," Braxium said, as Jasce stifled a yawn.

"Never can before a battle."

"Drexus's army hasn't even crossed Graythorn Forest."

Jasce rubbed the back of his neck. He hated waiting. The forest wasn't large, but it was dense and to move an army through it would take time. But for his plan to work, the Paladin Guard needed to wait until Drexus's soldiers were in the fields. He'd compensate the farmers for the damage to their crops and destruction of their lands, but there was no way to avoid it. Everyone lost something when it came to war.

"When I was a Hunter, I never worried about the others fighting alongside me. All I cared about was myself." He looked up and found Braxium analyzing him, worry crinkling the edges of his eyes. "There are times, like now, where I'd give almost anything to go back to the way things were. I'd take the pain, the whippings, even the destruction of my soul to guarantee I wouldn't lose anyone I loved."

Because I didn't have anyone to love, he thought.

The admission cost Jasce, but he had to be honest with his uncle and with himself. Kenz, Kord, Jaida, his team, his friends, his family—all could die in the upcoming hours. Would he survive it? If he did, the ruination he'd bring would make Drexus's war seem like child's play.

Braxium eyed the coffee mug on the table and then laid a large, scarred hand on his shoulder. "You're a good man, Jasce Farone, and I'm proud of you. Proud to be your uncle. You're a survivor, and I have the utmost faith in you."

Jasce swallowed past the lump in his throat that didn't seem to want to budge. "I'm glad we found each other again."

"Me too." His uncle stared at the map. "Myself and a few Vaulter friends will do whatever you need us to."

"Vaulter friends?"

Braxium smiled but kept his focus on the map. "There aren't many of us left who fought in the Vastane War, so we keep in touch. We may be old, but we're wily."

Jasce fisted his hands. Now one more person, one more family member, was putting their life at risk. He hadn't thought Braxium would fight, but in the brief time he'd known him, he should have guessed the blacksmith wouldn't back down.

"Wily Vaulters, huh?" The corner of Jasce's lip tugged as a plan formed in his mind. Between the Shade Walkers, Braxium's friends, himself, and a few Vaulter recruits, they could cause a little chaos for Drexus and his army. Add in a Fire Spectral with a propensity to blow stuff up, and they might have a chance.

"What are you concocting in that brain of yours?" his uncle asked.

"I'm in need of some wily Vaulters."

Braxium tilted his head. "Okay."

Dawn was still a few hours away, but they needed to act quickly. He gently kissed Kenz on the forehead, not wanting to wake her, and stared down at her peaceful face. Jasce hated having to call upon the assassin lurking inside him, but to survive this war and protect those he loved, he needed to bury all his emotions, his doubts, his fears, and focus on the mission.

He tightened his brace and tugged his armored chest piece over his head. After securing the straps, he slid his two swords into the scabbards on his back, tied back his hair, and slipped his throwing knives into his boots. He wore spiked metal gauntlets on his forearms and reinforced leather protected his legs. His dagger rested comfortably against his thigh. He closed his eyes and breathed deeply, flexing and relaxing his hands, envisioning the fight ahead of him and donning the figurative mask of a Hunter.

Braxium's eyebrows disappeared behind his shaggy hair as he scanned Jasce's face and posture. "So that's what an assassin looks like."

"Indeed," Jasce said, striding for the door.

Breakfast in the mess hall was a noisy affair. Jasce leaned against the wall and observed his soldiers enjoying the food and camaraderie. Braxium and his Vaulters, soot collected in the wrinkles lining their faces, ate with some older soldiers they must have known from the first war. His uncle, as if sensing Jasce's stare, smiled and lifted his mug of coffee in salute.

His mission had worked beautifully. After waking an extremely irritated Flynt, he met with the Vaulters, young and old, along with Nicolaus and his two Shade Walkers, Renier and Chloe—a brother–sister team who had enjoyed the trickery way too much.

Loading satchels with Flynt's bombs, fire and magic-snuffing, they had used their magic and traveled to the forest. Since he didn't want his soldiers in danger longer than necessary, the attack was short and fast, but effective. Green smoke had snaked through the tents while fire engulfed wagons carrying supplies. Drexus's army didn't know what hit them, and because they weren't experienced in warfare, the chaos that ensued was almost comical. Unfortunately, no one had seen Drexus or Vale, which meant the army must have been sent ahead.

Jasce tamped down his anger. Drexus was using these created Spectrals, sending them like lambs to the slaughter, all for his desire for domination. At least the mission had thinned their ranks, even causing some to flee.

Kenz's laugh brought him back to the boisterous dining hall. Kenz, Kord, Flynt, Jaida, and Nicolaus had gathered around a table, all laughing at Tobias, who waved his hands in the air, most likely imitating a wyvern.

He was content to watch his family and friends from a distance, to sear their faces and smiles into his mind. He had something worth fighting for, and when the darkness became suffocating, as it always did in battle, he'd remember this moment and the sound of their laughter, infusing the bleakness of war with pure light.

Jasce lifted his mug of coffee and froze. The liquid inside rippled, but his hand was steady. He closed his eyes and focused. A slight tremor vibrated under his boots.

He marched to where Kenz and the others sat and touched her arm. "Do you feel that?"

They all stopped what they were doing and stared at Jasce. Nicolaus tipped his head and frowned.

Jasce's gaze spun around the room, finally landing on his general, Seb, who was an Earth Spectral. Swearing, he sprinted from the dining hall and through the corridor, taking the stairs two at a time until he reached the top wall of the outpost. The sound of clomping boots trailed behind him.

"What is it?" Kenz asked, holding his hand.

Jasce spoke to Nicolaus. "Do we know how many Earth Spectrals Drexus has?"

"Including Vale, at least twelve."

Using the spyglass his uncle gave him, he focused on the forest. Birds squawked and flew from the trees as they shook and swayed. Dust billowed into the air, and trees were ripped from the ground and cast aside like chaff.

Kord leaned forward and peered toward the forest. "They're clearing a path."

"It seems so," Jasce said. "Flynt, get to the tower and give the signal. Drexus is here."

Cassie Sanchez

～

The destruction the Earth Spectrals left in their wake was disturbingly impressive. Drexus's army lined up on the vacant field where the Paladin Guard waited—the last line of defense into the city. Quite a few people had evacuated Orilyon, but many hadn't yet had the chance.

From his position on the balustrade, Jasce examined the field, which reminded him of King Morzov's game board, all the pieces strategically placed. Kord and his Healers occupied a nondescript tent on the southern side of the battlefield, in between the outposts. Two Shields stood guard, protecting those inside. Next to them was a shelter where Healers, along with Kiana, continued making the Inhibitor vials and Flynt's bombs. Even though their clandestine mission had been a success, they had lessened their store of magic-fighting weapons and needed more quickly.

Movement at the back of Drexus's formation caused cheers to erupt across the field. Jasce retrieved his spyglass and swore. A light green wyvern tied to a flatbed cart was being led between the soldiers. A rider on a horse galloped half the distance between the two armies and dropped a bag. With his fist raised, he returned to the safety of Drexus's army.

Dread pitted in Jasce's stomach. He suspected what was in the bag, which meant one thing. He vaulted to the wyvern paddock where Tobias was stationed.

Tobias jumped. "I hate it when you do that."

"You're going to hate this more. Hang on." Jasce gripped his arm and vaulted them to the field with his sword drawn.

The general stumbled but didn't vomit like most people who vaulted for the first time. "Why . . . ?" Darkness flickered across his face when he noticed the captive wyvern. The beast, upon seeing Tobias, pulled against its restraints and scraped the wood with its massive claws. A soldier jabbed a spear at its side, making the wyvern roar.

Jasce strode through the grass to the canvas sack, already stained a reddish brown, the smell of blood pungent. He knew before picking it up what lay inside.

Tobias marched toward him and yanked the bag out of his hands.

Conquering the Darkness

Tearing it open, he peered inside, and quickly shut it. The Gemari they had sent to Terrenus for aid never made it. Help would not be coming from the east.

"Damn him," Tobias said through clenched teeth. The gem in his chest glowed, and a crossbow appeared in his hands along with a quiver of arrows.

Jasce vaulted Tobias from the field before an arrow could be loosed, before the Gemari prematurely started the war.

Once they reappeared, Tobias shoved Jasce, putting distance between them. "He won't get away with this," he said, striding to his wyvern.

Jasce marched after him. "No, he won't. But I need you to stop and think. We have a plan. We need to stick to it."

Tension strained the muscles in Tobias's broad back, and his hands opened and closed. He finally turned and dipped his chin. "We'll be ready."

Jasce returned to the wall to find Jaida scanning the battlefield. Jeers from the enemy soldiers sounded, but he still hadn't seen Drexus or Vale. He was done waiting, though. It was time.

"Jaida, I want you with Kord at the Healer's tent." He took hold of her hand. "Please. I can't be worried about your safety. It's already killing me that the people I love are fighting in this war."

"You can't protect everyone. But I love you for wanting to try." She rested her hand on his cheek. "I'll stay with Kord."

Jasce leaned into her touch. "I love you, Jai."

Her eyes glistened. "I love you, too."

His magic pulsed and then settled into its normal rhythm as she walked down the stairs. Her golden hair disappeared around the corner, and he prayed that wasn't the last time he would ever see her.

Kenz and Nicolaus waited near the tower, where Flynt would soon send the signal.

"Nicolaus, gather your Shade Walkers and meet me at the front lines," Jasce said. The Alturian nodded and then kissed Kenz on the cheek. He arched a brow when Nicolaus chuckled and merged with the shadows.

He double-checked the straps of Kenz's armor. "Do not hesitate. I know they are Spectrals, but Drexus has twisted their minds. They will not offer you any mercy." He gazed into her eyes, memorizing every detail of her face. "This isn't goodbye. Survive, you hear me?" He crushed her against him and closed his eyes.

She wrapped her arms around his waist. "You too. Don't do anything stupid, please."

"I never do anything stupid."

"Ha." Her voice wobbled as she tightened her hold and then pushed away, walking backward, her eyes never leaving his. Before she disappeared down the corridor, she said, "I love you, Jasce Farone."

"I love you, too," he whispered into the empty hallway. He shoved every emotion down, locking them behind the wall he hadn't needed in months, one he'd rebuilt over the last few days. He fisted his hands, focused on his magic, and embraced the darkness.

Chapter Forty

The sound of war was deafening: Steel crashing, wyverns roaring, the cries of the wounded haunting those who were still alive. Fireballs hurled through the air, along with cyclones of dirt and rocks. Shields ignited, and fierce winds and streams of water knocked soldiers off their feet. The ground quaked as every type of magic exploded across the burning field while Drexus remained on a distant hill, content to observe, with Vale at his side.

A squadron of Jasce's men and women had charged first and drew the enemy from the safety of the forest. Caston's and Alyssa's soldiers split into two smaller groups and attacked from behind and to the north, blocking off any retreat. Tobias and his Gemari struck from above. The wyverns' roars and dagger-sharp claws instilled terror in Drexus's Spectrals while Paladin archers launched the magic-suppressing vials into enemy territory.

Jasce had chosen twenty of his best warriors, a combination of Naturals and Spectrals, to kill or capture Drexus and Vale. He'd outfitted them in head-to-toe black leather, with even their hands covered. They wore tight fitting hoods and black masks that protected those with magic from the effects of the Inhibitor bombs—and all the masks were blank except one. Jasce had a gleaming white skull painted onto his. He figured it was a little theatrical, creating his own style of Hunter, but witnessing the terror on the faces of Drexus's soldiers and the rage twisting his ex-commander's face as they cut through the line was beyond satisfying.

Jasce slashed through any who stood in his way, combining his vaulting with his skills as an assassin. Even those with two types of magic weren't a match for him.

He snuck a quick glance behind him and spotted Kenz's indigo shield while the shadow of a wyvern drifted overhead. An arrow zinged past him. He spun around, and a soldier's wide eyes gaped as he gripped the arrow in his neck and fell to the ground.

Jasce searched the sky. Tobias flew his wyvern with Nicolaus riding backward, unleashing arrows into the fray. Even from this distance, he saw Nicolaus give him a mock salute.

A multitude of screams, followed by a roar that was all too familiar, pierced the air. Soldiers from both sides streaked past him.

"Snatchers!" an Amp yelled through the throng of falling warriors.

Jasce had wondered if the creatures would make an appearance with so much magic gathered in one place. Thankfully, as he continued yelling orders, his soldiers instantly paired up, just like they'd been trained to do to fight off the beasts.

Three Snatchers circled the green wyvern trapped by Drexus's army, hissing and baring their jagged yellow teeth. Jasce vaulted and removed the heads of two creatures with a crossing slice of his swords. The remaining Snatcher reared back with its claws extended. He lunged out of the way, spun on his knees, and whipped his blade around. Blood splashed onto his armor as the creature fell.

The screech of more Snatchers sounded, their clawed feet pounding across the field, with their white eyes focused on him and the ensnared wyvern. He quickly slashed through the restraints trapping the wyvern. It extended its wings and escaped into the sky with Jasce on its back.

The hoard of Snatchers darted through the soldiers, using their massive claws to swipe at anyone with magic. Jasce cursed as men and women from both sides fell and a breach formed in the line protecting the city.

Conquering the Darkness

Jasce flew over the carnage, searching for Drexus, who'd abandoned his position on the hill along with Vale. He veered toward the compound and spotted Vale and another Spectral appearing out of the shadows near the Healers' tent. Vale launched glowing daggers at the Shields guarding the tent, while fire spewed from the Spectral's hands.

A Shield pivoted, and a firebomb ricocheted off his glowing wall and collided with the shelter next to the medical facility.

Jasce forgot to breathe as the entire structure exploded along with Flynt's bombs.

The blast knocked the Shields off their feet, and their protective walls disappeared. Vale and the Spectral strode past the fire spreading toward the Healers' tent.

"Jaida," Jasce said. He focused on Vale and vaulted, crashing into him just as Jaida came sprinting out of the tent. Using the Balten magic of speed and strength, Vale threw Jasce toward the burning structures. Thinking quickly, Jasce vaulted midair and landed in a heap inches from the searing flames.

Vale stood, the black lines on his skin swirling at a dizzying rate and lifted his hands. Jasce got his feet under him and focused on his weakening magic, not sure how many more vaults he had in him, as Vale yelled and thrust his arms forward, releasing a multitude of glowing blades, all aimed at him.

"Stop!" Jaida stepped in front of Jasce and spread her arms. The daggers parted around her as she walked through the glowing blades. Her hair floated off her shoulders and Vale's feet left the ground.

The Fire Spectral shouted and shot a stream of fire at her. Jaida kept one arm raised, holding Vale captive. She stared at the approaching fire and tilted her head. The flames swerved and flew back toward the Spectral. He turned to run and smacked into Kord's fist.

"I've got this," Kord said to Jasce, nodding to the unconscious Spectral. Behind him, Kiana helped the remaining Healers and wounded escape before the fire and green smoke from the bombs consumed the tent.

Jasce wiped the dirt off his leathers and strode to his sister's side as Vale cried out, his arm twisting.

The sun peeked through the clouds and Jasce blinked as the gem strapped around Jaida's throat sparkled.

The sliver, he thought. Jaida must have picked it up in the Sanctuary and obviously not told him. But Jasce remembered what had happened in the streets of Orilyon. If she used its power, she might cause more harm than good.

She stalked toward Vale. His back arched, his arms and legs spread. Hatred marred his sister's face.

Jasce lunged forward and stepped between her and Vale. He grabbed her shoulders and gave her a shake. "Jai, stop. You don't want to do this."

Her eyes were wild as she bared her teeth. The Stone was not only enhancing her magic, but any anger she had turned into unadulterated fury.

Vale screamed as a bone cracked. Jasce looked behind him. Blood dripped from the man's mouth, the lines on his face had stilled, and pain-filled brown eyes stared back.

Jasce yanked the crystal off her neck. "I will not let you become a murderer."

Jaida blinked and lowered her arms.

Vale crashed to the ground, whimpering in pain.

She stared at the crystal in his hand and bit her lip. "I meant to give it to you, but . . ."

"We'll talk about this later." He forced the anger away. Now was definitely not the time for this conversation. "Are you okay?"

She nodded. "What about him?"

Vale groaned. He lifted his head and black eyes stared back. "I will kill you," he growled at Jaida. "And I'll make your brother watch."

Jasce shoved his sister behind him. "My sister's not a killer, Vale." He twirled his swords and widened his stance. "But I am."

"You are nothing!" Green daggers appeared out of thin air and shot toward Jasce, who blocked them with his swords. More blades appeared. "Drexus's pet project, a pawn, you're a failed experiment."

Jaida stepped out from behind Jasce. "Vale, please stop this. That magic is killing you. Can't you see?"

Conquering the Darkness

A Snatcher appeared out of the smoke, its maw spread, and claws outstretched as it stalked toward an unsuspecting Vale.

"Jaida, get behind me!" Jasce used his armguard to swat away another one of Vale's daggers.

Vale, unaware of the danger at his back, started melting into the shadows when the Snatcher pounced, stopping him from vanishing completely. Vale screamed as the creature sank its bloodstained jaws into his leg. He tried to create a weapon, but green smoke licked his heels, suppressing his magic alongside the Snatcher's venom. The black lines on his arms and face slowed.

The Snatcher released his leg and snarled. Its claws dripped with gore and its white eyes narrowed as it reared onto its hind legs.

Vale raised his hands. "No, please!"

Jasce used his body to cover Jaida, who whimpered as Vale's screams drowned out the sounds of growling and tearing flesh. Jasce tightened his hold until Vale's cries were forever silenced.

He peered at the carnage. The creature turned its white eyes toward them and snarled. Blood and gore clung to its razor-sharp teeth. It scratched its claws through the dirt.

A yell sounded and Flynt sprinted past with his sword drawn. With an impressive attack, Flynt leapt through the air and removed the Snatcher's head. The body twitched and fell to the ground.

Flynt's chest heaved. "Have I told you how much I hate these things?"

Jasce helped his sister to her feet. "That makes two of us."

"Try three." Jaida avoided looking at what remained of Vale's body and ran into Flynt's open arms.

Jasce stood over the beast and relief coursed through him. He had prevented Jaida from becoming like him. She didn't need the weight of regret haunting her for killing someone who had once been her friend. And even though the Snatcher was a horrible creature, it had kept Vale's blood from staining Jasce's hands.

Flynt released Jaida and looked to Jasce. "Caston and Alyssa need help. Drexus's army has infiltrated the city."

Jasce returned his swords to their scabbard and slid the chain holding the sliver of the Empower Stone over his head. His waning magic immediately pulsed to life. "Kenz?"

Flynt shook his head. "I haven't seen her."

He briefly closed his eyes.

Jaida grabbed his arm and squeezed. "Thank you."

He knew what she meant—for saving not just her life, but her soul.

"That's what big brothers are for. Now go help Kord." He stole one last look at his sister, Kord, and Flynt, and then disappeared.

∼

Flames engulfed the Textiles District and screams echoed along the narrow streets as Snatchers slinked through the alleyways in search of more prey.

Jasce, with his commanders and generals, had anticipated Drexus attacking the city. He'd hoped the Paladin Guard would have kept the army in the fields, away from the innocent, but the Snatchers had blown that plan to hell.

Tapping into the magic of the sliver of the Empower Stone, Jasce reappeared on the main street in front of the palace. Alyssa stood with her archers along the parapets, while Caston barked orders at his squadron of soldiers. He released a breath when indigo light shimmered from the far side of the street. Kenz, Delmira, and four more Shields blocked the entrance to the courtyard and the palace.

Jasce vaulted to his wife. Blood spattered her face and armor, but she seemed to only have minor injuries.

She arched a brow. "You're late."

"Got hung up with a Snatcher. Vale's dead."

"Can't really say I'm sorry to hear that."

Caston limped toward him, his magic-blocking collar peeking out above his chest piece. "Nice mask."

"Thanks."

Soldiers, young and old, Naturals and Spectrals, stood side by side at this final stand. Jasce recognized one of his uncle's friends covered in blood and dirt and scanned the other soldiers, searching for Braxium's familiar scowl.

Conquering the Darkness

Please, still be alive, Jasce thought. He squinted down the hill, where the sound of clomping boots reverberated off the cobblestone streets.

Drexus led the charge, his eyes sparkling in victory. A thick chain of iron hung around his neck, and attached to it was a glowing circular crystal. The Creator Stone sat at the top, its black liquid swirling through the clear crystal. Below it was the amber-colored Abolish Stone. On the sides lay the light blue Empower Stone and the green Inhibitor Stone. Ripples of magic surrounded Drexus, making his body practically shimmer.

A wake of destruction followed Drexus, caused by his Spectrals and the Snatchers. Smoke and dust darkened the sky as buildings surrendered to fires and earthquakes.

Drexus stopped at the end of the street and gazed at the palace. He sneered when his eyes met Jasce's. "Have you come to welcome me home?"

Jasce turned his back on his former commander and stared into the faces of his soldiers. Fear and exhaustion filled their eyes. This was their last stand, and one they couldn't afford to lose.

"Remember who you are," Jasce said. "You are warriors. You're stronger, smarter, and have something or someone worth fighting for." He peered at the men and women on the front lines. "We will not give another inch. The line is drawn here and you will fight. You will defend our home and our freedom. Remember who you are!"

The Paladin Guard cheered and raised their swords.

Drexus lifted his arms, and with a yell, his army sprinted up the hill toward the palace. The two forces collided with an ear-splitting crash. Jasce drew his swords and entered the fray, with Kenz on one side and Caston on the other.

Jasce and Caston, their fighting skills exceeding those around them, cut through the soldiers with lethal grace. But every time they drew near to Drexus, he disappeared.

The wyverns and their riders flew through the smoke and attacked the Snatchers in the streets. The creatures ran straight through the men and women fighting on a direct course for Drexus, who had reappeared behind a line of his soldiers. Since the creatures were attracted to magic, Drexus's new power lured them like a beacon.

Drexus's face twisted in fury. He placed his hand on the Heart.

"Shield!" Jasce commanded.

Kenz immediately enlarged her shield while ordering the others to do the same. Jasce grabbed Caston and vaulted him behind the glowing protection.

Drexus yelled, and a shockwave of magic blasted across the streets, knocking soldiers off their feet and exploding the glass in the windows of the surrounding buildings. The shields flickered, and Jasce's magic, normally a steady hum, fluttered. He glanced at the pendant on his neck. The sliver of the Empower Stone pulsed.

Drexus focused on the Snatchers and lifted his hands. The beasts rose into the air mid-run. With roars of pain, they collapsed in on themselves with a sickening crunch.

A Gemari dove their wyvern straight for Drexus while he was distracted, but he disappeared before the deathly claws snatched him.

Jasce's magic fluttered again, and Kenz's shield dimmed. He and Caston both reached for their daggers as the shadows shimmered.

Nicolaus raised his hands. "It's me." His hair was windblown, his sleeves torn and bloodstained. A bruise was quickly forming around his eye.

"What's happening?" Kenz asked, frowning at her bracelets, the indigo glow now a light blue.

"The Stones of the Heart have limited power before they need to be recharged," Nicolaus said, his face grim. "I believe every time he uses magic, the Heart drains ours to fuel its own."

Caston rubbed a hand down his face. "Well that's just great."

Arrows flew across the sky and crashed into a black shield.

"Look." Nicolaus pointed to soldiers on both sides, who gaped at their hands. Fire snuffed out, spinning rocks fell, and daggers made of ice shattered on the ground.

"What happens if we hit the Heart?" Kenz asked. Her arms shook as she maintained her weakening shield around the soldiers.

"That would not be wise," Nicolaus said.

Jasce spun in a circle.

Blood.

Conquering the Darkness

Bodies.

Cries from the wounded.

Too many were dying on both sides, and the Baltens still hadn't arrived. His plan wasn't working. Drexus, with the Heart of Pandaren and the ability to control all ten types of magic, was too powerful. He had to cut the head off the snake, and he could only think of one option, one plan that might save them all.

"Our magic is fading and we're easy targets." Jasce glanced at Kenz, who briefly closed her eyes. "It's time for Plan B."

Nicolaus stared at them. "What's Plan B?"

Caston swore and wiped his mouth. Jasce had spoken to him and Kenz privately if it came to this, and although neither one of them liked the idea, they agreed in the end that it would have to be done.

"Take this," Jasce said, wrapping the cord holding the sliver of the Empower Stone around Kenz's wrist. Her shield immediately brightened. His magic hadn't drained thanks to the sliver, but how long he had until it did, he wasn't sure.

"Please come back to me," Kenz said to him, and then she and Caston ran on an intercept course for Drexus. Delmira ignited her shield and joined them. She and Kenz rammed soldiers out of their way while Caston carved a path with his swords. Nicolaus used whatever magic he had left to Shade Walk through the enemy line, taking out soldiers every time he reappeared. Members of the Paladin Guard yelled and formed up behind them.

Black fire swirled, and the earth shook as Drexus concentrated on the incoming attack.

Jasce sheathed his swords and focused his mind. The execution and timing would have to be perfect for this to work. He couldn't afford to make a mistake. And he had to trust his team to clear the way. Even though everything in him screamed to do this alone, he knew his wife wouldn't let him down, nor would Caston.

Drexus touched the Heart, and a wall of fire erupted from his hand. Jasce felt his magic waver.

A scream sounded, and Delmira's shield disintegrated.

Jasce swallowed the fear and grief, felt the tug, and vaulted.

Cassie Sanchez

Through the darkness he traveled, and in less than a heartbeat he appeared behind the fire, out of Drexus's line of sight.

As if sensing him, Drexus turned, his dark eyes wide.

Jasce wrapped his arms around him and vaulted him away from the battle, away from those he loved. As they disappeared into the void, the sound of a Balten horn echoed across the land.

Chapter Forty-One

They materialized in an abandoned corridor of the Bastion, Jasce moving before Drexus could orient himself. Drexus swore as Jasce shoved him through an open door, and immediately shut it behind them.

"You vaulted us away from the battle to die with no witnesses?" Drexus laughed as he stalked toward him, his eyes manic. "It's futile. Once I kill you, your little band of Spectrals, your precious Paladins, will surrender. And you will have died for nothing."

Jasce removed his mask and drew his sword. "You may have missed the sound of a horn when we disappeared. The Baltens have arrived. Your army is defeated."

"I have the Heart. I am invincible!" Drexus touched the Heart and lifted his other hand. His brows furrowed as he stared at the gem, no longer glowing. He glanced around the room. "No," he whispered, finally realizing what surrounded them.

Jasce had tested a theory after Maera died, wondering if this room might be more useful than simply growing plants. There was enough Brymagus in here to render the Heart useless. When Maera had created a new way for the plants to survive, little did she know she'd also built a Spectral prison.

Jasce pointed his sword at him. "It's just you and me. Steel against steel."

Drexus's face twisted in rage. "You seem to have forgotten the last time we fought. You're weak and broken, and I will destroy you." He drew his blade and stepped into his fighting stance.

Jasce hadn't sparred with his former commander in years, but the man had taught him everything he knew, and he recognized the confidence in his black eyes. He recalled the fight at Hillford, when Drexus had defeated him, and then his inability to kill him during the Battle of the Bastion. The victory that had shown in Drexus's eyes when he disappeared with the Empower Stone. The pain and humiliation after they found the Creator Stone.

His goal for over fourteen years, his reason for living, had been to destroy the Spectral with the black fire, the one who'd murdered his mother in cold blood. And with every chance, he'd failed.

"You can't beat me." Drexus's lips curved into a sneer. "You think you're so clever, bringing me here, taking away my magic. But you will still fail. It's what you do."

Jasce slowly lifted his head and tightened his grip on his sword. "You talk too much."

"So be it." Drexus charged, slicing his blade in a downward motion. The vibration shot up Jasce's arms as he parried the attack. He kicked Drexus in the stomach, knocking him into the shelves. Plants crashed to the ground, sending soil across the floor. Jasce extended his arm and thrust his blade, aimed at Drexus's stomach, but Drexus side-stepped and deflected the strike.

Swords crossed and their feet remained in constant motion, creating a fluid dance of steel and muscle. Sweat dripped down their faces as they continued to stab, spin, and maneuver, trying to get past the other's defense.

Jasce lunged diagonally while Drexus counterattacked with his sword, at the same time slashing his dagger. Jasce had to drop to his knees and twist sideways to avoid the strike. The movement shot fire through his spine and leg, despite his brace.

He struggled to his feet as Drexus performed a roundhouse kick. Jasce blocked the impact with his arm and swore as his sword fell from his grip and slid across the stone floor. Drexus leapt forward with his metal claw and connected with Jasce's temple.

He grunted, blinking back stars, and reached for his other sword. But Drexus had already countered, his blade whipping around at an accelerated speed, intent on carving him in half. The sword connected with his ribs, the force of the strike dropping him to a knee.

Drexus stalked toward him. "You should thank me for ending your miserable life."

Jasce grabbed his side in anticipation of blood and pain, but when he looked at his hand, it came away clean. Drexus's eyes narrowed at Jasce's torn armor, revealing the leather and steel brace he and his uncle had made. The brace that had just saved his life.

Jasce smiled. "Looks like you missed."

With a roar, Drexus pounced, knocking Jasce onto his back and thrusting his dagger toward his face. He grabbed Drexus's forearms before the blade pierced his eye. Drexus bared his teeth, spit dribbling across his lip, as Jasce's arms shook, thwarting the dagger's trajectory.

Jasce had come too far, worked too hard for his life to end like this. His training with the Baltens and Nicolaus—learning how to balance and control his body, adjusting his fighting techniques because of his injury, working with weakness instead of ignoring it. He closed his eyes and breathed, focusing on each muscle, blocking the pain, and pushing with all his might.

Drexus cursed as Jasce shoved him to the side. He used the momentum and struck with his elbow, cracking Drexus in the jaw. Rolling away, he retrieved his fallen sword and sprung to his feet.

Drexus rose and spit blood on the floor. "We could have ruled side by side. But you had to grow a conscience." He wiped the sweat from his eyes. "What a waste."

Jasce removed his other sword from the scabbard on his back and twirled both blades. "I'm happy to disappoint you." He controlled his breath and combined everything he learned from the first day he stepped into the Bastion until now. Fourteen years of training, sparring, bleeding all amounted to this one moment in time.

But then he saw Kenz walking down the aisle, pledging her life to his, loving him no matter how many scars he had. And Kord, who had always stood by him and encouraged him to be a better man. Not just images of his past, but his present, too, and a future he desperately wanted. Revenge had dominated his life for so long, but his family and friends empowered him. Protecting them had become his new mission, one he was proud of.

Jasce attacked. Drexus retreated and parried his strikes. Jasce kicked off the wall, flipped, and spun. He completed the move with a perfect roundhouse kick to Drexus's chest, knocking him backward. Jasce feinted with one blade and slashed with the other. Drexus cried out, dropped his dagger, and held his thigh. Blood oozed through his fingers.

"I'm going to kill you," Drexus growled as he advanced with his sword.

Jasce side-stepped and pivoted. His blade slashed through the armor protecting Drexus's chest and cut the chain attached to the Heart.

Drexus yelled and dropped to a knee as the Heart clanked across the ground.

Jasce shoved the tip of his blade into the hilt of Drexus's sword and twisted his wrist. Drexus's weapon flew from his hand and smacked into the shelves.

Jasce crossed his blades on each side of Drexus's throat and stared down at him. "Do you yield?"

Hatred filled Drexus's dark eyes and the muscle in his jaw ticked. "You won't kill me. I can see it in your eyes." His other hand inched toward his boot. "Don't forget, you were a sniveling, weak boy when I found you, and I made you into someone everyone feared. The Angel of Death had power, worth, respect. And you're willing to trade all of that for compassion? Love?"

Jasce shook his head and tore his gaze from Drexus's face. The Angel of Death was a broken man, but Jasce had endured the flames of adversity and come out the other side stronger and whole.

A sparkle of silver caught his eye. He tilted his head and held his commander's gaze. "I don't think so." Drexus whipped his dagger from his boot just as Jasce swiped both blades across Drexus's neck, and his headless body fell sideways with a sickening thunk.

Jasce's chest heaved as he lowered his swords and stared at the man who had caused so much damage and destroyed so many lives. And for

Conquering the Darkness

what? Power? To rule? He supposed he could understand Drexus's motive. In his twisted mind, Drexus longed to make Pandaren and its Spectrals a force to be reckoned with so other lands, like Vastane, wouldn't dream of attacking. But Drexus lost his way and sacrificed everything that had once been admirable in his quest for dominance.

Jasce could have easily followed the same path, driven by revenge and power, if not for a blacksmith, a Healer, and a Shield who believed in him and never gave up on him.

He glanced once more at his former commander and released a deep breath. Twirling his swords, he slid them into their scabbards and let his hands hang empty at his sides.

Chapter Forty-Two

The door swung open and Jasce immediately reached for his weapons. Relief poured through him as Kenz ran into the room and threw herself into his arms.

"You're alive," she whispered.

"As are you." He tightened his grip, his heart overflowing with gratitude that she survived.

She scanned his face, looked to where Drexus lay, and grimaced. "What is it with you and removing heads?"

Jasce chuckled and led her away from the blood. "My method leaves no doubt."

"True." Kenz held both his hands. "It's over. With the arrival of the Baltens and Drexus disappearing into thin air, they surrendered."

His shoulders sagged with relief. The battle was won. They were victorious. His head shot up. "Jaida, Kord, the others?"

"They're all fine." She lowered her gaze. "Except for Delmira. She didn't make it."

"I'm so sorry." Jasce pulled her into another hug. He had a feeling he would be holding her constantly for the foreseeable future, to comfort her and himself.

She sniffed and wiped the tears from her eyes.

"Wait. How did you get here so fast?" Jasce asked.

Behind them, someone cleared their throat. He released her and turned. Why wasn't he surprised?

Nicolaus leaned against the door. His silvery black clothing and armor were filthy, and his normally perfect hair stood up in all directions, but his eyes sparkled.

He pushed off the wall and extended his hand. "Well done."

Jasce gripped the Shade Walker's hand and then pulled him into a hug. "Thank you for all you did. I can never repay you."

"I'm sure I'll come up with something." Winking, he retreated into the corridor, stepped into the shadows, and disappeared.

Jasce and Kenz stared at the empty doorway. He squeezed her hand. "Let's get out of here."

"What about the Heart?"

He leaned down and searched under the shelves until he found it. Standing, he held the Heart of Pandaren in his hands. All this power could be his. Ten types of magic, invincibility. No one would ever threaten those he loved. He'd be able to protect them.

Small fingers gripped his hand. He tore his gaze from the enticing lure of the Heart and stared into the most beautiful green he'd ever seen.

He didn't need unlimited power or a throne. All he wanted was the woman standing by his side. With her believing in him, smiling at him like she was doing now, he could do anything.

"You already have my heart. Might as well take this one, too."

She pursed her lips and retreated a step. "Your heart is enough, thank you very much." She led him from the room and out into the hallway leading to the vacant training area of the Bastion.

Once they cleared the effects of the Brymagus plant, the Heart glowed and thrummed with energy. Kenz removed the cord holding the sliver of the Empower Stone from her wrist.

The sliver dangled and, as if pulled by an invisible force, drifted toward the Heart.

"Together," Jasce said.

"Together."

They both pressed the sliver into the Heart. The Stone vibrated and a blinding light shot out from its center.

Conquering the Darkness

Jasce dropped the Heart and pulled Kenz behind him as a fierce wind blew through the empty training yard. He turned his head to keep the dirt from pelting his face.

The wind settled, and he opened his eyes. His mouth dropped open while Kenz jumped back and swore.

Two beings, each easily ten feet tall, towered over them. The male wore golden armor with a black leather baldric across his chest. Sharp edges lined his harsh face, and purple flames burned in his eyes. He gripped a sword with lightning swirling along the blade. The female had hair the color of midnight that fell past her waist, and her cream-colored armor shimmered in the sun. Red lips curved into a smile and golden eyes sparkled.

"You have restored the Heart." The male's voice resembled thunder.

Jasce swallowed and glanced at the blazing sword. He suspected who stood before him, but his mind was still playing catch-up. He rested his hand on the hilt of his dagger. The female arched a brow while the flames in the male's eyes burned brighter.

"Maybe we should bow?" Kenz whispered, peeking over his shoulder.

"Your woman has some sense." The male approached, and Jasce drew his dagger, but kept it at his side.

"Are you Theran?" Jasce asked the male.

His fiery eyes widened as he glanced at the female. "You know of us?"

Jasce nodded slowly. "And you're Cerulea."

She smiled. "I am."

"The magical beings from the legends," Kenz said, moving to stand next to him. "But I thought they were just a myth."

Jasce gripped her hand. If he needed to vault, he'd have to do it quickly.

Cerulea followed the movement. "You are a Vaulter, and you a Shield."

"How can you tell?" Kenz asked.

"She has all the Mental magics," Jasce said. "Am I correct?"

"You are."

Theran bent over and picked up the Heart. "Your people have abused magic. We should destroy all of you and start over."

Footsteps sounded, and both beings turned their heads. Kord stopped so suddenly that Flynt grunted as he ran into him. Jaida and Caston slid to a halt.

Theran lifted his sword, the earth trembled, and fire erupted in his palm.

Jasce rushed forward with his arms raised. "No, please. They are innocent."

Cerulea stepped in front of Theran, resting her hand on his arm until he lowered his blade. She took the Heart and closed her eyes.

When she opened them, she stared at Jasce. "You were not the one who wielded the power, were you?"

"No, but . . ."

"Even though the Empower Stone has left its mark on you, and"—she pointed at Jaida—"that girl."

Jasce again stepped forward. "Please, Drexus hid the sliver inside her. She didn't know."

"And what's *your* excuse?" Theran narrowed his eyes, making the purple flames more menacing. "You used the Stone for your own glory."

He lifted his chin. "Yes. I sought power and vengeance and used the Empower Stone for my benefit alone."

Kenz rushed to his side and gripped his hand. He shook his head at her and was about to tell her to stand with the others when Theran spoke.

"Your woman seems to think otherwise."

"First, I'm his wife, not his woman."

Kord had inched closer, but Cerulea waved her hand, and he and the others disappeared from the courtyard.

Kenz opened her mouth, but Cerulea said, "They are safe, for now."

Theran paced, swinging his sword back and forth. "We should kill them, take the Heart, and remove magic from this land."

Jasce's blood pounded in his ears. He hadn't just waged a war and escaped death to lose it now, not when they had won, not when his future lay ahead of him, untainted and whole.

"Please, have mercy." He dropped to a knee. Kenz followed suit.

Conquering the Darkness

"Why?" Cerulea asked.

Jasce lifted his head. "We didn't respect the power you gave us. But we can do better." He glanced at Kenz. "A second chance with the woman I love. Please."

Kenz squeezed his hand. "Whatever happens, know that I am so proud of you."

Cerulea stared at them with her golden eyes while Theran crossed his arms, a bored expression on his face. Cerulea turned and faced Theran, where it seemed they had a private conversation.

Theran uncrossed his arms. "Do what pleases you."

"Rise," Cerulea said. Jasce and Kenz rose to their feet. "Your name?"

"Jasce Farone."

"Very well. Jasce Farone, you have proven worthy. You protected the Heart and those you love. I can see a substantial loss in you, but also hope for a better tomorrow. For that, you will continue on with magic and have the life you long for."

Jasce released a breath, and the tension coursing through his body eased, until Cerulea fixed her gaze on Kenz.

"Your name?"

Kenz licked her lips. "Kenz Farone."

Cerulea nodded. "Kenz Farone, your loyalty and strength are admirable, and because you have stood by your husband and believed in him, you will also continue with your magic."

Theran peered down at them. "The Heart will disappear, hidden so no one can ever discover it again, and anyone who searches for it will find their life forfeit. And no one must learn of our existence. If they do, I will return, and you won't find me to be so agreeable. Do you swear it?"

"I swear it," Jasce and Kenz said at the same time.

"Very well."

Theran drove his sword into the ground. Another blinding light shot forth, and Jasce pulled Kenz to his chest and closed his eyes. The wind blew and dust circled them.

Cold lips pressed to his ear. "Know your worth, Jasce Farone."

Jasce jumped and opened his eyes. Cerulea disappeared along with the wind and blinding light.

Kenz pulled away and stared. "What the hell just happened?"

Movement to Jasce's right caught his eye as Kord, Flynt, Jaida, and Caston ran into the courtyard—again.

"There you are." Kord wrapped his arms around Kenz and lifted her into the air.

Jaida hugged Jasce. "We were so worried."

"Everything's fine. We're all right." Jasce smiled down at his sister.

Flynt scanned the courtyard. In the center, scorched cobblestones formed a perfectly round circle. "What happened?"

"Where's Drexus?" Caston asked at the same time Kord asked, "Where's the Heart?"

"Drexus is dead and the Heart magically disappeared," Jasce said. "We'll tell you everything later."

Kenz lifted to her toes and whispered, "Almost everything."

Jasce chuckled and pulled her into his arms, kissing her deeply. Kord groaned and Jaida made a gagging noise. Flynt and Caston laughed as they left the courtyard. As Jasce led Kenz through the archway, he glanced at the blackened cobblestones. He didn't like keeping secrets, but this was one he'd take to his grave.

Chapter Forty-Three

The following week was a blur of meetings, memorials, and rebuilding. The destruction to the city by Drexus's army and his use of the Heart required all uninjured members of the Guard to assist the townspeople in repairing the wreckage.

If only it was as easy to heal the emotional damage.

Days after the battle when the celebrations ended, the council agreed it was time to alert the kingdom of Queen Valeri's death. Lord Rollant reported her ship lost at sea because of the storms that had plagued the land. They sent messages to all the towns with the news, including the naming of Jasce as King Regent.

Queen Valeri's funeral was a grand affair attended by all who could make the trip, including the Alturian king, Thaleus Jazari. Nicolaus wasn't pleased to see his father arrive on the shores of Pandaren. Kord, however, was thrilled when Tillie, Maleous, Emile, and Lander returned with magical stories of the brief time they spent on the island. Maleous was already keen to go back, especially when he described the water dragons living off the coast.

Braxium, a little banged up but breathing, sat with Jaida and Flynt during the queen's memorial service. The relief Jasce experienced upon seeing his uncle limp into the Bastion after the battle had almost overwhelmed him. He was fortunate to have his loved ones by his side as they honored the queen.

King Morzov and Consort Lekov stayed through the service, but before they left, the king requested a meeting with Jasce. One he wasn't thrilled to take.

Jasce, with Kenz at his side, met them in the War Room. He eyed the throne but declined to sit there, instead choosing a seat in the middle of the table. An action the king noticed.

"I knew Lorella would make you King Regent," King Morzov said with a smug look on his face. The consort rolled her eyes.

"That makes one of us." Jasce had been worried about this meeting since he hadn't followed through with his deal regarding marrying his daughter. The marriage proposal finally made sense, if the king really had suspected Queen Valeri would promote him to King Regent. "I can't thank you enough for coming to our aid. Without you and your warriors, this war would have ended differently."

"You're welcome. I'll come up with a way for you to reciprocate, yes?"

"Just so you're aware, I'm already married." Jasce glanced at Kenz, who smiled at him.

"Yes, yes. I heard. Besides, Irina doesn't want you as a husband. Gave me quite the earful after you left. However, I may require your assistance in the future." He fiddled with his beard as his eyes drifted to the map of Pandaren. "Some of my enemies across the mountains are getting aggressive with their exploits. That's why my children are not here. They have their hands full."

The knot in Jasce's stomach untied itself. "Whatever you need, Pandaren will provide support. I may not be in this position, but either way, you have our aid."

Consort Lekov pushed back from the table. "What are your plans now?"

Jasce rose to his feet. "Tie up some loose ends and establish stability in the land. With the announcement of the queen's death, we've had some fires to put out."

King Morzov chuckled. "Ruling is always a headache, yes?"

Jasce huffed out a laugh. He couldn't agree more.

Conquering the Darkness

Jasce and Kenz escorted King Morzov and Consort Lekov to the palace courtyard. Their carriages awaited, along with the king's Khioshkas. The guard who held the snowcats' leashes looked relieved when the king whistled for his pets.

"Don't be a stranger," the consort said, kissing him on both cheeks. She did the same with Kenz.

King Morzov dipped his head to Jasce. "Until we see each other again."

Jasce watched the carriage roll through the gates and down the hill.

Kenz blocked the sun from her eyes. "I really like them. Too bad they can't live on a tropical island."

He snorted. "Speaking of tropical islands, have you seen Nicolaus?"

She shook her head. "With him sneaking around everywhere, who knows."

"I'm offended by that remark."

They both turned as Nicolaus stepped from the shadows. Kenz swore and smacked him on the chest. "I hate it when you do that!"

Nicolaus chuckled, but the normal sparkle in his eyes was missing.

"What's wrong?" Jasce asked.

Nicolaus gripped a roll of parchment. "The king has summoned me home." His father had left immediately after the queen's funeral. Jasce didn't even get the chance to meet with him.

Jasce frowned. "You don't want to return?"

"It seems there's some unrest in my kingdom." His gaze traveled around the courtyard with its splashing fountain and swaying palm trees, up to the spires of the palace where silver flags flew in honor of the lives lost. "I suspect my life just became much more complicated."

"You are welcome here anytime you need a reprieve." Kenz wrapped her arms around him. He peeked over her shoulder and wiggled his brows at Jasce.

Jasce rolled his eyes. "You really are an incessant flirt."

"I really am." He held Jasce's forearm. "Thank you, for everything."

"You too." He would never admit it out loud, but he was going to miss the Alturian prince. Maybe when life settled down, he and Kenz could travel to the island. He did, after all, owe her a honeymoon.

"I take my leave, then." Nicolaus dipped his head and stepped into the shadows.

"You two disappearing and popping up out of nowhere really is annoying," Kenz said, crossing her arms.

Jasce kissed her hard on the mouth. "I take offense to that."

~

Once again, Jasce stood in the field where scorched grass and charred wood was all that remained of his friends and fellow soldiers. The sky glowed with the colors of dawn and the rhythmic crash of the surf provided a balm to his aching heart. His mother's words filtered through his thoughts.

Here it comes, the light chasing away the darkness.

Memorial services were held the day before for Maera, Delmira, and any other soldiers who didn't have family nearby. Rowan had stood next to Jasce, his back straight and his eyes hard during the entire service. He'd monitor the kid in the months to come and help him grieve his mother properly, not that he had it figured out. At least he knew what *not* to do.

Caston remained stoic during the funeral. It seemed anger and purpose drowned out the sorrow, for now. But after the service, Jasce wandered into the training yard to find Caston in the sparring ring, holding two swords.

Jasce approached him. "Is someone in a mood?"

"I can't believe she escaped," he had said through gritted teeth.

With the chaos of the battle, Kiana had fled. When Caston found out, he hadn't been pleased. He still wanted her to pay for her crimes, but deep down, Jasce knew he really needed her to figure out a way to remove his magic.

Kord was working on it, but he'd warned the procedure might kill him. It was a risk Kord was not willing to take. In the meantime, they'd find a safer solution to suppressing the magic besides him always wearing a collar.

Jasce walked into the ring, cracked his neck, and twirled his sword. "Well, come on then."

Conquering the Darkness

The two stepped into their fighting stances and the crash of steel resounded off the stone walls. Once again, recruits gathered to watch their King Regent and commander spar. Was it the best example? Probably not, especially when Lord Rollant and Lady Darbry watched from afar.

The Hunter training Drexus imposed on Jasce and Caston, although harsh, gave them the skills to move forward. And Jasce had a feeling Caston would need his help and guidance in the days and months to come.

The roar of a wyvern brought Jasce back to the charred field and the rising sun. He turned to find Tobias approaching him and extending a hand. His soldiers were already mounted on their wyverns, ready for the long flight home to Terrenus.

Jasce shook the Gemari's hand. "Thank you for your help."

"We have a lot to sort out now that the archduke is no longer with us." Sadness flashed across his face, but disappeared as quickly as it came.

"If you ever need anything, let me know." He eyed the archduke's black wyvern. The majestic beast lifted its head and fixed its golden eyes on him. "Of course, I'll need a way to travel to Terrenus."

"Consider him a coronation gift." Tobias bowed his head.

Jasce snorted. The "coronation" had lasted all of ten minutes and only the members of his team and the council were present. He meant what he said to Lord Rollant. He didn't want this position and would only stay in the role until other measures were established.

Tobias nodded once and strode across the field to where Commander Alyssa Nadja waited. Jasce saw the blush on her cheeks while she and the general talked. Tobias reached for her hand and brought it to his lips, then patted the black wyvern's long snout and mounted his own beast.

Alyssa walked toward Jasce with her hands in her pockets. Her brown hair hung loosely down her back and a smile brightened her face.

"You're blushing, Commander," he said, trying not to laugh.

"Oh, shut up."

Their hair blew off their faces as the four wyverns took to the skies. While Alyssa watched them disappear behind the clouds, he approached the black wyvern and gazed into his enormous eyes. "Thank you for staying."

The wyvern puffed air out of his nostrils and then dipped his head.

"You need a name." *And a place to live,* he thought, thinking the horses wouldn't enjoy sharing their stable. He'd figure something out. For now, the creature seemed happy to remain in the field and heal from his wounds.

Later that evening, Jasce leaned against the wall in the dining hall. As he'd done before the Battle of the Heart—which it was now called, and which he thought was a stupid name—he was content to watch his family and friends rejoice and grieve together. Kenz waved him over, but he shook his head and mouthed, *I'll be back.*

He escaped to his rooms, craving a quiet moment alone. When he plopped down on the couch, he landed on something hard. Reaching behind him, he pulled out Amycus's journal. Earlier in the week, he'd been reading of Amycus's exploits and had fallen asleep. With the events of the last few days, he'd forgotten all about the journal.

He flipped to the last page and tried to swallow the lump in his throat.

Dear Jasce,
I only have a short while. I can see the battle raging between you and your former self. Azrael is winning, and the events with Kenz and the Snatchers and Evelina's manipulation finally pushed you over the edge. I feel it's my responsibility to save you, for my debt to Lisia and my love for you. Please understand, it is my idea to remove your magic when this is all done. I know you don't approve, but this is the only way to free you, even if you have to live without magic.
You are stronger than you give yourself credit for, and you are a good man with a good heart. I have faith you will do everything in your power to rescue Jaida, and I hope one day you'll marry Kenz. You are the other half of her, as she is of you. I'm sorry I won't be there to walk her down the aisle, but I fear my time is quickly fading.
You deserve a chance at happiness. Seize this, Jasce, and never let

Conquering the Darkness

anyone or anything get in your way of achieving it, for you are worthy.
Tell your sister she looks just like her mother, acts a bit like her, too. Stubborn and a fierce protector of those she loves.
I'll miss working by your side in the forge, as those are some of my fondest memories. I wish we had more time together, but I'm thankful for the relationship we shared.
Know that I love you as a father loves a son.

Jasce wiped away the tear that escaped down his face. Even with all his mistakes, Amycus had believed in him and loved him. Now, more than ever, with the war behind him and the responsibilities ahead of him, he longed for his mentor to be by his side. A rock he could lean upon, a pillar of strength and decency.

He closed the journal and ran trembling fingers down its cover. He'd never forget the blacksmith who altered the course of his life.

"Thank you," he whispered.

Epilogue

Carhurst, Paxton
Ten months later

The sound of a hammer striking metal filled the early morning hours. Sparks flew and heat from the forge made Jasce wipe the sweat from his forehead. The small practice sword he was creating was almost finished.

Unbeknownst to Kenz, Amycus had bequeathed his cottage and the forge to her. She'd shown Jasce the letter, and when they returned to Carhurst they'd moved in and made it their own. Except the forge. Jasce hadn't changed a thing. Keeping the room the same kept the old man close to his heart.

The sound of laughter drifting from the paddock he and Kord built brought a smile to his face. Most of the townspeople in Carhurst weren't thrilled with the idea of a wyvern becoming a permanent resident, but Jasce had been determined to keep the black wyvern, since flying was the fastest method of travel to and from Orilyon. Keeping Spero, a name both he and Kenz agreed upon, was sound logic. Kenz saw through his reasoning in an instant, though, and Bruiser hadn't quite warmed up to Spero's presence.

Cassie Sanchez

Another squeal came from the paddock, followed by a low rumble. Jasce wiped his hands on his apron and hung it on the hook by his worktable. "I'll be back. Want anything?"

Braxium grunted something about coffee while he worked on a set of throwing knives. He'd moved to Carhurst but retired from blacksmithing, even though he often tinkered around in Jasce's forge, which didn't bother him in the least.

Jasce leaned against the wall and watched his wife and one-month-old daughter, Lissy, feed Spero the strips of meat he liked most. The first time he held her, joy and fear had enveloped him, unable to comprehend the beauty he and Kenz had created. Kenz suggested they name her after his mom, which had filled his heart.

Kenz looked over her shoulder and caught him staring. She waved at him.

Jasce walked past Bruiser, eating his breakfast, and scratched the horse's ear. "You're still my favorite." The horse nuzzled his hand and returned to his food.

He sat next to Kenz on the bench and held Lissy, smoothing back the tendrils of her onyx hair as he gazed into gray eyes.

"So, how does it feel to turn twenty-nine?"

Jasce ran a finger down the bridge of his daughter's small nose. Her eyelids grew heavy. "Just like it did when I was twenty-eight."

Kenz arched a brow. "You're not still irritated about your birthday party today, are you?"

He sighed. "No, it's just been a long time since I've had one." So long, in fact, that he really couldn't remember the last time anyone celebrated his birthday. The only reason he agreed to the party was to see his sister and Caston. The last time he'd been in Orilyon, he'd been so busy with voting in Lord Rollant to his new position as governor, he hadn't had a chance to see either of them.

"Did Jaida get the time off?" Kenz asked.

Kord had promoted Jaida to Pandaren's chief physician, despite not being a Healer. Her efficiency in running the staff and her caring touch made her the obvious choice.

"Yes. She arrives this afternoon." He picked at a loose thread on his tunic. "She's bringing Flynt."

Conquering the Darkness

Kenz arched a brow and then shook her head. She had told him many times to mind his own business regarding those two. He wasn't sure of their relationship status, since both were busy. He'd promoted Flynt to captain of the Spectrals since the Fire Spectral was a natural leader, and the recruits seemed to love him.

He stretched out his long legs and gently rocked Lissy. Winter was on its way out, with spring welcoming the chirp of birds and the budding of trees. The past ten months had been hectic with transforming the monarchy of Pandaren into a democracy, and there were still a lot of issues needing to be resolved. Kord had remained by his side every step of the way, a steadfast refuge of wisdom and strength. The Healer continued his role as Spectral Liaison, but spent most of his time in Carhurst, creating furniture with Kenz or helping Tillie in the bakery.

Thankfully, Jasce's responsibilities as King Regent were coming to a close, and he couldn't be happier. He wasn't a king, and he was no longer the commander of the Paladin Guard. Both Caston and Alyssa worked as co-commanders, recruiting and training the soldiers. Even with Drexus defeated and the Heart of Pandaren hidden, hopefully where no one would ever find it, there was still the concern of other lands and potential enemies to consider.

So they worked to strengthen their relationships with Alturia, Balten, and Terrenus, and plans for another Gathering were in the works. The Vastanes were still rebuilding, but a new king was in place. Jasce hoped King Vacillo wouldn't be as ambitious as his predecessors.

The gate to the paddock opened and Kord and Tillie came in, followed by Mal and Emile. The kids ran to Spero, who lowered to the ground and allowed them to climb onto his back.

"No flying, not without the saddle Uncle Jasce made," Tillie said, pointing to the wyvern and then her son. If wyverns could roll their eyes, Jasce was pretty sure Spero did. Most people would frown upon letting children play with a wyvern, but Spero had proven to be more of a lover than a fighter.

Tillie wiggled her fingers at Jasce. "Give me my niece."

Jasce knew better than to argue with Kord's wife, especially when it came to holding Lissy. Tillie snuggled the baby and walked to the other side of the courtyard with Kenz. Both whispered, and a flush filled Kenz's cheeks. Jasce had a sneaking suspicion what those two were discussing, especially with the nausea that had plagued his wife the last few days.

"Happy birthday," Kord said, handing Jasce a steaming cup of coffee and one of Tillie's scrumptious pastries.

"Thanks."

"Are you ready for your big bash?"

Jasce froze mid-drink of his coffee. "Bash? I thought only family and Caston were coming."

Kord chuckled. "The look on your face. Relax, it'll be fine."

"Fine, huh." Jasce bit into the chocolate confection and almost moaned. *Damn, that woman can bake*, he thought.

Kord watched Spero stroll around the paddock with Mal and Emile. "Speaking of Caston, have you noticed anything different about him?"

Jasce frowned. Caston had been present at the birth of his daughter and had seemed okay. Kord, using Maera's research with the Brymagus plant, had developed a serum to help counter the effects of having four types of magic coursing through his veins. "I saw him last month. Your serum seems to be working."

Kord chewed the inside of his cheek. "I'm worried about him. Something seems off."

"I'll check in with him when he gets here."

Tillie rocked Lissy in her arms as she walked out of the paddock toward Jasce and Kenz's cottage. Jasce smiled, thinking of this family he finally had. His smile shifted as he felt Kord's penetrating gaze.

"You know I hate it when you look at me like that."

Kord huffed out a laugh. "You're a good dad and an even better husband. Not too shabby of a brother-in-law, either. I knew you would be."

"Well, I've had a great example."

Kord stood and placed a hand on Jasce's shoulder. "Your journey was filled with twists and turns, but you navigated them and came out a stronger man. I'm proud of you." With a squeeze, he walked away in the direction his wife had gone.

Conquering the Darkness

"Finally, a saying I understand," Jasce mumbled as he watched his wife approach.

Kenz sat next to him and nudged him. "What's on your mind?"

"Just content." He wrapped his arm around her.

He never could have imagined how his life would have ended up. When he'd been strapped to Drexus's table, receiving the Amplifier serum and thinking he might not survive, not once did he see a happy ending. He only saw revenge, and eventually death. But now, he had found joy, along with a fierce and loyal woman who loved him. Family and friends surrounded him, and he had a beautiful and healthy daughter. Plus, he was doing what he loved most—creating weapons in his own forge. Finally, a normal life.

He kissed Kenz on the cheek. "I love you, Kenz Farone."

She smiled and rested her head on his shoulder. "I love you, Jasce Farone."

He lifted his face to the rising sun and thought of his mother and father. They'd be proud of the man he'd become.

Peace settled into the soul of a warrior, and hope had emerged. The future shone like dawn breaking through the clouds, with fingers of light illuminating the way. Jasce watched the sky turn from a dark purple to a brilliant gold.

He had finally conquered the darkness.

Author's Note

Thank you so much for reading *Conquering the Darkness*. I hope you enjoyed your journey through the Darkness Trilogy with Jasce, Kenz, Kord, and Amycus. If so, please consider leaving an honest review with your preferred retailers, on Amazon, and/or Goodreads. As an indie author, I rely on my amazing readers to help spread the word about my books. Your support means so much—thank you!

To stay in the loop with upcoming books, please stop by website and sign up for my newsletter at CassieSanchez.com.

Acknowledgments

Five years ago, when I first stepped into my creative writing class, I never would have thought I'd be sitting here today with a completed trilogy. My own adventure in writing, publishing, and marketing resembles a rollercoaster of highs and lows, but what an amazing journey it has been.

I want to first and foremost thank God, who has given me a purpose and the creativity to write fantasy. As Kenz is Jasce's lighthouse in the storm, so is the Lord, always guiding and watching over me.

Here's to my fabulous Beta readers. I can't tell you how much your encouragement, ideas, and mostly, your time with reading and providing feedback meant to me. Thank you, Alyssa, Anna, Darin, Janine, Karla, Linda, Lacey, and Tracey. I also want to thank my sensitivity reader, Kimberly, for your insight, but mostly your trust as we delved into the topic of alcoholism. You are truly a brave warrior.

To my editor, Rachel Oestreich. Thank you for keeping me from walking off the clocktower and helping me finish Jasce's story well. I couldn't have done all of this without you and your expertise.

Laurisa, it's such a comfort to have one last set of eyes on this bad boy before sending it out into the wild. Thank you for proofreading Conquering and making it even better.

Thank you to Karen with Arcane Covers for creating my beautiful covers and bringing Jasce to life. And for formatting my books—they'd be a mess without you.

A big thanks to my ARC Readers and Street Team – you know who you are. Your promotion, support, reviews, and encouragement have kept me moving forward. Thank you for spreading the word about the Darkness Trilogy.

I want to thank my mom and my two men-children for being in my corner, cheering me on. Your support means more than you can know, and I'm truly blessed to have you in my life.

As for you, dear husband, none of this would be possible without you. You are my fierce protector and believe in me when the doubt creeps in. The Darkness Trilogy would never have seen the light of day if not for you.

Lastly, to my fans, thank you for believing in my world, my characters, and this story. Here's to more adventures and keeping the magic alive.

About the Author

Growing up, Cassie Sanchez always wanted superpowers and to be a warrior princess fighting alongside unlikely heroes. Suffice it to say, she lost herself in books, from fantasy to sci-fi to a suspenseful romance. Currently, Cassie lives in the southwest with her husband, Louie, while pestering her two adult men-children. She can usually be found drinking too much coffee while working in her office with her dogs, Gunner and Bullet, warming her feet. When she isn't writing about magic and sword fights, she enjoys golf, spending time with friends, or partaking in a satisfying nap. You can visit her online at Cassie Sanchez.com.

facebook.com/cassiesanchezauthor
instagram.com/CassieSanchezAuthor
tiktok.com/@cassiesanchezauthor

Made in the USA
Monee, IL
08 February 2025

11358705R10225